She blinked, qu
really you?"

He bobbed his head. "Gail? Why, you look pretty as I remember."

"It's been ten years," she said, brushing off his compliment. "People change."

Sensing displeasure in her voice, he dropped his gaze. "I know I left without saying anything. I should have stayed in touch."

Launching a frown, Gail folded her arms. "That's a poor way to say you're sorry."

He toyed with the hat in his hand. "I guess I owe you all an apology."

She offered a tight nod. "You do."

When Levi had run away, she'd been on the cusp of fourteen. His departure had crushed her. He didn't know it, but he'd taken her heart with him.

Now he was back.

And so were the feelings she'd believed she'd let go of…

Like the Amish, **Pamela Desmond Wright** is a fan of the simple life. Her childhood includes memories of the olden days: old-fashioned oil lamps, cooking over an authentic wood-burning stove and making popcorn over a fire at her grandparents' cabin. The authentic log cabin Pamela grew up playing in can be viewed at the Muleshoe Heritage Center in Muleshoe, Texas, which was donated to the city after the death of her grandparents.

Cathy Liggett is an Ohio girl who never dreamed her writing journey would take her across the world and to Amish country, too. But she's learned God's plans for our lives are greater and more creative than the ones we often imagine for ourselves. That includes meeting her husband at a high school reunion and marrying three months later—nearly forty years ago. Together, they enjoy visiting kids and grandkids, and spoiling their pup, Chaz.

PAMELA DESMOND WRIGHT

&

CATHY LIGGETT

Their Amish Second Chance

2 Uplifting Stories

The Cowboy's Amish Haven and
Her Secret Amish Match

LOVE INSPIRED
INSPIRATIONAL ROMANCE

LOVE INSPIRED®
INSPIRATIONAL ROMANCE

Recycling programs
for this product may
not exist in your area.

ISBN-13: 978-1-335-50831-7

Their Amish Second Chance

Copyright © 2023 by Harlequin Enterprises ULC

The Cowboy's Amish Haven
First published in 2021. This edition published in 2023.
Copyright © 2021 by Kimberly Fried

Her Secret Amish Match
First published in 2021. This edition published in 2023.
Copyright © 2021 by Cathy Liggett

This is a work of fiction. Names, characters, places and incidents are either the product of the author's imagination or are used fictitiously. Any resemblance to actual persons, living or dead, businesses, companies, events or locales is entirely coincidental.

For questions and comments about the quality of this book, please contact us at CustomerService@Harlequin.com.

Harlequin Enterprises ULC
22 Adelaide St. West, 41st Floor
Toronto, Ontario M5H 4E3, Canada
www.LoveInspired.com

Printed in U.S.A.

CONTENTS

THE COWBOY'S
AMISH HAVEN

Pamela Desmond Wright

For Tamela Hancock Murray, who believed.

For Melissa Endlich, who made it happen.

Acknowledgments

I would like to thank my fellow writers and buddies who are always there to encourage and cheer me on when the going gets tough.

Sara Reinke, Sascha Illyvich, Claire Matturro,
Vanessa Hawthorne, Marie Blackwood,
Sherri K Briles, Christie M Allen,
Ang and Sherry Baca.

I'd also like to thank my mother for suffering through endless revisions and telling me everything I wrote was good (even though it often wasn't).

Love you all!

And the king said unto the man of God,
Come home with me, and refresh thyself,
and I will give thee a reward.
                          —*1 Kings* 13:7

Chapter One

Rubbing tired eyes, Levi Wyse breathed a sigh of relief. Days of hard travel were finally nearing their end. Mile after mile disappeared beneath the tires of his truck.

Goodbye, Montana. Hello, Texas.

Gaze focused on the road, he drummed his fingers on the steering wheel. To stay awake for the last leg of the journey, he'd slammed down a few cups of coffee. Buzzed on caffeine and adrenaline, he felt tiny ignitions spark off his nerve endings. If only his blood didn't feel so hot and his skin cold as ice.

Sleep. All he wanted to do was close his eyes and hibernate for a week.

Levi glanced at the child sleeping in his car seat. Seth stretched out as much as the cramped interior allowed. Thankfully, his son could bunk out anywhere. Teddy bear locked in the crook of one arm, Seth mumbled in his sleep.

Emotion squeezed Levi's throat. The little guy was trying to be a trouper, but it was clear the last few months of hard travel had taken a toll. Instead of being dragged down the road, the child needed to be settled in a stable, normal routine.

Levi blinked to clear away the blur overtaking his vision. The white lines dividing the highway were running together. Pressing his fingers against his thudding temple, he pulled in a breath. To say he felt terrible would be an understatement.

He eased down the window and tipped back his head, allowing the cool night air to caress his stubbled face. The cobwebs and shadows inhabiting his mind thinned, but not enough to chase away his headache.

Feeling a twinge in his neck, he rolled his shoulders to loosen knotted muscles. His skin felt tight. A tremble threatened to overwhelm his fragile composure.

He had to find somewhere to pull over before he wrecked the truck.

Insides knotting, Levi clenched the wheel tighter. His destination was still miles away. He'd planned to find a place to set up the RV in Burr Oak. That wasn't going to happen. He was too tired to keep going.

A familiar landmark came into view.

Recognition seeped into his fogged mind. The ranch he'd worked at as a teenager was just a few miles away.

Maybe the Lord was watching out for him after all.

Even though he hadn't had contact with Samuel Schroder or his family in ages, he was pretty sure the man would let him park his camper for a day or two. As he remembered it, Samuel was always up before the sun, so pulling in early should not be a bother. Maybe he could even pick up some work doing odd jobs around the property to pay back the favor.

The next rodeo he planned to compete in was still a week away, so he'd have some time on his hands.

Spending a little time in one place for a while would be nice.

Stirring, Seth opened his eyes. "Are we there yet, Daddy?" Yawning, he squeezed his stuffed bear tighter.

Sucking back a sigh, Levi brushed a few stray locks off his son's forehead. *"Ja."* Unwilling to risk falling asleep behind the wheel, he decided to head for the nearby ranch. "We're getting close."

Gail Schroder sprinkled flour over the cutting board and flattened out a ball of sourdough. Every morning she baked fresh biscuits, a task in which she took great pride. True, the recipe was a common one, but she'd made it her own with a few special ingredients.

As was her custom, she had risen before the sun. Dressing quietly, she eased down the stairs, preparing to wrangle the ancient monstrosity dominating the kitchen. Feeding a fair amount of wood and kindling into its belly brought the old cast-iron beast to life.

Breakfast was her first task. Fire stoked, she started an old-fashioned coffee percolator. The scent of burning oak and a dark roast brew filled the air with a delicious aroma.

Gail pressed out a dozen biscuits and brushed the tops with home-churned butter mixed with honey from the beehive. After opening the oven, she slid the first batch inside.

Stepping back, she swiped a hand across her perspiring brow. The old stove took no time at all to heat the first floor. As was the layout of most Amish homes, the kitchen, dining room and living room all inhabited a single large living space.

A rectangular wooden table covered with a pretty,

ivory-colored lace cloth waited for stoneware dishes handed down through generations. The long picnic-style table with chairs on each side provided plenty of room for everyone.

A single wooden chair sat at its end, reserved for the man of the family.

Gail's head dipped as her eyes misted. The painful grip on her heart grew tighter, burrowing deeper. Oh, how she missed her *daed*. Her *mamm*, too, was gone, leaving only herself and her younger sisters.

Gail glanced out the nearby window. The yellow-pink sliver appearing over the horizon was widening and brightening. Out in the henhouse, the rooster's sun-rise song cracked the silence of the night.

A new day was dawning, and a long list of chores waited. Cleaning, gardening, mending, tending the chickens, rabbits and goats that provided fresh eggs, meat and milk were just a few of the things that needed to get done.

The unexpected odor of charred bread and over-perked coffee singed her nostrils.

"Oh no!"

Gail snatched a flannel potholder and lifted the per-colator. Liquid bubbled out of the spout. After setting the scorched thing aside, she fished the biscuits out of the oven. Twelve black circles greeted her eyes.

I ruined everything.

Biting back a sob of frustration, Gail stared at the disaster. Her emotions scattered in a thousand differ-ent directions. Without warning, her mask of stoicism and strength fell away, revealing deep cracks in her composure.

Grief. Loss. Confusion. They came at her from different directions, pecking at her like hungry ravens attacking carrion.

A tear rolled down her cheek. And then another.

Had her morning been normal, her *daed* would have been sitting in his chair, coffee in hand, Bible in front of him.

Gail swiped away her tears with a trembling hand. Since his passing, the family had left his Bible undisturbed. No one could bear to move it.

Walking over to the window to let in the morning breeze, Gail pulled in a hearty breath. Her focus was slowly returning.

Catching a glimpse of her reflection in the depths of the glass, she pulled a face at her image. Critical of her looks, she believed her eyes too wide set, and her mouth too generous. Her nose and cheeks were splattered with too many freckles. And no matter how tightly she wound her bun, a few brown curls always managed to escape her *kapp*.

I never look well put together, she thought, tucking her hair back into place.

A heavy rap at the back door interrupted her thoughts.

"Miss Gail?" a male voice called.

Gail recognized Ezra Weaver's voice. A visitor so early in the morning didn't bode well.

"Oh, please, Lord," she murmured. "I can't handle more bad news." Being the boss was hard. Harder than she'd ever imagined. She had a multitude of problems, the least of which was the ranch manager who had just quit without a word. Overseeing the homestead, which included the breeding and sale of Longhorn cattle, was considered a man's work. Now she had no guide, and no idea what to do.

Another knock sounded, louder and more insistent. "Anyone there?"

Glancing down, Gail sighed over the mess. She was hot and perspiring, her dress was wrinkled, and her apron stained by spluttering coffee grounds and flakes of dough.

"Just a minute!" She slid back the chain and unlatched the bolt.

Ezra Weaver waited outside. Mechanic, plumber, welder and jack of all trades, he'd come to work for the family seven years ago. If it broke, he fixed it. His wife, Ruth, took care of the cowboys, cooking and cleaning for the men who lived in the bunkhouse. An *Englischer*, he smoked a lot. Gail tolerated his bad habit because he was an honest man and a good worker.

"*Guder mariye*, Mr. Weaver." Gail angled the door so he could step inside. "Please, come in."

Battered straw hat in hand, Weaver offered an apologetic nod. "Sorry to disturb you so early, ma'am."

Gail smiled. Whatever he threw her way, she wouldn't flinch. It was up to her to make the decisions now, she thought, then sent up a silent prayer. *Gott, please help me make the right ones.*

"Not at all," she said. "How can I help you?"

"I'm not the one needin' your attention," Ezra Weaver drawled before jerking his thumb in a vague direction. "There's a man down by the gate, and he's askin' to see your daddy."

Surprised, Gail laughed in disbelief, then sobered when she realized Ezra Weaver was serious. Puzzled, she shook her head. Why would someone be asking to see her father? Three months had passed since Samuel

Schroder's death. Burr Oak was a small town. Surely word had gotten around by now.

She was curious as to who would make the inquiry, and why they had come so early in the morning. Visitors were not common. Weeks might pass before they saw a soul aside from family or hired hands.

"Do you know who it is?"

Ezra shook his head. "Nope. I ain't never seen him before."

"Did he say what his name was?"

"He said Samuel would know him."

"Well, in that case, I guess I need to find out what he wants."

"I'll come, too," Ezra Weaver offered.

Gail untied her apron and hung it on a peg by the door before brushing the flour off the front of her dress. She wanted to look mature, in control. Her efforts only added more smudges and wrinkles.

She opened the door and stepped outside. Nudged by the wind, the hanging chair on the veranda creaked.

Pulling back her shoulders and leveling her chin, Gail walked down the steps. Gravel crunched under her heels as she marched toward a white fence with a wrought iron gate that kept people from entering the property. Ezra Weaver dutifully followed.

Pasting a polite smile on her face, Gail peered through the bars. *"Guder mariye,"* she said, out of habit using the language she'd been raised to speak.

The driver slid out of his truck. Tall and blond, he was dressed in jeans, boots and a plaid checkered work shirt with the sleeves rolled to the elbows. He looked like any cowboy roaming the open plains.

"Guder mariye," he returned, tipping the wide brim of his straw hat.

Her brows rose. His pronunciation was decent enough. "Can I help you?" she asked, switching to English.

The visitor shifted to get a better view through the gate. His gaze widened, as did his grin. "Gail? You sure grew up."

The fine hairs on the back of her neck rose. "Do I know you?"

The man took off his hat, giving her a better view of his face. A blond layer of stubble roughened his skin. "Well, I hope so."

Gail searched for recognition. His eyes were his most arresting feature. Irises the shade of an icy arctic lake sparkled. Wry amusement slanted his mouth.

Noticing her lag, he took a step closer. "It's Levi," he prodded. "Levi Wyse."

Blood drained from her face. No. It couldn't be. This man didn't look like the boy she remembered. A thin scar marred his right cheek, and the slightly crooked set of his nose indicated a break or two throughout his life. His skin was deeply tanned, and small lines etched the outer corners of his eyes. A few character lines touched his mouth and chin. His voice, too, was deep, but mellow.

An image she'd put away long ago flashed across her mind's screen. When she'd last laid eyes on Levi, he'd had a huskier build and still wore his hair in the bowl cut favored by most Amish men. Now he had the lean and hard frame of a working man, and his hair was cut in the sleek combed-back style favored by most Texas cowboys. He'd replaced the clothes he'd once worn as one of the Plain folks with Western-style wear. Shedding his past, he'd gone *Englisch*.

She blinked, quizzical. "Levi?" Saying his name felt odd. "Is that really you?"

He bobbed his head. "Gail? You look as pretty as I remember."

"It has been ten years," she said, brushing off his compliment. "People change."

He dropped his gaze. "I know I left without saying anything. I should have stayed in touch."

Launching a frown, Gail folded her arms. "That's a poor way to say you're sorry."

He toyed with the hat in his hand. "I guess I owe you all an apology."

She offered a tight nod. "You do."

When Levi ran away, she was on the cusp of fourteen. His departure had crushed her. He didn't know it, but he'd taken her heart with him.

Now he was back.

What did he want?

An awkward silence widened the distance between them.

A boy with tousled blond hair popped up on the passenger's side. Rubbing sleepy eyes, he looked around in confusion.

"Dad," he called in a panic. "Daddy!"

Walking to the passenger side, Levi opened the door. "I'm here, calm down, son."

Gail caught a glimpse of the child as Levi unbuckled his car seat and lifted him out. "Your *boi*?"

Pride sparked in Levi's gaze as he cradled his son in his arms. "*Ja.* This is Seth."

Curiosity prodded. "And your *ehefrau*?"

Levi's mouth twisted wryly. Unease shadowed his eyes. "I'm sorry to say that Seth's mom isn't with us anymore."

Gail stood for a moment, locked in surprise.

Oh, no! How unkind of her to allow past resentments to control her emotions. Instead of welcoming him, she'd greeted him with an icy heart.

Shame filled her.

Unlatching the gate, she stepped through. "Forgive me for treating you so badly. Welcome home, Levi."

Chapter Two

"Thank you for inviting us in. I promise we won't stay long," Levi said as he and Seth followed Gail into the house.

"Please, sit." Face breaking into a smile of good humor and grace, she gestured toward the waiting table. "Can I get you anything to drink? Tea? Coffee? Maybe Seth would like something, too."

Hanging his hat on a peg by the door, Levi settled his son in a chair at the table before taking a seat. "Coffee would be great. A glass of milk for Seth, if it's not too much trouble."

Cranky after their long trip, Seth squirmed impatiently. "I'm hungry, Dad."

"Seth, don't be rude." Levi looked to Gail. "Sorry. I haven't had time to get him any breakfast this morning. I'd planned to stop somewhere in town."

"Well, I certainly can't let my guests go unfed. I insist you both stay for breakfast." Reaching for her apron, Gail knotted the ties around her slender waist. "Let me get the child something to tide him over."

Attempting to rub the exhaustion out of his eyes,

Levi nodded gratefully. "That would be a real treat. Been a long time since I've had a home-cooked meal, so I am going to say yes."

"I remember you used to eat like you had a hollow leg. *Mamm* couldn't fill you up," she said as she opened a bread box. Slicing off a piece of sourdough she toasted it on top of the stove before adding butter and a smear of pure strawberry delight. Stopping to fill a stoneware mug with milk, she delivered the items to the table with a deft hand.

Abandoning his bear, Seth grabbed the toast and stuffed in a large bite. "Mmm," he said, smacking his lips.

Levi frowned. "Mind your manners, son."

Mouth stained with jam, Seth used his sleeve to wipe away the mess. "Sorry, Dad."

Levi rolled his eyes. "He didn't learn that from me."

A flicker of amusement passed over Gail's face. "Now don't be too hard on the *youngie*," she said. "A good appetite is a good sign he'll grow." She turned her attention to Seth. "Do you like eggs with bacon and hash brown potatoes?"

Seth bobbed his head appreciatively, licking sweet strawberry jam off his fingers. "Mmm-hmm," he said before gulping down a mouthful of cold milk.

Gail returned to the stove, emptying the coffeepot and discarding inedible pieces of charcoal welded to a pan. Whatever she had attempted to make earlier had turned into a disaster.

"Problem?"

"Not my best morning." Exasperation knotted her brow. "I've got a lot on my mind."

"Oh?"

Gail waved off his concern. "It's nothing," she insisted. "Let me get some fresh coffee going."

Filling the pot with cold water and home-ground coffee beans, she set it on the stovetop to heat before rolling out more sourdough with a deft hand. The scent of a strong Colombian roast soon filled the air.

As she was otherwise occupied with her task, Levi snagged a mug off the counter before claiming a pot holder. "May I?"

She lifted hands covered in flour. "*Ja*, help yourself."

He tipped the metal percolator over. No modern machine could beat coffee brewed over a wood fire.

Looking up from her dough, she eyed him. "I'd forgotten you were so tall."

Levi gazed down at her. Her features were strongly etched, and her eyes evenly spaced over the slope of a perfectly straight nose. Dusty freckles spattered her cheeks.

"Guess if I say you're pretty again, you'll slap me."

Her cheeks heated, going ten shades of red. Her mouth twisted wryly. "Flattery won't get breakfast on the table any faster." Biscuits rolled out, she slid the pan into the oven.

Levi took the hint, backing off. It probably was not right to be saying such words to her anyway. Surely she had a husband somewhere nearby? And he most likely wouldn't take to a strange man making eyes at his wife, no matter their past connection.

He sat at the table and added cream and sugar to the tarry brew before taking a hearty sip. He let his gaze wander. Throughout the living space, sturdy handmade furniture filled the rooms. Crocheted afghans covered the sofas. Beneath the vaulted ceiling, the floor was solid oak with a scattering of handwoven area rugs. White lace curtains framed wide bay windows.

Save for Gail, the kitchen was empty, Normally, the house would be bustling with activity. Now it was strangely quiet, almost tomblike.

Having finished his snack, Seth yawned. His eyes drooped, struggling to stay open.

"Do you mind if I lay Seth down?"

"Not at all."

Levi slipped his arms beneath his son and carried him to a nearby sofa. He put him down and snagged an afghan to lay it on the boy. While Seth napped, it would give him a chance to talk to Gail.

Little pitchers have big ears, he reminded himself.

"Is he *oll recht*?"

Levi returned to his chair, finishing his coffee. "He's just worn out. I think being on the road so much is grinding him down. Getting to be time for a break."

"Oh?"

"We just drove down from Montana for some events here in Texas," he explained. "There's one in Eastland this coming Sunday. Then we'll head to Fort Worth for the rodeo there at the end of the month."

A faint smile haunted her lips. "*Daed* said that was what you would do. Join the rodeo."

"I know Samuel wasn't crazy about the idea." He shrugged. "Just something I had to do, I guess."

Gail's expression tightened. "*Daed* did the best he could by you, Levi."

As he caught sight of Samuel's Bible, guilt gave him a sharp prod. "I guess he'll tell me that when I see him."

Gail sliced off a slab of bacon with a sharp knife and added it to a cast-iron skillet waiting on the stovetop.

The meat sizzled, sending out the enticing aroma of pork cured in applewood. "I guess no one's told you, but he isn't with us anymore."

Surprise lifted his brows. *"Mein beileid an sie und ihre familie."* His pronunciation was rusty, but his offer of condolences sincere. "When did he pass?"

"Three months ago."

"How?"

Her expression remained cautiously neutral. "Unexpectedly."

Levi felt a twinge at the back of his throat. As hard as the old man had been on him, Samuel Schroder was never unkind. Gruff, maybe, but that was his way. "I know that must have been hard on your *mamm*. How is she?"

Gail's lips momentarily flattened. "Cancer took her, shortly after you left."

More news he had not expected. Sarah Schroder had always treated him well, sharing an uplifting thought or an encouraging word whenever he was discouraged or felt out of place.

"They were both good people. It doesn't seem right they're gone."

"It was *Gott*'s will." Quiet resignation tightened her words. "We can only accept it and pray they are at peace."

Levi swallowed hard. Hands circling the large stoneware coffee mug, he tried to draw some comfort from its warmth. "How have your *schwestern* been?"

Gail's gaze lifted from her cooking. *"Gut.* They've gone to town to deliver the morning produce, but they will be back soon."

"They are all well, I hope."

"Ja. Rebecca is a teacher. She is engaged and will

be marrying in November. Amity has a little shop of her own. Her homemade soaps and candles are popular with tourists."

Levi nodded. "The things she made were always too pretty to use."

"She's had a place in town for about two years now, and her business is starting to grow."

"Dare I ask about Florene?"

Gail rolled her eyes. "*Ach*, that girl. She's been trouble lately."

"Really?"

A rueful smile flicked across her lips. "Seventeen and thinks she knows everything. Right now, she's testing the waters of *Englisch* ways."

Leaning into the table, Levi brushed his fingers through his hair. "Been there, done that."

She eyed him. "I hope you will be honest if she asks you about your time away from Burr Oak."

"I've got a story or two I could tell," he said, but declined to elaborate. "And you? You are married now. *Ja*?"

Throwing up her hands, Gail made a scoffing sound. "Who has time to find an *ehmann* with all this to tend to on the ranch?" Claiming a fork, she deftly turned the frying bacon without missing a beat.

Levi had no chance to reply. A series of hard knocks hammered the front door.

"Well, aren't we popular today?" Frowning, she lifted the skillet off the stove. Setting it aside, she wiped her hands on a dishrag. "Who could this be?"

Levi shrugged. "Guess you'd better find out."

Gail straightened her *kapp* and smoothed her apron before greeting the visitor.

Glancing past her, Levi caught sight of the man standing on the veranda. Clad in an impeccably tailored three-piece suit, he looked to be a portly man in his late forties, with dark hair gray at the temples. His face was round and cheeks unusually ruddy for his pale complexion. His deep-set eyes peered through the rims of stylish gold wire-frame glasses. Beneath a thin, dark mustache, his lips compressed into a line. By the look on his face, he'd not come for a social call.

"Is this the Schroder property?"

Gail nodded. "Yes."

Levi bristled. Something was not right. Men in dark suits didn't show up out in the middle of nowhere in Texas to chat. Not wanting to pry into her business, he nevertheless turned an ear toward the conversation.

The stranger grumbled. "Even with a GPS, these county farm roads are confusing. I hate being out this early, but it was necessary."

"I'm sorry for the inconvenience. It is easy to get lost." Stepping back, Gail invited him in. "Come in, please."

Entering, the man didn't offer his hand or a smile. His features were guarded, his eyes intense in their perusal. "My name is Andrew Wilkins. I work in the loan delinquency department for the bank in Burr Oak. I was hoping you could explain why the mortgage payments haven't been made in the last three months."

"I—I don't understand."

Wilkins's gaze narrowed, as if she were a hardship he had to force himself to tolerate. "The payments on this property are ninety days overdue." Reaching in a pocket, he extended a white legal envelope. "Your notice of default is enclosed. This will be your final notice."

Puzzled, Gail accepted his offering. "I'm sure there's some misunderstanding, Mr. Wilkins. *Daed* never missed a payment."

"Samuel was always a good customer," Wilkins said. "We've never had any qualms loaning him money over the years. When he passed, we had every confidence his survivors would honor his debt."

"Of course, we intend to keep paying," she said with quiet determination. "We wouldn't cheat the bank."

"Then perhaps you might explain why the account the payments are debited from has not had adequate funds in months." Pausing, he gave a prod. "I sent out written notices, but no one responded."

Gail shook her head. "That's not right. We sent cattle to auction after *Daed* passed and collected over a hundred and fifty thousand dollars for their sale. That was at the beginning of March and should have been more than enough to carry us through next year. Our manager, Mr. Slagel, should have taken care of it. He always has."

Wilkins's lips pursed into a sneer. "No significant deposit has been made to that account for months. Certainly not anything close to that amount."

Gail visibly paled. The unopened envelope slipped from her fingers, but she didn't retrieve it. "Oh no…" Barely able to speak, she pressed shaking hands to her mouth.

Wilkins's brows rose. "Excuse me?"

She took a breath to steady herself. "Slagel must have taken the money."

"Now, hold on—" Andrew Wilkins held up a hand. "Are you accusing him of embezzlement?"

Seeing Gail flounder, Levi's protective instincts

kicked in. Having followed the conversation, he didn't have to struggle to put together the story she was trying to tell. He didn't know who Slagel was, but he intended to find out what was going on.

Rising to his feet, Levi stepped up, towering over the shorter man. "She has no reason to lie." Hands fisted at his side, he moved to shield Gail. "If she says the man took the money, it's true."

Blinking behind the rims of his glasses, Wilkins huffed. "Excuse me. I don't believe I was talking to you."

Levi refused to back down. The man was a bully, and he was using his position to intimidate. He refused to be cowed.

"Well, you are now."

Wilkins sniffed. "And you are?"

"A friend of the family," Levi returned in a cool tone. "A knowledgeable man could easily forge a bill of sale on livestock and collect a check in his own name. I doubt anyone would have questioned it if he was someone people trusted." Unfortunately, the theft of cattle was common.

Peeved, Wilkins responded, "What do you mean *was*?"

Moving like an automaton, Gail retrieved the envelope. Her composure hung by a thread. "Mr. Slagel disappeared. I don't know where he went."

Unmoved, Wilkins leveled her with a stare. "What you have going on with Walter Slagel is a legal matter you'll need to settle with him," he snapped. "Regardless of the circumstances, you will still need to make restitution for the amount owed."

Levi bristled. "What if she can't?"

"Then the bank will foreclose." His unrelenting gaze scraped every inch of the room. "Of course, that will include the house. Samuel put the primary acreage up as collateral, so this entire property will go to the bank."

"You would take our home?" Gail asked, aghast.

Wilkins unleashed a snarky grin. "Unless you catch up, I certainly intend to."

Struggling to keep his expression neutral, Levi looked over the rude man who apparently no had problem treating people like dirt. The entire situation left a bad taste in his mouth. He'd never had a stomach for fighting, but there came a time when a man had to stand up and do what was right.

Angling his chin, he folded his arms across his chest and stared the agent down.

"No, you won't," he returned with calm precision.

Still unable to process what had just happened, Gail stood rooted to the spot. Shock buffeted her from all sides. Her ability to think, to speak, had deserted her. She could only stare, numb with dismay and disbelief.

Levi, on the other hand, didn't seem to be affected.

Taking control, he grabbed Andrew Wilkins by the elbow. Propelling the shorter man across the room, he escorted him out of the house.

"We'll be in touch," he said, shutting the front door with a slam. Deed done, he brushed his hands together with satisfaction.

Relieved, Gail forced herself to relax for the moment. She gave him a grateful look. "Thank you for making him go, Levi."

"It was no problem. How could he come in here and speak to you like that?"

Gail's gaze dropped to the envelope in her hand. No need to open it. Wilkins had made it perfectly clear what the paperwork inside would say. "Does it matter? The bank is going to take our home if we don't catch up."

"Now, hold on. Don't panic just yet."

Her facade of composure cracked, revealing her fear. "How can I not?" A shiver curled up her spine, causing her to tremble uncontrollably. Her vision blurred, misting with tears.

Levi stepped forward, grasping her arms and giving her a little shake. "Just calm down and tell me what's going on. Who is this man you're talking about?"

"His name is Walter Slagel. *Daed* hired him last year to oversee the cattle operation. His health was beginning to decline, and he needed the help."

As she broke free of Levi's hold, guilt pummeled her. When her father had needed her most, she had let him down. In so many ways. At her age, she should have been married. A son-in-law might have been able to take the burden off her father's shoulders.

"You said Slagel was gone," Levi said, prodding for more.

"Yes. He packed his things and left a few days ago. Before that, all our ranch hands quit."

"They give any reason?"

An anxious sensation squeezed her insides. "They were upset because he was behind on payroll. They complained about having to wait for their money."

Levi's brows furrowed, and the lines between his eyes deepened. "That doesn't sound right. There's no good reason to pay your crew late."

Dropping her gaze, Gail bit her lip. Through the last few weeks she'd had the strange feeling something was not right with Walter Slagel. He'd become secretive, brushing off her questions about the day-to-day operations of the ranch. Her inquiries about the cattle, the crew and the books had gone unanswered, leaving her with a bitter taste in her mouth. But there was no chance to speak with him as to why he wasn't doing his job. He vanished without a word.

Regret choked her as she looked back. She should have acted sooner, confronted Slagel when the chance presented itself. "I know I made mistakes."

A somber look darkened Levi's gaze. "Sounds like walking out was probably the best thing he did."

"I was planning to fire him and hire someone else." She lifted the crumpled envelope. "But how do I fix this? How do I run a ranch without any money?"

Levi fished the envelope from her fingers. Tearing it open, he unfolded the papers inside. "I am no expert, but I do know how banks work, and how ranching works. It isn't as dire as Mr. Wilkins made it sound."

Grateful someone had answers, Gail relaxed. If Levi had the knowledge to help her, she would listen.

"You want to tell me what's going on with the bank?" he prodded.

Lowering her gaze, she sighed. "A few years ago, *Daed* was offered the chance to buy some acreage from our neighbor, Abram Fletcher. Abram wanted to retire, and he offered a fair price for his land. *Daed* saw it as a chance to expand the herd because beef prices have been good and there is a high demand for Longhorn meat. Mr. Fletcher wanted to be paid in cash, so *Daed* borrowed the money."

Levi nodded. "And Samuel put up his own land as collateral?"

"Yes. I can't see how we can keep the property now."

"You would be surprised what you can accomplish when your back is against the wall. Where there is a will, there's a way."

"Really? Then there is a chance we won't lose the house?" Grateful, Gail reached out, laying a hand on his arm. "Oh, Levi, if you would help me through this trouble, I would be so grateful."

"I think I can advise you," he said but didn't have a chance to explain.

The sound of footsteps on pavement stone and a rustling of skirts filtered in through the open window over the kitchen sink.

"The girls are back from town," she said, and pressed a single finger to her lips. "For now, we will keep this between us."

Surprise registered on his face. "You're not going to tell them?"

Fresh anxiety knotted her insides. Deception was unforgivable, but for now she was determined to shield her younger sisters from the betrayal Slagel had committed against their family.

"Not yet." Gail thought fast and made a quick decision. Claiming the paperwork, she stuffed it deep into a pocket of her apron.

Chapter Three

Stunned by Gail's request, Levi watched as she hurried back to the stove. "Please, say nothing to my sisters until we have had a chance to talk further."

Moved by her desperate tone, he nodded. "Of course." How Gail chose to conduct her business was just that. Her business. An outsider with no ties to the property, he had no say one way or another.

The back door opened. Faces bright and cheerful, the Schroder sisters entered the house.

Catching sight of him, all three women went silent.

Bending to retrieve the biscuits, Gail pasted on a smile. "Look who's come to join us for breakfast."

Puzzled, the women stood silent. No one recognized him.

"It's Levi," Gail prodded.

Blinking myopically, Rebecca was the first to respond. "This is certainly a surprise." She squinted behind a pair of wire-frame glasses.

"Yes, I guess it is."

Rebecca's smile broadened to fill her face. "You've

been gone a long time." She offered a hug, brief but heartfelt.

"Didn't mean for it to be that way," Levi said, more than a little ashamed he'd never considered the feelings of others when he'd decided to run off. Through the three years he'd lived there, the girls had treated him decently.

"You've changed," Florene blurted in a robust, forthright manner. "You look so old now." Tiny and fragile, she barely touched five feet. Her features, like her frame, were delicately etched.

Hovering in the background, Amity elbowed her younger sister. Soft and doughy, she had a round face with expressive brown eyes and red cheeks. "Mind your manners," she scolded. "Just because it's on your tongue doesn't mean you should say it."

Florene blushed. "*Vergib mir.* I meant no offense."

Levi offered a smile. "None taken. I guess I've changed a lot."

"You have," Amity said.

"But we are glad to see you," Rebecca added.

Awakened by the commotion, Seth sat up, rubbing his eyes. "Daddy?"

The women lit up.

"But who is this *kleinen* I see?" Rebecca asked, giving a little clap. "Your *sohn*, Levi?"

If there were anything good and right in his world, his child was the reason. "This is Seth." Crossing to the sofa, he ruffled his son's hair.

Squirming, Seth dropped his head and buried his face. Since his mother's death, he'd become reticent around strange people, especially women. "Nooo," he murmured, barely loud enough to be heard.

Levi placed a hand on the back of Seth's neck, massaging lightly. "Please excuse Seth's manners. He's been cranky these last few days."

Finishing the bacon, Gail turned her attention to making the hash browns, adding grated potatoes to the hot bacon grease. While those cooked, she cracked several eggs into a bowl, adding a dash of butter, milk, salt and pepper, before whipping them into a froth. She poured the mix into a second pan. "A *gut* meal will fix him right up." Remarkably composed, she acted as if everything was normal.

Settling Seth back at the table, Levi tucked a napkin under his son's chin. "You mind your manners around these ladies, now."

Seth nodded. "Yes, Daddy."

"Anything I can do to help?"

"Sit down, Levi," Gail invited. "We've got this."

Greetings done, the conversation drifted as the sisters bustled around, helping get breakfast on the table.

"Who was that man in the car?" Rebecca asked. "He came tearing down the drive so fast I thought he was going to hit the buggy. Beryl was so frightened she nearly bolted."

"He's from the bank," Gail answered, speaking noncommittally.

"Why would he come to the house?" Amity asked.

"He said there was an issue with how Mr. Slagel was handling the ranch account," Gail said, carefully choosing every word. "I told him that man was no longer working here, and that I would take care of the problem. It's nothing."

Rebecca frowned. "It seems to me like the man did nothing after *Daed* died. Thanks to him, we lost the cowhands." Claiming the coffeepot, she filled mugs with the steaming hot brew. "I'm so glad Ezra and Ruth have stayed on, or we would have no one."

"I'm going into town as soon as I can," Gail said. "I'm going to post a notice for hire and take care of a few other things."

"You've had so much to do," Amity said. "I don't see how you've kept up."

Gail pursed her lips. "Not well enough," she said in a self-deprecating manner. Hash browns done, she piled them into a heap on a plate. The scrambled eggs soon followed. Next was the gravy, which she made up from a roux of bacon grease and flour. Adding milk, she mixed up a thick country-style gravy.

"I never liked him," Florene piped up. "His eyes were tiny, seemed dishonest." She set plates heaped with food on the table. Fluffy biscuits and the gravy followed.

"My goodness, you've outdone yourself this morning," Rebecca said, sitting and spreading a napkin neatly across her lap.

"There's enough for at least ten people," Florene said, eyeing the food on the table.

"Everything looks wonderful," Amity said.

Gail tucked in her skirt before taking a seat. "We've got two hungry men to feed," she announced. "I haven't had a chance to tell you everything, but Levi's offered to help me hire a few cowhands and advise me about the cattle." She raised a brow, giving him a look. "Aren't you?"

Levi's own brows rose. In a way, it was true. Gail had asked him for help. He couldn't very well say no. If nothing else, he owed the Schroder family a debt of gratitude. Samuel Schroder had put a roof over his head and food in his belly when he needed it most. The older man had also given him a steady profession, teaching the ins and out of keeping cattle.

Making a quick decision, he backed up her words.

"I'm happy to help out in exchange for a few home-cooked meals." He'd planned to ask if he could park his trailer on their property a few days anyway, so her request just cemented the deal.

"That's so generous of you," Rebecca said. "None of us know a thing about the cows."

Levi nodded. "Glad to lend a hand."

Giving him a grateful smile, Gail unfolded her napkin. "Would you say grace, Levi?"

Her request caught him off guard. He had not bowed his head over a meal in years.

Conscience gave him a kick. It wouldn't be right to sit at their table and not respect their ways. "I'm not—" Feeling strangely embarrassed, he gulped in a breath. "I'm not very good at praying anymore."

Rebecca smiled. "I always tell my students to just say what's in their hearts."

Levi looked around the table. Each nodded encouragingly.

"Please," Amity invited. "I know it's been a while, but there will always be a place here at the table for you and Seth."

A twinge touched his throat. "Thank you. I appreciate the welcome." He wished now he'd made an effort to stay in touch. A postcard or short letter. He believed that once he was gone the family wouldn't give him a second thought.

Rebecca added, "When *Daed* welcomed someone to

his table, they were always *familie*. It isn't blood that binds people together but love and respect."

Giving each of them a look, Levi stretched out his hands. Seth sat to one side of him, Gail to the other. His son's small hand easily accepted his grip, as did hers. Beneath his touch, her skin radiated warmth and acceptance.

Levi bowed his head and closed his eyes. Reaching back in his memory, he tried to recall the many meals he'd eaten at this very table. Then, Samuel Schroder had sat at the head of the table, a strong man who was humble enough to give thanks for the many blessings he received.

Pulling in a deep breath, he fought to keep his voice steady. Somehow the words came easily, naturally.

"Dear Lord, thank You for welcoming me back to this table. Please keep Your guiding hands over those who are here and help us remember those who have passed…"

"Amen," the sisters murmured when he was done.

Blessing over, everyone tucked into their meal.

After cleaning his plate, Levi exclaimed, "If I eat another bite, my pants will burst."

Wiping his mouth, he pushed his now-empty plate away. The food Gail had prepared was not just delicious, it was a downright feast. The meal he'd just eaten was all harvested from the gardens and livestock kept on the property.

"There's still some bacon and hash browns left," Rebecca said.

"What about another biscuit with jam," Florene suggested.

"I'd like more bacon," Seth piped up.

Levi frowned at his son. "Remember your manners," he reminded, using his stern dad voice.

Seth grinned. "More bacon, *please*."

Sitting next to him, Amity chuckled. "I think that child has hollow legs."

Gail added another slice of bacon to Seth's plate and then refilled his empty glass. "The *boi* has a *gut* appetite."

Levi let out a sigh. "Don't be greedy. You don't need a stomachache later."

Chewing a piece of bacon, Seth grinned. "It tastes good, Dad," he said before releasing a loud burp.

Levi groaned. Once Seth had gotten over his shyness, he'd become the center of attention. All the sisters doted on him, encouraging his tales of rodeo life to grow bigger and wilder with each telling.

"Please, son. There are ladies present."

Amity chuckled. "He's quite the little storyteller."

Having grown up around the rough-and-tumble atmosphere of the rodeo arena, Seth had gotten an earful. Like a parrot, he memorized and repeated much of what he heard. "Don't get him started, please. He can tell tall tales all day."

Readjusting her spectacles, Rebecca snickered. "Oh, he's harmless compared to some of my students."

The sound of the grandfather clock chiming from its place in the sitting room interrupted further conversation.

"Oh my! The time got away," Amity said, gulping down the last of her coffee. "It's already nine."

Rebecca pushed back her chair. "I've got to go. I promised Noel I would help him at the butcher shop today. One of his clerks is feeling unwell, and he's shorthanded. Now that school is out for the summer, it will give me something to do," she explained, hurrying to the foyer to gather her bags.

Amity also put some speed into her steps. "If the horse trots fast, we can make it into town in twenty minutes," she said.

The two disappeared, gone for the day.

Seeming in no hurry, Florene dawdled at the table. "I'm so tired," she yawned. "I could sit here all day."

Gail passed her youngest sister a stern frown. "Haven't I warned you about staying up late on the phone?"

Levi's brows rose. "Phone?"

"The *Ordnung* allows phones for business or emergency nowadays," Gail explained. "It is not for social media and communicating with boys."

Florene blushed bright red and dropped her gaze guiltily. "I was just texting a friend," she mumbled.

Gail's hands settled on her hips. "And putting off your work," she scolded. "Don't you have rabbits and chickens to feed?"

Florene slumped as if she carried the weight of the world. "I feel like I'm tied down," she complained, crossing her arms with defiance. "I want to go places and do something more than tend animals and work in the garden. Someday I'll live the way I want—like Levi did."

Levi held up a hand. "Don't be so quick to use me as an example."

"I wish I wasn't here," Florene pouted.

Lips pressed flat, Gail shook her head. "Be careful what you wish for," she countered. "The world out there isn't easy, and some people aren't as friendly as you'd like them to be. You might find yourself handed a slap instead of a smile."

Florene returned a typical teenager's moody expression. "I'll find out. My birthday will come soon, and you can't stop me."

Annoyance filled Gail's face. "While you're under this roof, you'll still do your chores and mind the way you were raised." Her tone brooked no argument.

Shoving away from the table, Florene tossed down her napkin. Expression stormy, she headed out the back door. The wooden screen clattered back against the door frame.

Watching her go, Gail bit her lower lip. "How can I deal with that child?"

"Looks like someone is going through a little rebellion," Levi chimed in.

Gail sighed with weary patience. "I don't know what's happened. She has been like this since *Daed* died. I've tried and tried, but I can't keep her in line."

"You've all been through a tough time," Levi said. "Losing a parent isn't easy, I know."

"I'm sorry. I'd forgotten you lost your own family when you were young," Gail said.

Levi's stomach tightened. He'd lost his parents and siblings in a single day. "You know as well as I do, the hurt never really goes away."

"You're right." Gail's face mirrored her feelings. "The wound heals but the scars are still on our hearts."

Having sat remarkably quiet, Seth piped up. "My mommy died," he announced matter-of-factly. "Daddy says she's in heaven." He tilted his head back. "I look in the sky, but I never see her."

Sorrow wove its way through Levi's memory. Now

five years old, Seth was too young to recall much about his mother, or her tragic passing.

"Mommy knows you're looking," he said, forcing a lightness he didn't feel. "Remember what I told you?"

"When I see rainbows, Mommy's smiling at me."

"What a nice thought, Seth." Bending over, Gail cleared the dishes off the table. "I think I'll borrow it, if you don't mind."

Seth nodded. "I like rainbows. They're pretty."

"I agree," Gail said. "Perhaps you'll draw us one. I believe Rebecca keeps extra paper and colored pencils on hand for her students. Maybe I can get them out for you later. Would you like that?"

Seth clapped eagerly. "Yes, please!"

"Let me finish my dishes and I'll find them."

Levi stood. "Can I help?"

"I've got it. You just sit and rest a bit." Piling the dishes in the sink, Gail ran hot water into the basin. "I'm sorry to hear about your *ehefrau*." Washing each dish carefully, she sorted and stacked them to put away.

"Thank you." Helping himself, Levi replenished his coffee. "Seth's mom passed a few years ago. Since then, it's been just him and me."

Sliding out of his chair, Seth began to fidget. "Can we go out and play, Daddy?"

"In a minute, son. The grown-ups need to talk."

"Why don't we take a walk outside?" Finished with the dishes, Gail shook out her rag. "I could use a breath of fresh air."

Levi set his cup aside. "Good idea. I need to stretch my legs and walk off this meal."

Seth bounced up and down. His blond hair stood on

end, looking as downy and fine as the fuzz on a baby chick. "Yeah!"

"Calm down, buddy. Let's not get too excited."

"It's nice to see some excitement around here for a change." Hanging her apron on a peg, Gail opened the screen. "Come this way."

Outside, the three walked down a cobbled path, each stone laid by hand and perfectly aligned.

The house nestled in the center of a copse of towering oak trees mixed with some cedars and pecan. Providing welcome shade in the summer, the trees offered a break from the fierce winds often whipping across the wide-open plains. Thick grass blanketed the yard, the type that greened up in the spring and took on a straw shade come winter's frost.

The backyard was a delightful place for children. A set of old-fashioned flat seats attached to ropes hung from sturdy branches. A playhouse perched among the branches of the sturdiest tree, accessible by a rope ladder. A patio overhung by an awning promised a cool place to spend the days when summer's heat chased everyone out of the house.

Seeing the swings, Seth ran ahead and climbed into a seat. His stubby legs pushed against the ground. Within seconds, he was soaring back and forth.

"Look at me!" he giggled hysterically. "I'm flying."

Worry touched Gail's expression. "Take it easy."

Levi couldn't suppress his smile. For the first time in months, a touch of joy had lightened Seth's mood. The kid rarely got a chance to play.

"I was planning to have Ezra cut them down," Gail explained. "No one's played on those in quite a few years."

"I'm glad you let them stay. Seth's having a ball." He glanced around, taking in the neatly fenced gardens and pens where domestic livestock roamed. "Gosh, it's like I was here yesterday."

The corners of her mouth widened. "You've been away so long. I wondered what you'd remember."

"I know it must seem like I was ungrateful for leaving, but I didn't mean it that way."

"I guess there comes a time when a man has to choose his own path and follow it."

"I was seventeen, and far from being a man," he corrected.

Looking around, a rush of emotions tightened his throat. Losing his parents at such a young age had cost him the security of a home and family.

Taking him in, Samuel Schroder had given him a foundation under his feet where he had, after a time, began to grow and thrive. The older man had treated him fairly, encouraging him to stay on.

As long as a man has a piece of ground under his feet, he's got a home, Samuel had often said.

When he was younger, the idea of living in one town his whole life sounded boring and dull. Now that he was a father, Levi recognized the wisdom behind Samuel's words. Like a tree, a man also needed to set down roots.

Abandoning the swing, Seth ran up. A wide grin split his youthful face.

"I like this place," he said, throwing his arms around his father's legs and holding tight as he looked up with bright eyes. "Can we camp here, Daddy? Please?"

Gail laughed. "Of course, you can. I insist."

Levi felt a tug on his heartstrings. Glancing down at Seth, he returned his gaze to her face. Despite her cheerful demeanor, he knew the bank agent's visit put a heavy weight on her spirit.

"I think that's a great idea, son," he said, and gave Gail a knowing wink.

Nodding, she offered a smile. "I'm thankful the Lord sent you today, Levi. It's an answered prayer."

Chapter Four

Seth skipped ahead as they walked across the barn-yard. The youngster was delighted with the variety of animals in their pens.

"Dad, look, there's bunnies and chicks!" Spotting a handful of pups trailing their mother, Seth clapped his hands. "And puppies!"

"I see, son, I see." Giving his head a shake, Levi rolled his eyes. "You'd think the boy hasn't ever seen animals before."

Halfway hiding her grin, Gail soaked in the child's delight. Like most self-sustaining properties, the ranch looked like a petting zoo. Goats, chickens, rabbits and a few milk cows grazed behind the safety of barbed wire fences. A handful of mutts lounged nearby, keeping an eye out for predators. A barn with a nearby corral housed the horses, a sturdy breed of cow ponies bred to work with cattle.

Blue-eyed like his father, Seth was small for his age, with fine, delicate features. A ball of energy, he ran around to take in all the sights.

"Anything small is cute." Basking in Seth's delight,

she laughed. "That's the appeal of babies. They are born adorable for a reason."

Levi guffawed. "Can't say I saw much adorable in the red, squalling baby Betheny delivered. Seth was born with a good set of lungs and he used them a lot when he was hungry, that's for sure."

His comment perked Gail's curiosity. This was the first time Levi had mentioned Seth's mother by name. She knew the boy's mother was deceased but didn't know what had happened, or when.

A myriad of questions crowded into her mind. The desire to know more gripped her harder, but she decided not to pursue the topic. It would be rude to go prying into his private business. If Levi had something to say, he'd say it.

Have patience, she counseled herself. As the Bible said, all would be revealed in its time.

Having chased down a puppy, Seth caught the squirming canine in a bear hug. The canine wiggled with delight at the attention, covering the boy's face with wet, sloppy kisses. "Oh, Daddy, he loves me!"

Levi's mouth curved upward in the tight half smile parents often gave their children right before the word *nein* rolled off their tongue. "Looks that way."

Seth trotted up. "Can I have him? Please, please!"

Levi reached out, ruffling the pup's downy fur. "I know you want a dog, but we don't have room for one in the RV."

Seth's face fell a mile. Fat tears welled in his eyes. "But…but…you told me we could get a puppy…" he blubbered, hugging the animal tight. Squeezed within an inch of its life, the pup yelped with displeasure.

"Son, I said not right now. When we get a house of

our own someday, we will look into it." Sighing, Levi bent and pried the dog out of his child's protective grasp. "Turn it loose before you hurt it."

The mutt hightailed it back to its mother, disappearing among its littermates. A low growl rolled over the mama dog's taut lips.

Seeing his dream dash away, Seth bawled harder.

A little embarrassed, Levi grimaced. "Sorry. Someone's still on the cranky side."

Unable to bear the disappointment in the boy's eyes, Gail knelt, coming down to his level. "The pup belongs to no one, so he can be yours if you want him," she said. "But since your RV is small, maybe you should keep him outside. And while you are here, you can play with him every day in the barnyard. Will that work?"

Tears drying up as fast as they had appeared, Seth reluctantly nodded. "Can I name him, too?"

"Of course." She glanced up at Levi. "Does that sound like a plan to you?"

Giving her a look, Levi lifted the brim on his straw hat, giving his forehead a rub. "I think you just bamboozled me into getting a dog, though I'm not sure how yet."

Seeing him smile with genuine delight, Gail felt a pulse deep in her heart. Its beat shifted from steady to double time, sending warmth through her veins.

Back when he was a teenager, nothing ruffled Levi. He was courteous to a fault. Whereas she would grumble when saddled with household chores she had no love for, Levi had always done as he was asked. He never argued and had completed his work with quiet contemplation.

Standing, Gail brushed at her skirt to straighten out

the wrinkles. No matter how much starch she put into the ironing, her dresses never failed to look like she wadded them up before putting them on.

"You never could say no."

A shrug rolled off his shoulders. "It's easier just to tell a woman *ja* and let her have her way. What is the old saying? 'Happy wife, happy life.'"

Looking into his rugged face, Gail felt a blush warm her cheeks. She dipped her head and folded her arms in front of her chest. If things had been different, if she'd been older, would she have had a chance of winning his heart? As it was, she was barely on the cusp of fourteen when he'd departed.

Blinking hard to still her racing mind, Gail pushed the unwelcome thought out. No matter which path she walked, the outcome would always be the same.

Levi had left the ranch, going on to have a wife and child. She had remained single and, it seemed, would never have a *familie* of her own.

Gott gives us what he wants us to have, she reminded herself, shamed by her uncharacteristic resentment of a woman she'd never met. A woman taken much too soon from her husband and son.

"I will pray you know happiness again, Levi."

A moment of silence stretched between them.

Levi opened his mouth, but he never had the chance to reply.

Chattering to herself, Florene rounded the barn. She held a wicker basket of garden clippings, and a billy goat trailed at her heels.

Spotting the trio, she raised a hand as if to wave. "I'm doing my chores," she grumbled, heading toward the rabbit pens.

A bell tinkling around its neck, the goat kicked up its heels when a playful puppy nipped at its fluffy tail.

"Hey, now! Leave Sassy alone." Florene shooed the pup away. "Gail, control your dogs, please."

Entranced by the miniature goat, Seth ran up. The puppy no longer held his interest. "Can I pet it?"

Florene shrugged. "Sure."

"It's so cute and soft," the boy enthused, running his hands gently over the goat's neck and back. "Does it follow you around all the time?"

"I suppose it does."

Gail found reason to smile. Watching Florene interact with her animals was always a pleasure. Though her younger sister had taken on a teenager's rebellious streak, deep down inside Florene was a kind and caring person. She had a way with four-legged creatures, and had successfully nursed many orphaned animals to maturity, even when they had no hope for survival.

After the goat's mother had rejected it, Florene had taken the lonesome baby to raise, bottle-feeding it around the clock until it was old enough to be weaned. Whenever she was outside, wherever Florene went, the goat went, too.

She unlatched the gate and stepped into the rabbit pen. "Come on, bunnies."

Snow-white save for their black-tipped ears and noses, the ruby-eyed rabbits hopped around, foraging through their morning breakfast, a selection of trimmings from the flower beds and gardens. The hares were voracious.

Since they were old enough, each girl had a specific chore that would teach the value of work. To earn her pin money, Florene sold her rabbits, chickens and eggs at the local farmers' market. She took great care choosing her breeding stock and selling the rest. She kept a few select rabbits and chickens as pets.

"Can I feed the bunnies?" Seth asked.

"If he's being a bother—" Levi started to say.

Basket empty, Florene shrugged again. "He can help with the chickens. I've got a lot of eggs to gather."

Wanting to speak with Levi alone, Gail said, "I need to go to town so I can clear up the business Mr. Slagel left undone." As much as she wanted to forget the whole sorry mess, the bank's threat loomed at the edge of her mind. "Levi," she continued, "would you give me a ride?"

Catching her hint, he nodded. "Sure. Can Florene keep an eye on Seth?"

Gail nodded. "Of course."

"I'll put the *boi* to work," Florene promised. "Can always use more hands."

Waiting until the two were out of earshot, Gail said, "Thank you for helping me."

"I'm honored you trust me," he said.

"I do. More than you know."

Sliding behind the wheel of his pickup, Levi reached for the ignition. "I think you've made the right decision," he said as he started the vehicle. The engine roared to life, humming smoothly. Having unhooked and set up the trailer, he no longer towed the heavy 5th wheel.

Gail climbed into the passenger's seat, with a manila folder in hand. It had taken her an additional hour to gather the paperwork she would require proving Slagel's theft. She still needed to go to the bank and get copies of the statements he'd concealed.

"I hate going to the police, but I don't think I have any other choice."

"If the man took that much money, you have to."

She clicked the seat belt into place and sighed. "The Lord says we are never to avenge ourselves."

"If I recall correctly, the Bible also says men shall be subject to the governing authorities. This is not vengeance, Gail. It is justice. This man's actions put your home and your living on the line. You might forgive him, but you also need to let the sheriff do his job."

Gail settled her hands calmly in her lap. "I know you're right. Even so, I can't help but wonder what would drive Mr. Slagel to steal from us. *Daed* always paid him fairly, as he did every man who worked here."

Putting the truck in gear, Levi guided it down the drive. "Some people are only honest until they find a way to take advantage. He probably wouldn't have tried it if your father were still alive."

Gail lowered her gaze. "I feel like such a fool."

Eyes going narrow, Levi sidled a look her way. "Stop blaming yourself. You are not responsible for that man's actions. You were unknowledgeable, and he took advantage of that."

"In other words, I am stupid."

Turning off the county road and onto the main highway that would take them into Burr Oak, Levi blew out a frustrated breath. "That's not what I said. If anyone is at fault, it is Samuel. He should have prepared you to take over, especially if his health was getting bad."

Her mouth went flat. "I am the one who failed him. *Daed* expected all of us to find suitable *ehmann*."

"You're what now—twenty-four?"

"Ja."

"Surely you've had suitors. Don't tell me you didn't kiss a few boys during your *rumspringa*? At least one of them should have been worth marrying."

Gail's expression grew taut. *"Mamm* passed away when I came of age and there was so much to take care of. I never had a true *rumspringa."*

Levi gave himself a kick. If there had been a hole nearby, he'd have crawled into it.

As the oldest unmarried daughter, Gail would have naturally stepped up to take over the household. She also had three younger sisters to care for. Instead of running around and exploring life outside the Amish community—as well as having the chance to socialize with other *youngies* and find a potential mate—she was firmly and inextricably bound by her commitment and loyalty to her family.

"Well, you didn't miss much."

Giving him a knowing look, Gail cocked her head. "Does that shoe-leather taste good?"

"Delicious," he muttered under his breath.

She straightened her shoulders. "I have had a few beaus. Why, I could have married Albert Dekker last year if I'd had a mind to."

Levi dragged a hand over his mouth. "Albert Dekker," he repeated slowly. "Wasn't he the red-haired guy with the big ears who used to help deliver the hay?"

Gail bristled. "Albert's quite handsome now. He's proposed twice."

Levi sidled another look her way. "So why haven't you said yes?"

Temper flaring, Gail said, "Why are we even talking about my love life?" She struck the dash with a hand. "Can't you make this thing go faster? I believe my buggy could outrun this rattletrap."

Aware he'd hit a nerve, Levi backed off. It was one thing to josh around for fun, but quite another to hurt someone's feelings.

"We're getting there." To distract her, he turned on the radio to his favorite rock and roll station.

Arms crossed, Gail sat stiff, still stewing in her anger. "I like classical," she said, reaching out to switch the channel.

Remembering her mention of a cell phone, Levi said, "So, tell me what else had changed since I left."

A smile crept across her face, softening her serious expression and crinkling the corners of her eyes. "Many things," she said. "We might be Plain folks, but we're not the backward hicks some people still think we are."

Levi shook his head. "I never would have imagined your father would allow a cell phone and the like in the house."

"There is nothing in the Bible that says we can't have modern technology to make our lives more comfortable and our work less trying. It helps that Bishop Harrison is fair about what we may use and how. We live simple lives, but we are not stupid. Just—" she shrugged "—different."

"Nothing wrong with different."

"I suppose not." The questioning look returned to her gaze. "Do you regret leaving Amish life?"

Looking into her eyes, so clear and green as a field of clover, Levi felt an odd twist to his midsection. In the depths of her gaze was an openness that said she accepted all and would judge none. "Sometimes." He shrugged. "I mean, I thought I had the world figured out when I was younger."

"Did you?"

"Oh, not by a long shot." He chuckled, not in amusement but in wry regret. "In fact, in hindsight, I can say I knew nothing. Less than nothing. When I left the ranch, I was as shaky as a newborn colt."

"So that grass…was it greener in the *Englisch* world?"

"Let's just say I took a couple hard knocks. More than my share." His reply, a bit rueful, was also truthful. Life had not been easy or trouble free.

"So you haven't been entirely happy?"

Her question gave Levi pause. If he could go back and rewrite the pages of his life, he'd do some heavy editing. Other pages, he wished he could tear up and throw away.

"I'm happy I have Seth and that I'm healthy enough to earn us a living. Past that, I'm just grateful to be standing upright and going forward."

"Have you ever given thanks to *Gott* for keeping a hand over you and your *sohn*?" Gail asked quietly.

Levi had no reply. Nevertheless, her question gave him food for thought. Perhaps the belief that he'd gotten himself through the tough times wasn't entirely accurate.

"Maybe I should," he said, not sure he was ready to commit one way or another. He'd sat in church long enough to have a good knowledge of the Bible, though years had passed since he'd been compelled to crack one open.

Gail, on the other hand, had no qualms about seeking divine guidance. Before making a decision, she'd sat down at the table in front of her father's old Bible and prayed for *Gott* to give her the wisdom she needed. Obedience to the church was a cornerstone of the Amish faith.

Despite his cynicism, Levi had to wonder if his own life would have been a little easier if he'd laid his burdens at the feet of the Lord?

The thought, fleeting as it was, burrowed into his mind.

More miles disappeared beneath the rolling wheels of his pickup. Passing over a low rise, the town came into view.

"Recognize it?" Gail asked.

Levi glanced around, looking for familiar landmarks. Even though he sometimes passed by when following the rodeo circuit through Texas, he'd never stopped long enough to take in all the changes to his hometown.

"So much has changed. It seems…bigger."

With exactly ten blocks and nary a stoplight in sight, the community grew up around a group of Old Order Amish families branching out from Pennsylvania in the 1930s. Seeking to take advantage of cheap and plentiful land, the settlers found the northern part of the state perfect for farming and ranching.

Through the years the population had expanded, as had the need for more public amenities. A courthouse and a post office had been established, as was an independent school district and a public library. Newer additions included a shining new stop-n-go convenience store with a row of gas pumps and a dollar store.

A sense of nostalgia tugged at his heartstrings. Driving through his hometown resurrected many of the good times he'd experienced when living with the Schroder family. What he'd once viewed as a boring and mundane were now cherished memories.

Shaking off his thoughts, Levi glanced toward Gail. Going silent, she stared out the window. Face pinched with worry, her mouth curved down, Walter Slagel's betrayal had clearly taken a toll on her.

Though he wanted to comfort her, Levi resisted the urge to reach for her hand. It wouldn't be proper to display such familiarity.

That she turned to him in her time of need had roused his protective instincts. He'd promised to help her untangle this mess, and he intended to follow through.

"Everything's going to be all right," he said attempting to lighten her mood.

She forced a smile. "I pray you are right."

"We'll figure this out," he returned, injecting confidence into his voice. "You have my word."

Chapter Five

Sheriff Evan Miller slid the paperwork across the desk toward Gail. "Please sign here."

Stomach knotted with anxiety, Gail looked over the typed documents the lawman had prepared. Hesitating, she didn't reach for the pen Miller offered. "What happens when I do?"

Miller leaned back in his chair. "Well, we'll take the complaint to the judge. Once he determines a crime has been committed, he will issue an arrest warrant. After that happens, we'll keep an eye out for Slagel."

"And then?"

"When he's arrested, the DA will file charges and it will go to court," Miller said. "Given the evidence against him, he'll probably get some lengthy prison time."

Looking at her old school friend Gail hesitated. While she had only gone to the eighth grade, Evan Miller had left the Amish and followed a career in law enforcement.

"I've never put a man in jail before."

"We can't do anything if you won't sign these," the

lawman prodded. "It's entirely your decision, of course, but I would say you'd be making a grave mistake if you decide to let him walk."

"You have to do it, Gail," Levi said softly. "If he's stolen from you, he'll steal from others."

She nodded. Knowing the Amish were reluctant to involve the law when they were victims of crime was probably why Walter Slagel believed he could walk away unscathed.

"I understand your hesitations," Evan Miller continued. "On one hand, you were raised to be forgiving of trespasses. On the other hand, Mr. Slagel didn't take just a few hundred dollars, which would be a petty misdemeanor. However, what he did was commit first-degree felony theft. Under Texas law, that adds up to a long stretch in prison."

"Is there no way to catch him and just make him repay the money? Then we wouldn't have to press charges."

Evan Miller shook his head. "It doesn't quite work that way. We can't put out an arrest warrant unless you sign—" he tapped the pages with his index finger "—these papers so we can file charges. No complaint, Slagel walks. Simple as that."

The invisible weight on her shoulders pressed harder. Her family had worked hard through many generations to build Schroder Ranch into one of the most highly sought Amish suppliers of prime organic meat. Schroder Longhorns were not just cattle; they were lovingly bred with an eye toward excellence.

Losing the money brought operations to a halt. True, she still had the land, equipment and cattle. But all that was now heavily mortgaged to the bank. And without cash to pay the vendors who supplied the machinery, feeds and other necessary items to run the operations, and cover payroll, Schroder Ranch was, effectively, spinning its wheels.

Stupid. Stupid. Stupid.

The word echoed repeatedly in Gail's mind.

If only she had been born a man instead of a woman, her father would have taught her the skills it took to run the ranch. Because she was a woman, all she was allowed to learn was cooking, cleaning and tending *kinder.*

Her mind flitted back to an earlier thought. If there was a way out of this disaster, she intended to learn how to run the ranch on her own. Not only the books, but everything about the cattle. Knowing Levi wouldn't be staying long, she must be prepared to stand on her own two feet.

Many an Amish widow had stepped into the business their husbands had established. Moreover, more and more single Amish women were branching out into business, running farm stands or small retail shops of their own, like her sister Amity.

Why couldn't she do the same? A daughter couldn't carry on her father's name, but she could certainly keep the Schroder legacy alive.

Things are going to change, starting today.

Expression going hard, she reached for the pen. Writing in her careful script, she signed the papers. She pushed them back across the desk and gave the sheriff a direct look. "I'll pray for Mr. Slagel's salvation. Until then, the law needs to deal with him here on earth."

Sheriff Miller collected his paperwork. "And that we will do." Standing, he came around his desk to shake hands with her and Levi, and escort them out. "I'll be in touch."

Gail nodded. "I hope we hear from you soon."

Levi accepted the sheriff's gesture. "Thank you for all you've done. We appreciate your time."

"I'll head over to see the judge as soon as I can," Miller promised. "Once he puts this in motion, we can put out an arrest warrant for Slagel. Hopefully, the information Gail provided will aid us in tracking him down. People usually run back to the places that are familiar, and knowing he has contacts in Oklahoma will help a lot."

"I know you'll do your best."

He offered a smile. "It's good to see you, Gail."

Gail touched the sheriff's arm. "You, too, Evan. And thank you for helping us through this."

Task complete, she departed the sheriff's office, stepping out into the afternoon sun. Levi fell into step beside her.

"I'm proud of you. That was brave of you to do."

Gail swallowed thickly. "I should have been wiser, more discerning. Instead, I let my own ignorance blind me."

"You were in mourning," Levi said gently. "This Slagel—for one reason or another, he saw an opportunity and took it."

"If he had troubles, all he had to do was ask for help. We would have given him anything he needed." She looked at him. "I know the Lord commands us to be forgiving, but I'm struggling with that."

"It's only right that you feel betrayed," Levi returned gently. "That's part of life. It might take time, but those feelings will pass."

Gail closed her eyes, and then opened and rubbed them. Her nights had been sleepless ones since Slagel disappeared. Allowing anger and disappointment get the better of her would only drag her down into despair.

"I hope so."

"Slagel dealt you a blow, but you don't have to let it beat you," he continued. "You've got resources."

She nodded. "It's been difficult for me to realize that because I felt like I was gazing down a dark hole with no end in sight. Now, I see I had it wrong the entire time. I need to look up, toward the Lord and the light of His grace and guidance. There will be a way to overcome this. I have to have faith."

Levi offered a smile of encouragement. "Amen to that."

Levi glanced around as he and Gail headed back toward the lot where he'd parked his pickup.

The downtown area was a pleasant one. Trees and neatly clipped hedges bordered part of the town's center, reserved as a rest area. Shaded benches and a gazebo overlooked a stone fountain and walkway fashioned out of natural stone.

The town impressed visitors with the quaint, old-fashioned ambience that harkened back to a gentler era. Small businesses prospered along the main street, a mix of Amish and *Englisch* that blended together in harmony. Just as they were about to cross the street, a man dressed in a short-sleeved white shirt, coveralls and boots jogged up. "Gail? Gail Schroder?"

Stopping mid-step, Gail turned. "What can I do for you, Mr. Yost?"

Levi recognized the owner of the local feedstore,

Linus Yost. No longer a rail-thin teenager, Linus had grown into a bear of a man with muscles developed from years of hefting sacks of heavy feed and massive bales of hay.

Pushing back his straw hat, Yost offered an apologetic smile. "I hate to bother you, Miss Schroder, but your account at the store is overdue and hasn't been paid in months."

Gail pasted on a smile. "I apologize for making you wait for your money," she said. "Mr. Slagel has left, and I've been trying to hire a new manager."

"I understand things slip through the cracks, and that you've got your hands full, what with your *daed*'s passing and all. But I have got a business to run, and if people do not pay their bills, I can't stay open."

"I understand completely. I—just—"

Levi stepped forward. "I'll be in to pay the bill this afternoon."

Linus Yost scratched beneath his lower lip. His beard indicated him to be a married man. "Levi?" he said behind a squint. "I didn't recognize you there for a minute." He offered his hand. "You sure have changed."

Levi accepted his gesture. "Nice to see you, too, Linus."

"I had no word you'd come back."

"Thought I'd stop by and stay a few days and catch up."

"Didn't know you were still in touch with anyone around here," Linus said.

"I let a lot of water go under the bridge, but I'm trying to make up for that."

"We're all very glad Levi has come home," Gail added. "Truth be told, I need the help."

Linus beamed. "Well, I'm glad to hear that, too. Your *daed* always said he was the best hand that ever worked cattle on his ranch."

"I don't disagree," Gail said.

"I have to get back to work." Tipping his hat, Linus offered his hand again. "Come in any time."

Levi waved a hand. "I'll be in to settle that bill."

After the man was out of earshot, Gail tossed him a look. "Levi, you're not responsible for our bills."

"The animals still have to eat and you're going to need supplies to keep them fed." He shrugged. "I've got a little money tucked away, so it's not a problem. I will pay the bill." To make her feel less beholden, he added, "You can pay me back when you've sorted through this mess. Until then, let me take care of things."

"I—I don't know what to say." Gail's eyes looked like they were starting to well up with tears.

Not comfortable with any shows of emotion at that moment, he rummaged for his keys, then glanced across the street. A small café beckoned.

His brow crinkled. Years ago, the space had been an empty lot. Now a business flourished there.

"Come on," he said, checking his watch. The morning, so full of activity, had given way to late afternoon. Lunch had come and gone, and his energy was beginning to wane. A good jolt of caffeine would give him a much-needed boost. Gail, too, could probably use a chance to sit down and rest.

"I'd like a cup of coffee. How about you?"

"A cup of tea would be wonderful about now." Acquiescing, Gail allowed him to lead the way.

Levi pushed open the front door, and they walked into a small but cheery dining area. Composed of an eclectic mix of brick, wood and other stone, the decor had a sweet, old-fashioned ambience.

Though the lunch run had apparently ended, the café buzzed with activity. Patrons talked and laughed, attended by waitresses.

A variety of tantalizing aromas wafted from the kitchen. From the day's specials listed on a blackboard on the wall, he could see the café served a mix of traditional Amish and *Englisch* foods. It seemed to be a popular spot for locals and tourists alike.

A slender young woman in a neat dress and apron was ready to help. Her blond hair was tucked under her white *kapp*, and her bright eyes sparkled with welcome. The pin she wore identified her as Alma.

"Guten nachmittag," she greeted as she guided them to a booth.

"Thank you," Levi said after they'd sat down. "Could I get some coffee—and bring whatever the lady would like."

"Hot tea," Gail said. "With honey and lemon."

A moment later Alma returned with their beverages. "Please let me know when you're ready to order." She left two menus on the table.

Levi took a sip of the hot brew. "That hits the spot."

Dunking her tea bag into the hot water, Gail looked around. "Been a long time since I've sat in a café. *Mamm* always said why eat out when we've got food at home."

He lowered his cup. "True. But sometimes a person needs to get out and enjoy themselves a little, just to socialize. How long has it been since you've been out?"

"Why, I go out fairly often," Gail said in her own defense.

"Where?"

She thought a moment. "Well, I go to church. There's always a potluck, and a singalong or other games."

"Yeah, but those are mostly for the kids," he said. "What do you do to relax, cut loose?"

"A couple of times a month I go to the library. And there's always a quilting bee going on."

Levi rolled his eyes. "None of that really sounds like fun."

Gail bristled, giving him a narrow look. "It is fun to me."

Levi was about to respond when the door of the café opened. A couple of rough-looking men shuffled inside. Their conversation was loud and coarse.

Catching sight of him, one of the men raised a hand in greeting. "There you are," he called.

Levi waved back in a half-hearted manner. These men were part of the same rodeo circuit and they often traveled in a group from event to event. Before leaving Montana, they had all agreed to meet up in Burr Oak, but he'd gotten sidetracked.

The men, Bill Reece and his brother, Shane, ambled up.

"Levi," Bill greeted. "Thought we'd lost you and Seth."

"Got tired and pulled over," Levi said, offering no further explanation. Cowboys were worse than women when it came to gossiping and he liked to keep his business to himself.

"Looks to me like you ditched us for some female company," Shane observed, and winked.

Levi bristled at the assumption. Bill and Shane Reece were single and ran with the partying crowd, one that he'd definitely had to step away from after becoming a parent.

"It's not that way at all," he said, immediately correcting the notion. "I just stopped to visit friends."

"Oh?" Bill released a snort of disbelief. "And who might this lady here be?"

Wanting the men to move along, Levi hurried through the introductions. "Gail Schroder, this is Bill and Shane Reece."

Both removed their hats.

"Nice to meet you," Bill Reece said.

"Sorry to interrupt," his younger brother added.

Clearly uncomfortable with their comments, Gail nodded politely. "Gentlemen."

"Gail is Amish, so mind your manners," Levi warned, making his displeasure clear. "Please, remember you are in the presence of a lady."

"Of course," Bill Reece said, and looked to Levi. "You ready for this weekend?"

Levi waved a hand to interrupt. "Gail hasn't got any interest in the rodeo or in bronc riding, fellas," he said and shot them both a look. "We'd like to get back to our conversation, if you don't mind."

Much to his relief, both men took the hint to move on.

"We'll catch up later," Bill said.

Shane tipped his head. "See you around."

"Maybe," Levi countered, offering no firm commitment.

The cowboys walked off, taking a booth at the opposite end of the café.

Suddenly self-conscious, Levi turned to Gail. "Sorry

about that. I didn't know they were going to show up. They can be a little uncouth, if you know what I mean."

"It's not a problem," she allowed graciously. "I enjoyed meeting your friends."

"Not really my friends," he corrected. "Just some guys I know from the rodeo circuit."

"I see." She pursed her lips. "I hope I'm not keeping you from anything important."

"I'd rather visit with you than hang out with those fellas," he insisted.

"I appreciate that, Levi." Pushing her tea aside, Gail slid out of the booth. "Would you mind if we go? I feel I should be home. There's so much work to do, and we have no hands."

"Of course." Standing, Levi took out his wallet and dug out a five-dollar bill, which he left on the table to cover their drinks and the tip.

They strolled toward the exit.

"I'd still like to post a help-wanted notice in the local newspaper," she said. "Would you mind driving me there?"

"Not at all." Pausing to open the door for her, he added. "Sorry I was teasing you before Bill and Shane interrupted. I didn't mean to make you angry."

"I'm not angry, Levi. You gave me something to think about." Her expression grew pensive. "I think you are right. I do need to get out more. Once we have straightened out things with the bank, I might get out and kick up my heels, so to speak."

He exhaled, relieved she wasn't upset. "I'm glad to hear that."

Gail offered a smile. "Thank you for all you've done.

I wouldn't have gotten through this morning without your help."

"I'll do what I can," he promised.

Escorting her outside, Levi considered the task ahead. It would take a lot of effort to put the Schroder ranch back into the black, but he had no doubt about Gail's determination to save her family's homestead.

Holding up his own plans a week or two to help her sort through the mess Slagel had left behind wouldn't cost him more than a little time. His schedule wasn't carved in stone.

Truth be told, now that he and Gail had reconnected, he was looking forward to spending time with her.

Staying on to lend a hand gave him the perfect excuse.

Chapter Six

The evening was subdued as Gail and her sisters gathered in the living room after a light supper. Because the entire day had been chaotic, she'd rushed to put something to eat on the table. After the meal, everyone settled into their favorite chairs. Never ones to let their hands be idle, each had some ongoing needlework project they worked on.

Levi sat among them, quietly sipping his coffee. He'd promised to say nothing about the bank agent's visit, and he kept his word. Given some paper and colored pencils, Seth stretched out on the thick, handwoven rug in front of the black-grated fireplace. Within minutes, he was asleep. The puppy he'd commandeered earlier in the day lay contentedly nearby, basking in the warm glow.

Gail knew Levi didn't approve of lying to her sisters about the state of their finances, but from her point of view it wasn't exactly a deception at all. More like a delay. She'd wanted to explore all her options before settling on a course of action. The news she had to deliver would be upsetting enough. Being able to present a solution would help allay the trauma.

Lowering her needlework, she cleared her throat. "I have something I need to say," she began slowly.

"It has to do with why that man was here earlier, doesn't it?" Rebecca asked presciently.

"I knew something was wrong," Amity added.

Florene barely glanced up. Her attention was tied to her smartphone.

"There's no easy way to say this, so I will just spit it out. The reason Walter Slagel ran off is because he stole the money from the last sale of cattle we sent to auction."

Rebecca's mouth folded into a frown. "I didn't have a good feeling about that man. No one honest packs up and leaves in the middle of the night."

"How much did he embezzle?" Amity asked, surprisingly calm.

"All of it," Gail said. "I've filed a report with the police, and now we wait for the law to do its work."

Sorting through swatches, Rebecca pushed her glasses back up on her nose. "Will the money Slagel took be recoverable?"

Levi glanced up. "Cash rarely is."

"The news doesn't get better. The loan *Daed* took out hasn't been paid for months." Reaching in her apron pocket, Gail produced the paperwork outlining the foreclosure threat. "Unfortunately, he mortgaged the homestead. The bank intends to take it in a month's time."

Florene finally glanced up from her smartphone. "So we're going to be homeless. Fantastic." Her voice smacked of sarcasm. "Great job."

Stung by her words, Gail felt her insides clench. "I

did the best I could," she said in her own defense. "I had no reason not to trust Mr. Slagel."

"When *Daed* was alive, he always kept a close eye on him," Rebecca chimed in. "Nothing got past him."

"Slagel clearly saw the opportunity after *Daed*'s passing and took it," Amity pointed out. "That shows a devious mind at work.

"He sold the cattle as his own," Gail confirmed. "And kept the money. The check and bill of sale he showed me was fake."

Amity nodded knowingly. "With a computer and a few clicks of a mouse, you can make anything look real nowadays."

Rebecca's lips thinned. "I understand technology can be a useful tool. But I'm glad the bishop bans us from having computers in our homes." Turning her head, she shot a look of disapproval at Florene.

Catching her sister's insinuation, Florene turned her cell phone facedown. "I don't think texting with my friends is wrong," she countered. "Besides, I'm not baptized, and I'm not staying Amish." Crossing her arms in front of her, she gave them a defiant look.

Unruffled by her younger sister's outburst, Gail didn't blink an eye. "That's fine." Needing something to do with her hands, she picked up her mending and nipped the thread to break the connection from the needle. "When are you moving?"

"What?" Caught by surprise, Florene stammered. "M-moving?"

Gail calmly continued. "As in packing your bags and leaving."

"Well...n...not until I'm eighteen," Florene answered, looking flustered.

"That's still a year away," Gail countered. "So, while you are still living under this roof, you will live by the rules of this house. And as the bishop said, cell phones are only for emergencies. Spending hours texting or on social media is not life-or-death."

Florene's expression darkened. "That's not fair! It's my right during my *rumspringa*."

Ever the peacemaker, Amity waved her hands. "Hold up," she said, calling for a time-out. "We're letting petty things distract us from more important issues." Turning to her younger sister, she put out a single finger. "It's true you're not baptized, but you are still part of an Amish family and were raised to be courteous to your elders. Have enough respect to put your phone aside when you are with family. Take it elsewhere if you want to message your friends."

Florene pouted as she turned off her phone and slid it into the pocket of her apron.

Amity then turned to Gail. "Now for you."

Gail's brows shot high. "Me?"

Amity pierced her with a frown. "*Ja*, you. For months you've been acting like life is a great burden."

"We've all tried to help you, but you've pushed us away, insisting you could handle things here on the ranch," Rebecca chimed in. "Well, I have news for you. You can't do it all, and now we're in a fine mess."

"But—" Tossing her mending back into the basket at her feet, Gail threw up her hands in frustration. "There's so much to do! How do I handle an entire ranch?"

"Learn!" Amity snapped.

"I intend to," Gail said, speaking more calmly than she felt. "I've talked to Levi and there is a solution."

Amity crossed her arms. "We're all listening."

"What are you going to do?" Rebecca asked.

Gail nodded to Levi. He'd been quiet throughout the entire exchange. "Please, explain."

Setting aside his coffee, Levi stood up. "Cattle aren't called *money on the hoof* for nothing. The best thing to do is cull some cattle from the herd and take them to auction. That will put money back in the bank. You won't get top dollar, but it should be enough to carry you through until the spring calves are ready for sale in the fall."

"How long will that take?" Amity asked.

"I'll need a little time to go through the herd and make my choices," Levi said. "You'll want to keep the cows that are of breeding age and cut those that haven't rebred on schedule. If they are not expecting or haven't got a spring calf by their side, they'll be on the chopping block."

"I wouldn't have known what to do," Gail admitted. "Levi is the one guiding me. Even though he has commitments of his own, he's agreed to stay and help us get the cattle to auction." She paused and then added, "He's also been generous enough to loan us a little money. Some bills were also unpaid, and he's been kind enough to cover them."

"Thank *Gott* you came, Levi," Rebecca said.

"I owe your family a debt of gratitude and I intend to repay it," Levi said softly. "I promised Gail I'd help out, and I will."

Amazed, Gail felt her heart fill with hope. The bank agent's dire warning was no longer a threat, but a challenge to be overcome. As she was the eldest of the sisters, keeping the family together, both physically and spiritually, would fall on her shoulders.

"I think now would be a good time to have a Bible

study," she said quietly. "It will be a good reminder that *Gott* is always with us, even through difficult times."

"I heartily agree," Rebecca said. Laying aside her project, she reached for the Bible on the end table. Opening the pages, she read from a passage. "See here in Matthew: The rain came down, the streams rose, and the winds blew and beat against that house; yet it did not fall."

"A house divided will," Amity added with some emphasis. "We must remember not to claw at each other's eyes like angry cats."

"*Daed* would be so disappointed in us," Rebecca added.

"*Mamm*, too, wouldn't want to see us talking down to each other," Amity added. "I think we should all make the promise that from now on, we will think before we speak in anger."

"That would be nice," Florene said after a moment. "If it means anything, I'll try harder not to aggravate you all with my cell phone."

"Well, that's a good start," Rebecca said drily.

Looking at her younger siblings, Gail felt her heart overflow with gratitude. Despite their quibbling, she loved them with all her heart. No matter what happened, they would always be sisters. And as sisters, they would always stick together no matter what might happen in their lives.

Her gaze turned to Levi.

The teenage boy she remembered had grown into a man. When she'd panicked over the banker's visit, he'd kept his wits, analyzing the situation and finding a solution that would keep the property out of foreclosure.

I am so blessed to have my family, she thought.

And that included Levi.

* * *

Stretched out in his bunk in the RV, Levi found rest eluded him. He desperately needed sleep, but every time he shut his eyes, they popped right back open. He was too keyed up.

Myriad details rustled through his head like the cattle he'd be tending. The Longhorns were the backbone of the entire operation. Without those cows, the ranch wouldn't be viable or profitable. Though he'd been away for over a decade, it was easy to recall most everything he'd learned as a young cowhand. *It was only a couple of weeks,* he reminded himself. *And then they'd be rolling down the road, on their way.*

But the idea of leaving didn't seem so enticing. Restless, Levi swung his legs over the edge of his bunk and stood up. Taking care not to disturb Seth, he slipped into the adjoining bathroom and shut the door. Splashing hot water on his face to revive his flagging energy, he stared into the mirror above the narrow vanity. The reflection of a tired man stared back.

Having spent most of his working career on the road, he had to admit that he was getting worn down from the constant travel from state to state. He and Seth rarely stayed in one town more than a few weeks.

When he was single, he'd enjoyed living a nomadic lifestyle. Marrying Betheny had settled him somewhat, but it was not destined to last.

Now that he was a father, the needs of his child preyed on his mind. Seth was growing like a weed. Every time he parked the RV, the trailer felt smaller and more cramped. Soon the day would come when the two of them would need a more permanent living arrangement. And Seth was almost old enough to start first grade, but the child could barely read or write. Despite that, Seth was a smart kid. Given a chance, he'd probably excel in school. He deserved a stable home and a decent education.

"It's getting time to do something else," Levi muttered to himself.

But what?

Having competed in the rodeo most of his adult life, he had limited experience in the working world. Not many people had a use for men who rode wild horses. Nearing thirty, his youth was fading. Time would soon become an enemy. Eventually, he'd have to walk away from the sport. A man could only take so much wear and tear before the mileage started to register on his body.

Hanging up his towel, he sighed. Going *Englisch* had expanded his knowledge about the world, but the fact remained that he still only had an eighth-grade education. There were not many employment options for a man of his age or experience.

Knowing he'd have to make some hard decisions soon, he cracked the door to check on Seth. The child slept in his own small bunk, surrounded by a multitude of toys. But not all the animals were inanimate. The pup Seth had set his cap on had somehow found its way into the RV. Already, a mat with a food and water dish sat out in the tiny kitchenette, along with some newspapers for accidents. Snuggled in the boy's embrace, the mongrel had made itself quite at home. By the looks of it, it was not going to be a small dog, either.

Levi shook his head. Of course, the kid had gotten his way.

His gaze shifted, taking in more details. A picture

frame welded to the wall and decorated with the word "Mommy" hung above Seth's head. A nightlight was nearby, illuminating the image of Seth's mother. Seth believed his mother watched over him from heaven, so he always wanted the light on so she could see him. In the child's mind, it made sense.

If only Seth knew Betheny didn't want him...

Chest going tight, Levi crept to the front of the RV. Thinking about the past would do no good. He could never undo or rewrite what had happened.

Filling the coffee maker with water, he added a scoop of pure Colombian roast to the basket. There was nothing better than a good strong cup of coffee to clear a man's head.

Pouring himself a cup a few minutes later, he sat down at the table. Around him, the kitchen and living room blended into a single living space, separated by a counter serving double duty as a breakfast bar. Down a short hall was the bathroom and a bedroom with two bunks and other storage spaces.

There had been no reason to hang on to the house he and Betheny had bought on the outskirts of Reno, Nevada. Sitting on a few acres of land, the house was picture perfect with its white picket fence and large fenced-in yard. All the hopes and dreams he'd had for his wife and child had gone up in smoke.

He pushed the thoughts away, refusing to think about all the mistakes he'd made. It was better to leave that past behind and walk away.

Sipping his coffee, Levi glanced out the window. After unhitching the trailer, he'd parked it just opposite the barn. Despite the thick line of trees bracketing the main house, he had a clear view of it through the backyard.

Looking at the place he'd briefly called home, he thought about all that had happened since he'd pulled into the drive. Samuel and Sarah Schroder were gone now, and Gail was the head of the house. A blind man could see she was struggling. She'd never been taught how to deal with the cattle. As a daughter, it was not her place to work out on the range.

Levi had to wonder what might have happened had he stayed in Burr Oak and gotten baptized. More than once, Samuel Schroder had hinted that he'd be willing to have him join the family as a son-in-law. Surely, out of his four daughters, Levi might find one of the girls to be a suitable bride.

Remembering how he'd brushed Samuel off, Levi frowned. Though it was common for the Amish to be married and starting their own families at a young age, his attention had always been fixed on his own ambitions.

Ambitions that didn't include getting married.

At least, not right away. There was a big world outside of Burr Oak, Texas, and he'd wanted to see it. Back then, he'd never paid any girl any attention. Certainly not Gail. All willowy limbs and pigtails, she was about eleven when her parents had taken him in. One thing he remembered most about her was her inability to keep herself tidy. Her white *kapp* was always askew, her braids always unwinding. Wearing her heart on her sleeve, she'd trailed him like a lovesick calf.

But he never gave her a second look. Having discovered the world of cowboying, he'd gotten pulled into the excitement of the rodeos. From his point of view, horses were far more interesting than gawky little girls.

Ashamed of how he'd treated her, Levi frowned. Had he hung around the ranch long enough for her to mature, there was no doubt in his mind he'd have sat up and taken notice.

What a fool.

Viewing her in a whole new light, he shook his head. Running off, he'd blown it. No doubt there. He couldn't court Gail now even if he wanted to. They walked in two different worlds.

Setting aside his empty cup, Levi felt a sense of longing settle deep inside his chest. He'd been raised by people who were models of self-sufficiency. Most of their food came from the garden and meat was plentiful enough. Chickens and rabbits were regularly served, along with beef, pork and lamb. Working from sunup to sundown, the Amish only purchased what they couldn't make or grow themselves. As for clothes, most everything he'd worn as a kid was handmade. The biggest treat of the year was a new pair of boots at Christmas. Everything else was made with love.

Faith. Home. Family. It all sounded so good.

Swallowing against the lump building at the back of his throat, Levi blinked hard. He wanted that again.

He just wasn't sure how to go about getting it. He'd always chosen the wrong path and burned the wrong bridges, a flaw he needed to work on if he ever hoped to achieve any sort of stability for himself and his son.

Chapter Seven

By the time her busy day ended, Gail wanted nothing more than to collapse on her bed. All the stress and activity the day had piled on her psyche made the space behind her temples thud. She'd been going nonstop since early morning. Dropping into bed at the scandalously late hour of 10:00 p.m., all she wanted to do was close her eyes.

Sleep, however, eluded her.

Tossing and turning, Gail struggled to find a comfortable spot on the bed. Another long night stretched ahead. Constant worry over her many responsibilities had worn her down to a nub. Exhaustion dogged her every waking moment.

For months, she'd been unable to find solace in her prayers, feeling every bit like a pilgrim lost in the wilderness. Levi's unexpected return had given her a sign *Gott* had heard her plea.

Rolling over onto her side, Gail attempted to regulate her breathing. Her mind kept racing, going off in wild directions. All the emotions she'd believed extinguished had come down on her like a ton of rocks. Banked embers of feelings had reignited.

Levi was home.

It was almost too good to be true.

Her thoughts drifted back to a time when she was younger and still innocent. Of course, she'd had a crush on him as big as the state of Texas, practically since the first day her parents had announced they would take in the orphaned boy. From the moment she'd laid eyes on him, she trailed him like a puppy, wishing he'd look her way.

Alas, he never looked at her twice.

As it inevitably did, time had unwound itself, disappearing into the ether. One year rolled into another, and then a decade had passed in the blink of an eye. She and Levi had changed: strangers becoming friends who'd again become strangers when he'd chosen to pursue the ambition that would take him far away from the prairie and lakes region surrounding Burr Oak, Texas.

Suddenly, she sat up, pressing a hand to her chest. "Dear *Gott*, help me stop thinking about Levi."

Knowing sleep would be elusive for her, she pushed aside the heavy covers, swung her legs over the edge of the bed and turned on her bedside lamp. She rubbed her eyes and glanced around the familiar space.

Like most Plain people, she preferred her private space to be neat and simple. Though the smallest, her room was the most comfortable, filled with a half bed and side table, an armoire, a rocking chair, and a shelf for personal items. A vanity with a deep porcelain basin and matching pitcher occupied one corner. Most every piece of furniture in the old house was an antique, handcrafted by Amish carpenters. The quilt on her bed was handmade, stitched before she was born.

A squat, flat-top iron stove also sat in one corner of the room. As the rambling old farmhouse didn't have central heating, the stove was very much in use during the cold season. Not only did it provide much-needed heat to the upper floor, but it was also a convenient way to make a quick cup of tea or heat water when she wanted water to wash her face. During the winter, the fire inside its black belly crackled, radiating with a reassuring warmth.

Pouring water from the pitcher into the vanity basin, she splashed her face before combing out her hair. She wove the thick, unruly mass into a tight bun. As usual, a few stubborn tendrils escaped, framing her face with stray curls.

Avoiding her usual drab choice, she chose a fresh dress sewn in peacock green. It was one usually reserved for socializing, but rarely worn. As an unmarried woman she could wear brighter colors, as a signal to men that she was single. Might as well get some use out of it instead of letting it rot on the hanger, unused. She slipped on the dress and tied a clean white apron around her waist. Last was her *kapp*, pinned into place.

Though the hours of night had begun to pass away, it was still too early to go downstairs.

Pulling up a chair, Gail set down and opened her Bible. A few hours of prayer and meditation on the coming day ahead would help clear her mind. Months had passed since she had spent quiet time, giving praise and thanks to *Gott* for his wisdom and the many mercies he'd granted her family through the generations.

By time the sun began to peek over the far horizon,

several hours had passed since she sat down to read. For her study, she'd chosen to revisit the story of Job. Job had lost everything, but he'd never given up his faith, and for that the Lord had blessed him twofold.

Feeling humbled and inspired, Gail put her Bible away.

I give my burden to you, Lord. Please bless the day ahead.

Humming under her breath, she went downstairs. Time was getting away and there was a lot of work ahead. After coaxing the old cookstove back to life with a bellyful of wood and lots of kindling, she set to putting together breakfast. She had two extra people to cook for now.

One by one, her sisters filtered downstairs to tend to their morning chores before breakfast. Eggs would be gathered, the cows milked, and other sundry tasks would be taken care of before anyone ate a single bite.

As a surprise, Gail made bread pudding. Mixing a bowl of fresh eggs, milk, diced apples, raisins, cinnamon, sugar and a touch of nutmeg, she poured the mixture over leftover bread from yesterday's baking, and then sprinkled over a generous helping of pecans. She slid the pan into the oven and then whipped up a vanilla sauce to drizzle on top.

She put on a pot of freshly ground coffee to brew, and then set to frying up several thick slabs of ham. She prepared double the amount, planning to make sandwiches for lunch. But sandwiches were not any good without fresh bread, prompting her to prepare a loaf of sourdough to go into the oven. Within half an hour, it filled the kitchen with a scrumptious aroma.

Drawn by the amazing scents filling the air, her sisters gathered back in the kitchen, ready for the morning meal. Florene had brought in plenty of eggs and Rebecca had a bucket of fresh milk. Later, the milk would be churned into butter, and the leavings would become fresh buttermilk.

Dunking a tea bag into a mug, Rebecca blinked. "My gosh, I haven't seen you in that dress in ages, Gail. You hardly ever wear it."

More interested in food than fashion, Amity hovered near the stove. "Something smells wonderful."

"Bread pudding." Gail slid a pair of mitts onto her hands and opened the oven to retrieve the pan. The pudding had set, perfectly browned. She placed it on the counter to cool.

Amity bent over the pan. "You rarely make this."

"I know why," Rebecca said behind a knowing grin. "It is Levi's favorite, and we all know the way to a man's heart is through his stomach."

Amity rolled her eyes. "*Ach*, now I remember the torch you carried for that boy."

Cheeks going hot, Gail dipped her head. When they were younger, her sisters had teased her unmercifully over her infatuation for Levi. It didn't help that one of them had found a page that once dropped from her school notebook, the one on which she'd written "Mrs. Levi Wyse" and "Gail Wyse" in her neat, angular schoolgirl script.

"That was ages ago. I was just a child," she countered. "We all had our silly moments then."

"If he asked you now, I bet you would marry him," Florene teased.

"Oh, don't be foolish!" Gail exclaimed.

Florene's smile dropped. "Take a chill pill," she

tossed back at her, sliding into the slang she picked up from her *Englisch* friends.

Rebecca's gaze rose sharply. As a teacher, she rarely countenanced inappropriate behavior, and would quickly call out the offender with a stern warning. She often acted as the peacemaker in the family. "Hold on now," she said, stepping between the two sisters. "There's no reason to get snappy with each other."

Florene dropped into her chair. "Can't have a bit of fun around here," she grumbled.

Rebecca waggled a warning finger. "Don't, Florene." Whirling on her heel, she went after Gail. "And where did your ugly temper come from?"

Gail angled her chin. "I don't like being teased." Fuming, she turned back to her cooking, cracking eggs into a bowl. Fork in hand, she whipped them into a froth.

"Florene was just funning you," Amity added, anxiously playing the peacemaker. "We've all had our infatuations. Doesn't mean we're in love."

"Gail's not married because no man wants a mean old spinster," Florene stated, sticking out her tongue.

Gail was stung by the insult. Her throat suddenly closed, blocking her air. "Someone finish the cooking, please."

She set aside the frothed eggs. Blinking back tears, she hurried out the back door. The argument had entirely ruined her mood. Though she knew her youngest sister was just being a brat, the fact she was still unmarried and childless bothered her more than she cared to admit.

Hardly paying attention to where she was going, she plowed straight into Levi. His straw hat went flying.

"Oh!" Her voice squeaked with surprise and her heart slammed against her chest. As she attempted to get out of his way, her heel snagged on a paving stone lining the walkway. Arms pinwheeling, she landed in a heap.

"Are you all right?"

Dazed, Gail pressed a hand to her forehead. What a way to start the day, flat on her backside.

Embarrassment heated her cheeks. She wasn't sure if she should laugh or cry. Her breath caught in a hitch. "I—I'm fine."

Levi leaned down, reaching out to her. Slowly, he helped her get to her feet. "I'm such an oaf," he said by way of an apology. "I should have been watching where I was going."

Surprised by his strength, Gail tilted her head back and gazed up at him. Eyes the color of a clear morning sky gazed down on her. His irises were not just blue, they were dotted with flecks of gold. How had she never noticed this before?

Gathering her wits, she took a quick step back, catching a better look at him. Freshly shaven, Levi was dressed in jeans, boots and a plaid checkered work shirt with the sleeves rolled to the elbows.

Inhaling sharply to clear her head, she lifted a hand to straighten her *kapp*, which had shifted in the fall.

"It was my fault for being in a hurry. I just needed a breath of air." She fanned herself with a hand. "The kitchen is so hot this morning."

Levi bent, retrieving his hat. Running his fingers through his hair, he set it atop his head. "Sorry, we're late. Seth wanted to play with his puppy." He jerked a thumb toward the play area. She saw Seth perched on the tire swing, swinging himself around. The puppy bounced around, nipping playfully at his heels. Small barks and squeals of delight filled the air with joyful sounds.

The tiff with her sisters forgotten, Gail offered a smile. "That's all right. Breakfast is almost ready, so you two should come in before it gets cold."

He beamed at her. "Sounds good." Turning, he called, "Seth, come and eat."

Seth slid out of the swing and scooped up the dog. "Come on, Sparky." Crossing the yard, he gave his father a hopeful look. "Can Sparky have something, too?"

Levi shook his head. "Leave the dog outside."

Seth's expression clouded. "But he needs…" He stopped on the edge of blubbering, his bottom lip quivering.

"I think I can come up with a few bones for him to chew," Gail said, eager to soothe the child before the tears set in.

Seth's tears dried up. "Sparky would like that," he said, hugging his dog.

Levi opened his mouth and then quickly shut it. The expression on his face said he knew he'd been overruled again. He shook his head. "If Gail says it's okay, then it's fine by me."

Seth's antics brought out a smile. He was an adorable child with a lively personality. "He sure loves that dog," she said, leading the way back toward the house.

"He does." Levi easily fell into step beside her. His sideways gaze fell on her, registering appreciation. "I don't believe I've ever seen you in green."

Gail blushed. "I didn't think you would notice," she scoffed, bushing a nonexistent wrinkle out of her apron.

"Well, it sure looks nice on you."

"I'm sure in an hour, it will be stained and wrinkled," she said, referencing her penchant to turn every article of clothing she owned to tatters. Somehow, she always managed to attract every spill, smudge and tear the day's work in the kitchen and garden doled out.

Levi reached out, giving one of the ties to her *kapp* a little tug. "You'd look fine dressed in a potato sack."

The screen door opened, interrupting their conversation.

Rebecca stuck her head out, "Breakfast is ready," she called, waving a hand. "Come and eat."

Seth bounced in first, pup and all. "This is Sparky," he announced proudly. "He's mine."

Levi followed, admonishing his son to keep the dog out from underfoot.

Sighing over the magical moment, Gail dragged her feet. Levi Wyse had always made her heart beat a little faster. She supposed he always would.

Rebecca caught her arm as she passed. "You okay?"

Gail nodded. "*Ja*, fine." Drawing in a breath, she added, "I'm sorry I stormed out like that. It was wrong of me."

"It's all right." Relief lightened Rebecca's anxious features. "We shouldn't have teased you like that."

"It's okay." Gail added a smile. "Already forgotten."

After breakfast was done, the dishes were whisked away and piled in the sink. A last round of coffee was poured as everyone enjoyed the last few peaceful moments before hurrying off to the long day ahead.

Levi was the first to stand. "Guess I'd better head out. Those cows won't tend themselves." He motioned for his son. "Come on, Seth. We're going to work."

Seth grinned. "Yes, Daddy."

Gail readjusted her apron. "I'm coming, too." Whether he liked it or not, today was the day she was going to start learning how to do work on the ranch. Levi couldn't do the work of four men. The least she could do was help pick up the slack.

He gave her a look. "You're dressed much too nice to be going out in the pastures."

She glanced down. The frock she'd chosen to impress him with was entirely inappropriate for cleaning the barn, tending the horses and working with cattle.

I am such a fool.

"I'll change in a minute," she assured him.

Parked outside the barn, Ezra was tinkering with one of his old trucks. "Morning," he greeted, giving the newcomers the once-over.

Realizing the two had never been formally introduced, Gail remedied the matter. "Forgive my rudeness, Mr. Weaver. This is Levi Wyse."

Levi put out his hand. "Nice to meet you."

Accepting the gesture, Ezra Weaver barely concealed his look of suspicion. "Nice to meet you."

"Levi is going to help us with the cattle until I can hire some help. Please make him feel welcome," Gail said.

"I don't know if I'd agree with that," Ezra grunted. "What's this here fella know about runnin' cattle?"

Levi didn't blink. "I started working on this ranch when I was just a boy. Samuel Schroder put me on a horse and sent me out on that range from sunup to sundown. Everything I know, I learned from him."

"Is that so?"

"That's so."

Hostility settled between the two men, tense and awkward.

Gail stepped in, separating the two. "I won't stand for any arguing," she warned. "Mr. Weaver, I know you've been here a long time and I appreciate your concern. Of course, you do not know Levi. You were hired after he left. But Levi is a part of this family, and I won't have you treating him with any disrespect."

Ezra hesitated, then nodded, a sour expression on his face.

Unable to keep out of the conversation, Seth jumped protectively in front of his father. "My daddy's the best cowboy ever!"

Surprised by the child's outburst, Ezra Weaver raised his brows. His stern look began to fade. "You ready to fight it out, ain't ya?"

"Yes, sir!" Seth put up his fists. "I can beat you any day!"

Levi caught his son by the arm. "What did I tell you about fighting, Seth? That's never the answer."

Seth burst into tears. "He's being mean to you!"

Ezra Weaver crumbled. "Aw, now, don't cry like that. I didn't mean no harm. Us men, well, we gotta kick a little dirt to show who's boss."

Face swollen, tears dripping, Seth sucked in a breath. "My daddy can kick more dirt than you."

Levi took his son by the shoulders. "That's not an acceptable way to talk to an adult." He guided Seth around. "Tell Mr. Weaver you're sorry."

Gulping down a mouthful of air, Seth sniffled. Tears shimmered in his eyes. "I'm sorry," he warbled. "I didn't mean to do nothing wrong."

"You're okay, kid," Ezra groused. A humorless laugh pressed past his lips. "Got some spunk, that's for sure."

Having had enough, Gail folded her arms. "Don't you have chores to take care of, Mr. Weaver?" To make sure he got the message, she raised her brows.

"Yeah, I do, ma'am." Tipping his hat, Ezra Weaver ambled off.

Watching him go, Levi shook his head. "I apologize for Seth's behavior."

"Mr. Weaver is the one who conducted himself badly, and I intend to have a little talk with him later on. There was no reason to treat you that way."

"Don't be too hard on the man. He is right to be wary. He might be a little gruff about it, but he is just trying to make sure everything is okay. If our roles were reversed, I'd probably do the same thing."

Gail sighed. "I suppose I should be grateful for his loyalty."

"Loyalty goes a long way in this world nowadays." Giving her a smile, Levi turned his attention toward the work ahead. "If you can find a good man, keep him," he said over his shoulder.

Gail watched him go. Levi didn't know it, but she'd found her man, years ago.

He just didn't know he was that man.

Chapter Eight

"How long has it been since you've worked with cattle?"

Patting the neck of the cow pony he intended to ride for the day, Levi laughed. "It's been a while, but you never forget how to deal with those ornery beasts. It will be fine. I promise."

"You're not doing the work alone," Gail said, and doubled down. "I'm going to be out there, too."

Levi visually swept her slight figure. Truth be told, he needed the help. She had no hired hands, and it might take days or even weeks to hire replacements. Because the funds to cover payroll were mighty skimpy, all the job offered was room and board for the men and their horses; not exactly an enticement for such strenuous labor. The sooner they got the cattle sold, the sooner things would be back on track.

"I don't like the idea, but we have no choice."

"Mrs. Weaver is going to take over the cooking, and Florene has agreed to help out with household chores. Rebecca will also lend a hand. And Amity plans to keep the ledgers for the ranch, too. We're all going to learn what needs to be done and do it."

Pushing back his hat, Levi gave his hairline a good scratch. If nothing else, he admired her fortitude. Challenged, she'd refused to be defeated. "Sounds good."

"And I didn't forget Seth," Gail continued, refusing to waver. "Mrs. Weaver will keep an eye on him in the mornings, so you won't have to wake him early. At lunchtime, I will pick him up and bring him out to visit with you. Rebecca will watch him after she gets home." She offered an anxious smile. "I think we have everything covered."

He nodded. "Well, I guess there's no arguing with you. You're the boss."

"Mr. Weaver's getting the buckboard ready so I can follow you." Squaring her shoulders, she pulled herself up to her full height. "Today, I become a real cowgirl. All you know, I want you to teach me."

"Riding fences and looking for predators can be mighty boring. Not to mention looking for downed or weak cattle. That really isn't a woman's work."

Gail stuck out her chin. "Just because I'm a woman doesn't mean I am not capable of doing a man's job. Every day you're out there, I'll be there, too."

Levi glanced past her, looking outside the barn. "Then we'd best get going. Time's getting away and the cattle haven't been looked after in nearly a week. Best get out on the property and see what we find."

"You lead, I'll follow."

Levi tipped his hat. "Yes, ma'am." Slipping a booted foot into the stirrup, he mounted the horse.

"I think old Bob remembers you."

"Hope so." Levi checked his gear. A length of rope

was attached to the saddle's horn. A set of saddlebags carried the supplies he needed for a long day on the range, including a knife, a canteen of water, beef jerky, a rain slicker and a few bandannas used as face coverings when the dirt got up. A rifle scabbard hung on the off side of the horse, with the butt at horn height and the rifle's barrel angled toward the back.

"I'll meet you at the gate."

Gail watched Levi go, commanding the horse with a practiced hand. Hat tilted to shield his eyes from the sun, back straight, he handled the reins with experienced hands. His eyes sparkled, and a grin turned up one corner of his mouth.

Needing to get a move on, she adjusted her sunbonnet. Her normal everyday *kapp* was not suitable for work under a grueling sun, so she'd switched to a hat with an overhanging brim. A bit too tatty for church, it was too good to discard. Having taken the time to change her clothes, her old cotton dress with three-quarter-length sleeves would be light enough to keep her cool through the day. She completed her working ensemble with a pair of knee-high boots, hardly attractive, but practical.

Gail walked around to the side of the barn. Under a bright morning sun, Ezra worked diligently, loading the last of the supplies onto the buckboard. The wagon was outfitted with many of the same things Levi had.

Leading the horse and wagon forward, Ezra stated, "Not sure I'm agreeing with your idea. Your daddy would roll over in his grave if he knew you were plannin' to work cattle."

Gail climbed into the buckboard, settling on the hard

seat. The wagon was made for hauling, not for comfort. "Not to be disrespectful, Mr. Weaver, but *Daed* isn't here and we're shorthanded. I'm trying to hire a few men, but no one's inquired about the ad I placed in the paper. If we are going to make this work, we all have to make sacrifices."

"I could—"

Gail shook her head. A few years ago, Ezra Weaver had a heart attack, which meant he could no longer do strenuous work. The jobs he did around the ranch were things he could do at his own pace, without stress.

"Ruth would skin us both alive if you tried to get on a horse," she laughed. "So don't even think about it."

"If you say so."

Gail took the reins. She'd been driving buckboards and buggies since she was knee-high to a grasshopper and would have no problem handling the horse or the wagon it pulled.

"Giddyap, Bessie!" Unlatching the brake that kept the wagon from rolling, she gave the mare a tap with the reins. A complacent horse, not easily ruffled, Bessie knew just the pace to keep the wagon moving.

The buckboard rolled.

As promised, Levi waited near the gate leading out into the pasture where the cattle grazed. Dismounting his horse, he pushed the heavy iron thing aside, allowing Gail into the fenced acreage.

Waiting for Levi to re-latch the gate, Gail gazed over gentle slopes stretching as far as the eye could see. Leaning her head back so the sun warmed her face, she pulled in a breath of fresh air. The scent of mesquite tickled her nostrils. In the distance, she glimpsed the cattle grazing. As Longhorns had the ability to survive on the vegetation of the open range, this type of cow was an ideal animal to manage.

A smile widened Gail's mouth. Hope and promise wove their way through her heart, reminding her that *Gott* gave every living soul a fresh start with each new day, erasing all the misery and mistakes of yesterday.

She waved. "I'm ready. Let's go!"

Chapter Nine

Gail's first few days out were busy ones. The spring calves were ready for branding, a task that needed to be done right away. Rounding up and catching hundreds of the animals roaming across several acres of grazing land was quite a chore.

Riding on horseback, Levi located and herded the animals into a fenced-in corral. Once contained, the calves that needed to be marked with the ranch's logo were separated from the group and penned.

And then the real work began.

Standing with her hands on her hips, Gail looked over the group to be branded. Come late fall, they would be ready to go to auction. Part of ranching was knowing that some of the animals they raised would be bound for slaughter.

"I didn't know we had so many younglings," she said.

"Over two hundred, by my count," Levi said. "I'm sure there are some stragglers, but I'll catch them as I find them. Right now, we need to get these babies branded."

Lips thinning, Gail nodded. The theft of cattle and other livestock was big business to rustlers, and unbranded cows were ripe for the picking. It would be simple enough for anyone with a truck and trailer to cut through the barbed wire fencing and load up some cows in the middle of the night. That was why it was so vital to keep men riding the fencing and checking the property lines. The state police rarely patrolled the rural settlements, if at all.

"I'll do the hard part, holding them down," Levi said. "Think you can handle the brand?"

"I guess I haven't got a choice."

"Not really. The sooner we get started, the faster it will go by."

"Just show me how."

Nodding, Levi walked her to the branding station, which was a contraption designed to keep the cow immobilized while the hot iron tattooed its skin. A brazier filled with hot coals stood nearby. A couple of branding irons had been set to heat in the heart of the fire. A small table with a few other items sat nearby, as did a pail of clean water.

"Now, here's what you do," he said, and went on to explain. "I'll catch the cows and clamp them down. Once I do that, you will take the brand and apply it to the flank. Do not press too deep or hard, or you will burn them and that could set up an infection. You do not want to cause hide or muscle damage. You need to do it straight on, so the brand comes off clean and readable."

While looking over the items, Gail forced herself to overcome her nerves. The idea of branding an animal's skin was slightly unsettling. But it was necessary. She just needed to get on with it. The sooner they got started, the sooner it would be over.

"I'm ready."

* * *

Hours later, they were finally done with the first batch of calves. They were both sweaty and grimy, and near to exhausted.

Taking a break, they had settled beneath a few shady trees to have a bite to eat and something cool to quench their thirst.

"You've done really well today. I've never seen any man do the work better," Levi said, taking a sip of the lemonade she'd packed in a thermos tucked into a cooler filled with ice.

Gail shook her head. "I'm not made of glass, you know. I can handle it."

Tipping back his hat, Levi gave his brow a wipe before lowering it back into place. The hot sun was blazing down on them; the temperatures felt near to a hundred or more. "I'd forgotten what a trial this was."

"I guess you were happy to leave it behind," she commented behind a grimace.

He shrugged. "Oh, I had a couple jobs on other ranches after I left here. But I spent most of my time chasing the rodeos. Decided not to go into the events that would require me to drag a horse and trailer after me. Barrel racing and calf roping just didn't excite me that much."

"Why broncs?"

His expression lit up, and a grin split his face. "I know you probably wouldn't understand, but it's an adrenaline rush. And even though it's just eight seconds, let me tell you, I've had a few rides that felt like they lasted a century although the horse sent me flying the minute it got out of the gate. There have been times when I hit the ground so hard I was sure I was headed toward the hospital."

Gail shook her head, unable to comprehend the attraction men had to dangerous sports. Why would any sane person risk life and limb just to sit on the back of a wild animal for a few seconds? She couldn't understand why anyone would put themselves in harm's way on the hopes of winning some money.

As if able to read the expression on her face, Levi let out a little laugh. "It's a crazy way to live, I know," he admitted. "If I were a smarter man, I might have picked an easier sport."

"I remember how excited you were when *Daed* took you to sell the wild bulls." Now and again, Samuel Schroder bred a bull that grew up wild and completely out of control. These types of beasts were highly sought after by breeders of rodeo animals, and when a bull or horse showed a particular trait, it was usually sold off. Allowed to go with his friends to some of the local events, Levi had fallen in love with the sport. By age fifteen, he was hooked.

Now that they had reconnected as adults, Gail didn't hold out the hope he might change his mind about the rodeo. Levi was no longer a part of the Amish community, and it was doubtful he'd ever want to come back. And even if he did have any interest in her, there was no way they would ever be allowed to have a relationship.

If she left the church, she'd be excommunicated. Banned. Baptism was a permanent vow to follow the church. Taking the vow and then breaking it meant the entire congregation would shun her. That would mean no one could speak with her, share a meal with her, or conduct any business. Although it might seem unfair, it was a widely accepted measure and considered necessary to preserve the Plain community.

Torn in half by her thoughts, Gail blinked back unbidden tears. Why did everything have to be so complicated?

Oblivious to her feelings, Levi drained the last of his lemonade. "That sure was good. But we'd best get back to work We've got plenty more to do before the day is done."

Chapter Ten

By the time Sunday morning arrived, Gail was glad *Gott* had added time to rest at the end of a week. There was a lot more to wrangling cattle than just sitting on a horse, watching a herd roam the range, munching grass.

Riding down deeply rutted dirt roads—and often no roads at all—was not fun. The buckboard bounced and jarred across the rolling hills. Even on the flatter land, there were washouts, holes, cactus and other things that could take out a wagon wheel, not to mention deep holes dug by jackrabbits that could snap a horse's leg without warning. The rugged country was also chock-full of brambles, thorns and rattlesnakes, and skunks, scorpions and wild deer. She didn't know which was worse: the uncomfortable wagon, the blazing sun, the dirt blasting her eyes or the insects.

By the end of her first day, she was utterly exhausted, barely able to keep her eyes open as she cleaned up before dropping into bed. The smell of cattle clung to her clothes.

Up early the next day, she'd found herself in the barn, mucking out stalls and getting the horses saddled and ready to work. Then she headed out to check the fence line, looking for breaches. If there was a break or a weak spot, it had to be repaired right there. To her credit, she was handy with the wire cutters and pliers. Then back to the corral for more branding.

By day three, she'd gained a new appreciation for the cowhands, holding the men who could do such work without complaint in high esteem.

By day four she'd come to hate the pesky bovines and never wanted to see another cow ever again.

Day five was a repeat of the previous ones, except busier. There was always something to do.

Snuggled into a warm bed, Gail rolled over onto her side, dragging the quilt over her head.

Cracking an eyelid, she glimpsed her bedside clock. Much to her surprise, the hands read ten after eight! Church was at 9:00 a.m., sharp. That gave her exactly twenty minutes to get up, get dressed and make it downstairs in time to leave for the ride into town.

"I can't believe I'm late," she murmured, rubbing away the cobwebs of sleep blurring her vision. She had never overslept a day in her life. Never!

Throwing off her covers, Gail hurried to quickly wash her face before grabbing her clothes: a plain black frock, black hose and flats. Hair a tangle, she twisted it up and pinned it into place. A white apron and *kapp* added the last touches. The sun had burned her exposed skin, giving a pink glow to her nose and cheeks.

Hurrying downstairs, she discovered her sisters had already finished breakfast.

"Why didn't anyone wake me?"

Her sisters looked up.

"I guess we just got busy," Amity said, shaking out

the quilt she'd painstakingly designed and sewn on for close to a year. The pattern was a bright burst of yellow sunflowers on a white background and trimmed all the way around with lace. "The church's charity auction is today."

"We've been getting ready for this afternoon," Rebecca chimed in, unfolding a set of cotton sheets and pillowcases, all bearing a matching design. Embroidered by hand, each tiny petal was perfectly crafted with silken embroidery thread.

But that was not all the girls had prepared. Florene added a beautifully framed needlepoint canvas. Sunflowers circled a familiar saying: *Gott segne dieses Haus.*

God Bless This House.

Gail groaned. She'd completely forgotten about the events taking place after church today. Besides an auction to benefit Emma Kresh, an Amish woman who'd recently lost her *ehmann*, there was also a potluck meal afterward. She'd intended to bake Shoofly and sugar-cream pies for the meal. Both recipes had been in her family for generations and were popular among the Pennsylvania Dutch people. But since she barely had a moment to rest, let alone bake, the pies had fallen to the wayside. She had nothing to contribute.

Ashamed she'd failed to do her part for a needy member of the community, she pressed a hand to her forehead. "*Ach*, I can't believe I forgot it was today."

Minutes ticked away, and there was no time to sit down for breakfast and have a bite to eat. She opted for a cup of coffee. Though her stomach growled, she'd have to wait till later for a meal. She eagerly sipped the dark brew. Warmth filtered through her aching body.

Amazing what a cup of caffeine and sugar could do for a person.

"I think we can forgive you," Rebecca said. "You've been gone from dawn to dusk every day. When would you have time?"

Amity refolded the quilt, careful not to let the lace sweep the floor. "This is from the entire Schroder family anyway, not just me."

A knock at the back door interrupted conversation.

Glancing toward the screen, Gail saw Ezra and Ruth Weaver. Both carried trays loaded down with pies.

"Here we are," Mrs. Weaver called. "All done and wrapped to go."

Gail gaped in disbelief. She hurried to help with the trays. Neatly covered with clear plastic wrap, the pies looked perfect. She couldn't have done a better job if she'd baked them herself.

"Oh, thank you! You are a gem, Ruth. I would have felt awful showing up empty-handed."

"She's been up since the crack of daylight, baking," Mr. Weaver filled in.

Mrs. Weaver laughed. "I know you make them for all the potluck events." Her expression shadowed. "Terrible thing about Mrs. Kresh, losing her husband so young."

"I agree," Gail said. "It must be crushing for her."

"I used your recipes," the older woman continued. "And I made a couple extra so there would be dessert for the family later."

"Perfect."

"We need to leave if we're going to get to church in time," Amity prodded.

Cloaks and bonnets thrown on, arms loaded up, everyone headed outside.

Levi was outside the barn, getting the horse and buggy ready to go. Built to carry up to six people and their possessions, the buggy was one of the newer models, fitted with headlights, taillights, interior lights and turn signals, all powered by batteries.

Entranced by the buggy, Seth ran around, clapping his hands with delight. Sparky nipped at his heels, barking intermittently. Together, the two created a joyous ruckus.

Seeing the adults, Seth came to a halt. "*Gooder mogan*," he greeted, haltingly attempting to speak the *Deitsch* language as he'd heard the adults do.

Levi shook his head. "Almost right," he said. "But you pronounce it like this—*guten morgen*." He sounded out the foreign words slowly.

Seth tried a second time, a little more successfully. "It means 'good morning,'" he finished, beaming.

Gail smiled. "Much better."

Tousling his son's hair, Levi grinned. "I thought I'd teach him some of the language I spoke as a kid."

Rebecca looked pleased. "I think that's a fine idea. He's almost six, *ja*?"

"In December."

"Excellent. How is he with his reading and writing?"

Levi demurred. "He knows some letters and numbers, but he's behind on learning to read." He looked a little ashamed. "That's my fault for not working with him. I should have read to him instead of shoving a tablet with some games in his hands."

"It's never too late to get him started," Rebecca stated.

"I'm afraid the delay's going to keep him back in school," Levi said. "I wasn't ready to let him go, but I guess it's getting to be time."

"Speaking of going," Amity said, shifting from foot to foot. "We need to get loaded and be on our way."

"Of course." Stepping away, Levi patted the side of the buggy, painted with glossy black enamel. "I think this is one of the fanciest contraptions I've ever seen."

Of all the buggies they owned, it was Gail's favorite.

Ezra Weaver opened the carry space cleverly built into the rear. Resting on built-in shelves, the pies would travel safely. Amity often used the buggy to carry her goods to town, hauling jars of honey, eggs and other fragile perishables. To keep things from breaking, Samuel Schroder had had the vehicle specially designed.

"Are you coming?" Rebecca asked Levi.

Gaze taking on a wistful look, he shook his head. "I haven't been to church in over ten years."

"You were born and raised in the community," Rebecca reminded. "And even though you have not been baptized, you were a member in good standing. I don't see how that changed."

"And Bishop Harrison welcomes anyone who will listen to his sermons," Amity finished.

Levi's brow crinkled at the unfamiliar name. "Then Bishop Meyer isn't there anymore?"

"He passed five years ago," Rebecca said.

"I remember Clark Harrison," Levi said. "Didn't he run the hardware store?"

"That's him. He's bishop now." Florene rolled her eyes. "That man can go on for days and days with his preaching."

Gail shot her younger sister a warning frown. "Florene, please…"

"Well, it's true," Florene shot back "Those benches are hard to sit on for three hours."

Silently, Gail agreed with her sister. Come the final hour, her legs bothered her dreadfully from sitting in one place so long.

Levi appeared to give the matter due consideration. "There's a lot to be done here. I would feel guilty running off when there's so much work. I'd like to get it done before I head over to Eastland this evening."

"What's in Eastland?" Amity asked.

"Rodeo." He grinned, adding, "I'd planned to participate, but I got tied up with things here. I'd still like to go. I've got friends who will be there."

Remembering the meeting at the café with Bill and Shane Reece, Gail's spirits dropped. She knew Levi had plans he wanted to pursue after the culled cattle were sold off. Then, he would tip his hat and go on down the road.

"Of course," she agreed, attempting to sound cheerful. "It will be a nice break for you and Seth."

"Would you like to go?" he asked out of the blue.

She blinked. "With you?"

"Well, yeah. With me," he invited. "Matter of fact, why don't you all come? Then you can see what my life has been like since I left."

"What a fine idea," Rebecca said. "Except, I've got plans after the auction, so I can't."

"I'm also tied up," Amity groaned. She looked at Gail. "But why don't you go and have an evening out?"

"*Ja!* You've been so cranky lately, we could use a break from you," Florene prodded.

Gail turned the idea over. True, she would enjoy the chance to relax and do something fun. It would also give her a glimpse of the sport that had lured Levi away from the ranch.

"I'll make you a deal," she said to him. "Come to church with us today, and this evening I will go with you and Seth to the rodeo."

Levi grinned. "You got a deal."

Guiding the buggy up the street, Levi saw the church parking lot was packed full. The neat white building claimed a single block, separated by a neat, paved stone walkway leading to the nearby community center.

He gaped. The layout had changed a lot since he'd last attended services. Save for a single vaulted window on the face of the building, there were no markings, not even a single cross, indicating the denomination of the church. Smaller windows mimicking the design of the original helped illuminate the building in natural sunlight. Lawns and hedges bracketing the building were immaculately kept. A stone-paved sidewalk circling the building led to a set of double doors. The new building was pleasant, bright and welcoming.

"What happened to the old church?"

Sitting beside him, Gail gave a tight smile. "It burned to the ground quite a few years ago."

"Probably a good thing, because that old building was unsafe," Amity added. "This one is up to city codes."

Levi digested that bit of information. He well recalled the stone-and-wood building that had stood earlier, which was believed to be as old as the town itself. Dank, cold and dangerous, it should have been demolished years ago, but was allowed to stand as a historical edifice. The new church building looked much more inviting to the weary soul.

Though most Amish settlements in Pennsylvania

and other states hosted Sunday services in the homes of congregants on a rotating basis, the Texas-based Amish were one of the few that worshipped in a designated building. Given the distance many rural families had to travel, it made more sense to have one central gathering place. An extension of the church was the nearby community center, which often hosted events for all townsfolk.

Finding a place to hitch up, Levi climbed down, helping each passenger out in turn. Taking his young son's hand, he bent close. "You remember what I told you?"

Seth bobbed his head up and down. "I think so."

"Be respectful to your elders," Levi said, giving him a gentle reminder.

The boy's face took on a serious expression. "Yes, sir."

Levi walked holding on to Seth with one hand and carrying a pie in the other, as he trailed Gail and her sisters on their way toward the church. Enjoying the warm morning, families milled throughout the crowded parking lot, everyone murmuring with anticipation as they unpacked items they'd brought for the auction. While the women were loaded down with food and items of their needlecraft, the men carried heavier pieces of furniture crafted in their workshops.

From what Levi glimpsed, there were many fine samples of Amish handiwork. There was no doubt in his mind that every item would sell.

In the community center, smiling women in neat black dresses and white *kapps* greeted them, directing them as to where the items should go. Inside, men and teenage boys hustled to set up tables and chairs for the potluck meal. Other women worked on displaying the donated items.

"Is there anywhere I can help?" Levi asked, handing over the pie to a girl working behind a counter set up for food preparation.

Giving him a shy smile, she shook her head. "*Englischers* are our guests."

Feeling less comfortable, Levi tried not to let her comment affect him. Looking around, he saw most of the men were clad in black, a white shirt beneath their coats being the only speck of color they wore. Worn over a vest, the men's suit coats lacked pockets or lapels or a collar. Instead of buttons, hooks or snaps allowed the coats to be closed, and suspenders, rather than belts, helped keep the pants up. Broadfall trousers and black boots completed the look.

Feeling very much out of place, Levi felt the urge to slink off. With his work clothes and Western-style hat, he looked like a gate-crasher among the congregation. It only made sense everyone would wear their best for such a formal occasion. Open to all, the auction was a chance to show the community what the Amish were all about.

I do not belong here.

"Maybe Seth and I should leave," he whispered to Gail.

"*Nein.*" To the girl, she said, "Levi grew up Amish right here in town."

The girl offered a nod of apology. "*Entschuldigen sie*," she said, switching to *Deitsch*. "I meant no offense."

"*Keinegenommen,*" Levi said, tipping the brim of his hat. None taken.

Blushing to the roots of her ears, the teen turned her attention to the pies. "What have you bought for the lunch today?"

"Shoofly and sugar cream pies." Gail handed over the tray she carried.

"*Wunderbar.* They look delicious." The pies joined the growing selection of scrumptious desserts. Cakes, cobblers, Danish and so much more were stacking up, waiting to be served to a hungry public.

Leaving the desserts, Gail and Levi rejoined her sisters. Together, they walked toward the entrance of the church.

Bishop Harrison stood at the doorway, greeting every congregant.

Holding Seth's hand, Levi stepped up. "*Guder mariye,* Bishop."

The bishop's forehead scrunched up. "I don't believe I know you two young men," he said behind a wide smile. Impeccably neat in his Sunday best, he was a portly man in his early fifties. "Welcome."

To help his memory, Levi prompted, "It's Levi Wyse. I used to come into your store with Samuel Schroder for supplies when I was a *youngie.*"

Bishop Harrison's face brightened. "Why of course. I recognize you now," he returned, clapping his hand on Levi's shoulder familiarly. "I haven't seen in you in such an awfully long time. Have you come back to stay or are you just visiting?"

Standing nearby, Gail answered for him. "Levi is in town a few weeks, helping us with the cattle."

"How thoughtful of you to help the Schroder *schwesder,*" Bishop Harrison said, then turned his attention to Seth. "And who is this *kinder*?"

"This is my *boi*, Seth."

"Well, I'm glad you've both come," the bishop said. "I hope you will enjoy today's services and that you plan to stay for the auction."

Out of habit, Levi tipped his hat. "Thank you, sir. We're happy to be here."

"The day care is this way," Gail said, leading Levi through the unfamiliar building. They walked down a short hallway and entered a bright, cheerful playroom already bustling with children. An older woman was overseeing the kids, while a group of tween girls helped with the needs of the babies and toddlers.

"*Guten morgen*, Mrs. Halper," Gail said, greeting the Sunday school teacher. "We have a new little one for you today. This is Seth."

Blinking myopically, Greta Halper clasped her hands. "Aren't you Elias Wyse's *boi*?"

Many years had passed since Levi had heard his father's name spoken. "*Ja*," he said, perking up. "You knew my *familie*?"

Greta Halper laughed. "I did. Your mother was my *dochter's* best friend. I had hoped Grace would make a match with my son. Alas, it wasn't meant to be, and she wed your father instead."

Levi quietly tucked away the information. He'd lost his parents at a young age, and his memories had faded with time. There were no photographs of his parents, and the passage of years had blurred their faces and muted their voices. Now and again, a clear image from his childhood came to mind, but those were few and far between. It was almost as if they had never existed.

Nostalgia prodded. "I would like to know more about

my mother's youth," he said. "Perhaps you'll tell me a bit about her when you have time."

"Gladly." Greta Halper turned her attention to Seth. "What a s*chönes kind*."

Grinning, Seth shyly hung back.

Bending to the boy's height, Mrs. Halper pointed to a group of boys about Seth's age playing with wooden horses. "Would you like to join us?"

Seth glanced up. "Can I? Please?"

Giving the boy a little nudge, Levi nodded. "Go on. I'll be back to pick you up after services."

All energy, Seth zoomed off.

"I see you have an *ehefrau* of your own now," Mrs. Halper said.

Giving Gail a quick glance, Levi shook his head. "Seth's mother died a few years ago."

"I am so sorry." Mrs. Halper reached out, taking his hand in hers. "Please know we will take *gut* care of your *sohn*."

"Danke."

In the main chapel, Levi took a seat beside Gail and her sisters on the pews lining the chapel. Like the outside of the building, the inside was undecorated. Save for two rows of hard, straight benches and a pulpit, there was nothing else. Sunlight streamed through the windows, warming the room and providing natural sunlight. As parishioners seated themselves, deacons handed out prayer books. As Gail had predicted, he recognized many faces, some more familiar than others. Several people gave him a friendly smile. He had not been forgotten, and the welcome bolstered his confidence.

As was tradition, services were held in Pennsylvania *Deitsch*, a dialect of German spoken mainly in the Amish community. Though rusty in the language, Levi gleaned the day's lesson centered around grace and forgiveness. Now and again, he whispered to Gail to request a clarification.

By noon, services concluded with a closing song of hope, sung by all. No music accompanied the clear, ringing voices of the parishioners, but it wasn't needed. Everyone sang together in perfect harmony. Again, the words were sung in *Deitsch*, but that didn't bother Levi one bit. He remembered the hymns from his youth, and sang with all his heart, basking in the simple pleasure of praising the Lord.

"What do you think?" Gail asked as they stood, ready to file out.

"I'd forgotten how peaceful it was to just sit and think on the Lord's word," Levi said, glad he'd agreed to attend.

"I'm ready for a break," Florene said, clearly looking forward to visiting with her friends.

"Don't go too far," Rebecca warned.

As the church emptied out, Levi felt a hand on his shoulder.

Surprised, he turned around. Bishop Harrison grinned. "I hope you enjoyed the sermon."

Levi returned a smile. "I did. Your message almost felt like you meant it for me."

Bishop Harrison beamed. "*Gut, gut.* I know some people grumble I go on a bit too long, but I feel the words need to be said." He paused, then added, "I do hope we will see you again."

Not sure he should make the commitment, Levi hesitated. Getting the cattle ready for auction was his number one priority. Even though the bank had given Gail a full month to settle the late payments, the days were slipping away. He still had to hire a truck and trailer to transport the animals, as well as take care of getting them sold.

"It's certainly a possibility," he said. "The Lord knows I could use some more time in the pews."

"As we all could," Bishop Harrison continued. "I also host a men's study group on Wednesday evenings. It's nothing formal. Just some prayer and instruction for those who are preparing for their baptism. You are welcome to come."

"Thank you, Bishop. I appreciate the invitation."

And he did. The sermon had filled him with an inner peace he hadn't experienced in a long time. The singing had also lifted his spirits. He'd also felt the fellowship and acceptance of the other congregants. Most everyone had welcomed him back with kind words.

"No pressure." The bishop chuckled in his jovial manner. "Sit in a time or two and see how you feel."

Hat in hand, Levi nodded. "Maybe I will."

"Gut." Bishop Harrison gave him a wink. "Who knows? The Lord might yet put the Amish back in you."

Levi reached out to shake the man's hand. "That might not be a bad idea."

It was true. Even though he'd only intended to stay long enough to help Gail get the ranch back in the black, he'd rediscovered living on the homestead had given him a longing for simpler times, when a man led a purposeful life dedicated to his god, his family and his community. It felt good to sit down at the table and bow his head over a hearty meal, well-earned after a hard day's work.

He had to wonder: if he decided to stay in Burr Oak, could he rejoin the Amish community?

The Bishop had put a bee in his bonnet, for sure. Maybe it was time to settle down and build a real home for Seth and him.

The notion gave him a fresh rush of energy. A plan began to take shape. When he had time, he wanted to look around and see what the housing and job markets had to offer. He knew the area, and the people. Surely, it wouldn't be hard for him to put down roots.

If nothing else, he'd also be closer to the Schroder ranch. Being within driving distance would give him a chance to drop by now and again.

Just to keep an eye on things.

Chapter Eleven

"What did you think of the auction?" Gail asked as they walked back to the buggy. Most every item had found a buyer and the sale had raised a good amount of money for the widow. Levi had bid on some handmade toys for Seth and a few other decorative items for his RV. The Amish widow and her family would be taken care of for quite a while.

Arms full of his purchases, Levi nodded. "You won't hear any complaints from me," he said, putting his items away. "The meal and sing-along was great, too. And getting to visit with folks I used to know was a real treat."

"*Gut*, I'm glad." Smiling, Gail added, "You didn't believe me when I told you I socialized."

Items tucked away, Levi turned, adjusting his hat to shade his eyes from the sun. "I was a jerk for picking at you," he admitted. "I really had a wonderful time."

"Honestly?" she asked. "You're not just saying that?"

Levi shook his head and made a gesture. "Nope. I mean every word."

"Me, too," Seth piped up, eager to share his news. "I made lots of friends."

"Thank you for inviting us," Levi added. "Best day we've had in a long time."

"I'm glad you both came."

"Me, too."

Now that the auction and potluck meal had ended and people began to drift away to enjoy the rest of their day, Rebecca had suggested a buggy ride so he could see how much Burr Oak had changed since he left.

Amity had gone to talk with a few other shopkeepers about the bishop's new decree on the use of computers and the internet in Amish-run businesses. Some shopkeepers were against the idea, while others were eager to embrace the technology that would help expand their reach to more customers. Florene had joined a group of friends. All the older teens stood in a group, eyes glued to their smartphones.

Watching them, Gail shook her head. Why didn't they just talk to each other?

Levi loaded Seth into the buggy, adjusting his car seat so that the child would be safe. "Now be still and mind your manners while we ride."

Seth nodded adamantly. "Yes, Daddy." He gave his father a pleading look. "Can we come back? I sure did have fun."

Levi smiled. "The bishop has said we can come again, so I think so."

"Yay!" Seth clapped his hands. "I can't wait."

"Sounds like he enjoyed playing with the other *kinder*," Gail commented as Levi unhitched the horse.

"I know he did. He needs to be around kids his own age." Guiding the buggy away from others parked nearby, Levi offered a hand to help Gail climb in. "Step carefully."

As his fingers curled around hers, Gail felt her pulse speed up.

Caught off guard by the unexpected reaction, she grabbed a handful of her skirt to keep it from catching on anything as she climbed into the passenger side. Seated, she smoothed out the wrinkles, making sure the hem fell to its proper place.

"Thank you," she murmured, waving a hand to lessen the flush heating her cheeks.

"You're welcome."

Levi climbed up beside her. To meet common safety standards, an orange triangle and taillights were affixed to the rear. The buggy was also outfitted with a simple braking system that would stop it from rolling into the horse when the animal came to a stop.

"I've been looking forward taking a ride around," he admitted.

Gail primly laced her fingers, settling her hands in her lap. "Burr Oak has really grown in the last ten years. More *Englischers* are coming in, and even some Amish from the northern states. New faces are always welcome."

"Never thought I'd miss small town living," he said, giving the reins a tug. The buggy rolled into motion, swaying gently. "I'd forgotten what it was like to ride in one of these things. Not so bad. Kind of relaxing."

Her nose wrinkled. "Better than cars, I think."

"I agree. Though I can't say I'm ready to give up my F150 pickup just yet."

Guiding the buggy through the afternoon traffic, Levi kept a firm hand on the reins. Though the horse was accustomed to the sounds made by vehicles, some drivers were careless when it came to the slower-moving buggies on the roads.

As they traveled, Levi's head swiveled every which way, taking in the sights. The wind kicked up, ruffling his hair. "I hardly recognize some places anymore. Main Street has really changed. A lot more shops than I remember."

Sweeping a few stray locks away from her face, Gail said, "It's why Amity wanted to rent a storefront in town. Her business is really taking off. She has even been able to hire someone to help her set up a computer to take online orders now that the town has an internet provider."

"I'll have to stop by and see her shop sometime," Levi commented.

The buggy rolled on. Because of the horse-drawn buggies and other wagons, gasoline-powered vehicles were forced to move at a slower pace. This didn't deter visitors, however. Amish goods had always been popular, and the town boasted a thriving tourist trade. Vacationers flocked to Burr Oak to purchase fresh produce and other handmade goods.

"Authentically Amish" was the official slogan of Burr Oak. It was even printed on the signs posted at the city limits. Amish and Texas were close to being an oxymoron, something that left some folks scratching their heads.

Gail watched as a car full of young women sped by. Top down, music blasting, they laughed and chattered. A few snapped pictures of the buggy and of her and Levi with their smartphones.

She momentarily dropped her gaze. It bothered her

the way tourists sometimes treated the Amish as if they were a curiosity.

Watching them go, she felt a brief pang of longing. Not having had a chance to experience *rumspringa*, she had no idea what it would be like to wear fashionable clothes or paint her fingernails with bright polish, as many other girls did when they came of age. As it was, Amish women were not allowed to wear cosmetics. Jewelry, too, was *verboten*.

Rumspringa was the time when Amish youths ventured into the *Englisch* world, eager to take a bite out of the forbidden apple. Though each community had its own rules, it was generally accepted that a youth could spend two years living their lives as they saw fit. After that time, they were expected to decide whether they would stay or leave.

Even though most Amish waited until marriage to be baptized, she had chosen to make her vow to the church formal when she'd turned eighteen. Her commitment to *Gott* was unbreakable. She'd never leave her faith. And unless she could find an Amish *ehmann*, she'd never wed.

Sometimes Gail wished she'd waited. Her sisters had yet to be baptized and could still marry outside the faith if they wished.

Albert Dekker had asked for her hand in marriage, as had a few other men in the community. As much as she'd liked them, she had had a difficult time even thinking about loving them. And though the bishop had approached her with the idea of a "family formation" match, she rejected the idea. Marrying an older widower who needed a wife to take care of his *kinder* and home didn't appeal to her.

She sighed. *The heart wants what the heart wants.*
And her heart had always wanted Levi.

A brief surge of emotion tightened her throat.

But all they could ever be was friends.

"Are you looking forward to the rodeo tonight?"
Levi asked.

Shaking off her melancholy, Gail nodded. "*Ja*, very
much."

Taking a breath and going out for an evening would
be wonderful, and she looked forward to the experience.
Though she had no interest in sports, she knew a lot of
people did. Rodeos were usually attached to livestock
shows and fairs, which were attended by most everyone. Some Amish boys were even known to join in.
Levi could have easily remained in the local area and
still chased his passion.

*Perhaps he would have, had Daed allowed him more
leeway.*

Instead of encouraging Levi's ambitions, Samuel
Schroder had forbidden him to participate. He expected
the teenager to work the cattle, day in and day out.

"I'm sorry you aren't able to compete. I know you'd
planned to."

Levi lifted his shoulders in a shrug. "It's okay. This
one is not a large payout. Mostly I planned to ride just
to keep my skills up. The big event I have my eye on
isn't until July. That's the one I'm looking forward to.
If I do win enough, it will take me and Seth through
the rest of the year." He paused, and then added. "At
least, I hope it will."

"Oh?"

"As a PRCA member, I've been invited to compete
in the qualifiers for the richest one-day payout rodeo

event of the year. It's called The Big Texan, and the purse is three million dollars, to be divided between competitors."

Eyes going wide, Gail gasped. "Cowboys are paid that much to ride a horse?"

Levi grinned. "Yes, ma'am. The higher the scores, the more that money goes into the pocket. There's even an extra bonus to be split between those who perform well."

"That's a lot of money."

"I've worked my whole career to be invited to compete in something this big. The event's going to take place in Fort Worth on Independence Day. If I qualify, I compete. Events like this only come along once or twice in a rodeo cowboy's life."

"And you're not getting much rest wrangling a lot of cows, I'm afraid," Gail said.

"No big deal," Levi said. "We'll get them sold in plenty of time to pay the bank. I'd like to see the look on Mr. Wilkins's face when you write him the check."

Her spirits sank. "And then you'll be on your way."

"Maybe." A shrug rolled off his broad shoulders. "Maybe not." He paused, clearing his throat. "I've had some things on my mind."

"Oh?"

Keeping one eye on the road, he gave her a sideways glance. "I guess I've begun to realize that I can't keep dragging my son around like he's so much baggage. Seth needs to go to school, make some friends and have that dog he wants. I can't give him that on the road."

"I know you've done the best you can, Levi. I can't imagine being a single parent and raising a *kind* on my own."

His expression seemed to tense as his jaw tightened. "You don't know the whole story, Gail, and I'm ashamed to tell you. What I will say is I've been selfish—wanting my own way without thinking about the needs of my child. Or even the feelings of others. I feel bad about the way I've treated the good people in my life. You're one of those people, and I'm sorry."

"Me?"

"Yes, you." He paused to clear his throat. "When you were a kid, I used to think you were a silly little girl—always following me around the ranch."

Gail blushed. "I didn't think you even noticed."

"Oh, I noticed. But you were young. And I was too busy strutting around like a peacock to pay you any attention."

"Let's be honest, Levi, I was a big pest."

"You were." He chuckled, then sobered. "But not anymore. You have grown into a fine woman. One I'm proud to know."

His words touched her deeply. "I'll always be your friend."

He nodded. "Anyway, I'm thinking about looking around Burr Oak for a piece of property. I think Seth would like to grow up in a small town. If we settled down here, he could go to school full-time. And he could go to church, too."

Gail's heart smacked her rib cage. Had she heard him correctly? "I believe Seth would like that."

"And there's another thing I plan to look into," he said, adding a hopeful smile. "The bishop has invited me to attend the men's Bible study."

Having overheard some of the conversation as they

filed out of church, Gail was pleased Levi had brought it up.

A tiny ember of hope flared. Was it possible he'd rejoin the church and get baptized? He hadn't said as much, but that was what she hoped was on his mind.

"How wonderful of Bishop Harrison to ask you, Levi," she said, careful not to reveal too much of her feelings. "I hope you will give it some consideration."

"I'm going to." His gaze brushed her face, a look as intimate as any physical touch. The tone of his voice said he was pleased. "I've got a lot of plans for me and Seth. I hope you'll be part of them, too."

Struggling to keep control over her emotions, Gail angled her head. Had she misheard him?

She dare not ask.

Tensing, her heart sped up as her thoughts whirled through her mind like a flock of birds set free into the wide blue sky. Though her joy would have had her shout out loud, she forced herself to stay calm. She had no doubts that the Lord was doing mighty and powerful things in Levi's life.

Feeling blessed to be a part of his journey, she said, "I will pray the Lord blesses you and your decisions."

"Thank you." His grin widened as he checked his watch. "Hope you're ready for a rodeo tonight."

But it wasn't the rodeo Gail had on her mind.

Was there a chance she and Levi might have a future together?

Reaching their destination, Levi parked his pickup within walking distance of the arena.

Keeping a firm grip on Seth's hand so he wouldn't lose him in the milling crowd, he paused to study the arena where the events were taking place. The scent of soil, manure and anxious animals all mingled together in the air. The evening promised to be pleasant as the sun tipped toward the horizon. In the summertime, the day lingered on until well past eight in the evening.

"Well, what do you think?"

Gail's smile wavered. "So noisy," she said. "I can barely hear myself think."

"It can get pretty crowded," he said, leading her through the swarm of people gathering around the food and drink vendors. Selling everything from hot dogs and hamburgers to cotton candy and other treats, the booths usually made a killing. There was nothing people liked more than eating as they watched the entertainment unfold.

And Levi loved every minute of it.

"Would you like something to eat?"

Gail started to shake her head, then caught herself. "Yes, I'll have something."

"What would you like?"

"I love those big hot pretzels," she confessed. "I had one at the county fair one time and it was wonderful."

"Then you shall have one."

Seth tugged at his shirt. "Can I have some cotton candy?"

Levi mulled his son's request. Even though he didn't approve of allowing a child that much sugar so late in the evening, he could hardly deny the kid his favorite treat.

"All right," he agreed, and led the way to the vendor.

"What color?" the man asked when it was their turn to order.

"Blue!" Seth called, delighted to watch as the man

operating the equipment expertly twirled the spun sugar onto a paper cone.

Levi inwardly winced as Seth devoured his treat. No doubt he'd regret it later when his kid was bouncing off the walls.

As he chose a soft drink for himself, Levi's gaze fell on the people buying harder beverages from other vendors. There was once a time when he was inclined to have an adult beverage. Matter of fact, he and Betheny had bonded over drinks at a party they'd both attended after a particularly intense competition that had seen him walk away with a couple of nice wins.

Leaving the food court behind, Levi couldn't help but think about Seth's mother. Her party-girl ways had frequently gotten her in trouble with the law and had, ultimately, been the cause of her tragic demise.

Frowning, he refused to think of the event that had sent his and Seth's life into a tailspin. He glanced at his son, so cheerful and full of life. Every day he thanked God Seth hadn't been harmed by her foolish decisions.

"Something wrong, Levi?"

Shaking his head, Levi smiled. "Not at all. Why do you ask?"

"You looked so sad for a moment."

"It's nothing," he said, packing away the memories he found unpleasant. The past was in the past, and there wasn't anything he could do to erase it. Building a future for Seth was going to be his focus from now on.

Treats in hand, they pressed through the crowd.

Levi led them into the stands. He liked to be up in the higher seats so he could see all the action in the arena below. The announcers were warming up the crowd, getting ready for the events to come. Competitors were prepping themselves and their animals. Wild horses and bulls snorted and bucked, fighting the handlers unloading them from trailers. Though not a large event, it promised to be an exciting one.

Pulling off a piece of her pretzel, Gail bit it daintily. "So, this is what you ran off to?"

"Yep."

Fresh memories filtered into his mind. When he'd first begun to chase his ambition, he'd started at the bottom, as all greenhorns usually did. He'd been thrown off his first bronc, but he knew he couldn't quit. Determination kept him moving forward.

It had taken him a few years, but eventually he'd started climbing the ladder as a professional. The money began to add up, and he even gained a little prestige as a bronc buster.

Though he had not stopped believing in *Gott*, Levi hadn't exactly thanked the Lord for his successes, either. Somehow bending a knee on Sunday became less and less important. And even though he made a living, he'd never quite hit the big time. He was, and probably always would be, just another cowboy hoping for a record-breaking ride.

Levi shook his head. He'd made a lot of mistakes. But his life wasn't finished, and many paths branched out ahead. He'd come to a fork in the road, and now had to decide which way to go.

Go back on the road, or stay in Burr Oak?

Glancing at Gail, he knew which way he leaned. The idea of marrying again had taken up space in his mind. *What if* he stayed in Burr Oak? *What if* he rejoined the church and got baptized? *What if* he asked Gail Schroder to be his wife?

Levi pulled back the reins on his thoughts.

One thing at a time, he warned himself.

He always tended to run ahead. If he were truly going to make the changes he envisioned, he needed to let *Gott* guide his actions.

Resettling in his seat, Levi attempted to focus on the events unspooling in the arena below. Rodeo action consisted of two types of competitions—roughstock events and timed events. Bareback riding, saddle bronc riding and bull riding belonged in the first category. Timed events consisted of steer wrestling, team roping, tie-down roping and barrel racing. Cowboys and cowgirls competed against the clock, as well as against each other. A contestant's goal was to post the best time in the event. If a competitor didn't place, they walked away empty-handed. Rodeo was one of the few sports that required an entrance fee but gave its contestants no compensation if they underperformed.

Levi had settled on bronc busting early on. The challenge of overcoming an angry wild horse sent a thrill through his veins. To earn a qualified score, the contestant rode one-handed, attempting to stay on the animal for eight seconds. If the rider touched the beast, themselves or any of their equipment with their free hand, they were disqualified.

As the bronc riding came up, he was anxious to see how other riders would fare. Down in the arena he caught sight of Shane and Bill Reece, along with a few other guys he regularly competed against.

Behind the gate, Shane mounted a solid black beast known as Midnight Express.

Wincing, Levi leaned toward Gail. "He's a bad one."

She shook her head. "I don't understand why a man would want to get on such a dangerous animal like that."

"You take a chance when you climb on any horse," he said, brushing off her concern.

"I know. But this just seems like asking for trouble."

Eager to see how his rival would fare, Levi let her comment pass unanswered. Like him, Shane Reece had been invited to the massive event taking place in July. Wiry and strong, Shane was an expert rider.

Mounted, Shane gave the signal he was ready. A bell rang and the gate opened. The audience cheered.

Set free, the bronc took off like wildfire consuming dry prairie grass. As he leaped and twisted with manic energy, it took him barely a second to dislodge his rider. Shane hit the ground, facedown into the dirt, and lay there, unmoving.

A collective gasp went through the audience.

"Ladies and gentlemen, please stay calm," the announcer ordered as medics and other men rushed in to distract the animal and attend to the wounded rider.

Stomach turning, Levi watched as medics carried Shane away on a stretcher. Even though he knew the risk involved every time a rider mounted a wild bronc, it was still shocking when an accident happened.

"Do you mind if we leave?" Gail asked. Clearly shaken, unease shadowed her expression. "I think I've had enough excitement for one day."

Levi agreed. "I think me and Seth have, too."

Taking Seth by the hand, he escorted Gail out of the bleachers.

"Will Mister Shane be okay, Daddy?"

Levi dragged a hand across his face. "We don't know, Seth. Let's hope so." It pained him that Seth had seen him tossed from a horse more than once. Every time, he'd managed to walk away on his own two feet.

They wove through the parking area and found the truck. Levi buckled Seth into his car seat and then slid behind the wheel.

Gail, too, climbed in and pulled her seat belt into place. "Thank you for bringing me tonight, but if you don't mind, I think this will be my last rodeo."

Heart thudding, Levi turned on the ignition. The engine roared to life. By the look on her face, he knew exactly what was on her mind.

"Getting bucked off is part of the sport," he said, attempting to explain away the danger.

"What if something happened to you?" Lips going flat, concern laced Gail's tone. "What would happen to Seth? He's just a *kind.*"

Her tersely worded questions smacked Levi hard. "I'll be okay."

"Will you?"

"Of course."

Despite his flippancy, Levi's words sounded hollow to his own ears. Gail was right. He might have escaped with only cuts and bruises in the past, but what would happen if he were the one in an accident?

His gaze shifted toward his son, before settling on Gail. Seeing true fear on her face made shrugging off the danger of competition difficult. It was not just his own life that would be impacted if something bad happened.

Seth had no mother. If a bronc took him out, the boy would have no father. There were no grandparents to take him, either. Betheny had no family close enough to take an interest in her child. His own parents were also deceased. The few blood relatives he did have—distant cousins he'd never met—were back in Pennsylvania. If he were killed, who would take Seth?

The possibility his son might someday be an orphan all at once shook Levi to the core. He'd gone through the experience, and it had left him feeling rootless and at loose ends. The Schroders had treated him well, but he'd never quite felt like he belonged in the family. Perhaps that was because he was an older teenager, and not a small child. Had he been younger, he might have adapted better.

Still, it was nothing he ever wanted his own child to experience.

Gott willing, he hoped to be around to watch Seth grow up and have a family of his own. Perhaps someday he might even bounce his grandchildren on his knee.

Keep riding those wild horses and that might not happen.

Chapter Twelve

For Levi, the next few days passed in a blur. Between rounding up and selecting the cattle to be sold off and taking care of other chores, he'd barely had a moment to think. By the time Wednesday evening rolled around, he was looking forward to a pleasant evening. He'd decided that he'd be showing up for the men's Bible study group. Afterward, he hoped to have a moment to speak with Bishop Harrison alone.

Could he rejoin the Amish community? He'd never know unless he asked. If the answer was yes, the plan he had in mind could move forward.

The idea was exciting, and frightening. But it was also one he looked forward to pursuing.

So that he wouldn't stand out like a sore thumb, he dressed in a muted manner, pulling out a pair of dark slacks, a black shirt and a pair of boots that weren't Western-style. His colorful shirts and blue jeans just didn't mesh with the more conservatively dressed members. He wanted to show some respect toward the church and its congregants.

As he put on his clothes, Levi's thoughts shifted to

the news he'd received earlier in the week. The shadow of Shane's accident was still on his mind. His friend had suffered intense neck and back damage. The injuries had effectively ended Shane's career. With prayer and determination, he might walk again. But his days as a rodeo cowboy had ended abruptly.

Levi shook his head. *That could just as easily have been me.*

Not for the first time, he began to consider the fact that it might be time to retire. The idea of going back to a life he'd abandoned both frightened and excited him. Back when he was a teenager, he'd found the Amish lifestyle too restrictive and regimented. Now that he was an older man with some experience of the real world, he discovered that he liked the idea of leading a simple life: up before sunrise, putting in a hard day's work and giving the Lord thanks on Sunday.

Maybe there is a place for me and Seth here in Burr Oak.

A knock on the door captured his attention.

Buttoning his cuffs, Levi hurried to open the front door.

Gail stood outside. "I've come to get Seth." She lifted the book she held. "I've also brought you your Bible. I noticed you didn't have one last Sunday and I thought you might want the one *Mamm* gave you when you first came to live with us. It took a bit of digging, but I found it."

Surprised the family had held on to his belongings, Levi accepted her offering. When he'd packed to leave the ranch, he wasn't able to take everything he owned. Not much fit in his small suitcase and many items were left behind, including his Bible.

"Thank you for going through the trouble of finding it. And thank you for keeping it all these years. I won't leave it behind again."

She eyed his clothes, grinning. "You look nice. Almost Plain. Just need to grow your hair out and you'd look Amish again."

He ran a nervous hand through his hair, slicked back with a little gel. "Not too much?"

"Not at all."

Levi stepped back, glancing into the back bedroom. Seth lay on his bunk with his puppy, laboriously copying the letters Rebecca had written out for him on sheets of paper. Determined to read and write, he worked diligently.

"Seth, Gail's going to watch you while I go into town."

Putting aside his pencil, Seth slid off his bed. Agile despite the fact he was threatening to turn into all legs, Sparky followed close behind.

"Can we play checkers?" Seth asked, hopping down the narrow steps.

Gail smiled. "Of course. I've got some more games, too."

"I'm afraid Seth's fallen in love with those board games," Levi said.

"They're good for the mind." Gail tapped her forehead. "Keeps you sharp."

"A lot better for him than playing on his tablet," Levi said.

"We'll feed him some supper and keep him busy."

"Sounds good." Stepping out of the RV, Levi shut the door before bending to give his son a hug. "I'll be back as soon as I can."

"Have a nice evening," Gail said, waving him off.

Waving back, Levi headed to his truck. He climbed into his pickup and headed toward town. He pulled into the church parking lot. Aside from buggies and a row of neatly parked bicycles, there were not any other gas-powered vehicles.

Times really had changed. According to Gail, many of the Plain folks had updated to propane or gas-powered appliances, solar panels for lighting and other conveniences that wouldn't have been allowed under the former bishop. From what he'd seen, Bishop Harrison was in tune not only with modern times, but with ideas on how best to allow its conveniences to be used by the congregation.

A few other men were heading into the church, so Levi followed them inside. They gave him an odd look but said nothing. Passing the chapel and then the nursery where Seth had played the Sunday before, Levi stepped through a small antechamber leading to an informal conference room.

A group of men were seated in chairs set up in a circle. Everyone glanced up as he entered. The bishop stood in the center of the circle.

"*Ach*," one man said, whispering sotto voce. "Is that the *Englischer*?"

Bishop Harrison shut his Bible and stepped away from the gathering. "Levi, I'm glad you came," he said and directed him back into the antechamber. "I need to have a word with you for a moment." He closed the door behind him.

Puzzled, Levi glanced at the older man. "Was I not supposed to come?"

Bishop Harrison gave him a smile that didn't reach

his eyes. "I'm sorry to tell you this, but I have to re-scind the invitation."

Levi blinked. "Why?"

He hesitated. "An extenuating circumstance seems to have arisen."

Levi's insides knotted. "I see. And that would be?"

The older man sighed. "It has come to my attention you aren't exactly a widower."

His brows rose. "Who told you that?"

"One of my ministers—I won't say who—has a rela-tive living in Reno, Nevada—where I believe you also had a home a few years ago?"

Levi tightened his grip on his Bible. Telling a lie would be unacceptable on all levels. "Yes."

"According to what he tells me, you divorced your wife."

Levi's insides twisted. Now that the cat was out of the bag, there was no reason to lie about it. It was, after all, public record.

"I did," he said, and then added, "Betheny died a few days after the final decree."

Bishop Harrison's mouth puckered with disapproval. "Was there a reason you couldn't honor your vows to the woman you married and who bore you a *kind*?"

Well, here it was. The shame he'd so desperately tried to hide. No reason to lie or try to cover it up. The truth always came out.

"Yes, there was. Betheny was not a good mother."

"I see. Do you mind if I ask why?"

Levi refused to flinch. "She put our son's life in dan-ger more than once." Drawing back his shoulders, he pressed on. "I did what I thought was right to save my child. I won't apologize for that, either, Bishop."

Silent a moment, Bishop Harrison nodded. "Thank you for being honest with me, Levi."

"If I had to do it all over again, I would. And if what I did was wrong, then I will stand up on my judgment day and answer to *Gott*. I know I made a lot of mistakes, but I'm trying to turn my life over to the Lord in the hopes *He* will make me a better man. If the church of my parents and their parents before them will not have me, I'll find one that will."

Save for a few extenuating circumstances, divorce was frowned down on by the Amish. Once two people were married, they were expected to stay together until death parted them. That had been his intention when he married Seth's mother. Unfortunately, the union was a disaster.

"I'm not trying to punish you," the bishop said in his own defense. "Given what you've just told me, I'd certainly be willing to reconsider the matter of your suitability to be baptized."

Levi pursed his lips. "Don't concern yourself, Bishop. Seth's mother paid for her mistakes with her life, and I would prefer she be allowed to rest in peace. As for myself, after I get the Schroder cattle to auction, I think me and my son will be leaving town."

Levi walked out the church building, and back to his truck. He slammed a hand on the side of the vehicle, frustrated with the situation he'd just encountered.

"Here I am trying to make changes to my life, and no one will let me," he muttered as he slid behind the wheel. Insides knotting, he stared ahead, seeing nothing except the mess he'd made of his life.

Doubt crept in, devouring hope. Caught between two worlds, fitting in neither, what was he to do now?

What if *Gott* had written him off as a lost cause?

"Stop it," he whispered, heaving a fortifying breath. "There are no easy fixes."

Focusing on his heartbeat, Levi cleared his mind of negative thoughts.

Yesterday was gone. All he could do was focus on a new day. Maybe things would go right. Or maybe they would go wrong. But true faith meant putting aside ego and submitting his stubborn will to a higher power. He needed to show he was ready to live a better life.

Clasping his hands, he bowed his head. "Dear Lord, I've strayed so far," he whispered, struggling to find the right words. "I ask Your forgiveness. Please, show me the way I need to go."

Chapter Thirteen

Twirling and throwing his rope, Levi took only minutes to capture a wandering heifer and guide her back to the safety of the herd. His horse, a fifteen-year-old gelding named Bob, was trained to work cattle since he was old enough to be broke to a saddle. Wily in the ways of stubborn bovines, Bob had a knack for moving and cutting cows, and waded through an entire herd without blinking an eye.

"Hey, cow, be still."

Sliding off his horse to set the heifer free, Levi barely noticed the twinge in his left leg. Lowing with offense, the animal trotted off, slapping flies off her rear with a bobbed tail.

He gathered his rope and watched her go. Not having worked with cattle in years, he was a little rusty, but his aim was getting better. He caught more than he missed, which was a switch from missing more than he caught.

He hooked the rope to the side of his saddle and lifted his hat, mopping his brow with a handkerchief. It was nearing noon, and the heat had climbed. June was one of the wettest months of the year, but it could also be hot. Come summer, the temperature would easily climb past a hundred.

Levi gazed out over the pastureland. Miles of buffalo grass and other flora mingled with stubby bushes. Towering trees dotted the wide-open plains. During the high summer, the rich-soil bottomlands along the creeks and rivers were verdant and teeming with an abundance of critters. Known for their hardiness, Texas Longhorns could forage on brush and survive for days without water.

He sighed. "Better get back to it, Bob."

Tucking away his handkerchief, Levi resettled his hat before grabbing the saddle horn and hitching a boot into the stirrup. Getting up and down on a horse all day was a tough workout. For the first week, he'd gritted his teeth through the aches.

Giving his horse a little tap with his spur, Levi let the horse have its own lead, trailing cattle at a leisurely pace. Cows were stubborn critters, and they usually got their way. Had the ranch been at full staff, there would have been more than one man working. A good cowboy could handle several hundred cows, but there was more to keeping up with cattle than just sitting on a horse. A man had to keep an eye out for predators, pregnant cows and foundling calves, among so many other duties. Normally there were three hands working the range, now whittled down to one.

Having settled on which cattle would be sold, Levi had started to corral those that would be going. Next week, he'd load the bovines on a truck and take them to be sold. The money generated by the sale would put the ranch back into the black. After that, he expected to hook up the travel trailer and head to Fort Worth to wait out the finals for The Big Texan rodeo. Once that event was over, he'd continue to follow the summer circuit before finding a place to park for the winter.

Staying in Burr Oak was no longer an option.

Life had a way of throwing a wrench in a man's plans. All he could do was find another path to walk. The one he'd picked had come to a dead end.

Story of my life.

The breeze kicked up. Stray clouds swept across the sun, ominously darkening the sky.

Reining the horse around, Levi headed toward a nearby gathering of sturdy oaks. The overhanging limbs provided a break from the heat and a chance to rest. Sliding off his horse, Levi let the lead fall. Old Bob would graze nearby.

"Datt! Datt!" The sound of a child's voice in the distance caught his ear.

Levi hove around, glimpsing Gail guiding her buckboard along a dirt-packed road. His heart skipped a beat as the pleasure he felt from the sight of her warmed his soul. She was beautiful and generous to a fault.

Seeing him, Gail rose, waving. "Levi!" she called. "Come and eat!"

Levi returned the wave. Gail worked in the mornings checking the fence line, and usually headed home around eleven to change out horses and pick up Seth for lunch. Given the heat and miles ridden in a single day, the horses needed rest, as did the people. Gail and Seth were always a welcome sight. Taking an hour's break gave him a chance to spend some time with them. It was the best part of his day, and he looked forward to the precious moments.

Gail pulled the wagon nearby, setting the brake before climbing down. Seth jumped down, rushing to give his father a big hug. Seth's puppy barked to be let down from the buckboard.

"Hi!" he greeted, throwing his small arms around Levi's neck.

Levi ruffled his son's hair. At such a young age, the boy had no trouble learning a new language, and was well on his way to becoming bilingual. He'd even asked if he could dress like the other Amish boys in church. Though it pained him, Levi had gently explained they were not Amish, but that he'd think about it. His reply had satisfied the child for the time being.

"Hallo, mein sohn." Levi hugged his child back and put him down. The frisky young dog barked and jumped, begging for attention.

"He wants to play."

He laughed. "Then go play."

The two youngsters, boy and canine, bounded between the trees, running off some energy.

"Be careful, Seth, and stay away from the high brush," Levi called.

"I hope you're hungry," Gail said, taking out an old blanket and spreading it on the ground in a nice shady spot. "Mrs. Weaver outdid herself today." She headed back to the wagon and lifted the enormous picnic basket riding in the back of the buckboard.

Levi hurried to help her. "Here, let me."

"Danke."

Gail smoothed out her skirt and sat down on the blanket. As she untied her sunbonnet, her sleeve accidentally snagged a long bobby pin holding her *kapp* in place. Her carefully tucked bun unraveled.

"*Ach*, my goodness!" Searching for her stray pins, she hurried to put her hair back in place.

Watching Gail struggle with her hair, Levi shifted in his place. Even when they were children, he'd rarely seen her with her hair down. The locks fell halfway down her back, covering her shoulders with a cascade of glorious curls. With her hair up, Gail was a pretty girl. Now, she was stunning. Though she wore a bonnet to protect her face from the sun, her cheeks glowed with a touch of color. Working as hard as any man, she'd put her heart and soul into keeping her family's legacy alive.

Gail noticed his stare. "Something wrong?" Winding her hair back into a bun, she pinned her *kapp* back into place.

Realizing he'd been rude, Levi quickly dropped his gaze. "Nothing."

"It's such a fright," she said, blowing out an exasperated breath. "How I wish I could cut it off and wear it short."

"You wouldn't want to do that."

"Hair is for an *ehmann*." A momentary shadow of sadness flickered across her face as she exhaled sharply. "As I don't have one, I shouldn't have to worry about keeping it long. I wish the *Ordnung* would allow single women to cut their hair. Just as single men don't wear beards."

"Short hair on you would be a shame," he said, carefully measuring his words.

Opening the basket, Gail spread out a napkin and unpacked the food. "Maybe," she said, speaking noncommittally. "The bishop is working on putting together a pen pal program with a Pennsylvania-based congregation to encourage more matches."

Jealousy kicked in. Levi remembered the announcement but hadn't paid it much attention. Since the Burr Oak community was small, the idea was to widen the net in the hope of adding to the Amish population by encouraging matches with other members of the Old Order throughout the country.

"Are you going to sign up?" he asked, without directly looking her in the eyes.

Lifting the foil off a plate of fried chicken, Gail shrugged. "I've given it some thought. Amity has, too, and she's encouraged me to do so." She laughed, but the sound held little mirth. "She says if I don't find a man soon, I'll be an *alt maedel*."

Levi remained silent. He knew that he had no right to make a claim for her affections.

The brief silence that ensued was broken by Seth, who was ready to eat. Plopping down on the blanket, he settled Sparky near his side. "Can Sparky have a bone?"

Gail shook her head. "Chicken bones aren't good for dogs," she informed the boy. "But I've got a pork rib here from last night's supper that ought to do fine."

Levi gaped at the feast she unpacked. Besides fried chicken, she'd brought homemade potato salad, deviled eggs and slices of chocolate cake covered in a layer of thick icing. There was also a thermos of cold, sweet tea to wash it all down.

"That's almost too much for one man," he said, accepting a heaped plate. "If I keep eating like this, I'll need new pants soon." Neither Gail nor Mrs. Weaver believed in cooking light, and they loaded their food with tons of real cream, butter, sugar and bacon grease. Forking up a bite of potato salad, Gail chewed and swallowed before answering. "I'll just have to let those pants out so they'll fit."

Going after the drumstick on his plate, Levi bit into the crispy chicken. "I might have to take you up on that," he said, finishing it before helping himself to a glass of ice-cold tea.

Gail gazed into the distance, eyeing the grazing cattle. "You deserve to eat well. It takes a lot of effort, keeping this herd healthy. I must admit I never really knew how much work it involved in raising cattle. And you are one man doing the work of three or four."

Popping a deviled egg in his mouth, Levi swallowed and wiped his fingers on a napkin. "You work just as hard. Riding that fence line, looking for predators and downed cows and calves is not easy. Not only that, but you also run horses back and forth and take care of Seth. That can't be easy since I know he's a handful."

Catching his remark, Seth shook his head. "I'm being good, *Datt*. I help with the horses and the barn."

Her expression warming, Gail patted the child's shoulder. "It's true. He is good with the animals and doesn't mind a bit helping me muck out the stalls or curry the horses. Best little helper I've ever had."

Hearing her praise, Seth beamed with pride. "I'm a big kid now," he bragged. "Florene lets me feed the bunnies, too. Sometimes, they let me pet them. And the billy goat, it follows me around, too."

Levi laughed. "Just as long as you don't want to make a pet out of one, that's fine."

"We'll make a rancher out of him yet," Gail said, laughing.

Levi impulsively tousled his son's hair. He'd never seen Seth so happy or content.

Since the day they had arrived, Seth had easily settled down into their new routine. As the days passed, Levi had watched his fussy, tired child blossom into a bright-eyed boy full of energy and good cheer. The change was an amazing and welcome one.

All four of the Schroder sisters kept Seth busy. To get the boy up to speed on his letters, Rebecca had even set up a makeshift school, complete with a kid-sized desk and chalkboard. After breakfast, Seth dutifully showed up for instruction, eager to learn his numbers and letters. The child soaked up every moment and couldn't wait to go to school with the "big kids."

A lump rose in the back of Levi's throat. Five years had flown by in the blink of an eye. Raising him had been both joyful and bittersweet. Joyful because he was so proud to be the father of such an amazing boy. And bittersweet because Seth hadn't had a proper mother to love and nurture him.

"Thank you so much for all you've done for him. And for me."

Gail offered a shy smile. "You're welcome," she murmured. "It's been such a delight having both of you here."

Levi had no reply. Falling into silence, he glanced toward the sky, peeking through the branches of the trees shading them from the heat of the day.

A sigh pressed through his lips. There was so much he wanted to say to her. She was everything he wished he'd gotten when he'd wed Seth's mother; a good Christian woman who loved the Lord and her family without question.

Much to his regret, he'd never be able to pursue a future with Gail. As an outcast from the church, she was forever out of his reach.

* * *

Finishing her lunch, Gail set her plate aside. Conversation had dwindled away, leaving each to their own thoughts.

The quiet moment was soon interrupted.

"Is it all right if I go play with Sparky some more?" Seth asked.

Checking his watch, Levi nodded. "You've got fifteen minutes, then we've got to get back to work."

Seth grinned and roused his pup. "Come on, Sparky."

"Don't go out of sight," Levi called after the pair. "I want to be able to see you."

"Okay!" Seth called back.

A wistful smile played around Levi's mouth as he watched the pair romp away.

Sensing he had something on his mind, Gail leaned forward. "You've gone so quiet. Is anything wrong?"

Forcing a smile, he cleared his expression. "Just thinking how fast Seth is growing up. I wish Betheny had—" Catching himself, he returned to silence.

At the mention of Seth's mother, Gail stiffened. Though Seth often spoke of his mother, Levi rarely mentioned her. From what she'd gleaned from his rare comments, Betheny Wyse's death was sudden and unexpected. Past that, Levi didn't feel compelled to share.

She frowned in frustration. Time and experience changed people. In the span of ten years, Levi had married, had a son, and then tragically lost his young wife.

Feeling unworldly and insignificant, Gail pressed a hand against her middle. She imagined that after taking an *Englisch* woman as a wife, Levi found her to be too simple, too Plain.

Levi noticed her move. "Are you feeling unwell?"

Hand dropping away, Gail shook her head. "I'm fine," she said, forcing a smile. "I was just thinking about all the things I had to do this afternoon."

Levi's expression darkened. His gaze locked with hers. "I wish I could do more so you wouldn't have to."

Heart thudding, Gail felt her pulse speed its pace. Mouth going dry as cotton, she licked papery lips. "It hasn't hurt me, and I've learned a lot. Maybe even more than I wanted to know."

Slowly he leaned back, taking in the surrounding landscape. "You know, I didn't think I'd miss it, but I love taking care of the cattle."

"I'm glad. Without your advice, I wouldn't have known what to do. You've been a lifesaver, and I'm grateful every day that you're here, and I look forward to many more."

Despite the hard work, she'd enjoyed the time they'd spent together. They made a good team. Given their conversation a few days ago, she hoped that would continue if he stayed in Burr Oak. She'd even considered offering him the manager's job, but felt it was premature to do so right away. She wanted to make sure the ranch was on solid financial ground first.

"About that—" Levi scrubbed a hand across his lightly stubbled face. "You remember Sunday afternoon when we were talking?"

She nodded. "Of course."

"Well, I hope I didn't lead you to think I'd be settling down anytime soon. I was just thinking out loud, you know. Chewing over my options."

Giving him a look of disbelief, she stiffened. "So, you've changed your mind?"

He shook his head. "What I had planned on for the

future… Well, I don't think it will quite turn out the way I'd imagined. Think I'm going to stick with what works for me and Seth awhile longer."

Gail's insides twisted. The accident she'd witnessed at the rodeo was still very much on her mind. Thoughts of Levi being wounded by a bucking horse terrified her. Every time he climbed into the chute to mount one of the wild horses, he risked his life.

"I wish you wouldn't."

"It's my profession," he reminded. "I wish I had a better education, but I'm just an old cowboy. If I'm going to take care of Seth—and keep the bills paid—then I've got to compete."

Still a bit stunned, Gail silently digested his words. Apparently, what he'd said during the buggy ride meant nothing. He'd changed his mind, backing away from everything he'd said. Well, at least she hadn't made a fool of herself by offering him a permanent position at the ranch.

Lacing her fingers, she rested her hands in her lap. "I guess I'm not surprised. You've got a habit of walking away from the people who love you."

"That's not fair." Frustration knitted his brows. "You don't have any idea what I've had to deal with."

Heart sinking, she shrugged. "It's your life, Levi, and you have to do what is best for you and Seth. I am certainly not one to judge, nor would I." Lifting her gaze, she gave him a level stare. "Whatever plans you care to make don't concern me. At all."

Caught in the grip of disappointment, she turned her head away, gazing into the distance. The words he'd spoken had sounded so heartfelt, and so sincere. She'd believed every word.

I am such a silly fool, she thought.

Without warning, a child's frightened cry shattered the uncomfortable lull.

"*Datt! Datt!* Snake! I see a snake!" The sharp barks of a dog followed Seth's cries.

Gail jumped to her feet. Levi, too, sprang into action.

Both spotted Seth at the same time. Without meaning to, he and Sparky had wandered toward the wagon. A venomous snake lay curled near the right front wheel. Perceiving the child and dog to be a threat, the reptile raised its head, rattling its tail in warning.

Reacting like lightning, Gail snatched Seth off the ground, even as Levi hurried to retrieve the rifle holstered on his grazing horse. Sparky barked, jumping around, further agitating the dangerous reptile.

"Move, Sparky, move!" Cocking the rifle, Levi took aim.

Gail cradled Seth close. His small body trembled. Seth's dog remained steadfast, circling the snake until it twisted around. Instinctively finding an opening, the dog lunged and grabbed the snake behind the head, clamped it between sharp teeth and shook it violently before dropping it. Pleased with his kill, the canine nosed the dead thing.

Gail lowered Seth to the ground. "Thank *Gott* he's safe."

Reassured the danger was over, the boy ran over to examine the snake. "Good dog, Sparky."

Lowering the gun, Levi relaxed. "That was close."

Lifting Seth into the safety of the wagon, Gail pressed a hand against her chest to steady her pulse.

"Too close."

Just looking at the dead reptile sent a shiver up her spine. Despite the warmth of the sun, she'd gone cold.

Levi looked at her, as if there was something else he wanted to add before shaking his head.

"I'd better get back to work," he said, re-holstering his rifle. Changing his gear over to the fresh horse, he climbed into the saddle. "The cattle transport will be here day after tomorrow. I've arranged for the cows to be sold in Saturday's auction. Monday, you can take the check to the bank and settle your business with Mr. Wilkins. Once that's done, Seth and I will be on our way."

Nodding, Gail numbly returned to gather the picnic basket and blanket. "I'll be sure to pay you back the money you loaned us," she said.

"I'd appreciate that." Levi rode off on his horse.

Gail stood there watching as he got farther and farther away. Was it possible to have your heart broken twice by the same man?

Seems she was about to find out.

Chapter Fourteen

Returning to the house, Gail parked the wagon beside the barn. She put the brake on, hopped down and began to uncouple the horse from the harness.

Seth jumped down, as did his dog. He'd been strangely quiet during the ride back, and his little features were pinched. "Are you mad at *Datt*?"

Gail stopped cold. Seth had obviously noticed the tense exchange between her and his father. Observant and smart as a whip, he didn't miss much.

Wry irritation gave way to an exasperated sigh. "No, honey. I am not mad at anyone. I'm just sad you will be leaving soon."

Seth lowered his head. "I don't want to leave," he said, petting his dog. Tears welled in his eyes. "I want to stay here with you and Sparky." He threw his arms around her.

Dropping to her knees, Gail hugged his small body tight. She'd come to care deeply for the child. *I wish Gott had seen fit to make me his mamm.*

Blinking back tears, she lifted her head. As far as she was concerned, the spat with Levi was over. She'd apologize when she got a chance. She didn't want to lose him as a friend and hoped he would want to keep in touch after he and Seth went back on the road.

"I'll speak with your *datt* later," she promised. "Maybe I can talk him into letting you keep Sparky. Would you like that?"

Seth's troubled expression cleared. "Oh, yes. I sure would."

To distract him, she said, "Why don't you go inside and see if Rebecca or Amity have any cookies for you?"

He grinned. "Okay!"

Watching the boy go, Gail finished unhooking the horse, led the animal into the barn and brushed the mare down before putting her into a stall for the night.

With the cattle coming up for sale, she was anxious and out of sorts. The bank's threats weighed heavily on her mind. Being able to clear the back payments and return to some semblance of normal life would be a godsend. As for Levi, her emotions about him were conflicted and jumbled. Would it be better if he left? Or stayed? She was not quite sure.

Restless, she stepped out into the barnyard. A breeze winnowed through the trees shading the house. Unusually brisk, the wind had blown in scattered clouds that spat down a few fat raindrops.

Tipping back her head, Gail gave the sky a wary glance. Rain was coming. The trouble with Texas storms was that they could turn on a dime, going from nothing to seventy-mile-an-hour winds in the blink of an eye.

Keeping an eye on the storm's progress, Gail walked over to the swings. The limb creaked a little under her adult weight but held firm. Hands circling the ropes, she gave herself a gentle push. She'd played in this same place as a child, imagining her future. As the oldest, she'd always felt she'd be the first to snag a beau. She'd even planned her wedding, as all young girls did a time or two in their daydreams, picking colors for her dresses and building her future home.

Alas, it seemed her dreams of marital bliss would never come to anything.

The wind suddenly kicked up, howling through the trees with renewed energy.

Gail looked up. As much as she hoped it would clear out, the rain that had held off most of the morning finally made an appearance. Thickening clouds darkened the sky, obliterating the sun. The warmth of the day dissipated, the temperature suddenly dropping. A splattering of fat droplets struck the ground.

Protected by the overhanging limbs, she didn't move. The day had turned as dark as her thoughts. Across the barnyard, Levi came galloping up. Bringing his horse to a halt, he slid to the ground before walking the horse inside the barn. A few minutes later he emerged, heading past the animal pens toward the house.

Catching sight of her, he pulled off his hat and raked a hand through his hair before wiping perspiration off his forehead with the back of his sleeve. "Looks like that storm almost beat me back." He glanced at the clouds brewing above their heads. "By the looks of it, I'm thinking we might get a flood and some high winds."

"No telling what'll happen this time of year," she said, keeping her tone neutral. She wasn't really angry at him, just disappointed.

He replaced his hat. "That's what worries me. It's getting awfully black on the horizon, and with the heat clashing with this cool wind, I'm afraid that might mean tornadoes."

Gail shivered. When they came, tornadoes were one of the most devastating things that could tear across the landscape. Through the years, many homesteads had fallen victim to the terrible destruction of the twisters. The last storm had struck Burr Oak once, damaging several buildings along the main street before touching down outside the town limits and uprooting several large grain silos.

She grimaced. "I hate bad storms. They're so frightening and dangerous."

A shooting bolt of lightning followed by a clap of thunder warned things were about to get worse.

Gail jumped from the swing. "Better get out from under these trees."

Levi didn't have a chance to answer. The sky opened, releasing a torrent of water.

"Come on!"

Gail lost her footing, slipped and almost fell on the stone path. "Oh no!"

Levi made a grab, catching her before she hit the ground. "Careful, now." His arm circling her slender waist, he kept her on her feet.

Gail gasped as she regained her footing. "I'm okay."

By time they sprinted through the back door, the rain was pouring in sheets. Another crack of lightning, followed by a fresh blast of thunder, crashed in from all sides. The rain suddenly redoubled its frenzy. The wind kicked up, going from high to horrible. Clouds rolling overhead continued to conquer the sky.

Levi took off his hat and give it a little shake. Droplets of water flew everywhere. "So much for a nice day. Looks like the storm's here."

Close to soaked, Gail trembled. Strands of hair unraveled from beneath her *kapp*. "I haven't seen it come up this fast in a long time."

"It sounds horrible outside." Shaken, Amity hurried to get the battery-powered storm radio out of the cabinet. "Better find out what we're in for."

Florene was already on her feet, lighting all the lamps in the house. "Hope this passes fast," she commented. "I hate it when the rabbit pens get muddy."

Rebecca hovered over the stove, stoking in fresh wood. "Let me heat the kettle and get some coffee going. I think we're going to be in for a bad evening."

Cup in hand, Levi looked out the window. Though the wind had settled a little, rain continued to pour through the afternoon. Bolts of light illuminated the underbelly of the clouds, even as the electricity snaked toward the earth. Thunder boomed, rolling across the land like the feet of a mighty army advancing. The sheer power and force of the storm was a reminder of just how mighty and destructive nature could be.

After a light supper, Gail and her sisters sat in the living room, huddling around the fireplace. Tired from an active day of play, Seth was asleep on the sofa, covered by one of the many handmade afghans thrown across the furniture. Sparky had pressed himself against Florene's legs. Every time thunder boomed, the animal whimpered piteously.

Despite the incessant sound of rain thudding against the roof, the house felt cozy and safe. Kerosene lamps burning throughout lent the rooms a warm, comforting glow.

Gulping down the rest of his coffee, Levi cocked an ear toward the radio tuned to the local weather channel.

"The storm continues to advance," the announcer warned. "Several counties are under a tornado watch, including Tarrant and Brewer."

Listening to the rest of the forecast, Levi shook his head. "Looks like we're in for a long night. I should get out to the barn and get the horses fed and bedded down."

Gail looked up from her mending, needle paused midair. "But it's pouring out there. You'll get soaked."

Levi left his cup in the sink and reached for a rain slicker that hung near the back door. "The horses need to be fed," he said, slipping it on. "Besides, I'm not made of sugar. I won't melt."

Gail laid her needlework aside and stood up. "I'll go with you. I could use a break from sitting."

He shook his head. "No need for you to go out and get muddy, too."

But she insisted, slipping on a raincoat of her own and grabbing up a flashlight perched on a shelf nearby. "Nonsense. You will need someone to help you. Two of us working will get it done a lot faster than one."

Levi gave his chin a quick rub. "You're the boss."

Gail smiled up at him. "*Ja.* I am." She drew a fortifying breath. "Let's go."

Nodding, Levi opened the door. He was met with an immediate deluge of water. The rain smacked against his rubber coat. He smashed his hat down, lowered his head and dashed across the yard.

Gail followed fearlessly, keeping pace with every step. By the time they reached the barn, they were both drenched.

Teeth chattering, she flicked on the switch near the

door. Battery-powered lamps burst into brilliant light, courtesy of Ezra Weaver and his mechanical tinkering. She clicked off her flashlight. "At least we're not working in the dark."

Levi gave himself a shake, much like a wet dog would. He was cold, but hardly noticed it. His eyes were riveted on Gail. Her *kapp* drooped, and dripping strands of hair had escaped her tight bun to hang in wet threads around her face. Her skin was red from the cold. But with her sparking green eyes and upturned mouth, she was the most beautiful woman in the world to him.

His heart thudded against his ribs. Stepping closer, he brushed a few wisps of hair away from her forehead before tucking them behind one ear. "You're still pretty even when you've been out in the rain."

Gail blushed but didn't draw back. "*Danke*, Levi." A wayward smiled tugged up one corner of her generous mouth. "I'm sorry I was angry with you. No matter what you decide to do, I want you to know you and Seth are always welcome."

Levi swallowed hard. If only she knew...

"Gail, I—I—"

Unable to express in words how he felt, Levi gently touched her cheek with the palm of his hand. He moved closer, dipping his head. Gail leaned in, and he kissed her gently, sweetly.

He didn't know how long the kiss lasted, but abruptly, Gail pulled away from him. The meaning behind her actions was crystal clear.

"I'm sorry. I should not have done that. But I know how you feel about me," he said.

Visibly trembling, she searched his gaze with hers. "Maybe I loved you once, Levi, when I was younger.

But I was just a girl then. As for now… Anything between us, it is not possible, and you know it. We are friends. Nothing more."

"I know you're right. Forgive me for saying things I shouldn't have."

Regret momentarily shadowed her features. "It's all right. I had to know, just once, what it would be like to be kissed by a man. But I will never break my vow to the church. Not even for you, Levi."

He nodded. It seemed no matter how far he ran or how hard he worked to clean up his past, he'd always be shackled to the *Englisch* world.

Just then, a perilous crack of lightning, followed by a blast of thunder, crashed in from all sides. Gail jumped. "We'd better take care of the horses and get back to the house."

She was always the voice of reason. "You're right. Let's go."

He hurried to close the double doors, locking them in place with a length of wood placed crosswise into iron brackets. A smaller door on the right wall led to an open side shed. Another door on the opposite side led to an enclosed room where the tack and other supplies were kept. Horse stalls were built toward the rear of the barn, as was the second-story hayloft. Half a dozen horses waited for their evening meal. The beasts were restless, whinnying and stomping with nervous energy. A few reared on their hind legs when the thunder blasted hard enough to shake the walls.

"Guess I need to get these animals fed."

Gail nodded. "Seth helped me clean the stalls this morning, so that part is done. They had a bit of time out in the corral this afternoon before we put them up."

Levi walked to the row of barrels where the feed was stored. He lifted the lid and scooped out a bucket of pellets. "Glad you got them in before the rain. That place is waterlogged right about now, no doubt."

"I guess you know Seth is all about the horses," Gail said, turning on the hose attached to a plastic tank.

He nodded and began to fill the feeders in each stall. The scent of hay, feed and horses mingled together, creating a damp, earthy scent. "The boy's been crazy about horses since he could walk."

Gail came behind him, freshening the water in the troughs. "What about his *mamm*? Did she like horses, too?"

Crossing to the next stall, Levi paused mid-step. Any mention of Seth's mother always caused his chest to tighten. Since his arrival, he'd done his best to avoid mentioning his ill-fated marriage.

He cleared his throat. "Betheny didn't go to rodeos for the horses so much as she liked the men who rode them."

An odd expression crossed Gail's face. "Oh...oh, I see..."

Levi finished his chore and returned the bucket to its peg by the barrel. *"Nein, du nicht."* Hands on his hips, he heaved out a frustrated breath. "There's a reason I don't talk much about Betheny. Seth's too little to remember much about her and, frankly, I was kind of hoping her memory would fade as he got older."

She cocked her head. "Why would you say something like that?"

Remembering his terror the night Betheny crashed her car caused Levi's pulse to speed up. "Seth doesn't know the truth about his mother," he said, feeling a rise of bitter acid scorch the back of his throat. "And I can never tell him."

A disturbed look flitted across Gail's face. "Something happened, didn't it?"

Jaw going tight, he shook his head. "I hate talking about it. I just can't."

Instead of turning away, Gail stepped forward and reached for his hands. "I feel so terrible for you. But keeping everything bottled up inside will never lead you toward the path to salvation. The Bible says whoever conceals his transgressions will not prosper, but he who confesses and forsakes them will get mercy. You will never be free of the past until you let it stop haunting you."

Levi started to reply, and then stopped. The silence was deafening. It took him a minute to realize the rain and thunder had suddenly ceased. The wind, too, had gone dead-still. An eerie quiet had settled over the barn and animals.

"Something's changed," he said. "The rain has stopped."

Gail's eyes widened. "Oh, please don't let it be..." Rushing to the side door, she pushed it open and ran outside into the darkness.

"Gail, no!"

Hot on her heels, Levi sprinted after her. It took him a minute to orient himself in the dark. Fortunately, the lightning hadn't ceased, and a series of flashes lit the landscape. Guided by the light, he saw Gail run past the barnyard, passing the trees lining the driveway until the gate stopped her trek. A clear view of the open landscape stretched out in the distance.

Catching up with her, Levi grabbed her arm. "What are you doing?"

Jerking free, Gail pointed. "Look there!"

Frantically searching the gloom, Levi focused on the danger looming on the far horizon. The wind suddenly spun up again, ripping his hat off his head. It disappeared, lost to the relentless wind.

The sound of something much like a freight train blasted through the night. Small, bright, blue-green flashes flared again and again as powerlines along the highway snapped. Illuminated by the lightning, a thick gray funnel had touched down. Barreling across the landscape, the tornado sucked up everything in its path.

And it was heading straight toward the ranch.

Chapter Fifteen

"That's coming fast!" Grabbing Gail's hand, Levi pulled her away from the gate. "We need to get into the storm shelter. Now!"

They sprinted in tandem toward the house. The wind turned vicious, scratching at their skin and clothes, threatening to push them off their feet. Fighting their way forward, they barreled through the back door with a crash.

"Twister on the ground!" Gail shouted to her startled sisters.

Everyone but Seth jumped to their feet. Blissfully asleep, the child had no idea danger loomed.

"The radio station went off the air a few minutes ago," Amity informed them. "We've got nothing but static."

"We've got to get into the cellar." Levi rushed to the sofa and scooped Seth up.

Amity grabbed a flashlight and the radio even as Rebecca hurried to douse the fires in the hearth and oven. Florene snatched Sparky, causing the dog to let out a surprised yelp.

The frightened group dashed out the back door and around the side of the house. Fighting the wind, Amity and Gail struggled to pull open the metal door that would take them underground to safety. The rain attacked with fresh vengeance, pelting the earth with a shattering attack of icy hail.

Once the door opened, Amity led the way down into the dark cavern, shining her flashlight down the narrow steps. Without hesitation, they all descended to safety. Pushed back in place by the intense wind, the door slammed shut, sealing everyone inside. As if angered by the defeat, the hail continued to drum against the metal barrier, filling the cellar with its steady beat.

Relaxing a bit, Levi looked around the enclosed space. Originally dug as a root cellar, the space had been widened into a basement for extra storage. Several custom-built shelves and cabinets overflowed with canned vegetables. A few foldable cots and chairs were stacked in a corner. There was even a first aid kit and a fire extinguisher.

"That was horrible," Rebecca said, rubbing a red mark imprinted on her temple. "I don't think I've seen it hail that hard in years."

Gail glanced at the ceiling. "Levi and I saw a funnel. No telling how far away it was, but it looked dangerous. I know we got the horses in, but I'm worried about the cattle."

"They're out in the open pasture, but they have a good chance of coming through just fine," Levi said, attempting to allay her worry. "A few might be injured, but hopefully they will stay to the low areas and not panic." His words sounded hollow in his ears. Livestock were often injured or displaced or even died during storms.

"May the Lord protect everyone in the path of these twisters, including the animals," Rebecca said. "I know Ezra was saying earlier he thought we'd have a storm today, but I didn't think it'd be this fierce. The bunkhouse doesn't have a storm cellar, so they'll be over soon, I'm sure."

"Still no news." Fiddling with the radio, Amity tried to tune into the local radio station. "If they've gone off the air, it must be bad."

Florene released the dog from her arms. Frightened by the thunder, Sparky cowered, slinking off to a corner to hide. "How long do you think it will last?"

Levi, who was still clutching Seth, cradled his son against his chest. "This could be gone in a few minutes or it could last all night. As long as it sounds horrible up there, I think we should all stay down here, at least a few hours. Just to be safe."

Tornadoes and Texas went practically hand in hand. The central and high plains of the state were part of the area known as "tornado alley," part of a swath across the country most likely to be struck. The thing about the twisters was that there was not one certain time in which they might strike, though midsummer was the most dangerous.

Amity exhaled loudly. "Since we're stuck down here, we might as well be comfortable." She pointed to the cots and chairs. "Florene, grab some of those, won't you? And Rebecca, I think there's a couple of blankets in those bags on that far shelf."

Everyone set to work without grumbling.

"*Ach*, these cots are so uncomfortable," Florene grumbled, unfolding the narrow beds. She set down a few chairs nearby.

"Not the first time we've done this," Rebecca said, pulling out two heavier quilts that had gone into storage. She spread them over the foam mattresses.

Amity lit a few kerosene lamps, illuminating the chilled gloom with a cheery glow. The radio perched on a shelf spat nothing but static. "Music would be nice, but even the classical station is down."

Florene slipped her cell out of her pocket. "I've got no signal, either." She frowned at the display. "And my battery is almost dead."

Rebecca shot a look at the tiny glowing screen. "For once I wish that thing worked."

"The last text I had from Frida said the rain was flooding roads around town."

"If this keeps up and the old riverbeds start to run again, we could be trapped for a couple of days," Gail said.

"That's the trouble with the weather," Levi said, laying Seth on one of the cots. "Mother Nature's going to have her say. All we can do is hold on and pray hard."

Prodded out of sleep, Seth sat up, rubbing his eyes. "Daddy? Daddy?" Confusion turned his words into a high treble.

Levi sat down. "It's okay," he said, rubbing a hand across the nape of the boy's neck to soothe him. "We're down in the cellar waiting out the storm."

Seth's eyes widened with panic. "Where's Sparky?"

"Sparky's right here." Florene fetched the puppy and deposited him on the cot. All paws and ears, the shepherd mix was now at least thirty pounds.

Seth wrapped his arms around his dog, snuggling into the warmth of his fur. "I'm so happy you're here," he whispered.

Moved by the sight, Levi felt tight fingers squeezing his chest. Seth loved that dog probably more than he'd ever loved anything in his entire life. Sparky was his constant companion and rarely left Seth's side. The animal was intelligent, instinctively taking a protective role toward the boy. Better yet, having a pet to look after had given Seth a sense of pride and responsibility.

"We couldn't forget him. He's family, too."

The storm door opened, bringing in a fresh rush of wind and rain.

Ezra and Ruth Weaver descended into the cellar, a clatter of heavy feet and anxiety hurrying them along. The storm outside continued its assault, pounding furiously against the metal door. Icy pellets sounded like gunfire.

"Thought we'd find you all down here," Ezra Weaver said, hacking a little into his handkerchief as he shook off the wet.

Red hair blown into strings, Ruth Weaver clutched a covered pan in both hands. "Didn't think I'd have time to finish my baking."

Levi stood. "How's it looking out there?"

Tucking away his handkerchief, Ezra Weaver fished his pipe out of a pocket. "The twister didn't make it this far, and everything's holdin'," he said before sticking the stem between his teeth. "But there's no tellin' how many of those things are gonna pop up."

At least the news was good. For now. But that didn't mean the danger was over.

"We haven't had a terrible one in years," the older man said. "Last one I recall was over twenty years ago. Killed many people."

"Don't talk like that," Ruth Weaver said, frowning

at her husband. "This storm is going to pass us by, the Lord be willing."

"*Ja*," Gail agreed quietly. "We should take a moment to pray."

As everyone bowed their heads, Levi sat and curled a protective arm around Seth and his pup. His son snuggled close.

Gail spoke in a clear voice. "Dear *Gott*, You are our shelter when storms come, and we are secure, no matter the danger. You are our defense and we will not be fearful when the wind rages, for You are ever near us. We humbly beg You to keep us safe. Amen."

"Amen," everyone finished together.

"And Sparky says amen, too," Seth added.

Everyone chuckled, which lightened the heavy mood. The atmosphere in the cellar was warmed and strengthened by the shared moment.

Sniffing, Florene glanced around. "Do I smell chocolate?"

Ruth Weaver smiled. "I couldn't leave a fresh batch of brownies sitting on the counter," she said, holding out the dessert she refused to leave behind. "Is anyone hungry?"

Amity clapped her hands together and grinned. "I sure could use a treat right now." She patted her thickening waist. "And calories don't count tonight."

"Dibs on the corners," Florene called. "I love those edges."

Rebecca wrinkled her nose. "Too hard for me."

Amity fluttered around. "Don't we have a propane burner?" Rummaging, she located a little camping stove and matching metal pot.

"And if I recall rightly, we have plenty of tea bags and instant coffee, too," Rebecca added.

"We have some cups here," Gail said, pulling out an array of odd-sized mugs belonging to no particular set. She turned. "Levi, would you open one of the water bottles, please?"

He nodded. "Of course."

He lifted one of the heavy, five-gallon containers and carried it to the counter, to help Amity fill her pot. He liked the way the sisters bustled around, each keeping their hands busy and not focusing on the storm. Part of that, he felt, had to do with Seth. If the adults were afraid, Seth would be, too.

Amity lit the burner with a match and sat the pot on top of the little flame. "Tea will be ready soon."

Taking a seat at the foot of the concrete steps, Ezra Weaver made himself comfortable. "A soul could move in and live nice down here," he commented to no one in particular.

Ruth Weaver gave her husband a fond look. "You would be content burrowed in a hole."

Coughing, Ezra Weaver sucked on his unlit pipe. "Ah, yeah," he agreed. "I could fit it out real nice, add lights and even a little privy."

Mrs. Weaver sliced into the brownies and cut everyone a generous piece. "I made the old-fashioned kind, with plenty of walnuts."

Amity put bags into the mugs and added boiling water to let them steep. "Tea's ready for anyone who wants a cup. I hope you all don't mind Earl Grey."

Seth anxiously tugged Levi's shirt. "Can I have a brownie, Dad?"

"Just a small piece. And don't feed any to Sparky. Chocolate is poisonous to dogs."

"Okay." Seth hopped off the cot and went to claim his share.

Mrs. Weaver cut him a child-size portion. "Here you go."

Seth grinned up at her. "Thank you." Treasure in hand, he settled back on the cot. Sparky gazed at his young master through envious eyes.

Carrying two mismatched teacups, Gail offered one to Levi. "I think we all could use a little chocolate to help calm our nerves."

Giving her a smile, Levi accepted the plate. "Thank you."

They each claimed a chair, sitting side by side. Both ate in silence, listening to the chatter of her sisters and the Weavers trying to distract themselves from a stressful situation.

Though he tried not to stare, Levi's gaze gravitated toward Gail. Prodded by conscience and the need to make things right, he put his empty plate aside.

It's time. I have to tell her the truth about me and Betheny.

The storm carried on. The wind howled incessantly. Now and again, there would be an audible crack of lightning followed by an intense, thundering blast that shook everyone to the core.

Having perched herself near a kerosene lamp to read, Gail looked up from one of Rebecca's romance novels she'd dug out of a box. She enjoyed reading, and through the pages of books, she visited faraway lands, met fascinating characters and shared in their adventures.

Her father had passed along his love for reading. Once the day's work was done and the evening meal eaten, Samuel Schroder would read from the Bible, leading the family through their evening devotional. Afterward, as a treat, he read the girls a story, using different voices to bring the characters to life. Contrary to popular belief, the Amish didn't only read Bibles or other religious tracts. The library was a vital resource for members of the church.

Unable to concentrate on the plot, Gail lowered the book. Most everyone else had found a place to settle down, drifting off to sleep.

Except Levi. Having traded places with Ezra Weaver, he sat near the top of the stairs, wreathed in flickering shadows. Leaning forward, he'd clasped his hands, resting his elbows on his knees. Head bowed, he appeared to be deep in meditation.

Knowing he was unaware she watched, Gail took a moment to study him. He was clad in faded jeans and leather work boots, with the sleeves of his plaid shirt cuffed up at his elbows. Tanned and solid, he had the lean, muscular look of a mature man.

Completing his silent contemplation, Levi raised his head. His gaze caught hers.

Gail froze. Had he sensed her watching him? She wasn't sure.

Needing to stretch her legs, she stood. She laid the book aside and wove her way around the sleeping people, careful to disturb no one. Climbing the steps, she sat down beside him and cocked an ear toward the metal storm door.

"Sounds a little better out there," she said, leaning closer and whispering.

Levi scooted over to give her a little more room. "Sounds that way," he returned, glancing over their heads. "I hope the worst of it is over. The wind seems to be dropping."

"Let's hope so."

Levi shifted, his leg brushing hers. "Sorry."

Gail gave him a nudge back. "No need to apologize."

Pulling a breath, Levi blurted, "Actually, I do owe you an apology. I've been doing a lot of thinking, some of it out loud, and it led you to think Seth and I would be staying permanently."

She allowed a cautious nod. "Sounded that way to me."

"I meant what I said, Gail. I want to settle down and raise Seth, and I want to lead a better life. And I wanted to rejoin the church and get baptized, but that's not going to happen."

She shook her head. "I don't understand. I thought Bishop Harrison invited…"

Levi cut her off with a brief gesture. "I guess I'll just say it. The bishop told me at the meeting Wednesday night that I can't come back to church."

"Oh, Levi. Why didn't you tell me?"

"I was ashamed." Hesitating, he added, "I know you've never asked, but there are some things about Seth's mom I've never told you."

Gail nodded solemnly. "I suspected, but I never wanted to pry."

"I never wanted to tell you because I didn't want you to think less of me."

"Why would you think that? Whatever you've done, I'm sure you had your reasons." She laid a hand on his arm. "You're a *gut* man, Levi. I don't see you setting out to hurt someone deliberately."

He visibly grimaced. "You might not think so highly of me when you know the truth."

Meeting his gaze, she tightened her grip on his arm. She could almost imagine the wheels in his mind turning as he selected each word. "You can tell me anything."

Levi's mouth tightened, revealing his inner stress. "Um, there's a certain sort of woman who likes dating rodeo cowboys. The relationships don't last more than a season or two."

Gail instantly connected the dots. "I understand what you're telling me. I am not that innocent, Levi. I know some young folks sow their wild oats during *rumspringa*. It's only natural."

"I'm not proud of my past," he said.

"If that's the worst sin you committed," she continued, trying to lighten his burden, "I doubt Bishop Harrison would hold it against you. I know many couples who had to rush the wedding and then say the *kind* came early. It doesn't make them bad people. Just human."

He raised a hand. "There's more. To an inexperienced country boy, Betheny was beautiful, sophisticated and exciting. And I must admit, I was proud that a woman like her wanted to be with me. But then she got pregnant with Seth."

"Ah."

He grimaced. "Betheny and I had no business getting married or having a kid."

Gail shook her head. "Levi, that precious little *boi* could never be a mistake."

"*Nein*. I can't call Seth a mistake. He's everything to me. The two of us together created this unique little individual. I just wish Betheny had been more…"

Sensing trouble in his tone, Gail urged him to continue. "What happened, Levi?"

He sighed. "Betheny hated being a mom. She missed the party life, traveling with the rodeo. Staying home and taking care of a baby was not what she saw as her future. So she drank a little, and then a lot more." He bit off his words, unwilling to go further.

Heart stalling, Gail felt a rush of anxiety. "Levi, go on."

His mouth turned into a deep frown. "Betheny had a bad habit of drinking and driving. One night, she decided she wanted to get out of the house and meet up with friends. She had Seth in the car with her. She didn't get far from home before she ran a red light, plowing straight into a semitruck."

Gail's hand flew to her mouth. "Oh!"

"Thankfully, Betheny had enough sense to put Seth in his car seat." He paused, and then added, "Seth was bruised but unharmed. Betheny also survived. But after that incident, I decided I had to take him and leave before something worse happened."

Gail sensed the weight of his guilt, sorrow and regret. It took a lot of courage and strength for him to share his tragic story. "I see."

Levi visibly flinched. "No, you don't. I'm not a widower, like you thought I was. I divorced Betheny because she wouldn't get help for her addiction, and I was afraid for Seth's life. The accident that killed her happened after we'd split. The bishop knows this and, technically, in the eyes of the church I am a divorced man. And that is not acceptable."

His words caused Gail's breath to stall. In that moment, the hard concrete she sat on and the chill in the cellar faded. "I'm so sorry."

"It is what it is. I messed up my life in so many ways. And now that I'm trying to fix it, I can't."

Gail trembled as her composure melted. A ribbon of warmth curled around her heart. "I believe you."

Leaning closer, Levi caressed her cheek with gentle fingers. "I had so many plans for Seth and me." He paused a moment and then added, "I was hoping once I got baptized, I might court you. I know I can't do that now. But if there was any girl I would want to marry, it would be you."

Surprised, she blinked. "You want to court me?"

"*Ja*, I'd ask you right now to marry me, if I could."

Gail covered his hand with hers, squeezing tight. "If I could say yes, I would," she whispered, careful that no other ears but his heard her words.

His gaze deepened. "Would you do something for me?"

She nodded.

"Kiss me, again. Please? Just one more time."

Throwing caution aside, Gail leaned forward. With no hesitation, Levi's warm mouth claimed hers. In that single precious moment, there was only the two of them as the rest of the world fell away.

Chapter Sixteen

After their kiss ended, Gail glanced around at the others in the cellar. No one had stirred. It would always be their secret.

They sat in companionable silence, each lost in their own thoughts. Regret hung between them. What would happen now? How could they ever be together? It was something Gail couldn't answer.

Breaking the stillness, Levi tipped his head. "Do you hear what I hear?"

Shaking off her thoughts, Gail tilted her head. The incessant howl outside had ceased, as had the attack of rain. "Nothing. I hear nothing," she murmured. "Is it over?"

"I think so."

Standing, Levi reached above his head, pressing the edge of the heavy metal. Rusty hinges protested with a screech. A thin sliver of light appeared between the door and the edge of the frame.

He peeked. "Sun's breaking the horizon. Storm's over."

Breathing in relief, Gail asked, "Can we go out?"

"I think so." He pushed the door open and looked around. She heard him catch his breath.

Gail stiffened. "What?"

"It's…" He hesitated, swallowing hard. "Bad."

Hurrying up the steps, Gail left the safety of the cellar and stepped back onto solid ground. The world she'd left behind and the one she returned to were two different things. The tornado had done its damage, tearing up the landscape. In the span of a night, her entire world had changed forever.

Gail's first thought was of the house. Running around to the front yard, she was relieved to see it remained standing. A few of the older trees around the perimeter had gone down, sending a spray of stray limbs through the front window.

She headed to the backyard and ran toward the barn and pens. Much to her relief, the animals appeared to have made it through all right. The rabbit hutches and chicken pens built against the far side of the barn still stood, as did the lean-to for the goats. Though muddy and wet, they had survived. Unfortunately, the barn itself had not fared so well. Part of the roof was entirely torn away, and the open side shed had crumbled.

Levi ran up beside her. "The horses!" he cried, hurrying to pull away the debris from the side door that would get them back inside.

Following close behind, Gail rushed to check the stalls. Pawing the ground and snorting, half a dozen skittish horses met her eyes. "They're on their feet."

"Good." Levi removed the plank holding the front double doors shut, pushing both open.

Together, they walked out. Across the barnyard, the bunkhouse also appeared to have suffered minor damages. But that wasn't all. The tornado had turned over Levi's RV, completely totaling it.

As she trembled at the sight, a sob broke from Gail's throat. "Oh no!"

Levi's jaw hardened. If he had any thoughts about losing everything he and Seth owned, he kept them to himself.

"We need to check the cattle." Leaving his small trailer behind, he turned and disappeared back into the barn.

Gail hurried after him. Inside, she found him leading a horse out of its stall. Still a little skittish, the horse whinnied. "I'm going with you."

Saddling the horse with quiet efficiency, Levi brushed off her words. "No, you should stay here. The others will wake soon."

"I'm going, even if I have to saddle my own horse."

Brows knitting, Levi slipped a boot into the stirrup and heaved himself into the saddle. He held out a hand. "If you think you have to, then come on."

Accepting his help, Gail slipped a foot atop his, using the leverage he offered to take a seat behind him. Pulling herself close, she wrapped her arms around his waist. "Let's go."

Levi spurred the horse into action. "Giddyap!" Galloping through the barnyard, he pointed the horse in the pastureland's direction. The path of the tornado was clear, for it had torn through the fencing and created a gaping hole.

Gail held on tight as Levi urged the horse to run faster, taking them into the heart of the acreage where the cattle normally grazed. Near one of the watering tanks, the windmill had been mangled, reduced to broken planks and twisted metal. But that wasn't all. They saw cows scattered across the landscape, unmoving.

Levi reined the horse to a stop. He slid to the ground and handed Gail the reins as she slipped forward to take the saddle. He knelt near one of the cows. "They're gone."

Not trusting her eyes, Gail tapped the horse. The animal lifted its head and neighed in protest but kept going. Without really looking where she was going, she rode through the pasture. By her count, most of the cattle had perished.

Gaping in horror and disbelief, Gail squeezed her eyes shut. "Please, no."

The Longhorns, the pride of the Schroder ranch, were no more.

Tears stung her eyes, but she refused to let them fall. Senses reeling, she thought about the consequences of the damage. With no cattle to sell, there would be no money coming in. With no income, there was no way to make up the missed payments.

Soon, the bank could legally foreclose on the property and there would be nothing she could do to prevent it.

It is all gone, she silently lamented. *We are going to lose everything.*

Gail looked down at Levi. Dark circles from a sleepless night bruised his eyes. Grim-faced and pale, he looked up again at the sky. Now that the storm had blown out, it was as clear and blue as a crystal lake.

"What do we do now?"

He frowned. "We call a rendering plant and sell the carcasses to them," he answered automatically. "You won't get a lot, but you will get something."

"How many do you think we lost?"

His brow furrowed. "Won't know for sure until we round up the stragglers. With the broken fences and acreage, might take a while to figure that out. Any loose cattle roaming have your brand, so we can reclaim them."

Hope flared. "Then there's a chance we can recover?"

"Depends on how hard you want to keep trying."

Gail dropped her gaze. "I—I'm not sure I can, Levi. *Daed*'s death, Mr. Slagel's theft, then this—"

She blinked, fighting back tears. So much had gone wrong this year. Everything was falling apart in front of her eyes.

Levi turned away to study the surrounding devastation. Then he said, "You should get back and let the others know what's happened."

"What about you?"

A shrug rolled off his shoulders. "I'll walk back. I need to check the fencing. No telling how much has been destroyed."

Reluctant to leave him, she nevertheless turned the horse around. "Go on," she urged, tapping her mount with a heel.

Spurred forward, the horse galloped across the plains.

Gail didn't glance back. She couldn't. All her hopes to save the ranch lay with the cattle, and now they were gone.

Along with the hope she'd nursed to carry on the Schroder legacy.

Hands on hips, Levi surveyed the remnants of his RV. Of all the items on the property, it was the worst hit. A total loss, there was no salvaging it. Everything he and Seth owned was inside. And now there was nothing. All they had was the clothes on their back and his truck. For the time being, he and Seth were homeless.

Holding Seth's hand, Gail stood nearby. "You and Seth can stay in your old room," she was saying. "We use it for storage, but Rebecca and Amity are cleaning it out. Mr. Weaver's also taken his pickup into town to pick up some new glass for the front window of the house. By this evening, things will be a little more normal."

Levi gave her half an ear. "Glad it's coming together."

Since the family had come out of the cellar and seen the devastation, everyone threw themselves into clearing away the debris. Shock passed quickly as the need to repair and restructure took over. Busy as an army of ants on the move, everyone had found something to do. There were still animals to care for, too.

As far as he could tell, instinct had moved the cattle to find shelter in the lower spots of the pasture, gathering in a tight bunch to shield the calves from the hail. The tornado had come straight through the herd, sending the animals into a panicked frenzy.

He shook his head. Once the radio station came back on air, the newsmen had reported the extent of the damage. The weather service confirmed the wind had reached over a hundred miles an hour, spawning a slew of tornadoes. Burr Oak and several surrounding towns had taken a lot of damage, not to mention the multiple farms throughout the region. Many people had lost homes and businesses. Thankfully, no one was killed, though livestock had not fared so well.

The Amish didn't believe in insurance. They relied on the collective community to lend a hand when times were hard. Given that the tornado had done a lot of damage to many families, resources would no doubt be stretched thin.

"Do you think that's okay?" Gail asked, trying to restart the conversation.

Levi transferred his gaze to her. "If you don't mind, Seth and I can stay in the bunkhouse until I can figure another RV. It has insurance, so I'll file a claim when there's time. It will be replaced. Might take a few weeks for them to settle. Meanwhile, it wouldn't be proper for us to move into the house with you and your sisters."

Gail acquiesced. "Of course, you are both welcome to stay there," she demurred.

Levi nodded. *"Gut."* It would be hard to keep his distance, but he resolved to do just that.

As soon as the insurance company sent a check, he'd be able to move on.

As for the ranch... Unless Gail could convince the bank to refinance the loan, Mr. Wilkins would most likely follow through with his threat to take the property. With the due date for payment rapidly approaching, there was no time to put the place up for sale and hope a buyer made an offer.

Seth broke away. "Daddy, can we find Mommy's book?"

Gail gave the boy a questioning look. "What is that? Perhaps it's something we can replace."

Though he didn't feel very encouraged, Levi offered his son a smile of reassurance. "I'm going to try to find it, bud," he said, eyeing the debris.

"Should you go inside?"

Levi considered the wreckage. "I should be able to at least reach Seth's bunk."

Passing through the remnants of the front door, Levi picked his way through the living room. The trailer was a jumbled mess. He navigated his way down the short hall and, entering their shared room, he kicked aside the rubble near the overturned bunks. It took him a minute to locate the white faux-leather photo album Seth wanted. Intertwined hearts and ribbons adorned the cover. Though dampened by the rain, it was still intact.

Levi's heart skipped a beat. It was his and Betheny's wedding album.

He didn't want to look, but couldn't help flipping open the cover. A myriad of images filled the pages. There were some of him from a few years ago. Others were of Betheny. There were some of Seth, too, after his birth. Pasted to the pages in vivid color were bits and pieces of his past.

A photo of him and Betheny on their wedding day gave rise to a lot of old feelings he'd believed were carefully packed away.

A closer look revealed something he'd never realized till today. Neither looked joyous. In fact, they both looked downright miserable.

I was never in love with Betheny, he thought.

Although his first impulse was to lie and tell Seth he couldn't find the photo album, Levi knew he couldn't do that to his young son. Even if his perceptions of his mother were hazy, Seth still loved his mother. Seth also believed Betheny had loved him. Whether he'd ever tell his son the truth remained to be seen. But for the time being he couldn't deny the child something he treasured.

Sighing, Levi closed the book. He looked around and saw a few of Seth's things that might be salvageable, including a few stuffed animals and some clothes. He picked through the items.

"Levi, are you all right?"

Hearing Gail's voice, he lifted his head. "Yes, I'm here."

"I'm coming in." Gail appeared shortly thereafter, tripping through the debris to join him. She offered a crooked smile. "I thought you could use some help."

"Where's Seth?"

"Florene took him to help with the goats."

"*Gut.* That'll take his mind off the RV and his stuff."

"Ezra just got back, too," she informed him. "He's brought word the church was damaged, too. The bishop's called a prayer session this evening, for those affected by the storm. Will you come?"

Levi bent, retrieving Seth's purple dinosaur. The thing was a soggy mess and would take days to dry. "No. If you don't mind, I think Seth and I will stay here. There's a lot of cleaning up to do."

She nodded. "We'll be leaving for town in about an hour, if you change your mind."

Even though the bishop had said he would give Levi's case due consideration, Levi didn't have much hope Bishop Harrison or his ministers would change their minds. In their eyes, he'd skipped out on his marriage vows. If he'd done that, they would probably be of the mind he wouldn't honor his vows to the church once he was baptized. The mistakes of his past had destroyed his future.

No one to blame but myself.

"Thank you, but I don't think I will. No reason for anyone to see my face around town right now."

Gail started to walk away and then stopped, visibly

struggling with indecision. An awkward silence hung, widening the bridge between them.

"I know we will probably lose the property," she said quietly. "The cattle are gone, and we have no money. Taxes and other expenses have to be paid." Wrinkling her nose, she forced a laugh. "I hated taking care of cows anyway."

Shaking his head, Levi stepped forward. When Gail was working the cattle, he'd seen pride and determination on her face. True, the work was hard, but she'd carried it with grace, never complaining. Given a little more time, she'd have grown into a fine cattlewoman.

"Now you know in your heart that isn't true."

Momentarily going teary, Gail blinked hard. "You're right. Even though it was hard, I finally had the feeling I was getting ahead of the problems plaguing us." Stepping forward, she tilted back her head, gazing into his eyes. "I couldn't have done it without your help," she continued in a soft voice. "Since your arrival, you gave me so much hope and the courage to keep going."

Touched, Levi reached for her hand. "You gave me a lot, too. Without you, I wouldn't have found my faith. You and your sisters bought me back to *Gott*, and I am grateful. I know I can't go back to being Amish, but please know you will always hold a special place in my heart."

Lower lip trembling, Gail forced a smile. Sadness and longing lingered in the depths of her gaze. "I'll always love you, Levi Wyse," she murmured softly. "Always."

Chapter Seventeen

Levi spent a fitful night tossing and turning on the narrow bed in the bunkhouse. No matter how much he tried, sleep wouldn't come. After another hour of fighting to still his racing mind, he finally gave up. He swung his legs off the mattress and sat up.

The gentle glow of a digital clock lit the small room. The time read five fifty.

He glanced at the bed across from his own. Covered by a heavy quilt, Seth lay snuggled close to Sparky.

Moving with stealth so he wouldn't wake the boy, Levi rose. He pulled on his pants and shirt, picked up a small duffel bag he'd packed earlier and crept over the threshold, closing the door to the bedroom behind him. He didn't want Seth to wake up until after he left.

Entering the shared living room, he sat down to put on his socks and boots. For the last week, they had been living in the bunkhouse, occupying the space that would normally house the cowhands.

Levi walked to the stove. He turned on a burner, filled a kettle with water and set it to heat. He spooned instant coffee and sugar into a mug. When the water was boiling, he poured it over the mix and then added a dash of milk from the small fridge.

He sat down at the dining table and sipped his coffee. The kick of caffeine and sugar helped perk him up. He thought about eating breakfast, but the knots in his gut wouldn't allow it. He was too nervous. The coffee would have to keep him going awhile.

He glanced around the empty room. Housing intended for a bunch of rowdy cowboys wasn't the fanciest place he'd ever lived, but it wasn't uncomfortable. The bunkhouse had private bedrooms for sleeping. Two of the rooms were widened into a single larger living space for the Weavers. An open gathering room that included a kitchenette with propane appliances gave the hands a place to eat and relax.

Seth had taken the temporary move easily. The child liked living like a "real" cowboy.

Levi grimaced. Cowboying was the last thing he wanted Seth to pursue. He wanted Seth to go to school, learn a trade. Had his own father lived, Levi probably would have been a stonemason. It was a steady job, and a man could make a good enough living to support his family. That was what he wanted for Seth. Stability and a sense of belonging to the community. He might not be able to settle in Burr Oak, but there were plenty of other towns. Other places where no one knew him or anything about his past, Amish or otherwise.

Meanwhile, a man had to make a living, and he had a job to do. Once insurance took care of replacing the RV, he and Seth would leave town. The summer was young and there were many rodeos ahead.

But first, he intended to make things right with Gail and her family.

Finishing his coffee, Levi washed out the cup and set it in the rack to dry. He wanted to leave before Seth woke. If his son found out where he was going, he would want to go, too.

Duffel bag in hand, Levi slipped on his jacket and hat before stepping over the threshold, closing the door quietly so as to not disturb the rest of the sleeping household. The horizon was dark, the sun not quite ready yet to throw off its dark velvet cloak. The night sky above his head was crystal clear, spattered with stars that glowed like jewels. A light breeze caressed his stubbled face.

Tightening his grip on his bag, he passed the barnyard, heading toward the main house. His truck was parked outside, gassed up and ready to go. As he suspected, the kitchen windows were already lit with light. Since the storm, Gail had resumed breakfast duties, reclaiming her kitchen from Mrs. Weaver.

After the storm, the surviving cattle numbered about sixty, a number any good cowboy worth his salt could manage. The good news was three of the prime male sires and several young heifers had survived. It took nine months for cows to deliver, so new calves would not be born until next March or April. Given time, it would be possible to rebuild the herd.

Good news, but still a problem. With the barn severely damaged and no cull cattle to sell, the ranch still had a serious cash flow problem. And the threat of foreclosure was now too close for comfort.

Drawing a breath, Levi tapped on the screen door before opening it. "Hope I'm not bothering you."

Gail, busy at the counter, turned her head. "Of course not. Why would you?" Up to her elbows in flour, she threw him a smile. "I hope you're hungry. There's coffee on the stove and I'll be finished rolling out these biscuits in a minute."

Shaking his head, Levi removed his hat and sat down. Gail was her usual messy self, her plain gray dress and white apron all wrinkles and stains. A tear ran down one side of her apron. Flecks of flour dusted her chin and forehead. Defying the efforts of bobby pins, stray curls peeked out from under her *kapp*.

As he looked at her, Levi's breath caught in his throat. No matter what Gail might think about herself, she was beautiful in every way. She was kind, good-hearted and generous to a fault. She also treated his son as if he were her own.

I let this family down once, but I won't do that again. Time to step up and be a man.

"I had a cup of coffee at the bunkhouse," he said. "But if you don't mind, I'll fill a thermos to take with me on the drive to Fort Worth. Maybe you'd even consider making some sandwiches for me?"

Gail froze. "The competition. I'd forgotten."

Levi nodded. "You have a lot on your mind right now."

She shook her head. "The bank agent won't work with us to refinance the mortgage. They seem determined to take everything we have."

"That's not going to happen," Levi said. "I'll make sure of it."

Dusting off her hands, Gail placed them on her hips before shooting him a frown. "After seeing your friend seriously injured, I don't understand why you would even consider getting on one of those horses."

"I know the risks and I'm willing to take them." Determined to convince her it was the right thing to do, he continued, "If I get through the try-outs today, I get to compete for a share of that prize money I told you about. This rodeo will be the biggest event in the state for the Fourth of July, and I intend to be a part of it."

Clearly upset, Gail threw up her hands in frustration. "I saw a man thrown off a horse and almost lose his life right in front of my eyes." Her gaze traveled to his face. "That could be you some day."

Levi dug in his heels. He'd made up his mind and that was that.

"Unless I show up and win some money, you're going to lose your home. If I win enough, I can catch up the mortgage for you. It's the least I can do…before I leave."

Stepping forward, Gail pressed a warm palm against his scarred cheek. "Oh, you silly man," she said, blinking misted eyes. "I think it's admirable that you're willing to risk your life for this *familie*. But I can't expect you to do that, nor would I ask you to."

Savoring her touch, Levi covered her hand with his. "I have to do this. If not for you, then for Samuel. I owe him, and I intend to pay back my debt."

Letting her hand drop, Gail stepped back. "I guess I can't talk you out of the notion."

"I sound foolish, I know." He laughed. "At today's events, they whittle down the people who have been invited to enter. That's why the prize is so big. It's the best of the best. They will choose only ten competitors in each category. Three chances each, to make the best time."

"And if you don't qualify?"

"It's over. I'm out." Pausing, he hurried to add, "But I'm going to final, and then I'm going to win."

The fighting spirit left the depth of Gail's gaze. Her expression went blank. Mouth turned down, she returned to the cabinet, rummaging around for a thermos. "Let me get your food ready. Give me a few minutes. I have some cold ham that will make good sandwiches."

Unwilling to leave without having the final say, Levi grabbed Gail by the shoulders, turning her around to face him. Slipping his fingers beneath her chin, he angled back her head. "Don't give up, Gail. You're not going to lose the land your family has worked so hard to keep for generations. Not as long as I have breath in my body."

Trembling, Gail wrapped her arms around him. "Promise me you'll come back in one piece, Levi. Promise me."

"You have my word."

Hugging her tight, Levi pressed his lips to her forehead. How he wished he could hold her forever and never let her go.

Driven by nervous energy, Gail tried to get through the morning without breaking down in tears. Ever since Levi left for Fort Worth, driving through the front gate in his old pickup, she'd been unable to think straight. Her thoughts were jumbled, jumping from one idea to another. What if Levi got hurt? One wrong fall, one strike from an angry horse's hooves might injure him permanently. Worse, it could kill him.

Please, Gott, keep a hand of protection over him.

Keeping her thoughts to herself, she glanced at Seth. The boy sat at the kitchen table with sheets of art paper and Crayolas, blissfully unaware of the danger his father faced. It was not unusual for Levi to go to work before he woke. As far as Seth knew, his father was out on the range with the cattle.

Having finished breakfast and shooed her sisters out for the day, Gail tried to distract herself with cleaning. Whenever she had something on her mind, it was best to keep her hands busy. Otherwise, she'd sit and fret until she was a nervous wreck. Come noon, she'd entirely cleaned and rearranged the kitchen and living room until not a single speck of dust or lingering cobweb remained.

Exhausted, Gail treated herself to a cup of tea. She sat across from Seth and studied the child. As she watched him, so innocent and unaware, her heart squeezed a little. She still couldn't wrap her mind around the fact the child's mother hadn't wanted him. He was the sweetest little *boi*, generous and kind. Exactly like his father.

Finishing the page, Seth lifted his head. "See what I made for you," he said, turning the book to show her his work.

Gail glanced at the page. Like most children his age, Seth's style was still mostly abstract. Nevertheless, she could make out three figures and some animals under a bright rainbow.

"That's beautiful."

Seth pointed at one of the people with a hat. "That's *Datt*." His finger moved to a girlish figure in a dress. "That's you." He pointed to the tiny boy. "And that's me." He picked up a blue Crayola, marking across a fresh piece of paper. "I wish you could be my *mamm*," he blurted out.

Gail was caught by surprise. "You do?"

Face serious, Seth nodded. *"Ja."*

Not sure how to respond, she replied, "But you already have a mommy."

"Mommy is in heaven," Seth said, his face pinched with thought. "She can't take care of me and Daddy anymore like you do."

"I'm sure she would if she were here," Gail said, keeping her tone noncommittal.

Seth looked up at her through imploring eyes. "I want you to be my *mamm*," he said. "Forever and ever."

Gail's eyes misted, and her chin quivered. "I wish I could be your *mamm*, too. But since I can't, maybe I can be your Aunt Gail instead. Will that be okay?"

Seth slipped out of his chair and ran around the table. "Oh, yes!" Arms open, he threw himself at her, wrapping his small arms around her neck in a big hug. "And can Rebecca, Amity and Florene all be my aunts, too?"

"I am sure they would be happy to," she said, gathering the child up and pulling him into her lap. "We all love you and your *datt* very much."

"I wish we didn't have to go," Seth murmured, burying his head in the crook of her shoulder. "I want to stay."

Gail stroked the child's downy hair. "I wish you could stay, too," she murmured.

A knock at the front door interrupted.

Gail's brow furrowed. Who could that be? Levi was gone. As school was on summer hiatus, Rebecca was working part-time in her fiancé's butcher shop. Florene had thrown herself across her bed, glued to her smartphone. The Weavers had gone into town for the weekly supplies. She expected no guests.

Her heart seized. What if something had happened to Levi? The drive to Fort Worth was only two hours. Texas highways sometime got crazy around the bigger cities. What if…?

Adrenaline flowing through her, Gail put Seth down. She rushed across the living room and pulled open the door. Her breath stalled.

A patrol car was parked in the drive, and Sheriff Miller stood at the door. "Good morning," he greeted. "I'm sorry to interrupt your day."

Butterflies taking flight inside her stomach, Gail stepped back. "Not at all, Evan. It's good to see you," she said. "Won't you please come in?"

"Actually, I haven't got time," he said. "I just wanted to stop by and let you know police in Oklahoma have picked up Walter Slagel. He's in jail now, awaiting transfer back to Texas."

Hardly daring to breathe, Gail forced herself to draw air into her lungs. "He's been caught?" she repeated, unable to believe her ears.

"Yes, he has. And there's more to tell," Sheriff Miller said. "Slagel had a duffel bag full of cash with him. It is not quite the amount he stole from you, but it's close. The legal process to return it takes time, but you will get your money back."

Gail's vision blurred as she took in the news. "Oh, thank *Gott.*"

"You can thank the officer who recognized him from the BOLO we sent out," Sheriff Miller said.

"I certainly do." Still processing the good news, Gail smiled and offered her hand. Her prayers had been answered. "Thank you. Thank you so very much. This is the best news we could have gotten today."

Evan Miller tipped his hat. "My pleasure. I'll be in touch."

Turning on his heel, the sheriff strode to his patrol car and slid behind the wheel. He'd barely exited the drive before another car pulled in. The vehicle was unfamiliar, but the man who got out of the back seat was not. Because he was a busy man, Bishop Harrison preferred to hire a car and driver rather than try to make his calls around the community in a horse and buggy. As long as he didn't drive the vehicle, it was an accepted practice. Many Amish often hired drivers when traveling a long distance.

Wondering what would prompt the bishop's unexpected visit, Gail greeted him with a smile. "This is quite a surprise."

Bible in hand, Clark Harrison offered a brief smile. "*Guten nachmittag*, Gail," he greeted politely. "I hope I'm not disturbing anyone."

"Not at all," she said, and stepped back to allow him entry. "Please come in."

"I'm just visiting the families impacted by the tornado. I heard you also had damages."

"*Ja*, the house and the barn. Mostly the barn. The horses have no roof over their heads." Filling the teapot with fresh water, Gail set in on the stove. "May I offer you a cup of tea or coffee?"

"Tea would be lovely," he said, and took a seat near Seth. "How are you, young man?"

"*Ich bin* okay," Seth returned in perfect *Deitsch*.

Clark Harrison's brows rose. "*Wunderbar*," he said, ruffling the child's hair.

Gail poured a cup of fresh tea and set it in front of her visitor. She glanced toward Seth. Perhaps the boy should not listen to what adults might have to say.

"Seth, why don't you go upstairs and show Florene your pretty drawings? I'm sure she would like to see them."

"Sure!" Bored with adult conversation, Seth grabbed a handful of pages and slipped out of his chair. His boots clattered on the wooden steps as he ascended the stairs.

"Your tea, sir."

Adding sugar, Bishop Harrison sipped his drink. "The reason I came is to assess the damages families suffered. The church has put together a coalition of volunteers who will help with homes and businesses that need rebuilding. I have also arranged deals with the suppliers of my hardware store to donate lumber and other necessary materials to complete the projects. We will do the work without cost to any family."

Freshening her own tea, Gail took a seat opposite him. "Oh, Bishop. That is wonderful. Such a blessing from *Gott*."

"I came to see if you and your sisters would be interested in donating a few dishes to feed the men as they move from job to job."

Gail dropped her gaze. "Of course. We will be happy to cook for them."

"Mmm, good." A pause. "Is Levi around? I'd like to speak to him if he has a moment."

"Levi is out." Unable to hold back her pent-up feelings, she blurted. "He told me he was turned away from rejoining the church."

"I see. Did he tell you why?"

Gail nodded. "*Ja*. He told me it was because he divorced his wife."

Setting his cup aside, Bishop Harrison cleared his throat. "Well, it behooves me to examine a person's past behaviors if they have left to live in the *Englisch* world awhile. Levi was away over a decade."

"Perfectly understandable. I don't disagree with your wisdom."

The Bishop gave his bearded chin a scratch. "True wisdom also means finding out all the facts before passing judgment."

"What do you mean?"

"I contacted a few people, to verify some details about Levi's past. It might be true he divorced his wife, but two facts stand out very starkly," Clark Harrison explained. "The first is that his wife was a danger to those around her, especially their young son. It is a parent's duty to protect the innocent, and Levi was doing all the law allowed in order to accomplish that."

"I see. And what is the second?"

"As he didn't marry in a church and his *Englisch* wife is deceased, my ministers and I agree there is no reason he can't rejoin the church. I believe he is sincere in his repenting and wants to make a better life for himself and his son."

Hope sprang up, circling Gail's heart. "Are you saying Levi can be baptized?" she said in a trembling voice, close to tears all over again.

Bishop Harrison nodded. "*Ja.* Of course, he will still have to take the baptismal classes, as everyone does before making such a life-altering decision, but I see no issues preventing him from rejoining our community."

Joy lifted her spirit. "Levi didn't think he'd be forgiven for what he did."

Clark Harrison took a sip of his tea. "Well, the Lord happens to be in the business of forgiving people. Once he rejoins the church, Levi's past is just that. In the past."

Inside, her soul soared. The dream she'd watched

turn to ashes came sparking back to life, rising like a phoenix from the flames. All she ever wanted to marry Levi Wyse and have his *kinder*—loomed as an actual possibility.

"Where is Levi? I would like to tell him the good news."

Her joy quickly drizzled away. "Oh, Bishop, Levi's gone to Fort Worth to compete in a rodeo there."

Clark Harrison's brows rose. "I see."

"It's not what you think," Gail said, and hurried to explain. "A few months ago, our manager stole money from the ranch account. He took every cent we had and disappeared."

The bishop nodded. "Is that why Sheriff Miller was here?"

"The sheriff came to tell us that Walter Slagel has been caught—and they've retrieved the stolen money."

"I had no idea you faced such troubles, my child. If you had only come to me with your issues, perhaps I could have helped."

Gail dropped her gaze. "I was so ashamed I let that man steal from us, Bishop. I didn't know what to do. Levi, bless his soul, was a saving grace. Everything was going so well. And then the storm happened, killing the cattle we planned to sell to keep the bank from taking our home." Pausing she took a breath. "Levi's trying to win the money he thinks we need."

"I admire his fortitude," Bishop Harrison said.

"I didn't want him to go. Not after seeing his friend injured at the rodeo last week."

"I heard about that tragic accident."

Gail pressed a hand to her stomach. "What if it hurts

or kills him? Where would that leave his *sohn*?" She tried to find more words, but fear stalled her tongue.

"I understand your concerns." The bishop took one of her hands in his. "If you like, we will pray for Levi's safety."

Gail shook her head. "Bishop, may I beg of you to do something for me?"

The kindly older man gave her a nod. "Of course."

"Please, take me to Fort Worth. We need to find Levi and stop him before he gets on one of those broncs."

Chapter Eighteen

Riding in the back of the car with the bishop, Gail tried not to focus on the traffic around Fort Worth. Though it would be hard for people to believe it, she rarely traveled far from Burr Oak. The city, with its massive buildings and soaring off-ramps, was mind-boggling, filled with so many people all determined to go somewhere.

Securely fastened with a safety belt, Gail didn't feel one bit better. Cars and trucks might be more convenient for long-distance travel, but she believed she'd always love the slow and steady pace of a horse and buggy. As for Burr Oak, the tiny Texas town suited her fine, having enough services and necessities to keep it from being labeled the boonies.

"You all right?" Bishop Harrison asked.

Gail offered a weak nod. She wouldn't say it out loud, but the automobile made her dizzy. "I'm fine," she said, forcing herself to keep her breaths steady. It didn't help that her nerves were all sharp edges.

What if we get there and Levi's already hurt?

Gail quickly banished the notion.

"Thank you for giving up your day to bring us," she said. "I'm so very grateful."

Bishop Harrison waved a hand. "Been a long time since I've gotten out of town. I rather enjoy a long ride. And I haven't been to a rodeo in ages." He chuckled. "I used to go with my own father when I was a boy. It will be nice to revisit some old memories."

Settled between the adults in his car seat, Seth looked up. "My *datt* rides broncs. The horses, they buck really hard."

"*Ja*, Seth, I know," Gail said, squeezing his little hand. Her own were cold as the arctic chill invading her heart and lungs. Anxiety beat double time through her veins. Images of the man injured in the Eastland rodeo kept replaying in her mind's eye.

As if reading her mind, Seth looked grim. A dark shadow touched the boy's face, erasing pride. "I hope the horse don't hurt him like it hurt Mister Shane."

Gail shivered. Seth, too, had been in the audience that night. He'd seen the accident and it had clearly affected him.

"That's why we're going to tell him to stop."

Seth bobbed his head agreeably. "I think *Datt* should come home. The cows miss him."

"Where exactly are we going?" the bishop's *Englisch* driver asked, navigating the van through traffic. "I need a destination."

Mind freezing, Gail blanked.

"I—I don't know," she stammered, anxiety scattering her wits. "All I know is it's in Fort Worth." She'd been so upset with Levi's plan that she hadn't gotten a single detail.

"No problem, I'll find out." Reaching in a pocket, Bishop Harrison pulled out a smartphone.

Gail gaped. She had no inkling the bishop himself would use one.

He noticed her stare. "This is definitely an emergency." He launched a verbal search app. Within seconds, he had an address. "Take us to the Sports and Livestock Arena," he told the driver, giving him the address.

The driver punched it into the GPS on his dash. "Got it. On our way." A few minutes later, he turned on to an exit.

Soon the entertainment center came into view. After paying the parking fee, the driver found a spot. A multitude of monster diesel trucks and horse trailers filled the parking lot of a massive, fenced corral overhung by a rectangular domed roof designed to protect it from the rain during the outdoor events.

The driver pulled into a parking space lined along the iron security fencing. "Here you go, Bishop. I'll wait here."

"Hopefully, we won't be long," Bishop Harrison said, opening the car door.

Gail unlatched her seat belt and then unbuckled Seth. Accompanied by the bishop, they hurried toward the entry gate. A uniformed security agent stopped their progress.

"Is this the tryouts for the rodeo next weekend?" Gail asked, not sure exactly what to ask.

The tall man nodded. "Yes, but it's not open to the public."

Gail's heart dropped to her feet. "Then we can't go in?"

"Not unless you're with one of the competitors," he stated, shaking his head.

Thinking fast, Gail tightened her grip on Seth's hand. "Levi Wyse is competing today. This is his son, Seth. I am bringing him to his father. I'm his sitter," she added for good measure. "And this is Bishop Harrison. He has some news that Levi needs to hear."

Seth seconded her words. "My *datt* is a cowboy," he proudly informed the man.

Mistaking the bishop's clothes for funeral attire, the man said, "I hope there's not an emergency."

The bishop chuckled. "Only if you consider salvation and the saving of a soul an emergency."

The security agent checked his clipboard. "That guy is here," he said, and made a quick decision. "Go ahead." He opened the gate. "Just don't say it was me who let you inside if there's any trouble."

Relieved they had made it past security, Gail tugged Seth toward the massive arena. Competitors waiting for their event milled around, preparing their animals for the events to come. Surrounded by iron fencing, a series of gates kept the horses and bulls penned in place until it was time for release.

Locating a man with a tablet and a badge that read "Judge," Gail tugged his arm. "Excuse me, sir. I'm looking for Levi Wyse. He is competing today."

Consulting his tablet, the man nodded. "Levi's up for his third run in just a few minutes." He pointed. "Just over there."

"Danke." Searching through the cowboys milling around, she spotted Levi talking to another man. The bishop hung back, letting her go ahead.

Spotting his father, Seth broke away from her grip.

"*Datt!*" Limbs in motion, he rushed to his father and wrapped his arms around Levi's waist. "I'm so happy to see you."

Shocked by the appearance of his child, Levi knelt and gripped Seth's shoulders. "How did you get here?"

Before the boy could speak, Gail hurried up. "Levi, praise *Gott* we found you."

Levi stood. "I'll be right back," he said to the man. Pulling her and Seth aside so they could talk in private, he gave her a strange look. "What are you all doing here?"

"I want you to stop this nonsense and come home," Gail blurted, taking in his battered appearance. When he'd left that morning, Levi was spick-and-span from head to toe. Now his clothes were badly wrinkled and caked with dirt. He looked like he'd hit the ground hard several times. He was dressed in well-used chaps and with spurs on his boots, and a single, fingerless glove covered his right hand.

Levi glanced over his shoulder. "I'm almost up for my third run," he said. "This is the one. If I make the numbers, I'm in."

"Putting your life in danger for money isn't worth the risk."

Tipping back his hat, Levi rubbed his temple. "I need to do this, Gail. No matter the consequences."

"Levi, I have something to tell you."

He hushed her. "I know what you're going to say. But the Bible also says you can do all things through *Him* who strengthens you. I have given this to the Lord, and I am putting it in *His* hands. Whatever the outcome, it's *His* will."

Seeing the set of his jaw and the glint of determination

in his eyes, Gail raised her gaze to his. "If that's what you feel you have to do, then I won't try to stop you."

"Wyse, you're up," a man barked, interrupting.

Levi waved a hand to acknowledge the call. "Coming," he answered back. "One minute."

"Go." No matter the outcome, she had to support his decision. "May the Lord ride with you."

A slow grin turned up one corner of his mouth. "Do I get a hug?"

Gail crossed her arms over her chest. Not because she didn't want to throw herself in his arms and squeeze him tight, but because the extensive number of men surrounding them embarrassed her. It wouldn't be proper to express affection in front of all these prying eyes.

"I expect you to come back in one piece," she said. "And then you'll get your hug."

Seth had no such reservations. "I know you can beat that bronc," he enthused, jumping up and down.

"You can bet I will do my best, son." Levi caught his boy in a bear hug, lifting him off his feet. "And for you," he said to Gail.

"Wyse," a voice called again. "Now or never."

Lowering Seth, Levi gave a final, crooked smile. "Take good care of him." Turning, he hurried away.

Gail stood rooted in her place.

A tap on her shoulder caught her attention. "I believe we can watch over there." The bishop pointed to a seating area. Having stayed at a discreet distance, he'd observed all that happened.

Legs trembling, Gail nodded. "Thank you."

Leading her to a seat, Bishop Harrison sat beside her. "I know you are worried. But there's something that pushes men into doing difficult or dangerous things, even when there's a risk of injury or death."

Smoothing her skirt across her lap, Gail shook her head. "I guess I will never understand."

Bishop Harrison patted her arm. "We men want to know we're strong and can take care of our women and children. This is Levi's way of saying he will take care of you and Seth, even if it kills him. Your job is to support his decision."

There was no more time for conversation.

Searching with an anxious gaze, Gail spotted Levi. He climbed over the fence and entered the small area keeping the horse pinned into place. A few men kept the massive beast settled as he climbed on to the wild animal's back.

An announcement came over the loudspeaker. "Next up is Levi Wyse." The male voice went on, giving out a few facts and statistics about Levi's career.

Hearing his father's name, Seth cheered loudly. "That's my *datt*!" He called to anyone who cared to listen. Face beaming, he stood up in his chair so he could better see the event about to take place. "He's a rodeo king!"

A few spectators sitting nearby chuckled over his enthusiasm.

"You tell your daddy to bring it on home!" one man called out, clapping.

Egged on, Seth clenched his fists above his head. "You can beat that old bronc!"

Gail glanced up at the boy. Having watched his father compete before, Seth didn't seem a bit concerned. All he focused on was the excitement brewing.

All she focused on was the outcome. Blinking back tears, she watched anxiously as Levi raised his left hand and nodded.

* * *

Sitting astride the bronc, Levi took a breath to calm his racing pulse. This was it. The moment he'd been waiting for. Make the magic number in the scores, and he'd be in next week's rodeo. Fail, and he'd be walking out a loser.

And the Schroder sisters would lose their home.

Not going to happen.

"So help me *Gott*," he murmured.

With only seconds to spare, Levi gazed toward the audience. He didn't see Gail, but he knew she'd be watching every second of his ride.

Tightening his grip and setting his knees against the sides of the horse, he clenched his jaw and gritted his teeth. His heart jumped to his throat, and his pulse beat at his temples. Anxiety shot into the red zone.

"Let's do this."

A bell rang out, clear and loud. Two waiting cowboys pulled the gate open.

Set free, the wild horse bolted, leaping straight into the air, a tangle of sinew and sheer muscle in motion. Levi held on for dear life, mentally counting the seconds he needed. After the third or fourth buck, he was not sure he could last much longer. Every bone in his body rattled. Heart pumping a mile a minute, he felt the blood rush through his veins.

Giving a final, manic leap, the horse sent Levi flying straight into the air. Losing his grip, he slammed into the nearby fence. He lost his ability to breathe before crumbling to the hard ground.

Levi landed on his side and lay there, unable to move. The onlookers gasped, even as two men on horses galloped in to control the roiling bronc. With the help of the rodeo clowns, they were able to distract the horse and lead it away.

Refusing to panic, Levi forced himself to breathe, taking in much-needed oxygen to clear his rattled brain. He wiggled his fingers and then his toes. As far as he could tell, he was in one piece and nothing was broken.

Reaching up, he grabbed onto the fence and pulled himself to his feet. The ride had lasted only seconds, but it felt like an eternity. Feeling his left ankle give out, he limped into the arena. Aside from a sprain, he'd survived the challenge intact.

The onlookers roared, cheering furiously.

Reclaiming his smashed hat, Levi signaled he was all right. A couple of competitors came in to lead him out of the arena to safety. As he walked, a voice came over the loudspeaker, "Levi Wyse, ladies and gentlemen. Judges will announce the score soon."

Just like that, it was over. Win or lose, he'd done what he came to do.

Caught between excitement and the anxiety that he'd upset Gail, he looked around outside the gate. Both Gail and his son waited nearby.

Seth burrowed in, grasping his legs. "You beat that bronc, Daddy!"

Ruffling Seth's hair, he gave Gail a crooked grin. "So how about that hug now?"

A reluctant smile turned up Gail's fine lips. "All right. But just this once." Leaning in, she circled his neck with her arms, squeezing tight. "You scared me so much," she whispered in his ear.

Levi nodded. "I know, and I'm sorry. I didn't mean to frighten you."

She let him go and stepped back. "I'm never going through that again," she said in a calm voice.

Before he could reply, a hearty hand clapped him on the shoulder. "Congratulations, my boy. You did well."

Recognizing the voice, Levi turned. "Bishop Harrison, what are you doing here?"

"I came to see you this morning, but you weren't home," the bishop replied jovially. "When Gail told me where you were, I offered her a ride to Fort Worth."

"Thank you for bringing her and Seth, Bishop. I appreciate it."

"I don't mean to impede on your celebration," he continued. "But I would like to speak with you when things have calmed down a bit."

Mouth going bone-dry, Levi felt his insides tighten with painful anxiety. Well, that didn't sound promising. He swallowed down the lump in his throat. "Whatever you've got to say, you might as well spit it out."

"Well, you can stop looking like I've just kicked your favorite dog and burned your crops," Clark Harrison said, adjusting the black frames of his thick glasses. "What I want to tell you is that I'm still planning to put the Amish back in you—that is, if you'll start coming to church again."

Levi struggled to find his tongue. "You—you mean I can be baptized?"

"*Ja*. My ministers and I have revisited your case and after going over the matter, we have ruled that you were acting in the best interests of your *familie*." Bishop Harrison glanced from Levi to Seth. "I know your heart is good and that you care for your son very much. I am honored you would want to raise Seth in the church, and hope that he, too, will one day want to join the community."

Emotion squeezed Levi's throat. "Thank you, Bishop," he said, reaching out to shake Clark Harrison's hand with grateful enthusiasm. "I intend to raise him to lead a good Christian life."

"*Gut*. Then I expect to see you both in church this Sunday." Clark Harrison fished out a pocket watch. "Well, as much as I have enjoyed my time in Fort Worth, the day is getting away." He looked to Gail. "I trust you will ride home with Levi?"

She smiled. "Yes. Thank you for bringing us."

"My pleasure." Bishop Harrison tipped his hat and bade them all goodbye. Weaving his way through the crowd, he disappeared.

The bishop had no more than disappeared from sight when another man holding a clipboard jogged up.

"Your numbers, Levi," he said, handing over a sheet of paper. "The judges gave you a score of ninety-five. You've set a new record. Congratulations. You've also qualified for next week's rodeo. You've hit the big time." He walked away, leaving everyone dumbstruck.

Levi looked at Gail and then back to the paper in his hand. He was speechless. The numbers on the page listed him as a finalist. He blinked several times to make sure he'd read it right.

Heartbreak in her gaze, Gail stared at him. "I'm so happy for you, Levi," she said, giving his arm a squeeze. "I guess you're going to want to compete next weekend."

Levi searched her face. "Why wouldn't I? This is my chance to get the money you need."

"You don't have to," Gail said, adding a wide smile.

"Sheriff Miller came by the house earlier. The police caught Mr. Slagel. He had the money with him."

Disbelief widened his eyes. "You're kidding? That's wonderful."

"He said we will get back most of what was stolen." She reached for his hand and clasped it in hers. "I want you to come home and help me rebuild the herd. I can't do it without you."

A grin split his face. "Are you trying to hire me?"

Frustrated, Gail blurted out, "*Nein*. I'm asking you to marry me, Levi Wyse." The words pushed past her lips before she could stop them.

He gave her a cockeyed look. "Did you just propose?"

A rush of heat flooded her cheeks. She couldn't believe what she'd just said. "I—I—" she stammered helplessly.

Laughing, Levi made a sudden decision. He tossed the paper away.

Gail's eyes widened. "What are you doing?"

"I'm saying yes. But we have to do this the right way. I'm the one who is supposed to do the asking." Then, untangling himself from Seth's hold, he placed his hands on her shoulders. "Gail Schroder, will *you* marry *me*?"

Gail burst into tears. "Oh, Levi. I thought I would never hear you say those words." She wiped at her eyes.

He pulled her closer. Placing a gentle kiss on her forehead, he looked down into her eyes. "I hope that means you are saying yes."

Gail cried harder. "*Ja*," she said, and laughed through her tears. "*Tausendmal, ja.*" A thousand times yes.

Epilogue

Two weeks later

Busy working at the kitchen counter, Gail wiped the back of her hand across her perspiring brow. She'd spent the entire morning baking fresh bread, then cutting up thick slabs of ham for the sandwiches she made. She needed at least two dozen, maybe more.

She glanced up to check the time. The clock read ten minutes to twelve, and a lot of hungry men would expect lunch soon.

"Is the lemonade ready?"

Spatula in hand, Rebecca scooped freshly baked cookies onto a waiting plate. "It's chilling in the fridge now, with plenty of ice."

Gail nodded her approval. "The men have been working on the barn since sunrise. They're going to be famished."

"I still can't believe Levi won so much money," Florene said, adding mustard and mayonnaise to the bread Gail had laid out before adding the ham. She stacked the sandwiches neatly on a waiting tray.

"Hard to believe, but it's true," Gail said. The surprise still had her reeling.

Even though Levi didn't compete in The Big Texan, he'd received a letter in the mail, recognizing his record-breaking ride at the finals. A check for fifty thousand dollars was included, part of the bonus prize all finalists shared. There was enough money to catch up on the mortgage payments and repair the barn. It would also tide them over until the court ordered the return of the money Walter Slagel had stolen. The criminal proceedings still lay ahead, and Gail was ready to testify against the man who had come close to costing her family everything they owned.

For now, the focus was on rebuilding the herd. To celebrate the joining of their families, she and Levi had created a new brand, incorporating the *S* and the *W* of their names. The Schroder-Wyse Ranch would go on.

Thinking of all that had happened, Gail smiled to herself. Once she and Levi had officially tied the knot, they would become a proper family. Faith and the power of love had brought them together. Their path had been a rocky one, fraught with tragedy and trying times. But hard work and plenty of prayer had delivered many blessings. Hopefully, the Lord would also bless her and Levi with many *kinder* of their own.

"We'd better get this food out there," Rebecca said, heading for the back door with a tray of her famous oatmeal raisin cookies.

"I know the men must be hungry," Gail said, picking up the tray of sandwiches while Florene grabbed the lemonade from the fridge.

The three of them walked outside.

Amity was directing a couple of *youngies* to set the picnic tables and benches under the shadiest trees.

"Now set them just there," she ordered briskly, before covering them with a pretty tablecloth and putting out a stack of paper plates and cups. Plastic coolers sat nearby, full to the brim with bottled water on ice.

The wives of the workers arrived in their buggies. Delighted with the arrival of his friends, Seth ran to play with the other children. The sound of laughing children and chattering voices filled the air.

Putting down her tray, Gail glanced up at the sky. The July day was warm, but not blistering. The breeze kicked up a skittering of clouds, scenting the air with the promise of rain.

"Through rain or shine, *Gott* will keep us safe," she murmured, sending up a silent prayer of thanks.

Standing close by, Rebecca smiled. "Amen."

At the strike of noon, the men laid aside their tools and headed into the backyard for their meal. Though it might seem an incredible feat, a crew of men could raise a new barn within ten hours. Every man there had volunteered his time as an early wedding gift.

Levi walked among the group. No longer clad in Western-style clothes, he dressed in the same dark trousers, boots and white shirt that the other men wore. As soon as he completed his studies, Bishop Harrison would perform his baptism, bringing Levi back into the fold of the Amish community. Not long afterward, he and Gail would stand before the entire congregation and share their vows.

Gail's heart swelled with pride as he closed the distance between them. She'd never been happier or felt more at peace. Levi was hers and nothing would ever part them.

"And there's the prettiest girl I know," he said as a greeting.

Flushing, Gail shook her head. "And the happiest." She'd smiled every minute since he'd proposed. And once the bishop pronounced them to be man and wife, she didn't ever intend to stop.

Reaching out, Levi caught her hands in his and leaned forward. "I'd love to steal a kiss, but there's too many people around," he whispered so only she could hear.

Gail felt her cheeks heat with a blush. "There will be time for kisses after we are wed."

Stepping back, his smile widened. "I hope you got what you wanted."

"Of course, I did," she said, and tossed him a saucy wink. "You forget, I'm not only Amish, but I'm also a Texan. And Texas women always get their man."

* * * * *

HER SECRET AMISH MATCH

Cathy Liggett

To my incredible husband, best friend
and forever love. Who would've ever imagined nearly
forty years ago that we would've found each other
again? I've got to say, I'm truly thankful
that God is the best matchmaker of all!

A new heart also will I give you,
and a new spirit will I put within you:
and I will take away the stony heart out of
your flesh, and I will give you an heart of flesh.
—*Ezekiel* 36:26

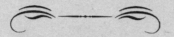

Chapter One

"I got the mail for you, *Daed.*"

Wrench in hand, Jake Burkholder looked up from the plow he was intent on fixing and saw his daughter Sarah standing close by, holding a handful of envelopes.

A slight breeze whispered through the open doors of the barn, causing wisps of hair to escape from her *kapp.* With her free hand, she pushed away the dark brown curly strands, revealing wide, blue-as-sky eyes that resembled her mother's. Even though nearly two years had passed since his wife, Lily, had gone to the Lord, there were moments when their daughter's similar gaze caught him off guard.

The children had spent the sunny Saturday morning gathering eggs and helping with other daily chores. After that, while he focused on his repair work, Sarah and the twins settled on the straw floor of the barn, hovering over the new litter of playful calico kittens.

At least, he'd thought that was what they were doing.

But apparently, Sarah had made her way down their stretch of driveway to the mailbox at the side of the country road that curved in front of their house. She'd also made her way back up the driveway without him even noticing her disappearance. Not that a trip to the mailbox in their part of Sugarcreek, Ohio, was anything close to perilous. But it did concern him to think he'd been so preoccupied with his work that he hadn't even realized she'd been gone.

"*Danke*, Sarah." He took the mail, stuffing the envelopes into the pocket of his black pants. "But next time, you must ask if you may go down to the mailbox."

The oldest of the children, Sarah was close to turning six years old. Yet ever since Lily had been gone, he could tell she had been trying to take on her mother's role as much as she could. Her willing heart, ready to assume extra responsibilities, touched him. And tore at him, too.

He hated to reprimand her for being helpful. Yet, as her father, he needed to be ever protective of her physical safety. That went for his four-year-old twins, too, who were looking up from the pile of kittens. "Do you understand, Sarah?"

"*Jah, Daed.* I do." She nodded solemnly. At the same instant she spoke, her stomach growled, causing them both to smile.

"It sounds as if there's a tiger inside you that would like to be fed," Jake teased. "Are you *hungrich*?"

"I'm hungry!" Eli answered before Sarah could get a word out.

"Me, too," Clara, Eli's twin, chimed in.

"I suppose it is close to mealtime," Jake agreed. Actually, he realized guiltily, since the mail had already arrived, that meant it was hours past their usual noon meal. He'd not only lost track of Sarah, he had totally lost track of time, as well.

"I can make peanut butter and jelly sandwiches for us, *Daed*," Sarah quickly offered.

He was almost tempted to let Sarah take charge. He hated to break away from his maintenance work, not knowing when he'd get back to it. Plus, there was a fence that needed mending. Horse stalls to be cleaned. And those were only two chores on a never-ending list. Pausing, he considered his options but quickly came to realize what he already knew. Children required their own kind of maintenance, and that was especially true when they were missing a mother's attention and love.

"*Nee*, Sarah. Let's go in and eat together."

While he put his tools away, Sarah gathered up the twins like the mother hen she was. Jake smiled at the way she cautioned them in the same manner he'd spoken to her.

"Eli and Clara, did you hear what *Daed* said before? Don't go to the mailbox without asking." Sarah paused to wag a finger at her siblings.

"*Oll recht*," Clara replied, and Eli gave a quick nod.

With that, the three of them scampered ahead of him down the walk toward the house.

After the dimness of the barn, Jake couldn't help but be struck by the brightness of the autumn day. Glancing at his surroundings—the golden colors of the changing leaves and the vibrant blooms on the chrysanthemums—he felt a surge of gratitude that he was able to move into the home he'd grown up in after Lily's passing. His younger brother, Samuel, had had his fill of caring for the property their parents had left to them, and had readily taken off with a friend to Kentucky and new opportunities.

Jake was also thankful for the ridge of pine trees that

separated his family's property from the Keims' land. All year long, those towering trees blocked the view of the house where he and Lily had been raising their family. But unfortunately, neither a row of trees nor anything else could block out the haunting memories of his and Lily's years together in that house.

Of course, it wasn't like he hadn't known their marriage was starting out with a lie. As it turned out, their marriage had ended with lies, too.

Jake felt relieved that Lily's brother, David, had put their family's property on the market soon after her death. Two years later, Jake wondered if potential buyers could feel a sadness still lingering in the walls.

As for the walls and rooms and land that now surrounded his children, he hoped to build as many happy memories as he could.

Just not with any indoor pets.

"Eli, leave the kitten outdoors," he called to his son, whose right pants pocket bulged with the furry creature he'd hidden there. Obviously, Eli hadn't thought he would notice, causing Jake to smile. Caring for three *kinner* surely kept him on his toes and was often overwhelming. Just keeping watch over his son was a job in itself.

For sure it would be good when his sister Esther, now all grown up herself and a teacher, arrived from Lancaster County to help with his children as she'd promised. As it was, every time he had a nanny from the community whom he thought would be a keeper, something would happen to pull them away and leave him stranded again.

Of course, Esther had made the same promise before and hadn't come through. He shook his head at the thought, not even wanting to consider the possibility of her changing her mind.

"Should we put Eli's kitten back in the barn with the others?" Sarah asked.

"That would be a very *gut* idea."

While the children took off on their mission back to the barn, Jake continued on his way to the house. He was almost to the front door when he heard the faint clip-clop of horse hooves. Immediately his trio of *kinner* broke out into a chorus of squeals.

"Hannah! Hannah!"

Jake turned to see Hannah Miller's spotted horse and buggy coming up the drive. The sight of Hannah always gave him much relief.

For months following Lily's passing, many kind people had brought meals, advised on childcare and tried to help in his new life as a single parent. But as time went on, they'd fallen to the wayside. Without any members of his family—or Lily's—living close by, there was no one consistent in his life or his children's. Except for Hannah.

Deftly hitching her horse to a post, Hannah gracefully stepped down from the buggy. Seeing her brought about a reaction in him just as when they were *youngies*. Back then, her chestnut-colored hair reminded him of milk chocolate, and her hazel eyes with their golden tint like fireflies lighting up on a summer's night. In a way, they still did.

He noticed hugging the *kinner* was Hannah's first order of business. The second was to unload the canvas sacks she'd brought. The children practically tripped over themselves, eager to help carry something into the house, each looking so happy to see her.

"Hannah, this is a *gut* surprise," he said, catching up with them. "Let me help." He reached for the covered pie dish in her arms, catching a whiff of it as he did.

"Cherry?" he asked.

"The *kinner*'s favorite. I was making a pie for worship at the Lapps' tomorrow, and I thought, why not bake two?"

Jake nodded. "Because managing Sew Easy and having your disabled aunt living with you isn't enough work for you, *jah*?" "How is your *aenti* Ruth, by the way?"

Hannah smiled. "Very *gut*, *danke*. As you know, she hasn't had use of her legs since birth and has been in a wheelchair all her life, but she can still run circles around me when it comes to most things."

"You know, you do need to take time to do things for yourself sometimes, Hannah."

"I am doing something for myself." She looked from him to his children. "I'm visiting my three favorite *kinner* in the whole wide world," she announced, causing the children to jump up and down with excitement.

"Daed," Sarah spoke up right away. "May Hannah eat lunch with us?"

"You're just now having lunch?" Hannah grinned at him curiously. "It's kind of late, don't you think? Closer to suppertime."

"*Jah*, we got a bit off schedule today."

"*Daed*'s been working on the plow," Clara informed Hannah.

"Oh, I can see how a person could lose themselves in such an interesting project." Hannah's eyes glimmered as she teased. "Sounds real fascinating."

"Verra." Jake smiled back. "So, will you stay and

eat with us?" He hoped she would stay awhile for the children's sake. And, honestly, for his sake, too.

"Ah. Well, I was just going to drop by with new dresses I'm stitching for the girls. I don't want you going to any trouble cooking for me."

"Please stay," Eli pleaded, and his sisters chimed in.

"We could have an early supper," Jake said, hoping to persuade her.

Hannah looked from his eyes to each of the children's faces. "I'd love to stay. An early supper sounds perfect."

After depositing the canvas sacks in the catchall room that also housed a sewing machine, they walked into the kitchen. The messy countertops and stacks of dirty dishes piled in the sink made Jake feel somewhat self-conscious. But Hannah said nothing. Instead, she started to wash her hands, obviously ready to help with the meal.

"Nee." Jake shook his head and pointed toward a kitchen chair.

"Have a seat and rest while we make the food."

The children were accustomed to helping him in the kitchen as best they could each day, but cooking for Hannah put a different spin on things. Jake noticed that suddenly they appeared far more earnest about their tasks. Eli squeezed the lemons mercilessly to get every drop of juice from them, only stopping when he needed to rest his arm from the workout. Sarah and Clara got busy deciding on the very best vegetable bowls and serving spoons, as if their lives depended on it.

Of course, they beamed when Hannah noticed their efforts. "Sarah and Clara, you do good work," Hannah complimented them. "And, Eli, you look as if you're a natural in the kitchen, just like your *daed*."

That comment drew a chuckle from Jake. "Oh, *jah*. I'm a natural, all right."

"You cook real *gut*, *Daed*," Sarah defended him.

"I'm only teasing your father, Sarah, because he wreaked havoc in a neighbor's kitchen when we were much younger."

"What happened, *Daed*?" Sarah's eyes widened. Eli and Clara glanced up from their tasks, looking concerned, too.

"One of the neighbors, Mrs. Fisher, was teaching your *mamm* and Hannah how to can tomatoes," he started to explain. "I'd gotten done with my chores early and—"

Hannah smiled. "He thought he might want to learn, too. But, oh, he made such a mess with the tomatoes."

"I did, didn't I?" He laughed at the memory. "I accidentally broke a few mason jars, too."

"*Jah*, indeed. Mrs. Fisher shooed you out of the kitchen and sent you into town to buy more jars."

"Poor woman. She was nice about it, too," he said. "Even though I'd tested her patience." He shook his head. "Well, I've gotten somewhat better around the kitchen since then."

He'd had to. But he didn't want to think about the reason why at that moment. The children were in a cheerful mood and he was, as well. He was glad when Hannah diverted the conversation.

"How about if I at least set the table?"

"That's fair. Girls, can you help Hannah find everything?"

The girls instantly went to work with Hannah, who

also oversaw Eli as he shakily carried his very full pitcher of lemonade to the table. Jake completed the meal with bowls of vegetables and a platter of leftover chicken.

As they all sat down, he looked around the oak table, taking note of the children's content faces and Hannah's serene expression. It felt somewhat strange, as it always did when Hannah visited, to look up and see her sitting at the table in Lily's seat. But after the past two years, he realized it was beginning to feel more comforting than strange. Hannah's company and spirit were truly a salve they all needed.

"Let us have a prayer yet," he said, then watched his children fold their hands together properly before he bowed his head and closed his eyes. Without a doubt, he was always ready to give thanks for *Gott*'s multitude of blessings. But on this day, at this moment, he felt moved to express his extreme thankfulness in a way he hadn't done in a long while.

After everyone helped clear the table and Jake coaxed little Eli into helping with the dishes, Hannah took Sarah and Clara to the extra room down the hallway.

Early-evening sunlight poured in the window, streaking across the girls' grinning faces, making it easy for Hannah to see how excited they were about their new dresses. To be able to do such a thing for her best friends' children tugged at her heart in a bittersweet way.

Thankfully she hadn't put off bringing the sample dresses for the girls—especially where Sarah was concerned. Hannah noticed the close-fitting dress she wore. She'd grown even more than Hannah had realized.

As both girls stood next to each other, Hannah slid the dresses over their heads. Clara's fit perfectly, but she'd misjudged Sarah's size. The new dress was as snug as her old one. But instead of focusing on the uncomfortable fit, Sarah looked up at her with the widest smile. "This is a real pretty green color."

"I thought it would go well with your hair and eyes, Sarah."

"What color goes with me?" Clara asked.

Clara's coloring was just like her mother's and father's, blonde with electric blue eyes. "I like blue on you, little one," Hannah told her. "But I have lots of fabric of other pretty colors, too. Once I get them all sewn, both of you girls will have plenty of warm dresses for the colder weather."

She stepped back and eyed them both once more. "Clara, your dress fits well. But give me a minute to place some pins for new seams, Sarah."

As she knelt on the ground in front of Jake's oldest, pinning the garment, Clara leaned up against her side.

"You like to sew, don't you?"

"*Jah*, dear girl, I do. I've been doing it since I was a young girl."

When Jake moved into his parents' old house, she'd been happy to see that he'd brought along the treadle sewing machine that had once belonged to Lily's grandmother. When Lily's parents, Noah and Rachel, kindly took her into their home after she lost her family at ten years old, Hannah had felt comforted to see the machine in the Keim household. Certainly, sewing had reminded her of her own *mamm* in a lasting, heartfelt way like nothing else did. She'd taken to the craft, making it her life's work.

For the past seven years, her job at Grace Newberry's Sew Easy shop had never been just a means to keep her and her aunt fed and to pay her bills. It was the very desire of her heart. She loved helping the customers. She loved teaching and being creative. The *Englisch* store owner had promised that the shop would be hers one day soon when Grace retired, which was far more than she could ever have hoped for. It was the perfect answer for her. Because knowing what it felt like to be orphaned, she never wanted to feel that way again. She yearned to be self-sufficient and not depend on anyone but herself.

"Will you teach me how to sew?" Sarah spoke up.

"*Jah*, I would love to teach you."

"Me, too?" Clara asked.

"*Jah*, you, too." Their interest warmed her heart. "I'd enjoy giving you both lessons if it's okay with your *daed*."

After Hannah resized the last of Sarah's seams, the girls helped her gather up the basted dresses and turn off lanterns. Then, skipping down the hall ahead of her, they rushed to tell their father their news.

"Hannah is going to give us sewing lessons, *Daed*," they announced gleefully.

Hannah also heard their father's reply. "That's nice, girls," he said, but his voice was alarmingly flat. Completely different from the cheerful way he'd acted an hour earlier. His reaction quickened Hannah's feet till she reached the family room, too. In the amber glow of the lamp sitting on the table next to him, she could see his stricken face. She could also see an envelope and a crumpled piece of stationery on top of the table.

"Jake, is everything all—"

"Girls," he cut her off, getting up out of the chair, "your *bruder* is getting ready for bed. Go do the same." He pointed to the staircase. "I'll be up to say prayers when you're ready."

Without another word, he stepped over to the window, staring into the darkening sky. The girls glanced at her, clearly puzzled. She couldn't help but feel the same way. She tried not to let it show.

"Good night, sweet *maedels*." She gave the pair a wink.

Ever obedient, the girls did as they were told. Not until they were up the stairs did Jake turn and look at her. There was no denying he was completely beside himself.

"Jake, what happened?"

He ruffled a hand through his blond hair. "It's Esther."

"Is your sister *oll recht*?"

"*Jah*, she's just fine. But once again, she's broken her promise to me. She says they haven't been able to find a replacement for her at her school, and she cannot leave her teaching position to come help her nieces and nephew. Can't come to help her own flesh and blood."

Hannah wanted to reach out and calm him, but he began pacing. It was heartbreaking to see the defeated slump of his broad shoulders and the darkness in his usually smiling, warm blue eyes. This was the man who had always been so confident and sure of himself, the good-looking boy that all the girls crushed on and all the other boys wanted to be like.

"Jake, I'm sure she didn't mean it like that exactly."

"It doesn't matter how she meant it. The point is, she's not coming."

Hannah didn't bother to ask about other family members in Lancaster who might be able to come to Ohio to help. They'd covered that ground before. Whereas Esther was better acquainted with all their aunts and uncles and cousins since she'd spent the first ten years of her life there, Jake had been only two years old when his parents had moved from Pennsylvania to Ohio. Plus, from what his sister had written, those distant relatives were busy with their own lives and families.

"Oh, Jake, I'm sorry it's not working out like you hoped."

"*Jah*, well…" He stopped pacing and shook his head, sounding half-angry and completely distraught as he spoke. "I really needed her help. I can't provide for my *kinner* and also watch over them. It's a problem I can't seem to solve. But what else is new?"

"You know, Jake…" She hesitated. "Maybe a nanny isn't the answer you're looking for."

His brows arched, all six feet of him stiffening. "Oh, *jah*, while I'm out in the fields working, I'll just have the mares watch the *kinner*," he said curtly.

"What I mean is, a nanny can be a temporary solution. But it's not a permanent one."

"Hannah, you're confusing me."

She was sure he'd forgotten that when some townsfolk spoke of her, they said she had a special gift. Namely, the way she matched a man and a woman together. She was thrilled to help others find love. It took the pressure off finding her own match while keeping her heart intact and not being hurt again. More like devastated, as she had been by the unaware man she was looking at.

Yet she'd never mentioned matchmaking to Jake before, knowing he was still getting his bearings after Lily's death two years earlier. She also knew, however, that the once most popular boy in their community had become a solitary man out of necessity and his chances of crossing paths with a mate were slim. So, she was happy to try to find him a match, if he was willing.

"Jake, I think your *kinner* need so much more than what you can pay a stranger to give them." From her own background, she knew that better than anyone. "They need a nurturing female who is always there for them. And always there for you, their *daed*. Someone who knows you all well and cares for all of you, too."

"And you're saying what?" His forehead pinched.

"What I'm saying is, I can help you find that someone. But let me tell you, Jake, it means you'll have to start dating."

"Dating?" His jaw slacked.

"Well, *jah*. How else do you think you can find a mate?"

"To be honest, I've been so busy working and raising the children, I've not thought about finding a new wife."

"Well, what do you say, then? I'll be your *verra* own matchmaker. Agreed?" She held out her hand, waiting for his handshake to seal their arrangement.

"I… I don't know… It seems mighty strange…" He stood, pulling on the gold-tinted beard that had and still did link him with Lily. Then he began shaking his head nonstop. She wasn't sure if he was declining her offer or couldn't believe the offer she was making. "So, then I'd be just like one of the other Sugarcreek couples that you've brought together?"

"You mean like the other happy Sugarcreek couples that I've successfully matched? Yes, Jake," she answered reassuringly.

He eyed her warily.

"Jake, who knows you better than me? I'm the perfect person to do this for you." she said.

"Sure, but…" He let out a long sigh. Then finally, slow as a turtle poking its head out of its shell, his right hand came out of his pocket. Hesitantly, he reached for hers.

"Agreed." He clasped her hand lightly. "I guess."

"*Gut.* I'll start looking for a match tomorrow, then." She began gathering up her canvas sacks, then put on her warm cloak.

"Tomorrow? So soon?" His face clouded with unease, and his eyes seemed wide with—fear?

She'd rarely ever seen her friend appear afraid. Could barely recall a time even when they were younger that he'd seemed frightened. The sight of him looking that way stirred her heart. "It's going to be all right, Jake," she said softly, placing a comforting hand on his arm. "You'll see. Have I ever let you down?"

Chapter Two

The next morning was as drizzly and cloudy as Jake's thoughts while he steered his buggy over the damp, narrow roads through Sugarcreek. What in the world had he been thinking when he agreed to allow Hannah to find him a *fraa*? As if finding a new wife was as easy as buying a bale of hay at the feed and seed store. And what would the *kinner* think about him bringing another woman into their lives?

"Daed..." Sarah drew out the word as her concerned voice came from the back of the buggy, interrupting his thoughts.

His hands tightened on the reins. *"Jah*, Sarah?"

"Eli doesn't have any socks on."

"What? No socks?" Puzzled, he glanced over his shoulder at the boy, who was wedged between his sisters. "Eli, I thought you knew how to dress yourself by now, *sohn*. It's forty degrees outside."

"I didn't have clean ones, *Daed*." Eli folded his arms over his chest defensively. "All mine are muddy."

"That's silly." Clara reprimanded her twin, sounding much like her older sister. "If I can have on dirty clothing extra days, you can have on dirty socks, too."

Jake was at a loss for words. Didn't know what to say or think—except he needed to get the laundry under control. If that was even possible.

Oh, dear Lord, I need Your help, don't I?

Currently, however, socks, clothing and every other soiled item would have to wait. Before he headed his *kinner* back home to do more chores, he needed to put up more flyers around town, announcing his availability to do handyman work.

After Lily's passing, he'd left his job at the lumberyard to work the fields of his farm. He needed to be close to home and his children, even knowing full well—like his brother, Samuel—that farming wasn't what he was best suited for. It was also no mystery that the yield from farming was uncertain. Thankfully, *Gott* had made sure that the first harvest was plentiful, while he and the children were still grieving and finding their footing.

But this year, the harvest had been mediocre at best. As a result, he'd had to find other income. Though he'd already taken on a few handyman jobs, he hoped to pick up more work during the winter months ahead.

Turning those hopes over to *Gott*, he hitched the buggy in front of McNab's Hardware Store, and the children hopped out eagerly. Why wouldn't they? Kauffman's Kitchen was right next door and he'd promised them a late breakfast there. Not that the money he'd earned days earlier from his repair work was burning a hole in his pocket, by any means. But he figured the change of scenery and something other than his own cooking would do them all good.

It shouldn't have taken long to guide Sarah and the twins through McNab's, tack up a flyer and then head to Kauffman's. Yet, herding his family always took more time than he thought it should. A dropped glove here. A tripped toe there. It was at least twenty minutes before they were seated at a table and ordering their favorite foods.

The outing could've been relaxing except for Eli's elbow knocking over a glass of chocolate milk, then Clara dropping her fork on the floor. Jake leaned under the table to pick it up, then heard his name, raised his head too quickly, smacked his skull on the edge, and looked up to see Seth Hochstetler standing next to his chair.

Seth, his former employer and owner of Hochstetler's Lumberyard, smiled at him as if he could empathize. "It's not easy, *jah*? But I know you can handle whatever *Gott* throws at you."

Jake laughed, rubbing his head. "It's not always easy with these three."

"Just wait till they're teens." Seth seemed to be talking from experience as he nodded over his shoulder at his wife and their son and daughter seated several tables away. Jake also noticed Seth's younger sister Emma seated with them. "I'm glad I ran into you, Jake. Your name's been coming up, and I've been meaning to ask you something."

At that point, a smile lit up Emma's face as she looked over at Jake and gave a little wave. He tentatively waved back. He hoped Seth wasn't about to set him up with Emma. Did he seem that desperate and ill-equipped, sitting there with his children?

Glancing around the room, he looked for signs of

spilled milk or utensils on the floor. But all he could see were families eating and enjoying themselves.

Yes, he probably did need all the help he could get from Hannah, Seth or whoever else. Realizing that, he looked at Seth, prepared to hear what his old boss had to say.

Hannah assumed it was the chilly rain keeping customers away from Sew Easy that afternoon. At least, she hoped the nasty weather was the cause and not the recent opening of the fabric chain store that people had been raving about.

So far, she'd waited on two older ladies, both only needing thread. Then, an hour or so later, the postman had arrived with several envelopes and parcels.

Her boss, Grace, had said she'd be busy with her retired husband for the rest of the day. Without her there to talk to, the store was virtually silent.

Normally, the solitude would've been boring. But all day Hannah's mind had been going a mile a minute, thinking about the prior evening and all that had happened with Jake.

As she stood at the counter methodically measuring remnants of material, rolling up the pieces and attaching a price tag, Hannah knew what she needed to do to get her thoughts in order. Closing her eyes, she bowed her head.

Dear Gott, I'm forever grateful that You found a home for me as a child. One day if and when I'm ready, I may have You find a home for my heart, too. But right now, things aren't about me. As You know, I made a promise to Jake to find him a wife. But my words can only come true if You're there to help, Lord. So, I'm thanking You in advance for finding a woman who will love his kinner *like I do—and the right person for Jake, too. In Your Son's name. Amen.*

She opened her eyes and sighed, immediately feeling more relaxed. It helped, too, when she spotted Anna Graber coming through the door. Rushing out from behind the counter, she hugged her friend, leaving enough room for Anna's protruding belly.

"Anna, how *gut* to see you! You look beautiful," she exclaimed truthfully. "When are you due?"

"Three months, and trust me, I'm not feeling anything close to beautiful." Anna grinned, massaging her round stomach. "But look at you, Hannah. So pretty, as always. When are you going to let a man snatch you up?"

Hannah felt the heat of a blush encircle her neck. After all, it wasn't like any men had been chasing her lately. And even if they had been, she wasn't much interested. After a few short-lived relationships, she'd realized she was far better at creating other people's happily-ever-afters than finding a match for herself. Plus, there was no wear and tear on her heart. The thing that really interested her right now was thinking about her future at Sew Easy. And as soon as she got Jake settled in a relationship, she could go back to concentrating on business.

"I've been so busy with work and teaching sewing classes. Oh, and helping *Aenti* Ruth organize an embroidery class here." Knowing those things might not sound like good excuses, she added, "And I've been helping Jake with Sarah and the twins."

"How is Jake?" Anna tilted her head, looking concerned. "Matthew and I only have the two boys so far, but it's endless work. It's so nice of you to be there for him. I don't know how he does it alone.".

"*Jah*, I know. That's why I promised to find him a match," she blurted out, without meaning to.

"You're his matchmaker?" Anna chuckled, her eyes growing wide. "Some things never change, huh? Remember when you and Lily tried to match me with Jake back when we were *youngies*?"

"How could I forget?" Hannah giggled. "We thought he should have a real girlfriend instead of always being with girl friends like Lily and me. And it might've worked if you had just shown up." She laughed again. When Anna didn't appear for their date, Jake had quickly brushed it off. Instead of being angry, he'd made them laugh, saying too bad for Hannah and Lily that they were stuck with him. On that day, he became everything she thought a boy should be.

"I couldn't. I was too shy back then," Anna admitted. "And Jake was the cutest *buwe* I'd ever seen." She shook her head. "Honestly, Hannah, I always thought you and Jake would end up together."

The words clutched at Hannah's heart, stealing her breath away. Still. After all this time. Because when it came to Jake, she'd simply been young and foolish. She'd taken his sweet words and smiles and turned them into big hopes for the future. And the time he held her hand in his before she left for Indiana to take care of her sick aunt? Well, she'd felt something she'd never felt before. But apparently, it had just been his way of saying goodbye. Because by the time she'd returned home with *Aenti* Ruth, he and Lily were about to be married.

She waved a hand at her well-meaning friend, much the same way as she shooed that past hurt from her mind and heart. "Jake and me? Oh, no, no. Jake and Lily were my best friends, you know that. Lily was like a sister to me." She paused. "I mean, I didn't see them as much after they were married. They were busy with their family. But whenever I stopped to count my blessings, I always counted my friendship with Lily and Jake twice. Now with Lily gone, well, I could never repay the kindness the Keims showered on me when I was a girl, but maybe I can help Jake and his children, you know?"

"It's a shame that Lily's *mamm* had a stroke right after Lily passed." Anna shook her head. "She was living with David up in Middlefield before that, wasn't she?"

"Yes, Rachel lived there ever since their *daed*, Noah, departed this world just shortly after Jake and Lily's wedding," Hannah replied.

"I remember him as a kind, soft-spoken man."

"That he was." Rachel Keim had never seemed thrilled with Hannah being in their home. But not so with Noah. All through their growing-up years, Noah and her father had been close friends and neighbors until they'd married and moved a couple of towns apart. When Noah heard she had lost her parents and two younger siblings in a tornado that crushed their home while she was at school one day, he had offered her a place in the Keim home. He treated her with love, like his own daughter.

Though it had hurt her immensely to have Noah leave this world, she'd found peace knowing he was with the Lord. "He was *verra* gentle and sweet."

"And so are you, Hannah." Anna placed an affectionate hand on her shoulder. "It's so kind of you to help with Rachel and Noah's grandchildren. And as for finding Jake a match…" She leaned closer. "I'm think-ing you may have your first candidate right over there."

Anna turned her head and Hannah followed, their gazes landing on petite Rebecca Fisher at the front of the store. Barely visible from the bolts of material sur-rounding her, she'd slipped in quietly. Anna was right— on a list of possible brides-to-be for Jake, Rebecca was a definite prospect.

"I'm just looking around today, so don't worry about me," Anna said. "Go talk to Rebecca, and I'll be keep-ing you and Jake's family in my prayers. Oh, by the way, Matthew's brother Zachary is moving back to Sugarcreek in case you're interested," she added. "Just a thought…"

Hannah had heard Zachary Graber had grown up, and was no longer like his younger, wilder self. But it was too much for her to think about at that moment, so she didn't bother to address Anna's parting comment. "*Danke*, Anna. I'll be praying for you and your family, too." She gave her pregnant friend another awkward sort of hug before approaching Rebecca.

"Rebecca, *guder daag*. Can I help you with any-thing?" She broke into her friendliest smile, all while taking a closer look at the woman. A few years older than Jake, Rebecca was surely not as lovely as Lily. But the good news was Rebecca was a wonderful cook, and she was always kind to everyone's children, giv-ing them extra goodies to take home after the worship meal. Most important, she was still single.

"Truth be told—" Rebecca leaned closer "—I'm not the most decisive person outside the kitchen. What do you think?" She pointed to two fabrics, one a washed-out blue and the other a blinding green.

"Well…" Neither color was a favorite of Hannah's. She tried not to frown. "It depends. What are you making?"

"I'm needing a new dress." Rebecca bit her lip.

"Why not come look at some new fabric we just got in. I'm thinking there's a color perfect for you."

Rebecca followed eagerly as Hannah led the way. Pulling out a bolt of plum-colored fabric, she thought it went well with Rebecca's blond hair and brown eyes. It was also a favorite color of Jake's.

"It's so pretty, Hannah." Rebecca gleamed. "I'll take it. It's perfect for my special occasion." Her voice sounded almost breathless.

"*Jah?* What occasion is that?" Hannah asked, making conversation as Rebecca followed her to the counter where Hannah began measuring out yards.

"It's for supper next week."

"That sounds nice."

"Honestly, Hannah, I'm hoping it's more than nice." Rebecca's eyes seemed to shine with a mixture of excitement and apprehension. "Remember when you tried to match Karl Riehl and me last year? Well, I guess the timing wasn't right then. But now…" She clasped her hands as if in prayer. "He and I have been seeing each other a lot lately. He wants me to have supper with his parents."

Scissors in hand, Hannah paused, feeling her hope for Jake and his *kinner* slipping away. "Oh, I didn't know. That sounds serious."

"I hope it is. I pray it's *Gott*'s plan," Rebecca confided. "I've spent so many years alone, and Karl is such a *wunderbaar-gut* man."

At Rebecca's admission, what could Hannah do but

reach out and pat her hand. "You and Karl would do well together, Rebecca," she said sincerely. "I'll be praying it's *Gott*'s plan for you both, too."

After Rebecca paid for her fabric and left, Hannah told herself that just as the Lord had brought Karl and Rebecca together, He'd surely be there for Jake and his children, as well. Still, it didn't keep her from sizing up the next few Amish women she waited on as possible matches for the Burkholder household.

Yet no one seemed to be a likely fit. It wasn't until later in the afternoon, when the rain had ceased and the skies were lightening, that the door opened once more and Hannah looked up, surprised.

Why, of course! Miriam Schrock, the school's elementary teacher. She was also single, and liked children, *jah*?

"Miriam," she exclaimed. "I'm so glad to see you!"

"You are?" Miriam shot her a puzzled look. The two of them had always known each other but had never been particularly close. Hannah tried to think why that was. At that moment, a reason escaped her.

"Yes, I am. It's been a long time, hasn't it? I'm happy to help you find whatever you might need. Come to think of it, I'd be mighty grateful if you could help me, too."

It had taken some convincing to get Miriam to say she'd come out to Jake's farm the next week for dessert. Oh, and just the smallest of fibs, too. Small because maybe if Hannah had thought to ask Sarah, perhaps the child really might say she was nervous about attending school the following year. Maybe if she'd asked, Sarah would say she wanted to meet her teacher in a comfortable setting like her own home.

A lie is a lie, no matter the size, Hannah. Her mother's voice rang in her ears. As she drove out to Jake's after work to tell him her news, she began praying again—this time for forgiveness.

At the muffled sound of horse hooves, Jake looked up from the pile of clean clothes he was folding and peered out the window. He didn't know what he'd done right to have so many pleasant visitors in one day, but he wasn't complaining. Especially not at the sight of Hannah's buggy not twenty-four hours after he'd last seen her.

Happy to take a break from laundry, he was eager to tell her his news. A gush of brisk air entered the house as he greeted her at the front door.

"Hallo." He smiled.

"I thought I'd stop and see if you have a minute."

"For you, more than one."

Slipping off her cloak, she gave him a crooked smile. He assumed she was wondering how he could be playful when he'd been in such a dark mood the night before.

"It's so quiet in here." She glanced around. "Where are the *kinner*?"

"Gone."

Her eyes widened. "Gone?"

"Jah, you wouldn't believe what happened."

Seeing her worried expression, he rushed to explain. "Don't worry. It's all good. At least, I think it will be."

She gave him a puzzled look.

"Seth Hochstetler's *mamm* came by for the *kinner* a bit ago, and I think it's all going to work out."

"What do you mean?"

"Well, I was in town with the *kinner* today putting up flyers, hoping to stir up some handyman work, and

I ran into Seth at Kauffman's Kitchen. At first I thought he was going to ask me about dating his sister—"

"Emma?" Hannah's eyes lit up. "I hadn't even thought of her."

"But instead, Seth told me he has an open position at the lumberyard, and he's really needing someone with experience. He'd like me to come back as soon as possible—tomorrow if I can."

"But what about the *kinner*?"

"When I was talking with him, I figured I could contact one of the nannies I've used before. Maybe for a short time, until I figure something out. Then Seth's *mamm* stopped by and said she could watch Sarah and the twins for the next month until she needs to care for her ill sister. She also said she'd help me find another nanny for them in the meantime." Hannah's pretty face brightened at his news, which erased the nagging doubts from his mind.

"Jake! That's great to hear!"

"And good timing, too. I wasn't quite sure how I was going to get through the winter financially," he admitted. "But *Gott* opened a door, and I need to take it on faith that something will work out long-term." He lifted his hands in surrender.

"And the *kinner* are with Mrs. Hochstetler now?"

He nodded. "*Jah*, they left just a little while ago. She wanted to spend some time with them so they could get acquainted."

"I'm sure it'll all be *gut*. Mrs. Hochstetler is a very nice woman, and your *kinner* are always delightful."

"Mostly." He chuckled before changing the subject. "Did you miss me already? Is that why you stopped by?"

"*Jah*. I mean *nee*. I mean—" Hannah stuttered as her cheeks bloomed with color.

"I'm only teasin', Hannah. You know, like you tease me."

Her lips eased into a more relaxed smile. "I actually stopped to let you know I have your first date set up."

"Already?" He almost audibly gulped.

"Well, not exactly a date, more like someone coming over for dessert next week."

"And who might that someone be?"

"Miriam Schrock is coming over to talk to Sarah about starting school next fall. And to visit with you, too."

"Miriam *Shock*?" He winced. "Really, Hannah?"

"Oh, that's right. People called her that for a reason, didn't they?" She cringed slightly. "Well, she's pretty as can be, Jake. And I'm sure she's changed by now. People do change, you know."

He didn't know if he quite agreed with that statement. From his experience he'd learned people only changed if they wanted to. Yet knowing Hannah was trying her best to help him and the children, he nodded assuredly. "All right, as long I don't have to make the dessert."

"Definitely not. I'll do the baking. You do want to make a good impression with her, don't you?"

He grinned. "I'll let you know when the time comes."

Just then, a noise sounded outside the window, capturing both of their attentions. Then he saw Mrs. Hochstetler's buggy pull into the yard.

Jake's good mood began sinking rapidly. "They haven't been gone that long."

"Maybe one of the *kinner* forgot something," Hannah offered. "Maybe one of them wanted gloves."

But by the time Mrs. Hochstetler got the children into the house and stood a good distance away from them, Jake knew the reason for their early return wasn't as simple as a pair of forgotten mittens.

"I'm sorry, Jake." Mrs. Hochstetler looked notably uneasy, wringing her hands. "I'm not going to be able to help you after all."

"I'm sorry, too, Mrs. Hochstetler." Sorely disappointed, he nodded understandingly. The three of them could be a handful at times. "Did you do something to upset Mrs. Hochstetler?" He confronted his *kinner*.

"Jake, it wasn't—" The older woman started to interrupt, but Jake held up his hand to stop her.

"If the children misbehaved, Mrs. Hochstetler, they need to apologize to you."

"But—"

He held out his hand to Seth's mother again.

"We didn't do anything to her, *Daed*." Sarah shook her head, looking sheepish.

"We only did it to us." Clara stepped in front of her big sister. "We scratched too much." She rubbed at the coat sleeve covering her arm.

"And I'm all hot." Eli began undoing his jacket.

Completely baffled, Jake finally did appeal to Seth's mother. "I'm afraid I don't understand."

"As soon as we got to Der Dutchman and the children took off their coats, they all began scratching. I started to notice red spots popping up on their necks and arms. Eli here is running a fever, too."

"Chicken pox?" Hannah stepped in front of him and felt Eli's forehead.

"I'm sure of it," Mrs. Hochstetler confirmed, looking apologetic. "And since I've never had chicken pox and need to be in good health to take care of my sister in a few weeks, I can't take any chances. Again, I'm sorry, Jake."

"No need to apologize, Mrs. Hochstetler. I appreciate you trying."

"Do you want me to tell Seth you won't be able to start the job after all?" She bit her lip.

Out of the corner of his eye, he noticed Hannah getting the children out of their coats and shoes before sending them upstairs to get into their bed clothes. She was taking everything in stride while he was feeling like the world had just crashed in on him. Again. And suddenly, as the children traipsed off, she was standing alongside of him, seeming to take charge of his situation, as well.

"I may be able to help," she spoke up. "I had chicken pox when I was little. I have some vacation time coming to me. If I took care of the *kinner* until they weren't contagious anymore, then could you come just like you'd planned? For the last couple of weeks before going to your sister's?"

Mrs. Hochstetler glanced at him and then Hannah. "I think I could do that."

"If you'll give me a minute…" Hannah began slipping on her cloak. "I'm going to call Grace right now and see if I can begin taking vacation tomorrow. Then we'll all know if we have a workable plan."

Before he and Seth's *mamm* could even answer, Hannah was out the door, making a beeline to the phone shanty across the street. After ten minutes or so, he was concerned there was trouble with her boss. He was just about to run and tell her it wasn't worth all that when she came trudging into the house. Slowly. Her face suddenly pale, and minus the glow of determination that had been there before.

He was sure she had bad news for him. He was just about to tell her not to worry, when she spoke up.

"I talked with Grace and I, um… I can watch the *kinner*," she said quietly.

"It's all settled, then." Mrs. Hochstetler began to gather up her cloak. "Jake, I'll let Seth know you can be at the lumberyard tomorrow. And, Hannah, let me know when the children aren't contagious."

"Well, I—I don't know," Hannah stammered. "I'm not so sure about anything now."

"But I thought you just said—" Obviously confused, Mrs. Hochstetler was looking closely at Hannah.

"What I mean is, it seems I have more than a week to spare." Hannah's shoulders slumped more with each word. "As of today, I no longer have a job."

Chapter Three

"Try not to scratch, Clara."

Hannah attempted to dab at the rash on Clara's right arm with a cotton ball soaked in calamine lotion. But Clara wasn't making it easy—she was busy scratching at the bumps on her left arm.

"But it itches." Clara pouted, and Hannah couldn't blame her. Though her experience with chickenpox was ages ago, she still had a vague recollection of what the children were going through.

"I know it itches something awful. But it'll get better every day."

"Promise?"

"I promise," Hannah vowed, as she tucked a strand of hair behind Clara's ear. Hopefully every night would get better, too, for the children and for her. She sighed. She'd only been on chickenpox duty twelve hours and she was already exhausted.

Settling into a chair in the children's bedroom the evening before, she'd listened to them fidget most of the night. She'd also checked on their fevers every few hours, even placing a cool, damp cloth on Eli's forehead.

Thankfully, the morning was starting out far better. Eli's raging fever had diminished to just below a hundred degrees, and the girls' fevers had subsided completely.

"I hope it's not too many more days," Sarah said, rubbing the sleep from her eyes.

"Sarah, try not to put your hands near your eyes." She strained to keep her voice calm.

Quickly, she finished dabbing Clara and moved to Sarah's side of the double bed.

"It's your turn, dear *maedel*. How about putting your arms straight out in front of you? And I'll get some lotion on you."

"On me, too?" Eli asked, sitting up in his twin bed.

"*Jah*, you, too." She smiled over at him while she finished covering Sarah's worst spots.

"Don't you have blue lotion for boys?" Eli asked the moment she sat down on the edge of his bed.

"Sorry, calamine only comes in pink." She began dotting the bumps on his neck.

"It's okay, Eli," his older sister chimed in. "Sometimes things just come in one color, but they're meant for everyone. Like the sky. *Gott* made it blue, but it's for girls, too."

"Sometimes it's pink," Clara chirped, which led to even more talk about all the various colors of the sky.

Hannah smiled at their conversation and was glad that between that distraction and the calamine, no one seemed to be scratching for the moment. Finishing up Eli, she let their chatter subside before mentioning food.

"Would anyone like breakfast in bed?"

"Did *Daed* get oatmeal last night at the store?" Eli asked.

"He did, but it's a kind of oatmeal that helps itching. You can take a bath in it later today."

"Fun!" Eli's eyes brightened immediately.

"But if it's oatmeal you want for breakfast, I spied some in the kitchen."

While Eli and Clara nodded, Sarah scrunched her nose. "My stomach doesn't feel so good. May I just have toast with jelly, Hannah?"

"Of course you may."

Placing the lotion and cotton balls on the dresser, she was just about to head to the kitchen when Jake appeared in the doorway.

"How is everyone this morning?" he asked.

It seemed he'd done everything he could to make a good first-day-on-the-job impression. His blond hair was neatly combed, his beard freshly trimmed, and his light gray shirt looked crisply ironed but wouldn't stay that way long while working with wood. She could detect lines around his eyes. That was understandable since it'd been after midnight before she finally convinced him to head to bed.

She wasn't about to mention anything he might find worrisome. Like how many times the children had woken up through the night. Or how many times her mind had kept her awake, while she cried over the fact that she no longer had a job to return to. It wasn't just the job. Her dream, everything she'd been working for, had disappeared in an instant. Jake had immediately offered his *dawdi haus* as a free place for her and her aunt to live. She'd accepted, but only after he agreed she would be the children's nanny for free. Even with that, she still felt orphaned all over again, her life out of her control.

She tamped down her disappointment for now and delivered good news instead.

"We're doing better," she said, injecting into her voice a note of optimism she didn't totally feel. "Eli's fever is under a hundred this morning, and the girls' fevers are gone."

"That's great." Jake's eyes instantly sparkled at her news and there was a lift to his voice. He was a caring father, for sure. "I thought I'd see if I could help with anything before heading out," he added.

"*Nee*. We're good. Ain't so, *kinner*?"

The three nodded, Sarah speaking for them. "Hannah is taking *gut* care of us, *Daed*."

"I'm sure she is." Jake glanced her way, giving her an appreciative smile.

"I was just about to head to the kitchen to make them some breakfast. Would you like anything?"

"I've eaten, but I can help you before I go," he offered, turning to the children first. "While I'm gone today, you *kinner* get some rest, and let Hannah get rest, too, you hear?"

"*Jah, Daed*."

Descending the stairs ahead of him, Hannah smiled at the sound of Jake's trio chiming in together. Once in the kitchen, she began pulling oatmeal and bread from the pantry.

"I can pour juice," Jake offered, coming into the kitchen. Reaching into the cabinet, he took out three glasses—which Hannah immediately took from his hands.

"Honestly, Jake, I can get this. You don't want to be late on your first day, do you?"

He glanced at the clock. She could tell he was anxious to leave, but he was stalling.

"It's okay." She nudged at his shoulder. "You need to be on your way now."

Still he didn't move, his eyes searching hers. "I feel badly about how things turned out, Hannah."

"I know you do, Jake. And as I've told you, losing my job wasn't anything to do with you. Or the children. Or even me. I should've seen it coming, honestly." She shrugged, thinking how naive she'd been. "And it's not even Grace's fault that she has to close the shop. The rent has nearly doubled. And with the opening of that fabric chain store…" She worked hard to put on a brave face. "And I'll tell you this, if you don't get out of here, you're not going to have a job, either."

His warm, grateful smile soothed her, kind of like how the calamine had seemed to help the children's discomfort. "All right. I'm going. Do you want me to pick up anything on my way home? Bananas or milk or—?"

"No, *danke*. The only thing you need to concentrate on is your job and having a *wunderbaar* first day. *Jah?*"

"But I could—"

She stopped him, pointing to the back door.

He held up his hands in submission, backing toward the exit. "Okay, I'm going."

She nodded.

But just as he was about to turn and grab his jacket and hat from the hook by the door, she called out to him. "Wait!"

"Jah?" He shifted around, looking eager. "Did you change your mind? What can I bring you?"

"It's not that." She shook her head. "It's your collar."

Stepping forward, she reached up and straightened

his crooked collar. Being accustomed to the feel of fabric at her fingertips, she couldn't stop herself from running her hands over his shoulders, smoothing the cloth underneath his suspenders just so.

"There." She patted his broad shoulders. "Perfect."

"*Jah?* You really think so?" He stared into her eyes, a teasing grin curving his lips. The kind of smile that always used to make her cheeks flush, and unfortunately, still did.

"Jake Burkholder. Go. Now," she said as sternly as she could. After all, this new living arrangement wasn't apt to work if she was going to blush like the young schoolgirl she used to be.

Seth and the rest of the Hochstetler clan were on hand to welcome Jake, kindly making him feel like he was doing them a favor instead of the other way around. After a bit of catching up, Seth escorted him to the section of the lumberyard where he'd be working, introducing him to new team members, both Amish and *Englisch*. He also insisted Jake take some time to get reacquainted with his former coworkers, which he was glad to do.

No doubt it was especially good to see Tom McDaniel again. Although from different backgrounds, he and the *Englischer* had easily become good friends when they'd worked together over two years ago. Jake very much enjoyed the man's sense of humor, which was every bit as clever as any Amish proverb. Often as the two of them worked side by side, they had shared stories about their children, their marriages and their faith.

He figured Tom might've felt glad to see him, too. When Jake reached out to give Tom a handshake, Tom took Jake's hand and drew him in, patting Jake on the back. It felt like an instant resurrection of the friendship they'd shared. Tom had been the only person Jake had ever dared to confide in—about Lily's drug addiction. He'd seemed safe to tell, since Lily had pleaded with him not to let anyone in their Amish community know about her issue, promising she'd try harder. Promising she'd get better.

"Man, it's been a while." About the same age as Jake but a few inches shorter, Tom stepped back, giving Jake a once-over. "You're looking good, brother. Good and healthy."

"It's by *Gott*'s good grace. It sure isn't because of my cooking." Jake chuckled. "You're looking good yourself."

"Ashley takes full charge of that and is all about fat-free, gluten-free and whatever-else-free." Tom smiled, rolling his eyes. "From time to time, I have to sneak a burger and fries."

Jake laughed. "*Jah*, I hear you. We don't want to get too thin and scrawny, do we?"

"Exactly," Tom readily agreed with a grin. "Hey, I have an order that needs to be processed ASAP, but let's catch up later. You've been missed around here, buddy."

"I've missed the job, too." Jake nodded.

As Tom walked away and Jake got settled in at the planer, he realized the job wasn't the only thing he'd felt nostalgic about. He'd also missed the camaraderie. Even the scent of the various woods, and the opportunities to help customers, instantly seemed to renew his spirit, giving him an ear-to-ear smile that made the hours slip by quickly.

In fact, he was so engrossed in his work that it wasn't until he sensed someone come up directly beside him that he shut down the machine, pulled down his goggles and turned to see a familiar face.

"Rosie! Is that you?"

Standing with her arms crossed over her chest, Hochstetler's longtime personnel manager Rosie Thatcher didn't look much different since the last time he'd seen her. Maybe a little grayer and slightly chubbier, but the *Englisch* woman still radiated the perfect blend of professionalism and friendship.

"It's me, still alive and kicking," she clucked.

"It's *gut* to see you." He meant the words sincerely. Rosie had been like a dear aunt to him when he'd been going through shakier times.

"Well, if it's so good to see me, Jacob, why didn't you stop by my office before lunch? I need you to sign some papers and fill out forms."

"Oh, *jah*. Sorry about that." He frowned. "I can come sign things now. Unless you'd rather wait until tomorrow?"

"Never put off till tomorrow what you already don't want to do today. It probably won't get done."

He grinned at the truth of her statement. "Lead the way."

Expedient as ever, Rosie already had the required employee forms on her desk. It didn't take him long to fill in his information and sign them.

"And last, but not least, is the community fund pay form." Rosie handed him another sheet of paper. "Don't feel forced to contribute, Jacob. Or if you want to, you can do it later, you know, when you've been here a bit longer. I can imagine that things have been—"

He cut her off, taking the form from her hands. "I'm happy to sign up now."

Years ago, employees at Hochstetler's had started an emergency fund for lumberyard workers and their families as well as for others in their small community. Each pay period an employee could chip in whatever money they wished, and that amount would come directly out of their paycheck and be added to the fund.

When Lily had passed, some monies from that fund were given to him, helping him make the transition from working dad to stay-at-home dad easier. Knowing that people cared had made all the difference.

"How are your children?" Rosie asked as he handed her the completed form. "Are they doing all right?"

"Ah…they have chickenpox."

"Oh, goodness." Rosie shook her head. "Been there, done that. It's no fun, but it'll pass quickly."

"*Jah*. They'll be fine. I'm just used to being there with them. I'm kind of feeling guilty that I'm not." He felt funny admitting such a thing, but it was true.

"I'm sure you left them in capable hands," Rosie responded.

"I did. A good friend, Hannah Miller, is watching them."

"Hmm…" Rosie squinted. "Why does that name sound familiar to me?"

He found himself telling his surrogate aunt all about what had happened with the nannies, the children's illness, and how Hannah had offered to help and then lost her job. "I'm still not feeling right about it," he admitted, to which Rosie simply smiled at him.

"You know what this gray hair means, Jacob?" She pointed to the lighter hair edging the sides of her face. "This gray means I've lived long enough to know and believe that God's timing is far better than ours. If you're feeling that badly about it, pick up some flowers for Hannah on your way home tonight," she suggested.

"Flowers." He blinked. "We have mums in the garden."

"I'm sure you do. But it's not the same. Every woman likes a bouquet of flowers that's just for her."

He shrugged, tossing Rosie's suggestion around in his mind. "Hmm... Maybe you're right."

"Jacob, you've known me long enough to know I'm always right." Rosie's eyes glimmered as she chuckled.

All the way home, he debated with himself about stopping to buy flowers for Hannah.

But then a memory came back to him. Of a day long ago, and a field. And the elated look on Hannah's face when he picked a handful of wildflowers from that field and presented them to her. If witnessing that look was all that had happened to him that day, maybe he would've bought flowers just like Rosie said.

But that wasn't all that had taken place. When he'd handed Hannah those flowers that day, an intense feeling had welled up inside him, making him want to give her every good thing there was on *Gott*'s blessed earth.

Yet, that wasn't meant to be. Not then, and certainly not now. He and Hannah were merely friends helping friends. Their situation was temporary, as it should be.

Even so, noticing the lights still on in Dee's Florist Shop, something inside him made him stop. Pulling into Dee's lot, he hitched his buggy to a post and headed for the store, thinking he'd buy a single rose. But right as he opened the shop door, the overhead chime jingled, and the sound brought him to his senses.

Closing the door swiftly, he walked away and guided his buggy straight home.

Chapter Four

❧

"Why, what pretty scenery, don't you think?"

Hannah was sitting in the back of the horse-drawn wagon, surrounded by boxes of her and her aunt's belongings. But close enough to hear *Aenti* Ruth chirp delightedly to Abram Mast, who was busy maneuvering the horses and their cargo up Jake's driveway. Hannah noticed how their former landlord, being a man of few words, merely scratched a graying sideburn then nodded before giving her aunt a shy smile.

"The *dawdi haus* looks *verra* nice, Hannah," her *aenti* continued, turning to her. "I haven't seen it in a while. I'm sure we'll like it here."

After living with her aunt for so many years, Hannah knew it was just like her mother's sister to make the best of things. It was a trait that reminded her so much of Hannah's own mother. Though she'd been a young girl when her mother passed, she could still remember times when the food spoiled, or the basement flooded, or a sibling was feverish and crying inconsolably, and how her mother would take it all in stride. *Mamm* would manage to find something to take away the hunger pangs, sweep up the floodwater without complaining, heal her siblings with hugs, and through it all, remind Hannah how important it was to count her blessings.

"*Jah*, it will be *gut*," Hannah agreed, trying to follow in her mother's and aunt's positive footsteps, and eager to convince herself, as well. Because while she'd been packing the night before and that morning, she couldn't stop feeling unsettled.

It wasn't so much that she'd miss living in town. Or that the rooms she'd rented for herself and her aunt in the Victorian house owned by Abram and his sister Susan had been all that spacious or irreplaceable.

But after so many years of being on her own, after working hard and being closer to achieving her dream using the talent *Gott* gave her, moving into Jake's property felt like a step backward. Now she had no idea what her future looked like anymore. And as much as she wanted to help Jake and his children—and knew he wanted to help her by giving her a place to live— she felt like she was depending on someone too much.

And didn't depending on someone usually lead to being disappointed somehow?

"Oh, Abram, look at all the colorful chrysanthemums and the beautiful, rolling hills," her aunt was exclaiming as if she'd never witnessed Sugarcreek's picturesque landscape before. "It's perfect!"

In spite of her mixed feelings, Hannah found her aunt's unbridled enthusiasm hard to resist, and began to look outside herself. Eyeing the land bordering Jake's property, she had to admit it did look mighty special.

The air might've been brisk, but the late-autumn afternoon sun sparkled on the outstretched fields and patchwork of hills in a way that could warm a person's soul—even hers.

"And there's our new landlord," *Aenti* Ruth said gaily, pointing toward the house. "Though you'll always be my first landlord in Sugarcreek, Abram." She smiled broadly at the man sitting beside her.

Jake's lean frame certainly wasn't hard to miss. Hammer in hand, he was bent over, and appeared to be putting the finishing touches on his latest project. It wasn't until he stood up that Hannah realized just what that project was. A wheelchair ramp that led up to the *dawdi haus* porch.

Hannah couldn't believe she'd been so wrapped up in herself the past few days that she hadn't ever considered how her aunt would get in and out of their new home. But clearly Jake had.

Right away, his thoughtfulness shifted her mood. He was such a kind, caring person. He truly deserved any happiness he could find and all that she'd promised to help him find.

Laying the hammer on the porch rail, Jake waved at them with a sly grin on his face. She easily recognized it from their youth as one that always meant he'd been up to something. This time, something good.

"It looks like you've been busy getting ready for my stay," *Aenti* Ruth called out to Jake as Abram brought the horses to a halt. As usual, her aunt was never one to be shy about her disability.

"And looking forward to it," he replied.

Feeling grateful that the two most important people in her life always got along no matter how much time passed, Hannah whispered, *"Danke,"* to Jake as he helped her down from the wagon.

He looked at her, puzzled. "I think I should be saying that to you, ain't so?"

Meanwhile, Abram had retrieved her aunt's wheelchair from the back before helping her settle into the chair. Hannah was surprised how he performed the task as if it was the most natural thing in the world. Any of the times she'd encountered her aunt and Abram together, either working on puzzles or people-watching from a porch bench, he seemed to be a quiet, awkward man.

"Jake, I don't know if you've met Abram Mast." She looked between the men. "And, Abram, this is Jake Burkholder."

"I think I've seen you at Hochstetler's Lumberyard," Jake said to the older man. "It's *gut* to see you again. Thanks for helping the ladies with their move. It gave me time to get the *haus* ready for them."

"*Jah.*" Abram nodded.

Abram also hadn't had much to say when Hannah told him about losing her job and their need to move abruptly. He and his sister had been nothing but kind. Susan had even offered Abram's help to get them moved. That meant moving clothes, embroidery accessories and puzzles for her aunt, and Hannah's sewing machine, patterns and material. Lots and lots of material.

"Jake, I haven't seen your beautiful *kinner* in a while," her aunt spoke up, bridging the gap in conversation. "Hannah said they're feeling better."

"*Jah*, much better. They still have some scabs here and there, but Hannah nursed them back to health."

"Where are they?" Hannah asked. It seemed odd they hadn't come running outside to greet them on their arrival.

"You'll see."

Jake waved them toward the *dawdi haus,* and they followed him up the freshly built ramp to the top of the porch. Once there, he opened the front door.

"They've been waiting for you," he said as he extended his arm, inviting them inside.

As Hannah entered the house behind Abram and her aunt's wheelchair, she realized just how true that was. In an instant, every area of the small home became illuminated with an amber light coming from all directions.

She gasped and her aunt let out a surprised "Oh, my!"

Sarah stood in the sitting room and had turned on a light there. Clara held a lantern that shone throughout the connected kitchen. Meanwhile, Eli was calling to them from where a light glowed from the bedroom.

"I'm in here!" he shouted.

Right away, with the girls scampering ahead of her and her aunt wheeling behind, Hannah walked over to the bedroom door. None of them could help laughing. There was Eli, sprawled out on one of the twin beds.

"I got tired of standing and holding the lantern."

"And I don't blame you," Hannah told him.

Glancing inside the room, she saw that the two headboards didn't match and neither did the quilts on the beds. Yet somehow, all the colors and designs complemented each other, giving the room a warm, homey feel. No wonder Eli had been tempted to get cozy while he was waiting.

As he jumped from the bed, Sarah tugged at Hannah's hand.

"Come see what else," she said, leading her into the bathroom. "We got you and *Aenti* Ruth washcloths and towels."

"And soap," Clara chimed in, holding on to the arm of *Aenti* Ruth's wheelchair. "It smells *gut*, too."

"And there's bread in the kitchen," Eli noted as they all ambled back into the kitchen and sitting room.

"It seems like you three have thought of everything," her aunt complimented the children, causing them to beam.

"*Daed* did lots," Sarah noted. "He brought the rug over since it was too heavy for us."

"I helped him," Eli added.

"No, you didn't." Clara dug in.

"*Daed*," Eli whimpered a protest. "I helped, didn't I?"

Jake stepped forward, laying a hand on each of the twins' shoulders. "You three are all big helps," he said, his words instantly defusing the squabble.

With the house lit up, Hannah could see just how much work Jake had done to get the place in shape. Not only was every surface sparkling clean, but the braided rug from the spare bedroom of the main house did make the sitting area look inviting. The curtains were pulled open and looked free of any dust. The windows had been wiped down, too.

"You even thought to bring over my pillow."

Among the throw pillows lining the couch was her favorite decorated with golden sunflowers that Jake's mother had embroidered. From time to time, he'd tease her about how she'd always hug it when they'd sit and read their Bibles some evenings. "Well, it's not *my* pillow, but—"

"It's yours now." He smiled. "Oh, and if you're wondering why I didn't put the couch in the center of the room, it's because I thought your sewing machine would work best over there." He pointed to a bare area on the other side of the room. "I know you'll still be using the machine at my house sometimes. But if you're sewing here, that corner faces south, and you should get more light coming in the window there."

"Do you like it?" Sarah squeezed her hand again, questioning Hannah with her eyes.

Hannah tried to answer but couldn't. Suddenly she was too overwhelmed. They'd all worked so hard to brighten the once-deserted house and turn it into a comfortable home. It was all so sweet, so thoughtful. Instantly, her eyes became misty and a lump formed in her throat. How had she ever thought it would be a mistake to live here?

"She must not," Clara insisted. "She looks sad."

"*Nee.* That's how Hannah looks when she's happy," Jake answered, knowing her too well.

"Your *daed* is right. I am happy. Like *Aenti* Ruth said, you all have thought of everything. Every little thing. Thank you, Jake. And Sarah, Clara and Eli. Thank you so much."

The children's eyes lit up at the sound of their names. It touched her heart to see how much they had wanted to please her. She opened her arms, and the three of them stepped into her embrace for a group hug. Until Eli wriggled away.

"And, Abram—" she looked over to where the man still stood near the front door "—thank you, too. We couldn't have gotten here without you."

"Do you like the house, too, *Aenti* Ruth?" Clara turned to Hannah's aunt.

"*Jah*, I do," *Aenti* Ruth assured all of them. "It's *wunderbaar*!"

"Perfect!" Hannah said, realizing she was repeating her aunt's earlier remark.

Right then, it struck her that her aunt might have had reservations about the move, too. Living at Jake's, on the outskirts of town, her aunt would surely miss seeing her friends as much as she used to. And without sidewalks or nearby stores to visit, she wouldn't be getting out and about as much as she was accustomed to, either. But *Aenti* Ruth had never complained at all. Not one peep. Without hesitation, she'd said yes and trusted where life and *Gott* were taking her. It was something Hannah needed to remember.

"Hannah, that makes no sense," Jake said a bit brusquely, but it was truly out of the kindness of his heart. He and Abram had barely gotten the boxes from the wagon moved into the *dawdi haus* when the woman started making dinner plans.

"Why cook when we can have peanut butter and jelly sandwiches? Wouldn't you rather be unpacking and getting settled?" he asked, knowing she usually was one for getting a job done quickly.

But apparently not this time.

"I can do that anytime." She waved a hand. "Besides, I only want to make some chili. Nothing complicated," she countered. "All the ingredients are in your kitchen, and the meat is defrosted. I thought I'd have a chance to make it yesterday, but I never got to it with packing and all."

"So why not make it at my house, and we can eat there?"

She scrunched her entire face as if he'd said something distasteful. "Because I'd really like our first meal to be here with everyone who helped. Don't you think that would be nice?" She looked up at him with that hopeful glint in her hazel eyes that he'd never been able to resist.

"Whatever you'd like."

"Oh, *gut*." A smile burst across her face. "And you'll stay, too, right, Abram?"

Jake watched as Abram blinked, then glanced at Ruth for his answer.

"Of course he will," Ruth confirmed.

Hannah clapped her hands together, her eyes shining even more. "Let me see what cooking utensils we have before we head over to the house."

"We? I get to help you cook?" With Hannah being at his house often recently, he hadn't been in the kitchen much. But he certainly didn't mind helping out.

"Well, I, uh…" She seemed to be searching for a way to spare his feelings. It almost made him laugh.

"Hannah, trust me, it won't hurt my feelings if you don't want my help."

"*Nee*, but I do. You can help me carry over the ingredients from the house."

The sun was setting, nearly touching the ridge of hills as they made their way across his lawn. It was a peaceful sight. Hannah must've been thinking the same thing.

"The *kinner* seem happy to have *Aenti* Ruth here," she said, sounding somewhat surprised. "They had her and Abram working puzzles with them."

"Why wouldn't they like her? She's a lot like you. Or I guess I should say, you're a lot like her. Very easy to talk to. *Verra* nice to be around."

She giggled at that. "Jake Burkholder, are you trying to sweet-talk me into baking a cake, too?"

He chuckled. "I think not. Remember, I was the one ready to settle for peanut butter and jelly sandwiches."

"Well, *gut*, because I'll be baking this week for Miriam's visit. You do remember she's coming, right?"

He couldn't help but groan.

"Was that a groan I heard?"

"*Nee*. Just cleared my throat."

She gave him a sideways glance and a wry grin, letting him know he wasn't fooling her. He gave her a half smile in return, while trying to push the thought of Miriam Schrock's dreaded visit from his mind.

Thankfully, that wasn't too difficult to do. As soon as they entered the house and walked into the kitchen, Hannah lifted an empty woven basket from on top of the refrigerator and handed it to him, putting him straight to work.

Without referring to a recipe, she pulled together a few cans of beans, canned tomatoes, spices and ground beef and placed them in the basket.

"Anything else?" he asked, the basket now several pounds heavier than before.

"Hmm." She tapped her forehead thoughtfully. "There was something I was just thinking of...oh!" She snapped her fingers. "I'm going to need a large container for the chili. A bowl with a lid would work real well."

She bent down and looked through the lower cabinets. A few random items tumbled out.

"Sorry," he apologized as he watched her attempt to stuff the items back onto the shelves. "The cabinets are overcrowded. I wasn't sure what to keep when we moved after Lily passed, and I didn't know what had been left behind here by my parents and brother. So I crammed it all in there," he admitted.

"It's a lot, for sure," she agreed. "If you want, when I have time, I'll go through the cabinets and pantry and organize things a little better."

"I'm sure my pots and pans and bowls and whatever else is in there would appreciate that. I would, too," he added, though he wasn't sure if she heard him with her head buried in the cabinet.

A minute later, she pulled out a large plastic bowl with a lid. "Here's exactly what I was looking for," she said, getting to her feet.

As she stood up, something rolled inside the bowl. In the silence of the kitchen, the sound caught their attention.

She looked up at him, her forehead pinched. "Wonder what that could be?"

He shrugged, acting as unconcerned as could be— while panic reared up inside him, a feeling he knew all too well. His heart raced. His chest tightened. And a familiar sick taste rose in the back of his throat.

Too many times he'd found Lily's pills hidden in strange places. During their marriage. After her death. Possibly now—in the bowl Hannah held?

He could never forget the time after Lily's surgery and shoulder recovery when Hannah had asked him if Lily seemed to be acting strange. A little more distant, Hannah had said. Not as much like herself.

Of course, he'd known exactly what she was saying, and he knew the pills were making Lily act that way. But he pretended it was of no concern.

At that time, he didn't know what to do. Whether to be dishonest with Hannah, his and Lily's dearest friend, or disloyal to his wife, who had begged him to keep her addiction a secret while promising to get better.

Standing next to Hannah now, knowing how he'd lied to her, he almost wished there was a pill bottle hidden in the bowl. Everything inside him wanted to unburden himself. He wanted to be cleansed of the lies and secrets that lay between them.

While Hannah started to pull away the lid, his thoughts were scrambled as he tried to think of the right words to say. But nothing came. Still he needed to say something. Anything.

"Hannah, there's a chance it could be—"

Reaching into the bowl, she pulled out a small plastic horse. "Eli loves to hide things, doesn't he?" She shook her head, clearly amused.

"Uh, *jah*. He does at that." He returned her smile with a feeble grin, feeling sick at heart.

What would Hannah think if she knew what he was hiding? What would she think of him for not doing better by her best friend?

Chapter Five

Monday morning had come quickly. Gathering her things so she could get to Jake's before he left for work, Hannah felt torn about leaving her aunt.

"*Aenti* Ruth, you know you're welcome to come over to the house, don't you?"

"*Jah.* I may do that later."

"I can always run back and get you," Hannah offered as she slipped on her cloak.

"Not necessary. I can easily roll down the ramp outside this house and roll up the one Jake kindly built onto the main house." She wheeled over to the front door and pulled it open, inviting Hannah to be on her way. "I'm taking it slow this morning."

"Are you sure you're all right? Are you feeling okay?"

"Why wouldn't I be?"

"I don't know." Hannah shrugged. "It's a lot of change. New people. New surroundings. New things to get used to."

"And who says new isn't a good thing?" Her aunt

cocked her head. "Besides, Abram may stop by later. He said I forgot something at the house during the move."

This time it was Hannah's turn to cock her head, as she stood in the doorway. "I thought our rooms were bare when we left."

"Me, too." Her aunt blinked. "I have no idea what he's bringing."

Hannah couldn't imagine. "Well, if you change your mind about coming over…"

"Like I said, I'll stop by if I get too lonely. And I promise I won't get lost on the way over."

"Now you're making fun of me."

"Maybe just a little." Her aunt chuckled, shooing her out the door.

Though it was a short walk between the houses, Hannah pulled on her hood and dipped her head to ward off the chilly wind. Her chin was still tucked when she entered the house, causing her to bump into Jake, who was about to reach for his jacket from the rack by the door.

"Oh!" She could feel her cold cheeks instantly warm the moment she brushed up against him. "Sorry."

Steadying her on her feet, he readily apologized. "It's my fault. I've been rushing around, running late this morning."

"Me, too."

"I guess we should both slow down some, huh?" Still holding on to her arms, he smiled into her eyes.

Feeling her cheeks burn even more, she swiftly slipped out of his grasp.

"Not if you want to be on time," she warned.

All business, she handed him his jacket and hat, then hung her cloak in the empty space.

"Are the *kinner* still sleeping?" She straightened her *kapp*.

"I haven't heard them yet."

"I'll wake them in a bit. We have lots to do today with chores, playtime and baking dessert for our special guest tonight."

"Oh… Miriam." He groaned loudly as he slid into his jacket.

"Are you clearing your throat again?" she jested. "You seem to be doing that lots these past days."

"Have you noticed that, too?" His expression grew serious. "Maybe I'm getting sick. I could be contagious."

Hannah couldn't help but laugh. "You know that's not getting you out of your first date, doncha?"

"I had to try." He pulled his wool hat way down on his head, conjuring up a most woeful look. "I'll see you after work. Unless I decide to run away from home."

"You wouldn't dare," she said.

"I know. I'd miss my *kinner*, and I'd miss teasing you." His eyes twinkled as he waved goodbye.

As she closed the door behind him, she couldn't stop thinking how he always left her smiling. She'd never felt that irresistible urge with Lucas Sutter, whom she'd courted briefly soon after she learned about Lily and Jake's engagement. And certainly, her time spent with good-looking but prideful John Lantz had turned out to be nothing to smile about. In fact, those attempts were just one—no, two—of the reasons she'd let matchmaking and her job fill her time.

But she and Jake had always communicated easily with one another. She could tell him whatever was in her heart. But that simply came from knowing each other so long, didn't it?

She was still musing over Jake's silliness when Eli shuffled into the kitchen. Per his usual morning greeting, he came close as if wanting a hug but was too shy to initiate one. She leaned over, embracing him the way she always did. "Good morning, sweet *buwe*. Did you have good sleep?"

He rubbed his clear blue eyes before speaking. "I had a dream."

"A good one?"

His golden-haired head bobbed. "I dreamed you lived in the house out there." He pointed toward the window. "And that a nice lady lives there, too."

"That wasn't a dream, Eli. It's true."

He backed up and looked at her guardedly. "Really?"

"Really."

The sparkle of relief and happiness that lit his eyes touched her deeply. When he reached out and hugged her around her waist, she was moved even more.

Just like with his twin, his four years on Earth had been wrought with endless change. True, she'd lost her *mamm* as a young girl, as well, but at least she'd been old enough to know her. The twins had only been two years old when their mother left their world. Ever since, a stream of nannies and neighbors had paraded in and out of their lives. But had there been anyone who could make them feel like they were safe and loved? No, there hadn't been anyone like that. And more than anyone, she knew how a child yearned for that.

That's why I need Your help to find the right mamm *for these* kinner, Gott.

She kissed the top of his head. "I hear your sisters chattering upstairs. Think they're ready for breakfast?"

"*Jah!* Pancakes?" He searched her eyes, looking hopeful.

"Sure, if that's what you'd like." She started toward the refrigerator. "Why don't you go tell your sisters to get dressed while I start cooking."

"Do we need to make beds, too?" he hedged. "Or is it washday?"

Walking toward the refrigerator, she couldn't help but stop and grin at him. How he reminded her of Jake as a young boy, always trying to wiggle his way out of things. "No, sorry. It's not washday."

Even the way he groaned in response reminded her of his father.

After they ate breakfast and cleaned up the blueberries that somehow got smashed on the wooden floor, the morning went by quickly. At lunchtime when she mentioned a visitor was coming for dessert that evening, and she needed their help to make a pie, the children were thrilled. Sarah donned an apron that fell past her knees and the twins tied dish towels around their waists.

"Who's coming?" Sarah asked.

"A person we grew up with. Miriam Schrock."

Sarah's eyes immediately went wide. "I've heard of her from girls at worship who have her as a teacher."

Hannah started to ask Sarah exactly what she'd heard about Miriam, but Clara changed the subject.

"What kind of pie are we making?" the twin asked.

"A pumpkin custard pie," Hannah told them. "It's *Aenti* Ruth's recipe."

"Is *Aenti* Ruth going to help?" Eli asked.

"*Nee*, it looks like she has company."

All throughout the morning, each time Hannah glanced out the window, she'd spied Abram's buggy outside the *dawdi haus*. Her first instinct had been to run over and rescue her aunt. But as her aunt had reminded her earlier, she was capable of wheeling to the house on her own. Even so, *Aenti* Ruth had to be bored beyond belief, entertaining the nearly wordless man for so long.

In a way, Hannah blamed herself. She needed to set aside some time to make an introduction between her aunt and Joseph Beiler, Sew Easy's former repairman. He'd be a much better match for her lively aunt than Abram.

But even now, time was running short for baking, and she still had soup to make for dinner. While the twins played with flour that they'd spilled out over the tabletop, she and Sarah got to work, measuring ingredients at the counter.

"I remember my *mamm* made a cake once with chocolate icing that she called a pie," Sarah said wistfully as she poured brown sugar into the mixing bowl. "It had custard that was this high." She measured at least twelve inches into the air.

"I believe you." Hannah chuckled. "Your mom had a special talent for baking."

"But *Daed* said he couldn't find any of her recipes."

"Hmm, I honestly don't remember your *mamm* using recipes much. Or if she did, she turned them into big, fancy desserts like you're talking about." Thinking about baking with Lily brought a smile to Hannah's face. "I bet that dessert was yummy, wasn't it?"

"And messy, too." Sarah grinned.

Hannah laughed. "I don't think this pie is going to

be that messy, but our kitchen is sure going to be." She leaned her head toward Sarah's younger siblings. Both were smacking their flour-covered hands together and laughing as the flour dust flew into the air.

"My *daed* says they rile each other up." Sarah shook her head, then rolled her eyes just like her *mamm* used to do.

Hannah had always noticed how the twins' features were a true combination of Jake and Lily. Yet when it came to Sarah, beyond her blue eyes, she didn't look like her mother or Jake, not with her dark curly hair and medium skin tone.

She didn't act like her mother, either. If it had been Lily in Sarah's position, she would've snuck into the kitchen and tried to figure out the missing recipe on her own, using up all kinds of ingredients without anyone's permission. Lily truly had a hard time sitting still and being patient, and not diving in and going after what she wanted.

Even now, Sarah wasn't tossing around flour like her *schweschder* and *bruder* or even like her *mamm* would've. She'd already grabbed a wet cloth and was trying to clean up the mess. Knowing firsthand what it was like for Sarah to have to grow up fast, Hannah's heart ached for the second time that day.

After sliding the pie into the oven, she wiped her hands on a dish towel and turned to the girl. "Sarah, if you'd like, we can try to make that dessert of your *mamm*'s some day."

"We can?" Sarah's smile was as bright as the sun shining through the window. "Do you know the recipe?"

"No, but I'm thinking we can find something close

and adapt it like your *mamm*'s. At least we can give it a mighty good try."

"That would be *gut*." Sarah grinned even more. *"Danke."*

The way Sarah's eyes glowed with such innocent appreciation made Hannah's eyes well up with tears. Partly because it felt *gut* to see the glimmer of pure happiness that shone on Sarah's face when Hannah offered to bring her *mamm*'s memory to life. But also because as she glanced around the kitchen at the *kinner*, she was earnestly praying once again. Praying with her whole heart for *Gott* to be beside her and to guide her to do the very best she could by them—no matter what.

Other than the prospect of enjoying one of Hannah's *wunderbaar* desserts, Jake had been dreading Miriam Schrock's visit all day. And even more, when she walked in the door.

"Why, Miriam, don't you look nice," Hannah greeted her. "Doesn't she, Jake?"

Jake was silent as Hannah took their guest's cloak and turned to look at him. Usually he agreed with most anything she had to say. Even when he didn't, he rarely put up much of an argument, preferring to let Hannah have her way. But this time he had a hard time being prodded into saying something he wasn't feeling.

After all, Miriam Schrock looked the same as he remembered. Coal black hair. Blue eyes that might've been pretty but appeared too piercing and judgmental behind her glasses. If only her lips didn't look so tight as if she hardly ever smiled.

Mercifully, he didn't have to answer because Miriam spoke up. "I look the same way I always do when

I'm finished with a long day of teaching." She peered over her glasses.

"I bet you could use a little something sweet, then," Hannah replied, thankfully, since he was still at a loss for words. "It can be a small reward for your hard work today. Isn't that right, Jake?" Hannah prodded him again.

"Dessert? *Jah*. I'm always in the mood for dessert."

Evidently, those hadn't been the right words to say. Both women eyed him, puzzled. Hannah even frowned, causing him to try again.

"What I meant to say is you deserve more than dessert. Teaching is no easy job. That's what my sister Esther says."

Miriam nodded. "*Jah*, if it were easy, everyone would be doing it."

Jake was ready to argue that *Gott* didn't call everyone to be teachers, but that everyone could teach children things. But he stopped himself, thinking better of it. "So, how about dessert?" He clapped his hands. "Hannah makes some *gut* ones. Doesn't she, *kinner*?"

His three children had been standing in formation like soldiers at the door when Miriam walked in. Sarah had made sure of that. He'd overheard her telling the twins that she'd heard Miss Schrock was hard, so they needed to act their best. He also knew she'd brushed their hair, replaced her and her sister's *kapps*, and had them all looking perfect.

Glancing down at his own rumpled work clothes, he realized he should've tried harder. Not so much for Miriam, but for the rest of his family, and for Hannah, since they were trying to be respectful of their guest.

"Why don't we all go into the kitchen and relax?"

Hannah's soothing voice broke through the tension. "I made a pumpkin custard pie to celebrate your visit, Miriam. The children helped."

"You did?" Miriam glanced at his children, and for the first time he noticed a glimmer of something bordering kindness in her eyes.

All three nodded in unison.

"Eli and I mostly played in the flour and rolled the roller," Clara admitted.

Miriam furrowed a brow at his youngest daughter before looking around at all of them. "I appreciate the effort, and I hate to disappoint you all." She stood staunchly. "But pumpkin gives me indigestion."

Hannah's shoulders dipped. "I'm sorry to hear that. Well, I, um…" She paused, obviously thinking. "There are a few oatmeal raisin cookies in the cookie jar."

Jake chimed in. "*Nee*, I packed those in my lunch today."

"Of course you did," Miriam said coldly, like she was already disappointed where he was concerned.

Hadn't he told Hannah this was the way things would go?

Still, for all of Hannah's effort, he needed to try to set things right.

"I'm really sorry about that," he replied. "But instead of dessert, why don't we all sit down and visit? It's been a long time since I've seen you, Miriam."

"Not really." She took a seat in the middle of the sofa. He and Hannah settled into chairs across from her while the children sat on the floor. "I saw you several weeks ago in town."

"Really? Why don't I remember that?"

"Because you didn't notice me. You were putting up

flyers and standing not ten feet from me, but you didn't see me. But that's how things have always been with us. Isn't it?" She glared at him.

Hannah clapped her hands, moving the conversation elsewhere. "So, Miriam, this is Sarah. She'll be in your class next fall." She pointed to where Sarah was sitting. "And we—Jake—thought it best to make sure she knows all she needs to before school starts. Isn't that right, Jake?"

"Yes. My Sarah is a sweet and sensitive *maedel*, and smart, too. I think you'll really enjoy having her in your class."

"You do know your ABC's, right, Sarah?" Miriam quizzed.

"Of course she does."

"I was speaking to your daughter, Jake."

"Yes, Miss Schrock," Sarah replied quietly.

"And how to add numbers together?"

"We've worked on that some, but we'll be working on it more."

"Again, I was talking to your daughter." Miriam turned from him to look at Sarah again. "You'll want to know how to add, how to write the alphabet and your name. If you're a good father," she said, casting her critical eyes on him, "you will have already taught her those things."

"Are you saying I'm not a good father?" He could feel himself getting defensive. "Because those aren't the only things a father needs to teach his *kinner*."

"I'm saying that being prepared would make her a better student than you ever were."

He could feel his face burn. Even if what she was saying were true about his school days, she needn't be saying it in front of his children. "You know what they say, Miriam. Teaching children to count is fine but teaching children what counts is better."

Hannah interrupted. "Would you all like some tea? Some soothing chamomile, maybe?"

Miriam shook her head. "I need to get home before it gets much darker."

"*Jah*, it's best you be on your way, then," Hannah said diplomatically, walking Miriam to the door.

As soon as Hannah closed the door behind Miriam, she leaned against it, letting out a long sigh. "All right…" She inhaled deeply. "Who wants dessert?"

"We do!" The *kinner* cried out and took off for the kitchen.

"Now do you remember why they call her *Shock*?" he whispered as they followed behind the children. "She has no filters. Just a stinging way about her."

"You're right." Hannah shook her head. "So right."

Once they were gathered around the table, Hannah cut each of them a healthy serving of pie. Before she could top the pieces with whipped cream, he pointed to the container, sitting on the table.

"May I?"

She smiled at him quizzically and nodded.

Reaching over to Eli's plate first, he sprayed an *E* on his son's wedge of piece. "What's that *E* for, *sohn*?"

"Eli." The boy grinned.

Leaning over to Clara's plate, he sprayed a big *C*.

"And what's that *C* stand for, *dochder*?"

"Clara."

"That's right."

"And you, *dochder*…" He swirled an *S* onto Sarah's slice.

"That's for me, *Daed*. Sarah."

"*Jah*, and *H* is for Hannah." He reached across the table and wrote an *H* on her pie. "Though I could've put an *M* for *matchmaker*," he said under his breath, giving her a conspiratorial wink.

"Not tonight, you couldn't." She grinned before getting up and grabbing another container of whipped cream from the refrigerator. She shook the can as she walked over to his side of the table.

"And here is a *J* for Jacob," she told the *kinner* as she sprayed away. "It could also be a *J* for *just right* because your father is just that. He is kind and considerate and loving and—"

"Fun!" he exclaimed.

With that, he sprang from his chair and began spraying more blobs of whipped cream on the children's pie and even on their noses, leaving them squealing. They were laughing even more when Hannah came at him, topping his nose with white cream, too.

As he chased Hannah around the table, and the two of them tried to spray each other, the children clapped and screeched. They were both laughing until finally, Hannah, nearly out of breath, called for a truce.

"You do know we have to clean up the mess after we eat, don't you?" he said as he and Hannah sat down, and they all dug into their pie. He didn't want his children thinking there wasn't a price to pay for silly behavior.

"But, *Daed*, we didn't make the mess." Sarah smirked. "You and Hannah did."

He laughed. "*Verra* smart, Sarah."

After the children were in bed, it didn't take long for him and Hannah to tidy up the kitchen.

"It was a fun night after all, wasn't it?" Hannah sighed.

"But I need to ask, you didn't really think Miriam would be a match for me, did you?"

"Nee." She giggled. "I just thought I'd give you a practice round."

"It was more of a workout," he scoffed. "I can't believe she said that about me and my school days…even if it was true."

She laughed. "Well, let's just say if I was the one handing out report cards on the subject of Miriam and first dates—"

"I would've easily failed, huh?"

"And I'm glad you did. Goodness, she's a tough one. However—" Hannah held up a delicate finger.

"Jah? I'm all ears."

"On the subject of parenting, I'd give you an A plus. You're a great father, Jake."

He was quiet at first, beyond moved by her words. "That means a lot coming from you, Hannah. What you think is important to me."

"I think you're the best, Jake, and you deserve to find the best."

Their eyes locked and, for a brief moment, held. Then Hannah turned to take her cloak from the rack, the day ending in the same place it had begun.

From her tone he knew she'd been sincere. But as he stood on the porch and watched her walk over to the *dawdi haus*, his past mistakes and overwhelming guilt pulled at him as it always did. Leaving him feeling that he didn't deserve the best, not at all.

Especially not someone as perfect as Hannah.

Chapter Six

Hannah had experienced many life changes in the past couple of weeks. But standing in Grace's former store, where she used to happily serve customers, was still a change that wasn't easy to accept. Sighing, she ran her hand over some material that she'd spotted in a packing box that hadn't been sealed yet. "I always loved this cotton muslin. It's so soft and came in the prettiest prints."

"I know," Grace Newberry agreed. "Remember when it first came in? You couldn't wait to make a baby blanket and put it on display for everyone to feel."

Hannah smiled at the fond memory. Yet at the same time felt sad that memories were about the only thing she could smile about as she glanced around her previous workplace. What once was Sew Easy looked nothing like the shop she'd helped Grace run. All the shelves and cabinets had been disassembled. Gone, too, was the counter that she'd stood behind for so many years. It had been the place where she'd greeted customers, helped them decide on material and yardage, and where she'd been happy to listen to whatever was on their minds or in their hearts.

Now the shop that she thought would be hers was virtually empty. All except for the stacks of boxes filled with material and sewing accessories that Grace wanted to gift to her.

"Grace, you're giving me so much. I appreciate it, but couldn't you make money by selling the material to another store or online?"

"Hannah, honey, I don't want this fabric to go to anyone but you," Grace said sweetly but firmly, laying a hand on Hannah's shoulder. "I know you'll make such beautiful things with it. And now that you're living at Jake's, you'll have more storage space, right?"

"Well...*jah*." She wasn't quite sure where that would be. In the basement or barn, maybe?

"Giving the fabric to you will make me feel better about things. At least a little." Glancing around the place, Grace sighed heavily. "I just never imagined things would turn out this way." She shook her head. "My dream was to help you with your dream. You deserved it after all your years of dedication and hard work. I never counted on that chain store coming to town. And dealing with that huge rent hike."

Hannah almost felt worse for Grace than she did for herself. "I'm going to hold on to this material," she promised, "and someday we're going to open another shop together."

Grace reached out and squeezed Hannah's hand, giving her a wan smile. "That's so sweet of you. But I have to say, this whole situation has tuckered me out. I've decided to retire earlier than I intended. Harry and I are moving to Cleveland to be close to our grandkids."

Admittedly, when Hannah first walked into the storefront, it had gone through her mind that Grace looked paler and somewhat grayer than she'd ever seen her. She seemed worn out from all the disappointment and changes.

"Harry's been trying to talk you into that for years, hasn't he?"

"Ever since he retired himself." Grace gave another weak smile.

"I'm sure your son and his family will love having you close." Hannah meant every word. "But doncha think you'll need some material so you can make your grandchildren a few things?"

Grace snickered. "Trust me, I've packed up plenty of boxes for myself. I couldn't resist, even though Harry has made me promise that from now on sewing will be just one of my hobbies, not my main one. He's ready for us to play golf and bridge. Honestly, I wouldn't mind having time to bake. Garden. Read. Things I've been far too busy to do."

"That sounds *wunderbaar*. Can I move with you?"

Grace laughed. "I'd take you in a second if you weren't so busy yourself. Taking care of Jake's children and your aunt—I'd say you have your hands full."

"Now I just need to find time to sew."

"You'd better." Grace wagged a finger.

After loading as many boxes as they could into every corner of Hannah's buggy, Grace promised that Harry would deliver the rest to Jake's place later in the week.

Then it was time to say goodbye. Hannah's eyes misted immediately as Grace reached out to hug her. Like her, Grace didn't seem to want to let go.

"Hannah, I'm sorry," Grace whispered into Hannah's ear. "So, so sorry." She let go of a sob.

"Grace, please." Hannah's voice trembled as she

patted the older woman's back. "There's nothing to be sorry about," she whispered in return. "You've always believed in me. You gave me hope for the future. Do you know what a comfort you've been in my life? You've been like a mother to me."

Saying that out loud surprised even her. But every word was true. In many ways, she couldn't remember feeling the same kind of closeness with Rachel Keim, even after living with the Keims for so many years.

"Now don't you go making me cry," Grace said, but as she loosened her hold and stepped back, rivulets of tears streaked her cheeks.

"But it's true. And I don't want you to be feeling bad." Hannah swiped at her own damp cheeks. "*Gott* will be there for both of us, I know He will. And we can always write to each other."

"And we will." Grace pulled a tissue from her coat pocket and wiped her nose. "Are you heading back to Jake's now?"

"In a bit." Hannah sniffled. "He suggested I put up flyers around town letting people know I'm available for seamstress jobs and to sew decorative home items."

"See, I told you that material would go to good use with you."

Grace beamed for the first time that morning. Still, Hannah's heart was reeling with emotion as she gave Grace a final hug and headed down the sidewalk with her satchel of tacks and flyers. She kept hearing her own words about *Gott* having a plan for her future swirling in her head. Some days she could believe that without question, with absolute faith. And then there were other days…she desperately longed to feel that trust completely.

As she tried to sort out that contradiction within herself, her thoughts were interrupted by a familiar-looking man walking toward her. Even though his head was somewhat hidden under his hat, she could see enough to be sure it was him.

She halted in her tracks.

"David?"

He stopped and looked up. "Hannah."

He may have been family, but their greeting was nothing like what she'd just experienced with her *Englisch* friend. Even though her hands were outstretched, David's remained buried deeply in his pockets.

True, they hadn't ever had the closest of relationships. She was never sure if that was because he was six years older than herself and Lily. Or because he hadn't been enthusiastic about her taking a spot at the Keim table. She'd also had a closeness with Noah that David never seemed to share. But then David always seemed to go up against his father while prodding his mother into taking his side. Generally, Rachel did.

Clasping her hands around her pouch again, she said, "I'm glad to see you're all right, David. I've been worried. You haven't answered my letters."

"I've been awful busy with my job and the *kinner* and *Mamm*."

"*Jah*, your *mamm*. How is she?"

"She's your *mamm*, too, Hannah."

Instantly, her face burned with embarrassment. "David, I'm sorry. I didn't mean that the way it sounded. She was—is—my *mamm*, and you do know I'd be happy to help you any way I can, don't you?"

He shrugged his shoulders. But deep down, he had to know she cared. Since he lived two hours away in

Middlefield, she couldn't do much. But she did send letters regularly to check in with him, even though she never received a reply. And she'd also hired an *Englisch* driver twice in the past two years so she could visit Rachel, and David's family. Though his wife had been sweet both visits, David hadn't appeared all that happy to see her. As for Rachel, the stroke had left her unable to speak. Hannah had no idea if she comprehended anything Hannah said.

She tried again. "I hope everything is well with your *kinner* and your *fraa*, Mary."

His response was a curt nod, causing her stomach to tighten. She never understood why there was always such an undercurrent of unease between them that seemed to have gotten worse over the years.

"Gut," she replied. "In case you're wondering, your nieces and nephew are doing fine, too."

Numerous times she'd asked Jake if he'd heard from David. His answer was usually no, and he never appeared to want to elaborate on that.

At the mention of Jake and Lily's children, David's jaw tensed. "Do you talk to Jake often?"

"More now since I lost my job. *Aenti* Ruth and I are staying in his *dawdi haus*, which has been quite a blessing. I'm taking care of the children while he's at work."

"Are you and Jake…?" He paused, and she could tell what he was attempting to ask, which seemed somewhat strange.

"It's only a temporary situation, David. One that's handy for us both right now. Once I find a job, and he finds a permanent nanny, *Aenti* Ruth and I will be moving."

"Humph." He blinked and looked at the ground before raising his head. But it wasn't to look at her. Instead he glanced across the street at the Highland Realty sign. "I have an appointment with a new real estate agent. I don't want to be late."

"*Jah*, I understand." She knew it had probably been a burden for him with his parents' home still for sale after two years. "Please give *Mamm* a hug for me. And if there's anything I can—"

"There's nothing, Hannah. But I…" He peered straight into her eyes, as if he wanted to say something more. But it was only for the briefest moment. Then it was gone. "*Mach's gut*, Hannah," he said. At the edge of the sidewalk, he looked both ways before jogging across the street.

Appointment or not, the way he appeared in such a hurry to be gone from her felt like he was trying to escape from something.

She'd gotten the same feeling from him around the time of Lily and Jake's wedding.

Only weeks before the ceremony, when she'd come back from Indiana to help Lily, David had already permanently moved to Middlefield after he and Mary quickly married. His decision to move away had disappointed, and even confused Noah and Rachel, who assumed their family would always stay close by.

Of course, David and Mary did come back for Lily's wedding, but they didn't stay long. Hannah remembered that even then, just like today, her *bruder* didn't have much to say to her.

The five-foot-tall double-door storage cabinet wasn't the most involved piece of furniture Jake had ever made. Even so, as he wiped a rag damp with Puritan Pine stain over its hardwood surface, he hoped Hannah would be pleased with it.

Ever since Grace Newberry had stopped by the lumberyard, asking him to let Hannah know about the boxes of material she had waiting for her, he'd been moonlighting in the barn each night, building the cabinet. He doubted the cabinet would come close to holding the amount of material Grace had mentioned. But at least it would be storage space for some of Hannah's favorite fabrics.

He just needed to get it stained before Hannah got back from Grace's.

Thankfully, at Ruth's request, Abram had stopped by to help Jake move the cabinet into the *dawdi haus* once Hannah had set out for town. Ruth had also been keeping the children busy all morning, playing outside and feeding the barn kittens.

The children were in on the surprise and knew he needed to finish the staining before Hannah returned. So why they were knocking at the door, and testing his patience, he couldn't imagine.

"Come in," he shouted. "No need to knock."

With that, he expected the door to burst open and one of his children to scamper in, either in search of kitty treats or in need of a trip to the bathroom. Instead, the door squeaked slightly, and he barely heard footsteps wandering in.

Curious, he lifted his head from his work and was surprised—no, shocked—by what he saw.

Standing in the glow of sunlight streaming in the doorway was a woman. A very pretty woman.

"Oh! You're not supposed to be here." She sounded as taken aback as he was.

"I'm not?" He blinked.

"What I mean is, Hannah's *aenti* said I could come in to leave Hannah a note. She didn't mention you were inside."

Whoever she was, the woman looked as fresh as the morning. Strawberry blond hair peeking out from her *kapp*. Green eyes. Freckles dotting her nose.

"She'll be back shortly. Do you want to wait?" He inclined his head toward the couch. "Or I can get a pencil and paper for you."

"I only had a quick question for her. But…well…" She rubbed one gloved hand over the other. "I suppose I can ask you."

He quirked a brow. Laying the stain-covered rag aside, he picked up a clean towel to wipe his hands. "You can try me."

"What time are you and I meeting for supper at Der Dutchman on Monday? Hannah didn't say."

"Dinner? Monday?"

She chuckled nervously. "I'm thinking you don't know about the date Hannah set up for us."

He didn't know which was worse. Telling the truth that Hannah had never mentioned it. Or acting like he'd misplaced his brain. He went for the latter.

"That's right. You're… I'm sorry, sometimes I have a hard time with names. I think because I meet so many people at work."

"I'm Catherine. Catherine Zook."

"Right. Catherine. Pleased to meet you." Again, he didn't want to hurt her feelings. "I believe Hannah said six thirty. Does that sound all right with you? Should I pick you up?"

"*Nee*, I can get there myself. Except…it will be dark.

And there might be a drop in temperature." She bit her lip. "Not that I'm that far from the restaurant, so I could walk. But then…if you're offering, that would be *gut*. Unless, of course, you're just saying that to be nice. Because then—"

He held up his hand. Surely, she was simply nervous to be talking so much? "I'll pick you up at six fifteen."

"All right." She grinned. "I live at 2020 Redbird Lane. The house is on the right side—well, that's only if you're turning off Bluebird. If you're coming from Songbird, then it's on the left. Oh, and there's a park bench on the corner of Blackbird that—"

Again, his hand went up. "I know exactly where Redbird Lane is."

"Okay, then I'll see you at six fifteen. On Monday. For dinner at six thirty. At Der Dutchman. That will be *gut*."

Catherine Zook repeated every bit of their plan as she backed out the door with a sweet smile on her face.

What a surprise! He'd never seen the woman before. Although in the past couple of years he hadn't been off his property much.

Maybe Hannah was onto something with her matchmaking after all, he thought, as he stood back eyeing each corner of the cabinet to see if he'd missed any areas. Though he had to wonder when she had time to think of him and to reach out to anyone on his behalf. She certainly was special, that was for sure. She was so good to her aunt. And great with his *kinner*. She was always putting someone else's needs first.

He picked up the staining rag and began smoothing over a few of the lighter spots, feeling glad he'd built the cabinet. In fact, he'd make as many as Hannah needed.

It was only right that she have the chance to do the thing she loved, and the time to devote to it.

Right then and there, he made a promise to himself that he would help make that happen.

Hannah felt like she'd been gone forever, but as she guided her buggy up Jake's driveway, she was glad to see the *kinner* were happily playing. It appeared they were running circles, literally, around her aunt, who was directing them in a game of Ring Around *Aenti* Ruthie. They were giggling as they all fell to the ground. Until they spotted her.

Her aunt said something that sent Eli dashing into the *dawdi haus*. Meanwhile, the girls stood still, watching as she unhitched the buggy and tied the horse to a post. It was so different than their usual greeting, leaving Hannah befuddled.

"Is everything all right?" she asked.

Before her aunt or the girls could answer, Eli came running out. "*Daed* needs you. Right now."

Immediately, her heart sank. What could've possibly gone wrong?

Hurrying toward the house, she could sense the foursome trailing behind her. When she opened the door, she braced herself for the worst, expecting to see a flooded floor, a burst pipe, or the remnants of a fire caused by embers escaping the fireplace. But there was no foul stench. No smoky odor hanging in the air.

Instead, there was only Jake's familiar soapy, balsam scent that never failed to catch her attention. That, along with the unexpected aroma of new wood and fresh stain coming from a cabinet that fit perfectly into her sewing corner.

She gasped, not believing her eyes. The aroma of the wood and stain heightened as she stepped close, and so did her emotions.

"*Daed* made it for you." Sarah said what she'd already guessed. "It's for your material and thread and whatever else you use to sew."

"I can't believe you made this, Jake. It's so beautiful," she said, surprised by her unpredictable friend. "How? When? It must've taken you so long."

"*Nee.* I headed to the barn a few nights to work on it after I knew you'd gone to bed."

"A few nights?"

He shrugged. "Maybe more than a few."

She reached out to touch the smooth surface, but he caught her hand in his.

"The stain is just drying, so you'll want to wait a couple days to touch it or use it. But it has four shelves, and I can make more if you need them. I can even make another cabinet if you want."

"It's perfect, Jake. So perfect that I don't even know what to say. *Danke, danke, danke.*" She started to give him a hug, but Clara tugged on her sleeve.

"*Aenti* Ruth bribed us."

Hannah glanced at her aunt. "You did what?"

"It's true." *Aenti* Ruth rolled her eyes. "I bribed the *kinner.* I told them we'd get pizza tonight if they'd keep quiet about their *daed*'s surprise."

"Well, they certainly did." Hannah chuckled. "It's pizza for dinner, for sure and certain. And I have a surprise of my own."

"Ice cream for dessert?" Eli asked.

"*Nee*, not exactly. It's more of a surprise for your *daed*." She turned to Jake.

"Do you mean the dinner you set up with Catherine?" His brows rose.

"Oh…" She swallowed hard. "How do you find out about that?"

"She stopped by asking about a time for Monday."

"I was going to tell you about her. I mean, ask you. But I was waiting for Miriam's visit to wear off." She gave him her most apologetic look. "I hope you're not mad."

"*Nee*, it's fine. I know you only want the best for me." He repeated the words she'd spoken to him. "And who knows? Maybe one day I'll be raving about your matchmaking skills like Simon Weaver."

"Ah, *jah*. Simon and Greta." She grinned, remembering. "But let me tell you, Jake, you have more skills than you know. Even besides creating beautiful furniture."

"I do?"

"Oh, *jah*." She could barely tell him fast enough. "You made those flyers for me, and I took them around town like you said. And when I was tacking one up in the *kaffe* shop, an *Englisch* woman who used to come into Sew Easy noticed. Right away, she hired me. She wants me to make several things for her children's rooms."

"Your first job?"

"*Jah*. What a blessing."

"Hannah, I'm so happy for you!" Jake exclaimed. Suddenly, he lifted her up with his strong, muscled arms and swung her around. Laughter sifted out of her and a few sentimental tears, too, as she found herself moved by knowing how much he wanted this for her.

"*Daed*, you're gonna make her dizzy," Sarah protested, watching them.

"Really?" Clara piped up. "I like when *Daed* does that to me."

"Me, too," Eli agreed. "But why are you twirling her, *Daed*?"

"Because Hannah has a job to do," Jake answered his son.

"A job is a *gut* thing?" Eli wrinkled his nose.

Hannah burst out laughing along with Jake and *Aenti* Ruth. As Jake set her back down to the floor, she noticed his arm still lingered around her waist.

"*Jah*, Eli, it's a *verra gut* thing," Jake said. "Wouldn't you agree, Hannah?"

As he looked down at her, she could see all the happiness he held for her in his sweet eyes.

"*Jah, verra gut.*" But even as she said the words, her heart fluttered.

Was she talking about her new job? Or how she certainly wasn't minding the close warmth of him?

Chapter Seven

Hannah could only hope, for Jake's sake, that he would have an easier time communicating with Catherine Zook on this Monday evening than she was having with his *kinner*. She had lost count of how many times she'd tried to explain to the children about their father's absence at the supper table.

"But why isn't *Daed* eating with us?" Clara asked again, her forehead crinkling like the sweet potato fries on her plate. "Aren't roasted chicken and fries his favorites?"

"You're right," Hannah said from across the kitchen table. "He likes roasted chicken and fries very much. But your *daed* is going to have dinner with a pretty lady in town tonight."

"But you're pretty." Eli's perplexed expression mimicked his twin's. "And you're not all the way in town."

She had to smile at his logic and sweet compliment. "That's nice of you to say, Eli, but your *daed* and I are only friends."

Instantly, a snicker erupted. It came from her aunt,

of course, who was sitting next to Clara. "*Verra, verra gut* friends," *Aenti* Ruth commented.

"And we've been that way for as long as we've known each other."

"That's what you've always said, over and over and over again…" Her aunt whispered the last part under her breath.

Hannah laid down her fork. "*Aenti* Ruth, is there something you'd like to say?"

"*Nee.*" Her aunt blinked with wide, innocent eyes. "I'm just agreeing with you, niece, and your claim that you two are just friends."

"And we are," Hannah assured her.

"But," Sarah spoke up, "you do things for us and live with us like a *mamm* does."

"No, I live in the *dawdi haus* with *Aenti* Ruth."

"It's still our house," Sarah was quick to point out.

"Well, *jah*, but…" All the questioning had squelched her appetite, and the children looked like they were only poking at the bits of food left on their plates. She got up from the table, hoping her movement could also move the conversation elsewhere. And it did—for the short time that she retrieved the ice cream from the freezer and scooped it into bowls for them. But as soon as the *kinner* began eating, the questions started again. This time directed at her instead of their *daed*.

"When are you going to court someone?" Sarah asked, scooping up a bite of vanilla ice cream.

The young girl sounded so much like her meddling aunt, who turned around from the sink where she was rinsing dishes. "That's a *gut* question, Sarah, and one I've also asked. I'm curious about that, too."

"I don't really have anyone in mind right now," Hannah stated. Which was an honest answer. One she assumed would immediately put the issue to rest.

"But when you do have someone in your mind," Sarah pushed, "will you still live here?"

"*Jah.* Will you?" Clara frowned, ice cream dripping from the corners of her mouth.

Eli looked up at her with questions in his eyes.

Seeing all three of their confused faces wrenched her heart, making her want to swoop them up into her arms. Glancing over at her aunt, she could see from her expression how the children's concerns tore at her heart, too.

"I promise you, *kinner*, I'm not planning on courting anyone for a long time. So you don't have to worry yourselves about that, okay? And you know what?" She attempted her second bribe of the evening. "The sooner you finish your desserts, the sooner we can have a practice session on the sewing machine, girls. And, Eli, you can be the man of the house and bring in firewood."

Each of them looked pleased with her answer as they focused on their desserts once more.

As she stepped over to the sink to help with the dishes, her aunt patted her hand. "They'll be *oll recht*," *Aenti* Ruth whispered, offering her most comforting smile.

"I know."

At least, that was what she kept telling herself. Right now, the *kinner* were confused and anxious about what was going on with their *daed* and her, as well. Under the circumstances, it was normal for them to worry that any security they felt could all go away in an instant. Yet she had to believe that when the time was right, and she did find a match for Jake, they would be happy, and their lives would feel more complete.

Although if that match happened to be Catherine Zook, she couldn't take much credit for it. It was Anna Graber who'd sent her cousin Hannah's way.

Hannah had to smile, remembering how Catherine had come all the way from town and knocked on the *dawdi haus* door one day while Jake was at work. She asked Hannah if she could 'try out for the position.' At first, Hannah assumed Catherine thought Hannah was still working at Sew Easy and was asking about a job at the shop. But *nee*. Catherine was asking if she could try out for the part of Jake's *fraa*, which Hannah thought was sweet. Even if the girl did chatter a bit much.

Of course, after the way Jake had looked when Miriam came to the house, Hannah wanted to make sure he presented himself in a better light for this first real date. She'd started by laying out his newest black pants along with his black suspenders and wool hat. She'd also ironed the shirt she liked best on him, his light blue one. The fabric was a soft denim and so was the shade of blue. Ever since she'd known him, any time he wore that color, she noted how it accentuated his sapphire eyes and blond hair.

Yet when he stepped into the kitchen before leaving for the date, her jaw dropped at the sight of him. He was wearing his black shoes, black pants—and a dull, washed-out beige shirt.

"I'm ready to go," he announced as he circled the table, kissing the children's heads. "You'll probably be asleep when I get home, *kinner*, so you be good for Hannah and *Aenti* Ruth this evening, you hear?"

She couldn't help but speak up. "You're not wearing it."

"Wearing what?"

"The blue shirt I ironed and laid out on your bed."

He shrugged indifferently. "Beige is fine."

"But it's too..." The word *boring* came to mind, but she searched for a kinder way to make her point. Laying aside the wet dishrag, she dried her hands with the end of her apron. "I don't know, Jake. That color looks like...well, like you didn't even try."

"Didn't try?" He held out his arms and looked down at his feet before pleading his case. "My shoes are freshly shined. I washed up, changed clothes and even trimmed my beard." He touched the golden hair that framed his strong jawline.

"Did you brush your teeth, *Daed*?" Eli asked, slurping ice cream from his spoon. "You always make us do that when we go somewhere."

"You're right, Eli. *Jah*, I brushed my teeth, too. So I'd say I'm ready. And I look fine, *jah*?"

Always the peacemaker, Sarah spoke up. "You look real nice, *Daed*."

"Danke, dochder." He nodded his thanks to Sarah then turned to Hannah for her final approval. "Miss Matchmaker?"

"Jah." She sighed, acquiescing. "You do."

What could she say? No matter the color of his shirt, Catherine Zook was sure to be attracted to Jake's captivating presence, his arresting good looks and his caring smile.

Which was what she wanted, wasn't it?

Jake wasn't tired when he left for dinner, but he sure was by the time he headed home. Catherine was a nice woman and as pretty as they came, but the hours he'd spent with her had worn him out.

Still, he hurried, hoping to get home before his children went to sleep. Yet by the time he got back to the house, he could hear their murmurings upstairs, sounding like they were already settling down. Not wishing to stir up things, he tiptoed up the steps and stood outside the bedroom door, listening in.

"Were you an older sister?" Sarah was asking Hannah.

"Or a younger one?" Clara wanted to know.

He wondered how Hannah would answer their questions. He was fairly certain she wouldn't share her experiences as an older sister with his children. At least not until they were old enough to be able to grasp and not be frightened by her horrifyingly sad story of loss.

Sneaking a peek into the room, he saw her thoughtfully eye his two girls as they lay side by side.

"Actually, for a while I wasn't anyone's sister," she said vaguely. "So I was *verra* thankful *Gott* blessed me with your mother's friendship. Your *mamm* was like a sister to me," she said. "And like sisters and brothers—" she looked over at Eli in his twin bed "—we watched out for each other just like the three of you always need to do."

Glancing back and forth between the children, she asked, "Now, who is ready to say prayers?"

"I am," Sarah declared.

"Me, too," Clara agreed.

"Jah," his son chimed in.

"Everyone ready?" She clasped her hands together, and he saw her wait patiently for his children to do the same before bowing her head.

"Dear *Gott*," she said in a reverent tone, "weary now these children lay to rest, please close their eyes in slumber blessed. Lord, may Thy loving, watchful eye, guard the beds on which they lie. *Gott* bless Sarah. *Gott* bless Clara. And *Gott* bless Eli. Amen."

Their little voices joined in with breathy *aemens*. Even outside the door, he sensed a special kind of peaceful stillness settle over him.

He was still in a tranquil state when Hannah gave kisses all around and came out of the bedroom. Startled, she gasped at the sight of him.

Without a word, they crept downstairs.

"You're back so soon," she said as they ambled into the kitchen. "That was a quick dinner."

"It didn't feel fast." He frowned. "Catherine kept talking and talking—and well, I can only listen so much. I guess it's not something I'm good at."

"Not true." Hannah readily defended him. "You listen, but you also like to take action. Look at how you've listened to me and knew I wanted to keep sewing. Then you made a beautiful cabinet for me. And if I'm being honest..." Her nose scrunched. "It did cross my mind that Catherine might be too chatty. But she also seemed so sweet and pretty."

He nodded. "*Jah*, I agree, but it's hard to get to know someone when you can't get a word in edgewise. You may hear all about them, but they don't have a chance to get to know you. Then you don't know how they'd react to you and if you two would be a fit."

Hannah's mouth suddenly went slack. "Jake, I've always known you're smart, but that's so insightful," she said, sounding astonished. "I'm impressed."

"Don't be," he said as a wave of guilt coursed through him and his years with Lily came to mind. "Unless... it would help my cause."

"Your cause?"

"Well, if you think I'm ahead of the curve," he hedged, "maybe this would be a good time for me to take a break from courting for a while."

"I wouldn't call what you've done courting exactly." She chuckled as she pulled her cloak from the wall rack.

He pulled his jacket down, as well. "How about I walk you home?"

"So you can talk me into backing off on finding you a match?" She quirked a brow.

"Of course not. It's dark and cold. I'm only trying to be polite."

She shook her head at him. "Hmm, why don't I believe that?"

As soon as they were out the door, he took the opportunity to change the subject.

"I wonder about you, Hannah."

"What about me?"

"Well, if you're a matchmaker, and a mighty good one from what I've heard, why not find a match for yourself?"

He noticed her stiffen at his question. "You sound like *Aenti* Ruth and the *kinner*. They were asking the same thing at dinner."

"Did you have an answer?"

"I'm happy being on my own," she said simply.

"Then why can't I be happy being on my own?"

That stopped her. "Jake, do I have to remind you about the night you were practically in tears saying you needed a woman in your life?"

"Me? In tears? Never," he countered. "And how did we get back to talking about me? I was asking about you."

She shot him a wry smile. "You're the one who changed the subject."

"Oh, you're right. That was impolite and would not be a good move on a first date. Would it?" he teased and enjoyed hearing her laugh. "*Oll recht*, back to you. Why don't you want to find someone?"

As soon as they reached the porch of the *dawdi haus*, they strolled over to the railing. Hannah leaned against the wood rail, looking away from him into the darkness. "I'm fine the way things are. Finding love for others has helped me find my place in the world. It seems that's *Gott*'s plan for me right now," she said matter-of-factly. "Plus, I enjoy taking care of your children, and I'm getting more sewing jobs all the time. Things are *gut*."

"That still doesn't answer the question."

"I know." She sighed before turning to face him. "Promise you won't laugh?"

"Promise."

"The reason I haven't tried to have a serious relationship is because…" She paused. "I'm scared."

"You, Miss Matchmaker? Scared?" He chuckled, then stopped himself instantly when he saw her disappointed expression. "Hannah, I'm sorry. That was rude of me. You're serious, aren't you?"

"I am." She tilted her head. "But I understand it must sound silly. Here I am pushing you and others into love, and I'm so afraid of it. But I've lost so many people I've loved. My mother. Father. Sister. Brother. Friends. Lily. Even when I saw David the other day it reminded me that I'd lost the Keim family, too. Noah is gone. Rachel is lost to me. And David and I were never very close, and still aren't."

Her answer stunned him. He thought she was going to say her reluctance to find love was because she'd been hurt in a relationship. Because he'd always wondered what had gone wrong with that love of hers while she was away in Indiana. The one that David declared to him without hesitation would soon be her *mann*.

At that time, hearing about her relationship with someone else had certainly hurt him. Because right before she left to take care of her aunt, he'd hoped to have a chance to talk, to see where they stood with one another. But she seemed so upset about her sick aunt, it didn't seem like the right time to ask. And then, the right time never came.

He was working up the nerve to ask about her old beau, until he noticed tears trickling down her cheeks.

"Hannah, forgive me." He took her hand into his. "I shouldn't have pressed you."

"*Nee*, it's not that." She sniffed. "Here I am feeling sorry for myself, and you've lost people, too—most of all, your *fraa*, the mother of your children." She gazed into his eyes. "I'm so glad *Gott* has filled your heart with your *kinner*, Jake."

Her compassion touched him to his core. Hannah could never think of herself too long. She was always caring for others.

"*Jah, Gott* has done that, Hannah." He squeezed her hand, rubbing his thumb gently over hers. "I thank Him for my children every day, and pray He keeps them safe." He paused, feeling torn. He wanted to say so much more but wasn't sure if he should. Finally, he couldn't contain himself.

"But I also have you, Hannah. We have each other. With everything that's happened in our lives, here we are together. I'm grateful for that. *Verra* thankful for you." He didn't mean to sound so serious, but the words spilled from his heart.

Fortunately, she didn't draw back from his earnestness. Instead, she chose to lighten the moment.

"*Jah*, I suppose we'll always be friends as long as I promise not to talk too much," she teased.

He laughed. "I still remember the time in seventh grade when you weren't talking to me at all."

"What?" Her head jerked back. "I have no idea what you're talking about."

But he could tell, by the exaggerated way she narrowed her eyes and then avoided his gaze, that she very well recalled the week that her silent treatment had been so rough on him.

"Ah, yes, you do."

"I know." She offered an apologetic smile. "I think it was my strange way of getting your attention."

"And it worked. I tried hard to find a way to make you laugh or speak to me, until one day I finally figured it out."

"*Jah*, you fell to the ground right in front of me, and I had to ask if you were okay." She chuckled. "I didn't know you'd fallen on purpose till you looked up with a big grin on your face."

"I knew you well, Hannah. And I still do."

"You really do, Jake." Her voice was soft. "And I know you, too."

They were quick to look away from each other. Standing in hushed silence, they gazed into the moonlit sky.

"It's a nice night, isn't it?"

In his heart, he meant more than the countless stars and the crisp white of the moon.

"It…it is," she agreed, her voice suddenly quivering. He looked over to see her shivering.

"You're cold." His first instinct was to protect her. To push up her collar to ward off the chill. But he stopped himself and dug his hands into his pockets. "You should go inside."

"I guess it is getting late." Her teeth chattered.

"It is. I'll see you tomorrow." He pulled open the screen door, urging her inside.

As he walked back home, he couldn't stop from musing about the evening. At the cozy restaurant with a plateful of delicious food sitting in front of him, he couldn't wait to get away from his date. Yet standing on a decades-old porch, when the hour was late and the air cold, he didn't want the time with Hannah to end.

He would've lingered with her until dawn.

Chapter Eight

"Is anything wrong?" Sitting next to Hannah in the buggy, Jake took his eyes off the road just long enough to glance at her.

"No." She shook her head. "Why?"

"You've been quiet the past few days."

"I have?" She pretended not to know what he was talking about. But it wasn't true, and on a Sunday, too, and on their way to worship.

Gott, *forgive me!* She lifted her eyes toward heaven.

Ever since their conversation on the porch Monday evening, she'd been going out of her way to avoid him. Because she couldn't stop thinking about everything that she'd really wanted to say. Namely, the real reason she had never tried to find love for herself and why she'd turned to matchmaking.

Because while she was good at pairing up the hearts of others, she certainly hadn't been good at judging love for herself. And where Jake was concerned, learning her love for him was all one-sided had been totally devastating, leaving her with a hollow heart and in a very dark place. And if that was how it felt to truly love someone and lose them, she wasn't sure if she could ever face that kind of misery again.

"I'm fine. Honest." She forced a smile. "I've just been *verra* busy."

"If I can help you with anything, let me know," he replied sweetly.

He was trying so hard to be there for her, she felt compelled to let down her barrier. "You mean like teaching you to sew so you can help with my projects?"

"Well…hmm. I think that's something I'll need to pray about this morning." He winked.

For the first time since Monday evening, she laughed. His teasing brought her back to the present, and she realized she needed to do everything she could to keep the past where it needed to be. Behind her.

Besides, she had so much to be thankful for.

Tiny flecks of snowflakes danced in the morning sunlight while staying clear of the roads.

She'd made it through another delightful week with Jake's children, who were chattering happily behind them.

By word of mouth, her client list was growing steadily, and because of Grace's generosity she had plenty of fabric and materials to use.

Aenti Ruth was happy to have Abram take her to worship with the families she knew from town.

And as Jake worked his way up the Hershbergers' driveway, she realized how happy it made her to worship with the circle of families he knew.

Plus, peeking out the buggy, she noticed the new acquaintances she'd made in past weeks were now familiar faces. And she'd had the opportunity to congregate with long-lost friends, too.

"Jake! Can you stop the buggy, please?"

"I was just going to park up there." He pointed to a piece of level ground where buggies were already lined up.

"But I just saw Beth get out of a buggy."

"Yoder or Lapp?"

"Yoder," she said. Though they both very well knew Beth's married name had been King, they'd always known her as Yoder.

"She's back in town?"

"I'm sure it was her. Do you mind letting me out so I can say hello?"

Jake pulled on the reins, stopping the buggy, and she slipped out, running along the edge of the drive toward her friend. Beth didn't see her. Instead, she was bent down, picking up a glove she'd dropped.

"Beth Yoder," Hannah called out.

Beth stood up, a puzzled look on her face. She swiveled her head around until her eyes lit on Hannah. Right away, she broke into a huge grin. "Hannah, is it really you?"

"It's really me." Hannah rushed toward her friend.

Lily had introduced Hannah to Beth when they were young children in school, and the three girls had played together. As teenagers they became even closer, sharing walks and talks, and had gone to plenty of singings and other *youngie* events during their *rumspringa*.

"I can't believe it! It's so good to see you." Hannah threw her arms around Beth.

"It's *wunderbaar* to see you, too. I've been meaning to come by and visit, but they've been keeping me busy at Kauffman's."

"Kauffman's Kitchen? Does that mean—?" Hannah hoped she was hearing right.

"*Jah*, that's another reason I wanted to stop by. I wanted to let you know I've officially moved back to Sugarcreek. I'm staying with *Mamm* and *Daed.*"

"Beth, that's wonderful. I'm so happy for you, for me, for everyone."

Beth's mother, Lovina Yoder, had come into Sew Easy every so often. When she did, she'd give Hannah updates on Beth's life. About a year before Lily and Jake had married, Beth had met a man named Aaron King when she was visiting her cousin in Pinecraft, Florida. They married quickly and happily stayed that way for many years. Until, their life together ended abruptly.

It had been an extremely sad day when Lovina visited the shop to let Hannah know Beth's husband had passed. He'd died from an unsuspected congenital heart condition. Husbandless, childless, Beth stayed with her cousin in Florida for a few years. Hannah could only suppose it had been easier on Beth to mourn in a place where she felt closest to her husband.

It was still so hard to believe someone so young was already widowed.

Just…like… Jake.

Her heart leaped. And an idea suddenly came to mind.

She knew Jake wanted to take a break from matchmaking. But with Beth it would be different. Beth wasn't someone new he'd have to get to know. He already knew her.

Then maybe, just maybe—she shuddered slightly at the thought—if Jake was brave enough to get settled into a new life and love, could she? Could she finally take a step, make a real effort and be courageous enough to find a home for her heart, as well?

"Beth, I'm sure we'll have time to talk after worship, but just in case, would you like to have dinner with me and Jake?"

Her friend's eyes lit up. "I think it would be *wunderbaar*. Let me know what I can bring. Dessert, a main dish, or something."

Hannah giggled at her friend's eagerness. "How about just yourself? I know Jake would love to see you."

"And Caleb Bontrager is in town this week. He's here at worship, in fact. What would you think if I invite him along?" Beth suggested. "The four of us together would be like old times."

Hannah knew the Bontrager and Yoder families had been close-knit friends for years. With Caleb, too, at dinner, Jake would be oblivious to her matching him up with Beth.

"I know Jake would love to see you both."

"I did hear you're helping Jake with his children and living with your aunt in his *dawdi haus*."

Nothing stayed a secret for long in Sugarcreek. "*Jah*, that's true."

"How *is* Jake?" Beth asked, as she glanced across the drive, eyeing him and the children exiting the buggy. "I'm sure he loves having you close by, Hannah. You two were so—"

Hannah held up both hands in protest. "We're friends who are helping each other right now. That's all."

"I think about him often." Everything about Beth's expression turned instantly empathetic, and Hannah detected fine lines around Beth's bluish-green eyes. "And about Lily, too. She was so full of life. Just like my Aaron." She shook her head and sighed. "Oh, goodness, we had some fun times with Lily, didn't we? Do

you remember when she got a hold of that pack of cig-
arettes during our *rumspringa*? She talked the cashier
at the gas station into giving them to us even though
we were underage and didn't have enough money between us to buy them."

That was Lily. She could charm a bird out of the
trees. "How could I forget? I've never been so sick."

"Oh, me, either." Beth chuckled. "But I don't think
Lily even coughed once. She seemed like a natural. A
part of me always thought she was more like some sophisticated city girl." She paused, looking away for a
moment as if conjuring up the scene again.

But Hannah didn't have to work at all to recall that
summer night. It wasn't so much for their smoking that
she remembered that day as for the way Lily had seemed
to be somewhere else entirely—even though she was
sitting on the ground right next to Hannah. Leaning forward with her elbows on her knees, Lily had taken long,
even drags on her cigarette, exhaling perfect swirls of
white smoke into the night air. While staring at the night
sky, she'd spoken about *Englischers* and *Englisch* boys,
as if longing for something more. That had always stuck
in Hannah's mind because it was hard to understand.
She'd thought Lily already had a perfect, blessed life.

"It's all so hard to believe, isn't it?" Beth said wistfully.

"*Jah*, it is. But I'm *verra* glad you're back, Beth."
Hannah sighed, thinking what a blessing it was to have
such a dear friend in her life again. And how she should
never question what *Gott* had around the corner for her.

"It took some time." Beth smiled. "But I'm glad to
be back, too."

"Well, it looks like everyone is starting to assemble." Hannah glanced toward the barn. "I should go help with the *kinner*."

"And I should catch up with my parents," Beth replied. "But I'll see you inside, and after worship, let's ask Jake and Caleb which evening will be best for dinner."

"That sounds *gut*." Hannah nodded.

Midweek, eyeing his reflection in the bedroom mirror, Jake buttoned the top button of his neatly pressed blue shirt. Then unbuttoned it. And buttoned it again, telling himself he was being ridiculous. But he couldn't seem to help it. This dinner with Beth and Caleb seemed mighty important to Hannah.

By the time he'd arrived home from work, Hannah had everything under control. The scent of a freshly baked apple pie, along with the mouthwatering aroma of a roast baking in the oven, had made his stomach growl the moment he'd walked through the back door. The kitchen was all tidied up, and the *kinner* had already been fed and were settled in the extra bedroom upstairs, where Sarah was supervising the twins, coloring and playing games.

Hannah had certainly done everything imaginable to make the evening special for him and their guests. The least he could do was look his most presentable. So—as for his shirt—the top button would stay closed, he decided, giving himself a satisfied nod in the mirror before heading downstairs.

"Don't you look nice," Hannah complimented him the moment he strolled into the kitchen.

He noticed how her hazel eyes seemed to shine with appreciation, making him glad he'd put some extra thought into dressing his best for the occasion. He also couldn't help but notice how graceful and pleased she always appeared to be. As if she felt blessed doing even the simplest of things, like making her way around the table with a pitcher in her hands, filling glasses with water.

"You look mighty nice, too," he said sincerely. "Is that new?" He nodded toward her dress. "I don't think I've seen that violet color on you before."

"You're right, you haven't." She gave him a surprised look. "I came across this fabric when I was making something for the Gentry family."

"It looks *verra gut* on you." He smiled.

"You know, if I'm remembering right," she said, barely glancing his way, "I'm thinking blue is Beth's favorite color."

"Ain't so? I wonder if it's Caleb's favorite, too?" he teased, pleased at the sound of her giggle.

"We'll have to ask him," she joked back.

He veered them away from their silliness. "Can I help you with anything?"

"Nee." Hannah set the pitcher on the counter and smoothed out her apron. "I think everything's set."

"It sure looks like it," he said, glancing around the perfectly cozy, clean kitchen. "And it smells way too *gut* in here." His mouth watered. "I say if our company isn't on time, we dig in and leave them the leftovers," he added, making her chuckle again.

"Jah, well, hopefully they will be on time. Because I'm just waiting for the rolls to finish baking."

The timer went off at the exact moment a knock came at the front door, leaving her to fetch the rolls and him the door. Then Hannah joined him and their guests quickly, and after hugs, handshakes and hellos, the visitors hung up their coats and she swept them all into the kitchen. Jake didn't know how she did it, but she seated them around the table, had them bow their heads for grace, filled their plates and had the conversation going instantly. It was as if she entertained all the time, causing him to marvel at her once more.

"*Danke* for going to all this trouble." Beth looked across the table at him and Hannah. "It's mighty nice to share supper like this."

"It was all Hannah," Jake confessed.

Hannah shrugged. "It's worth it, having the chance to see you both. After all these years, you two don't look a bit different. You still look wise behind those glasses of yours, Caleb, and you still have plenty of wavy brown hair that girls love."

"That's news to me." Caleb chuckled.

"And, Beth, you're still as pretty as a picture, don't you think, Jake?" Hannah turned to him.

Although Beth had blondish brown hair and blue eyes with hints of green, and features far different from Hannah's, both of their looks could certainly catch a man's attention.

"*Gott* has bestowed much beauty on both of you. Isn't that right, Caleb?" Jake asked his friend.

Caleb didn't have a beard to cover the flush of red that ran across his face. "I'd say so." To which the girls giggled.

"Caleb, I know Beth is back to stay, but will you be in Sugarcreek much longer?" Hannah asked.

"Only until tomorrow," Caleb replied. "Then I'll have to head back to Lancaster."

Beth let out a sigh. "This is like a reunion dinner and goodbye dinner all in one."

"I hate to hear that." Hannah held up the bread plate

to see if anyone wanted extra. Jake took a piece. "Jake said you're running a butcher shop up there. You've been in the meat business for a long time, *jah*?"

Even when they were younger, Jake thought Caleb had a bold business sense but was shy around girls. Yet, surprisingly, as soon as Caleb was old enough, he'd set his sights on a girl named Fannie. When her family moved to Pennsylvania, he moved, as well, planning their future together while learning the butcher trade there. Only problem was, Caleb hadn't had the courage to ask Fannie how she felt about him. As it turned out, she hadn't felt the same, but since he'd excelled at his job, he stayed there anyway.

"Since I left in my late teens." Caleb nodded.

"Well, maybe someday you'll come back here. Like Beth has," Hannah chirped.

Beth coughed on a piece of carrot, and she and Caleb both shot a glance at him. Jake couldn't blame them. It was like Hannah had read Caleb's mind.

After worship the Sunday before, Caleb had revealed everything to Jake, telling him how he and Beth had been writing to each other ever since Aaron's passing. At first their correspondence was courteous and innocent like their longtime friendship had always been. But over time, their letters became more personal, then romantic.

Because of that, when the company Caleb was working for had started talking about opening another butcher shop, he offered to set it up in Sugarcreek. That was why he was in town—to look for a storefront.

Beth knew about his plans to open a shop in town, but Caleb was keeping it a secret from his parents, wanting to surprise them. He'd only told Jake, hoping to hire him to build-out whatever shop space he found. What

Beth didn't know and what Caleb had shared with Jake confidentially was that when Caleb finally relocated, he was going to ask Beth to marry him.

Fortunately, Hannah didn't appear to notice their darting looks around the table. "Beth, I told you that Jake is working at Hochstetler's Lumberyard, didn't I?" Hannah asked. "So he's not too far from Kauffman's."

"You did tell me." Beth nodded.

"Oh, and he's so good at his job, too." Hannah leaned in. "They're talking about promoting him already."

"Is that so?" Beth smiled at him.

"Congratulations," Caleb said before lifting a forkful of potatoes to his mouth.

"It's only because I've worked in that same position before," Jake explained, as he carved the last of his meat into two bite-size pieces. "It happens to be good timing since another fellow is moving away."

"I'm sure that's not the only reason," Hannah broke in, appearing intent on speaking on his behalf, again. Especially to Beth. "It's also because they know he's good at whatever job he does, and he's mighty *gut* with people." She winked at her girlfriend. "Remember how Jake used to get the younger boys to help him with his chores, telling them they'd grow up to be big and strong like him?"

Beth covered her mouth with her napkin and laughed. "Do I ever!"

"I wish that had worked for me," Caleb jested.

"You all are embarrassing me." Jake chuckled, shaking his head.

But being embarrassed was the last thing on his mind as he suddenly realized that Hannah was up to her matchmaking antics again. Even though she'd agreed on him taking a break.

Otherwise, would she have ever mentioned blue being Beth's favorite color, Kauffman's being so close to Hochstetler's, all about his promotion, and even be talking about his physique?

Oh, but he could be just as sneaky and use her ploys to his advantage.

As Beth and Caleb pushed back their plates, complimenting Hannah on the meal, he did the same.

"And wait till you taste Hannah's apple pie," he remarked. "She makes the tastiest pies in the county, maybe even all of Ohio."

He was sure his praise would make her blush, but instead he noticed Hannah wasn't even listening. He followed her eyes, looking toward the staircase. Sarah was walking toward them, clutching her hands together tightly, her eyes wide with fright.

"*Dochder*, are you all right?"

Creeping up to the table, she stood on tiptoes beside his chair, bending close to whisper in his ear.

"That's not polite, Sarah." He shook a warning finger. "If there's something you need to say, let's— "

He started to scoot back his chair and guide her into the other room to talk privately. Before he could, tears filled her eyes.

"It's Eli, *Daed*. I tried to watch him best I could. I did!" She wrung her little hands. "But he—" She choked on a sob.

He leaped up, grabbing a hold of her shoulders. "He what, Sarah?"

"It's pills," she cried, taking a plastic bag from her pocket. "He found more pills."

Chapter Nine

Panic jolted through Hannah like a bolt of lightning.

The pills Jake snatched from Sarah's hand were the same color and shape as the ones she'd seen by Lily's bedside years earlier. No wonder that he raced up the stairs, two steps at a time.

Meanwhile, Sarah was standing, crying her little heart out. Beth and Caleb were both staring at her, wide-eyed and speechless. Exactly how she felt.

Tossing her napkin on the table, she jumped out of her chair and rushed to Sarah. Kneeling, she hugged the weeping *kind* tightly in her arms.

"It's going to be okay. You didn't do anything wrong," she said, as soothingly as she could manage, though her jaw felt clenched with fright. Looking into Sarah's fear-filled eyes, she tried to wipe away the girl's tears with a trembling hand. "Your *daed* will take care of everything. You'll see."

As she said the words out loud, those same words became a silent prayer, begging *Gott* with every part of her being for His help and presence where Eli was concerned. "But you need to go sit with Beth, child."

Thankfully, Beth was already at their sides. Still, Sarah clutched onto Hannah's waist, not about to let her go. "I want to be with you, Hannah. Please."

Hannah reached down, gently removing Sarah's hands and taking them into her own. "Sarah, it's important I help your *daed* right now."

With that said, Beth touched Sarah's shoulder, rubbing it ever so softly. "Let me get you something to drink, sweet *maedel*. Maybe some cocoa on this chilly night? I'm sure Hannah has some in the pantry. It was always her favorite."

While Beth led Sarah to a seat at the table, Hannah dashed up the stairs, rushing to a corner of the small room, where Clara stood bawling.

"*Daed*'s scaring me. He's scaring me," she cried, and Hannah knew why.

Standing in the middle of the room, Jake was roaring like a wild animal on a rampage as he hovered over a wailing Eli. Obviously, his ear-shattering rant was due to his own fear and desperation. But there was no way to explain that to a four-year-old.

Leaning over, she gently lifted the young girl's chin, looking into her eyes. "Guess what? My friend Beth is downstairs making hot chocolate for Sarah. Can you stop crying and go get some?"

Clara quieted some at her kindly touch. The mention of hot chocolate helped, too.

"With marshmallows?" Clara sniffled.

"They're in the pantry," Hannah assured her.

With Clara going downstairs and both girls in Beth's care, Hannah felt like she could finally go to Jake's aid.

Yet she was at a loss, not knowing what to do as he stood, shaking the bag of pills, frantically.

"Eli, tell me! Tell me now!" Jake demanded. "How many did you take?"

Clearly, the children weren't used to their father behaving like a monster gone mad. Just like his sister, Eli was wide-eyed and terrified. As he gasped and sobbed uncontrollably, Hannah didn't think he could speak even if he wanted to.

Finally, Jake seemed to realize the same thing. Attempting to calm himself, he tossed the pill bag onto the dresser, rubbing his hand over his face. Then he took in a deep breath and let it out slowly.

"All right, *sohn*. Let's both settle down," he said, his voice low and suppressed as he got on his knees. "Just say the number, Eli. How many pills did you swallow?"

Once more Eli shook his head, and Jake's panic suddenly flared again like a lit match thrown on gasoline.

"Answer me." Jake grabbed his son by his arms, shaking him. "You've got to answer me," he shouted.

No doubt Jake's own fear was scaring Eli into his mute state. Knowing time was of the essence in this situation, she realized they needed another approach.

Kneeling alongside Jake, she tried to keep her voice from quaking as she spoke as calmly to the child as she could manage. "Eli, we know you're a smart boy. Why, you can count way past ten." She reached out and pushed back a lock of fallen hair from his forehead. "Can you tell us how many pills you took? Was it one? Two? Three?"

Again, Eli shook his head through his tears.

"Oh, dear *Gott* in heaven, help us!" Jake yelled. "Are you saying more than three? We're leaving for the hospital right now. Hannah, get his coat."

"Nee!" Eli screamed. *"Nee!"*

Working to wrench his arms from his father's grasp, Eli cried even harder. Managing to free one hand, he raised it for them both to see. With his thumb and index finger, he made a zero.

"None? You didn't eat any?" Jake let out an audible breath. "You're sure? *Gott* wants you to be truthful. Please don't lie, *sohn*."

"*Jah*, Eli. Sometimes we get fooled," she interjected. "You may have thought the pills were candy. But pills can be dangerous if they're not medicine you need to be taking. I know your *daed's* not going to be mad if you swallowed some, Eli." She tried to reassure him. "Your *daed* loves you no matter what."

"I...didn't...swallow any." Eli's little chest heaved. And heaved some more, as he desperately tried to catch his breath.

"You're sure?" Jake tilted his head, his voice stern but quieter now.

Eli nodded, swiping at his cheeks.

Instantly, Hannah's eyes filled with tears of relief. Even more tears streamed down her cheeks as she watched Jake take his son into his arms.

"*Danke*, dear *Gott. Danke* for keeping my boy safe." His voice quaked as he rocked Eli back and forth.

After a few moments, he glanced at her. She patted his shoulder, as thankful as he was that their scare was over. But still she sat back on her knees and couldn't help but be puzzled. "I'm so sorry, Jake."

"For what?"

"Maybe I didn't clean as well as I should have. How did I miss those pills?" She glanced at the bag on the dresser, sick to her stomach at the thought of what might have happened. "Eli, where did you find that bag?" She needed to know.

After all they'd been through, Eli suddenly seemed eager to explain. "The girls were playing house, and I was the *daed*. And I saw that thing wasn't in all the way." He pointed to a finial topping the metal bedpost. "I took it off and I was going to fix it like you fix things, *Daed*."

At that, Jake got to his feet, striding over to the bed. "You took off this finial?"

"Uh-huh, and the bag was inside. I pretended I was bringing home food and gave it to Sarah to cook for us."

Jake unscrewed the finial and sure enough, he pulled off a piece of tape from the inside of the bedpost that had held the bag of pills in question. It was a bed he and Lily had had during their marriage. He'd moved it from the Keim house.

"Did you take off any other finial?" Jake's concern seemed to well up all over again.

"Nee." Eli shook his head rigorously.

She watched as Jake instantly began to move around the bed, unscrewing the rest of the finials. "Dear *Gott*, help me. I thought I found all the pills."

All the pills? He'd spoken the words under his breath, but still she'd heard them.

"Hannah." Eli tugged on her apron, pulling her attention toward him again. "I'm thirsty." He swiped at his runny nose.

"Let me guess. You want some hot chocolate, too?"

His response was a grin that lifted her spirits as much as it lifted his lips.

"Jake, I'm going to take Eli downstairs for some cocoa, *oll recht*?"

Jake stood up from looking under the mattress and

nodded. "Of course. Will you tell Beth and Caleb I'm sorry to cut the evening short? And I'm sorry for all your hard work, Hannah. I just don't think I can—"

She held up her hand. "Jake, it's fine. I understand." At least that part she understood. "Beth and Caleb will, too. Things don't always go as planned."

"Jah." He sucked in a breath and let out a heavy sigh. "Things don't always go as planned."

His eyes steadied on hers, and with that look she thought there was more he might have to say. But instead, he turned from her abruptly.

As she and Eli made their way down the stairs, she could hear Jake's footsteps overhead along with the clamor of drawers and closets opening and closing, as he continued his search.

After putting the children to bed, Jake descended the steps, not sure if he'd find Hannah still there. Since there was no sign of movement in the house, he assumed she must've headed back to the *dawdi haus* after cleaning up the kitchen. All was silent except for the fleeting crackle of burning firewood. All was dark, as well, except for the light coming from the fireplace and the glow of the moon filtering through the window.

He certainly couldn't blame Hannah for taking off. It had been a strange evening, indeed, he thought as he went over to poke the fire into submission. It had started well and ended well, but in between—

"Whose pills were those, Jake?"

Startled by the sound of Hannah's voice, he turned to see her sitting in the armchair, staring into the fire. Her cloak already on, she looked as if she'd intended to leave much earlier but hadn't.

"Please be honest with me," she pleaded.

Caught off guard, he collapsed into the chair alongside hers. More than anything, he wanted to be open and honest with her, but he couldn't find his voice.

"They were Lily's, weren't they?"

He couldn't make himself say the words. But then, he knew his silence would tell the truth on its own.

"I remember the days, weeks, before Lily passed," Hannah said softly. "I felt so distant from her. She felt distant from me. But I have to say, over the years of your marriage, it wasn't a feeling that was new. I mean…" Hannah paused to chuckle lightly. "Goodness, we were mighty close, the three of us, when we were younger. Silly me, I thought it'd be that way forever. Or at least that's what I'd hoped." She sighed. "But then your marriage changed things. And it took some time—" her voice lifted "—but I finally accepted that things had to change. You were raising a family, and I was helping *Aenti* Ruth and working at the shop…" Her voice trailed off.

He tried to think of how to reply, but then she spoke again.

"But I have to say, when you two first got married, there were times when Lily and I could still laugh, and she'd tell me things. But as the years went by… I don't know. It hurt me how things changed between us. She'd always been like a sister to me. But it almost felt like she wanted me to stay away more. So I did."

When it came to Lily, he knew exactly what Hannah was saying. From the time he and Lily had married, it seemed she started to pull back from him—from everything. Not that it was right, but then he'd concerned himself mostly with his work and the children.

"When she fell off the horse, after her shoulder surgery, they gave her painkillers," he said quietly. It was his turn to stare into the flickering flames. "You'd asked me about them, remember?"

He could feel Hannah glance over at him. "Of course I remember. I brought over soup when she was recovering—and, well, it doesn't matter what I brought. I saw the bottle and when I asked her about them, she said they were nothing. That they'd only given her a few to take. And when I asked you, you said the same. But I was worried because she—I don't know, she seemed strange."

"Her shoulder healed," he told her, "but her addiction to those pills devoured her."

"But why didn't you tell me?"

He held up his hands, feeling defeated all over again. "She kept promising she'd stop. And for the *kinner*'s sake, I begged her to. But then I'd find more pills hidden in all kinds of places. And money missing, too. She'd hire an *Englisch* driver to take her to some *doktah* in a rural area not too far from here who'd sell her more."

"Is that how she died, Jake? From the pills?"

Right before Lily passed, she'd sworn that she was finished with the pills. For the sake of their children, he'd chosen to believe her. But the night he was startled by a thumping noise and woke up to find her missing from their bed, he knew for sure she hadn't been honest with him or herself. He found her contorted body lying at the bottom of the basement stairs, the life breath gone out of her. Everyone assumed the fall was a freak accident. Even though he discovered a stash of pills hidden in a box underneath the same steps she'd fallen from, for his children's sakes and their dead *mamm*'s reputation, he never said otherwise. Only her brother, David, knew the truth about what happened and wanted it kept quiet, as well. Not having heard from David for a long time, Jake was sure he blamed him.

"She died from the fall."

"Of course. But because of the pills?"

"She wouldn't want anyone to know that."

Hannah's head jerked. She was silent for a moment. "You know, Lily was the world to me. You both were." Her voice quivered. "But now I know what role I played. I was just 'anyone.'"

"Hannah," he huffed out her name. "You know that's not true."

How could she even think that when only days ago he'd told her how much she meant to him?

"Do I, Jake?"

Not giving him a chance to protest, she jumped up and dashed for the door, shutting it tightly behind her.

Chapter Ten

Oblivious to the never-ending bustle of the lumber-yard, Jake fed another piece of white oak into the thickness planer, his mind still reeling from the dreadful events of the night before.

Hard as he tried, he couldn't suppress the bile rising in the back of his throat every time he thought about Eli's find and the harm that could've been done to him—and to his girls. Nor could he shake the anxious feelings reverberating through him as they had when Lily was still alive. Back when her addiction had taken over their home and lives. Back when he'd had to warn Sarah, who was barely four then, about the pills she'd discovered in Lily's apron pocket while trying to help him make soup for her listless *mamm*.

And now, to think what had happened the evening before could change his and Hannah's relationship tore at his very soul. To know that she was hurting…

Pain squeezed his heart as he recalled how they'd hardly glanced at one another when he'd left for work in the morning. As they'd crossed paths at the back door, they'd barely uttered a word.

Tormented, he grabbed another hardwood board and forcefully tossed it up on the machine. In doing so, he wished with all his might that life could be like a piece of wood that he could easily guide through a planer.

After all, hardwood comes from an oak tree that endures all kinds of conditions and a multitude of seasons, just like us, he mused. *Its trunk and limbs become marked and bruised. Yet in the end, the planer does its job. The wood gets sized just right, and each nick and blemish is stripped away.*

Engrossed in his thoughts, he lifted the finished board as it exited the planer, and rubbed his hand over its smooth, unmarred surface. As he did, he was reminded once again why he'd moved himself and his children. He'd hoped he would be rid of anything that tarnished his children's lives. He wished for a new future, a fresh start.

Yet, even being back in the house he'd grown up in, a place where he'd experienced happy memories, sometimes he couldn't sleep. He'd lay awake wrestling with his conscience, feeling remorseful about the way he'd handled Lily's problems.

Then Hannah had come along, and her presence had made such a difference in their lives. Truly, it felt as if everything around him had been cleansed, renewed. The *kinner*'s spirits were lightened. And the friendship the two of them shared seemed stronger than ever.

Until last night.

A tap on his shoulder jarred his thoughts. Turning, he saw Saul Hammond. Shifting his goggles to the top of his head, he pulled out his earplugs.

"Hey, Saul."

"You're whipping through those boards mighty

quickly, Jake. Be careful," his coworker warned. "You don't want to scrape your hands or wrench your shoulder."

"I'm *gut*," he said, barely glancing Saul's way. He started to turn back to his work when Rosie suddenly appeared at their sides.

"You both need to join Seth in the break room," she said tersely without any of her usual banter or smiles.

"Is everything okay?"

"Head there now, please." She didn't seem able to look them in the eye. "I need to go tell the others," she added glumly.

He and Saul traded puzzled looks and then did as they were told. With so much on his mind about the previous evening and previous years, he couldn't imagine what Seth might say that could make him feel any worse.

Seth Hochstetler stood in the front area of the break room, looking like the leader Jake knew him to be. But a rare, painful expression was etched on his boss's face. No doubt, something was taking a toll on him.

"Good morning, ladies. Men." Seth nodded. "My news will, um…will only take a few minutes." He hesitated, before speaking in a low tone. "Some of you may have noticed that we're missing someone on the floor today. Tom McDaniel isn't here, and there is good reason for that."

Pausing to clear his throat, Seth continued, "Last night around midnight a fire broke out at the McDaniel home while they were all sleeping. Sadly, their house is pretty much gone. But more important, one of their children—Tom's seven-year-old daughter—was severely burned," he informed the group.

There were gasps all around the room. Jake was instantly sickened by the news. Tom's daughter, Katie, was close in age to his Sarah. From the stories he and Tom had shared, the two girls were alike in many ways. He couldn't imagine the horror Tom and his wife were going through.

"Katie? Is she *oll recht*?" he blurted.

"Katie was immediately airlifted to a hospital which is renowned for their burn care," Seth replied. "From all accounts, it sounds like she will be *gut*, given time. But, of course, the family has asked that we keep her in our prayers. They also asked for prayers for their other little ones. Their two boys weren't burned but are traumatized by the event and very frightened for their sister."

"Seth, would it be all right if we pray right now?" someone in the front row asked.

"Absolutely."

All around the room, the men and women bowed their heads, silently praying for the McDaniels. It was minutes before heads were raised and Seth began to share more.

"As I said, there was extensive damage to the family's home and their belongings. Tom did mention that his mother-in-law is widowed and was all set to sell her home and move into a nursing home. So, for right now they have a place to stay and may work out something with her. Regardless, I think you'd all agree that our community emergency fund should go to the McDaniel family at this time."

Everyone in the room murmured their agreement.

Seth nodded. "All right. Good. Rosie will personally deliver a check to Tom's family. Also, just to let you know, given the fact that Tom will be losing hours at work, we plan to help him out. Our company will compensate him the best we can. Our hope is that we can keep his position open for him. But, of course, we know that's asking a lot..." Seth looked around the room.

"We're happy to do the extra work until Tom gets back," one of the older men spoke up.

Heads nodded as unwavering shouts of *yes* and *jah* filled the room.

"I thought you all would feel that way," Seth said. "We're *verra* blessed to have such a great group of people here at Hochstetler's. *Danke.* Thank you all very much."

Rosie took the opportunity to stride up front alongside Seth.

"One last thing." She held up her index finger. "Just so you know, I'll be placing extra collection bins for Tom's family in the corner by our other bins." She pointed across the break room. "As always, Seth's mother, Mrs. Hochstetler, will be emptying the bins weekly and delivering your gift cards, small household items, clothes or whatever you'd like to donate."

As Jake went back to his spot at the planer, his legs leaden and his heart heavy, he made a pledge to himself that he'd be helping to fill those bins. Even so, that gesture of kindness wasn't enough to override the shame he felt.

He chided himself for being so lost in his own concerns that he hadn't noticed his friend missing today. Not only that, he'd also been too wrapped up to stop and thank *Gott* for all the good he did have in his life. Starting with the Lord's unshakable, undeniable love.

It might've been years ago, but it felt like only yesterday that he had begged Lily to stop taking the pills.

When she wouldn't, not knowing what to do and wanting the situation to go away, as wrong as it was, he'd scolded her. He'd told her she needed to pray harder. He'd said *Gott* couldn't hear her because she wasn't praying hard enough to be free of the disease that had overtaken her.

Now he needed to take his own advice. He needed to pray harder. Not just for his own life, but also for the others *Gott* had placed in his life.

Hannah was about ready to take the *kinner* over to the main house and start dinner when Jake walked into the *dawdi haus*. His face showed every bit of strain and sadness that Hannah imagined it would. As if the prior evening hadn't been enough, he had to be agonizing about his friend's tragedy, and that broke her heart for him. When Beth had stopped by after her shift to let Hannah know about the McDaniels, she'd been filled with worry for all of Tom's family, too.

Barely glancing her way, Jake immediately strode over to Sarah, who had been playing school with the twins. Removing the blackboard from her grasp, he knelt and pulled Sarah toward him. He hugged her tight.

When the twins saw how their father was acting, Hannah knew they had to be confused. This wasn't the playful dad they knew. Jake beckoned Clara and Eli to come close. He opened his arms and brought them into his embrace, nestling his head against theirs.

After hearing about Katie's injuries, when her eyes fell on any one of the children, she'd wanted to hold them close, too. She'd felt so overwhelmed with gratitude, knowing they were well and safe.

Still, she had to turn away and pretend not to notice

Jake's intense display of love. Otherwise, she'd turn into a sobbing mess. Even *Aenti* Ruth, who was typically focused on her embroidery, was looking out the window, dabbing at her eyes.

As Jake pulled away from his children, he tugged a white bag from his jacket pocket.

"I know it's close to suppertime." He gave Hannah an apologetic glance. "But I brought home a treat for the *kinner*."

"Chocolate-covered pretzels!" Eli shouted and the girls were all smiles.

"It's fine by me," Hannah said.

As the children eagerly settled in at the table with their pretzels, Jake came over and touched her arm. "Can I talk to you, please? Outside?"

She nodded, and noticed Jake looked as relieved as she felt. Knowing her aunt would keep a watch on the children, she grabbed at the nearest warm thing, a thick shawl draped across a chair. Wrapping it around her shoulders, she followed Jake out to the porch.

The cold air instantly ran a shiver up her spine. Even so, she was glad to finally have a chance for them to talk. The day had felt endless as she'd waited for Jake to come home.

"Any more news about Katie?" she asked.

Not only had she heard Jake talk about the McDaniel family often, but she'd also met Tom and Ashley a few times when all the children had gotten together to play kickball before the weather turned colder.

"Nothing since I left work." He drew in a long breath and let out an equally long sigh.

"I'm so sorry to hear about them. It's awful."

"I know. All day long, I couldn't stop thinking about things. There's a lot I want to explain, Hannah."

"Jake." She laid a hand on his forearm. "It's not important."

He laid a hand over hers, intently staring into her eyes. "*Jah*, it is, Hannah. I need you to know that when all that was going on with Lily, I felt torn. I was trying not to betray her wish to keep things private. At the same time, I wanted to protect you from what was happening. I kept hoping that everything was going to work out and that you'd never have to know." He squeezed her hand. "But how I handled things was wrong in so many ways. Because of what I did—or more like didn't do—everyone got hurt, including you. I can't tell you how sorry I am, and—" His voice cracked. "Hannah, there can't be a wall between us. I can't lose you, too."

"You won't, Jake. You can't." She gently caressed his cheek. "Like it or not, you're stuck with me. Things changed years ago between the three of us, and I needed to accept that, and I have." She meant every word. "Although I have to tell you, last night…" She hesitated, not sure how much she wanted to share.

"Last night what?"

She shrugged. "I kind of felt orphaned all over again when I heard things about my two best friends in the world that I never knew. It made me feel the same loneliness I had when I lost my parents. And like maybe the relationships we had weren't everything I thought they were."

"I hate to think of you feeling that way."

"I know, and I don't anymore. I mean, it took some praying, crying, and lots of feeling sorry for myself.

But then I realized that wasn't the only thing that was making me hurt so much."

"I think I can guess… You were also hurting because you hadn't been there to help Lily. Trust me, Hannah. I have felt like that way more times than you know."

"But, Jake, you know what I realized?" She forced confidence into her voice. "I reminded myself that Lily was strong-willed, with a mind of her own. There wasn't much telling her what to do or how to do it, was there? Not about anything." Even though sadness gripped her heart as she thought of Lily being gone, a loving smile touched her lips when she thought of how she lived. "Even her *daed* shook his head at her time after time, and Lily and her *mamm* bickered constantly."

"*Jah*, they did clash often," Jake agreed.

"And pretty much always about nothing."

Jake chuckled. "I'm sure you're right."

"Lily's outgoing, impulsive personality drew some people to her, but it's also what hurt her and those around her. It had to be hard on you, Jake, living with lies. That's not you and deep down it wasn't Lily, either."

His jaw tightened in a flash. "She suffered with guilt, that's for sure."

"Guilt about the pills?"

"And other things," he said softly. "Even our decision to get—"

Hannah held up her hand, stopping him. "You know what? I don't want to know. Whatever went on in your marriage was between you two. It wasn't any of my business then and shouldn't be my business now. I just want to remember the three of us the way we were." She sighed. "That was a *verra* happy time in my life."

"Mine, too." He nodded, yet still looked troubled. "So, Hannah, will you forgive me?"

She felt humbled by his concern. "*Jah*, if you'll forgive me. I shouldn't have shunned you this morning. I felt bad the minute you stepped out the door."

"But, Hannah, you—"

She placed a finger on his lips. "No, let me finish. When I saw your *kinner* this morning, I felt even worse. It was then I realized how shallow I'd been. More important than anything I'm feeling are your children's feelings. Their well-being is crucial. By *Gott*'s grace they seem fine, and you've done a good job, Jake, of keeping them safe and happy. They never have to know about their *mamm*'s demons." She straightened herself, feeling stronger. "They only need to remember the way she loved them. And I promise, I'm going to do everything I can to make sure they remember her. We're going to make big, fluffy desserts and plant wildflowers in the spring, the kind Lily loved. And, *Gott* willing, I hope to find you a match who will love them like her own."

Jake stood staring at her, making her wonder if she'd said too much. But she had to. It was everything that was on her heart.

Suddenly, he took both of her hands into his gentle clasp. "*Danke*, Hannah."

"For what?"

"For being you."

Hearing his sweet words, she felt her cheeks heat. Quickly she tried to change the tone of the serious moment. "Just remember you said that when a group of women shows up here on Saturday."

"I already know what you're going to say." He grinned.

"When I stopped at the grocery store for the pretzels, I ran into Anna Graber. I'd forgotten her husband works with Ashley, so she knew all about the McDaniels' situation. She said you ladies are planning to cook and bake lots of things for Ashley to store away."

"*Jah*, Anna will be coming to help me and *Aenti* Ruth, along with Beth and Beth's mom, since the McDaniels' house was close to them. Marianne and Catherine from the bakery know the McDaniels, too, and they'll be helping out."

He winced.

"Don't you worry." She chuckled, patting him on the shoulder. "Catherine won't bother you. I promise. I took care of that. I mentioned to Anna that Catherine would be a *gut* match for Thomas Lehman. So now they're courting."

"You're right. I can see that. Those two can talk each other silly."

"Exactly." She nodded primly. "So we women will be cooking and baking, and it's perfect since we have two kitchens."

"Following in your footsteps, before I left town, I got a group of men to come over, too," he told her. "So many men that we'll probably be tripping over one another. We're planning to make bunk beds for the boys. It's something Tom had been talking about a while ago."

"And for Katie?"

"A bed, as well. A lot of their furniture was burnt up in the fire. And I think new beds may be comforting." He scratched at his beard. "I'm not certain of the design for Katie's yet, but it needs to be very special for Tom's princess. That's what he always calls her."

"I'm sure you talented men will come up with plenty of *wunderbaar* ideas."

"We hope to."

He paused, and even though the sun was setting, and a cool wind began to swirl around them, the way he gazed into her eyes warmed every part of her heart.

"Thank you, Hannah," he said, sounding just as sincere and heartfelt as he did before.

"For what?"

It took him a moment to answer.

"For helping me find my way. For helping me get back to being me again."

"Ah." She quirked a teasing brow, her best defense in slowing her rapidly beating heart. "And that's a *gut* thing?"

He pretended to be perturbed. "You know, you're not getting any pretzels if you don't start behaving yourself."

She waved a hand. "The *kinner* have probably eaten them all anyway."

They both glanced in the window, and she was sure he was as buoyed as she was to see his children enjoying themselves.

"True." He laughed. "Very true."

Chapter Eleven

Hannah stopped stirring another pot of beef stew being made for the McDaniel family just long enough to glance out the fog-streaked kitchen window.

"I feel bad being in this cozy kitchen while the men are working in Jake's cold barn," she said.

"I wouldn't worry." Anna chuckled. "I'm sure they're passing plenty of hot air between them, figuring out who's doing what to get those beds made."

"Thankfully, we're as organized in your kitchen as we are at Kauffman's." Beth held up a chef's knife triumphantly.

It was true, Hannah thought. The three of them were like a well-oiled machine, easily working together to make potpies, soups and stews for Ashley to freeze. They'd also already planned the supper they'd be cooking later to feed the volunteers at day's end.

"And it's a huge blessing the *kinner* are getting along just fine." Anna glanced into the other room, wiping her hands on the snug-fitting apron tied around her very pregnant belly. "I think that's mostly because Sarah has such a sweet way with them."

Before everyone arrived, Hannah hadn't been surprised when Sarah asked for help to make paper hearts, flowers and bears that she could have the twins and Anna's children color. Sarah thought it would make Katie and her brothers happy to receive cards from them.

"I think she's used to being in charge," Hannah told her.

The very thought saddened her some. More than once, Jake had also shared his dismay about how Sarah continually tried to step up and help.

If her dream had to be taken from her, Hannah was at least glad *Gott* had put her in a place where she might be doing another kind of patchwork and mending. She tried to do all she could to make sure Sarah got attention from her and Jake, as well. That was why she attended to the everyday things so Jake could have more time to spend with his children.

"Maybe I'll hire her to watch my *kinner*." Anna sounded excited about the prospect.

"I don't know, Anna," Hannah spoke up. "Sarah's too young to be alone with your *kinds*."

"No doubt about that," Anna agreed. "But if I had Sarah there in the house with me, I could be free to do something else. You know, something fun—like laundry."

They all laughed at that.

"I guess in some ways I'm fortunate," Beth said as she passed a cupful of chopped onion to Anna. "By the time I have any *kinner*, Sarah will probably be old enough to tend to a baby. Or even old enough to have one of her own." She scowled at her own statement.

"Oh, now, Beth, it may be sooner than you think," Hannah assured her.

"I'm praying that's true." Beth sighed longingly. "*Gott* does have a funny way of doing things. Like having a person whom you've known all your life come into your life again and seem brand-new to you."

Her words caught Hannah off guard. Not that they should have. Hadn't that been her plan? For old friends like Beth and Jake to discover a new love between them? Still, the idea that it was happening for real tugged at her heart in a strange way. She swallowed hard, trying to think of a reply when Anna spoke up, talking about something altogether different.

"I'm glad we're doing this," Anna said, holding an unbaked potpie in both hands. Hannah scooted out of the way so Anna could slide the glass dish into the oven. "I can't stop thinking what it would be like if the same thing happened to one of our *kinner* like it did with Katie."

"I feel so sorry for them," Beth said softly. "They're such a sweet family."

Fortunately, they had learned that Katie would be all right. Eventually. The worst burn she'd received was on her arm. It had been so severe it required a full thickness graft and at least a two-week stay in the hospital along with more recovery time at home.

"Speaking of sweet," Hannah said, "it's kind of Catherine to head up the baking projects in the *dawdi haus*."

"They've got a good group over there," Anna replied. "Catherine, Marianne, your *aenti* Ruth and Beth's mom. And Abram, too."

"He's a funny man." Beth chuckled.

"You mean funny as in odd," Hannah stated.

Beth's brows furrowed. "*Nee*, I mean funny. I've only seen him a few times at Kauffman's, but every time I do, he makes me laugh. Like the other day when he was there with your *aenti*—"

"They were together at Kauffman's? I didn't know they went out to eat," Hannah interrupted. "I thought they were running errands."

"Maybe their errand was to have a romantic breakfast." Anna batted her lashes.

"Anyway," Beth continued, "he told a joke that had me smiling all day."

"Abram? Abram Mast did this?" Hannah couldn't believe her ears.

"Would your *aenti* have been with any other Abram?"

Beth and Anna looked at her as if she was the odd one.

"Well, no. It's just…he hardly ever speaks…to me." She frowned.

Had she done something wrong to quiet Abram? She couldn't imagine what. But then, she also couldn't imagine what her outgoing aunt had in common with him. And every time Hannah mentioned inviting someone like Joseph Beiler to dinner, her aunt would say she wasn't in the mood for company.

Staring out the window again, she wondered why she felt so unsettled. First, by the success of the match she did make, and then by the one she hadn't.

"Hannah?" Anna's voice sounded in her ears.

"Hmm?"

Her friend nodded toward the pot of stew, which had gone from simmering to boiling.

"Oh!" Hannah quickly turned down the heat. She needed to concentrate on what was right in front of her, and the things she could control.

Jake hesitated knocking on the *dawdi haus* door. It seemed like he was going courting or something. Although it was closer to bedtime than a respectable going-out time. Still, he couldn't wait to share his excitement.

Hannah opened the door tentatively. "Jake." She clutched her robe closed. "Is everything *oll recht*?"

"I just got the *kinner* to bed. They fell asleep quickly, but I'm all wound up," he admitted. "I thought we could take a walk, but I'm guessing you must be tired, too, ain't so? You worked hard today, cooking, cleaning, serving."

Hannah grinned. "When you say it like that, I should be more tired. But I haven't been able to settle down. I can't seem to turn off my mind."

He looked past her toward the sewing corner. "You lost a day of sewing, didn't you?"

"Juh." She let out a sigh. "I sewed for about an hour after everyone left, then told myself I needed to rest. But that hasn't happened. A walk might be a good distraction."

Elated, he grabbed her cloak from the rack, holding it open for her. She turned and he slipped it around her shoulders. "Where are we headed?" she asked.

"To the barn."

She laughed. "Oh, not a long walk, then."

"I'm sorry to say no," he apologized. "Honestly, I haven't been able to turn off my brain, either. I'm still excited about the work the men got done today. With everyone here past suppertime, then bedding down the children while you cleaned up, I never got to show you the beds we made."

The walk was quick as they strolled to the barn, the crescent moon lighting their way. Once inside, Jake quickly lit two lanterns. He noticed Hannah's eyes light up as soon as he handed her one.

"Oh, Jake." She rushed over to the closest piece of furniture, the set of bunk beds for the boys. "I can't believe the work you men did. It's incredible."

"I work with some very talented men," he felt proud to say. "And men from town dropped in all day long to help. We decided on a stair-loft bunk. We're thinking Michael, their oldest son, can climb the stairs to the top bunk. And Jeremy can have the bottom bed."

"Plus, it has two drawers they can use." She ran her hand over the wood and even pulled out a drawer.

"Some bunk beds have ladders, but we decided the boys should have a set of stairs instead. We wanted everything to be as safe as possible."

"After all they've been through, that makes perfect sense," Hannah agreed.

"And then for Katie…" He put an arm around her shoulder, leading her to the other end of the barn.

She gasped again, her eyes wide with wonder as she gazed at the bed they'd built for Katie.

"One of the men found a similar design online."

"It's like a play castle with stairs leading up to a twin bed on top."

"*Jah*, for Tom's princess."

"The children are going to love these new beds, Jake. They're more than beds. They're special places where they can feel safe again."

He'd been eager to show Hannah what had been accomplished, but he hadn't counted on how much her response would mean to him. Instead of feeling ten feet tall, he felt at least eleven.

"We had quite a team. We still have more some painting to do, but we're close to finishing."

"Do you mind letting me know when you'll be delivering the beds?" she asked. "I'd really like to make some shams and spreads."

"I was hoping you'd say that. More than once, Rosie has mentioned how ladies in town are talking about Hannah Miller's designs." He smiled at her. "You're making quite a name for yourself."

"Hannah Miller's designs?" She chuckled. "That's funny. Grace gave me a mountain of beautiful fabric, and I had to do something with it. Plus, *Aenti* Ruth is an embroidery whiz, which helps."

"Well, word has gotten out," he assured her. "Rosie never stops talking about the pillow you made for her granddaughter's teacher. She said you came up with some saying on it about big hearts and little *kinner*."

"You mean 'It takes a big heart to shape little minds.' Trust me, Jake, that is not a new saying."

"It's new to me, and I thought it sounded very much like you."

"Are you trying to make me blush?"

He grinned. "It's not like I could tell in this light if you were." He paused. "Listen, Hannah, you have so many other projects on your plate. If you don't have time to make—"

"I want to very much," she interrupted him. "I'm not sure if I can do your woodworking justice, but I'll try. Like you, I'd like the McDaniel children to feel safe at night again."

Just then, Hannah yawned.

"Tiredness catching up with you?"

"*Jah*, but in a way, I don't want this day to end."

"I know what you mean."

"But you should get back to the house, Jake, in case one of the *kinner* wakes up."

"You're right."

Before exiting the barn, he extinguished the lanterns. They walked back to the *dawdi haus* in silence until they reached the porch.

"I can't thank you enough for arranging this day, Hannah." He paused to chuckle.

"What?" A curious smile curved her lips.

"I was thinking how you used to be the shy, quiet one in our group."

"Well, it was hard to compete with you and Lily. You were both quite outgoing and sure of yourselves." She defended herself.

"But things have shifted, don't you think? Now you're the town's matchmaker and popular seamstress. You've been my *kinner*'s lifeline and mine, too."

"You've been through a lot, Jake. It takes time to get yourself back on track. And when you think about the past, it all makes sense."

"What do you mean?"

She shrugged. "When we were young, you had the perfect family, people all around who loved you. You had every right to be sure of yourself. After losing my parents, I felt like I had to do everything right and keep in line for fear I could be orphaned again."

"Hannah, I never knew."

"And you didn't need to know." She laid a hand on his shoulder, once again making things easy for him.

"Everything has worked out, Jake. I've learned to trust *Gott* will help me make it on my own."

"You've helped others make their way, too," he told her. "In fact, I was thinking how the other day I thanked you for getting me back to being me. But I really should've thanked you for helping me be more like the person I want to be—and am trying to be."

She scrunched her forehead. "You mean caring and thoughtful of others?"

He nodded.

"But you've always been that person." She smiled, shaking her head. "Why, remember that time when Micah Stoltzfus was getting picked on by some *buwes*? You went right to his defense. You told the boys to stop and most of them did."

"All except for—"

"Willis Wittmer, who was the size of Goliath." She giggled. "Still you gave Wittmer a mighty big push."

"And thankfully he fell backward, knocked down a beehive and had bees swarming him." He laughed. "For a minute there, I was afraid Willis was going to get up and come for me."

"See? You've always been ready to help people, Jake." She gazed into his eyes, looking so earnest.

Right then and there, he wanted to tell her about Lily. The truth about why they married. It seemed like the perfect time. But it also seemed like it had been the perfect day, and he didn't want to ruin that. Or put an end to the way she was looking at him. After all, it had been a long time—many years in fact—since a woman he cared about looked at him so fondly. He had to admit, it felt *verra gut*. For the moment, he didn't want to put an end to that feeling, either.

Chapter Twelve

A couple of weeks later, Hannah had been sitting at her sewing machine since dawn, her Saturday just as busy as usual. She quickly realized that wasn't true for everyone.

"You're leaving, too?" she asked Jake, looking up from her sewing.

A half an hour earlier, Abram Mast had dropped by to pick up her aunt, saying they were going to take a buggy ride and maybe go shopping for a new board game. Well, Abram didn't exactly say that. *Aenti* Ruth had.

Now, here was Jake, saying he and the children were heading out, as well.

"Are you sure I can't fix breakfast before you go?" she offered.

"No need." He smiled. "I'm taking the children to Kauffman's. We haven't been there for a while."

Kauffman's Kitchen. Where Beth worked.

"Besides, you don't need to be cooking." He pulled gloves from his pocket. "You need to get your sewing done."

He was right, of course. News of her custom-designed, handcrafted decorative items kept spreading. Her client list had practically doubled, and with the holidays coming up, so had her workload. Busier than ever, after watching the children each day, she had been staying up, sewing late into the night.

"Oh, before you go, when do you want to take the shams and bedspreads over to the McDaniels'? I have the boys' linens done," she told him. "And I plan to finish everything for Katie's castle bed today."

In a way, she hoped it would be soon. She'd been missing having free time with Jake and the *kinner*. Beyond that, Jake said Tom had stopped by the lumberyard midweek to thank everyone for everything and to let them know Katie was back home. They'd moved into the house he and Ashley had purchased from his mother. Hearing that, some *Englischers* from Hochstetler's had rented a truck to haul the newly made beds to the McDaniels' new place the day before.

"How about we go after worship tomorrow?" Jake suggested. "Will that give you enough time?"

"That'd be perfect." She could feel her mood instantly lighten. "I'll see you and the *kinner* in a little while, then."

"Probably not until late today." Jake tugged on a glove. "Beth's shift ends early, and we're taking the *kinner* to her cousin Bridget's house after she gets off. It'll be good for them to play outside with her cousin's children and wear themselves out."

She couldn't deny the way her heart involuntarily sank at his news. Her heart obviously hadn't come to terms with what her brain already knew—that Jake and Beth were the perfect match. Obviously, the two of them must be thinking the same.

Even though the dinner she'd initiated with Beth and Jake and Caleb hadn't ended well, apparently it had been the beginning of something good. Ever since, Beth and Jake had been seeing each other regularly. And hadn't that been her wish—to have a woman in Jake's life who would love him and his children whole-heartedly?

Her heart really needed to get a grip.

She swallowed hard. "I'm sure the children will love that." She took a moment to think. "Well, then, I'll have supper ready when you get—"

Before she could finish, Jake laid a hand on her shoulder. "Hannah, stop. We have plenty of leftovers. You just keep busy. We can bring over food to you later if you get hungry."

"*Jah*, okay, I'll do that. I'll keep busy," she heard herself say. "And you go have a *wunderbaar gut* time."

"We will."

She was quite sure he would. Plopping his hat on his head, he was out the door in an instant, appearing quite happy to be on his way.

Meanwhile, it took a minute before she could refocus on sewing the last seams on Katie's pillow shams. Even then, her mind kept drifting, imagining how well Jake and Beth must be getting along.

Her heart and mind weren't in sync, though. Because while happy feelings for the two of them flitted through her, she couldn't dismiss the pangs of jealousy poking at her. Which was odd. When she'd fixed up Jake with Miriam and Catherine, she'd never experienced such a roller coaster of emotions.

The realization thrust her out of her chair.

Yanking open the cabinet door, she began to sift

through the yards of material, looking for fabric to match Katie's pillow shams. And a way to concentrate on something besides what she knew to be true.

Maybe a pastel floral for Katie's bedspread? Or just a light pink trimmed in lavender?

Yes, a pink to complement the pink crown topped with lavender hearts on the shams would work just fine, she decided. She started to lift the material from its spot, but then stopped. Instead, her hand seemed to have a mind of its own, running along the smooth wooden shelf…and remembering.

The day she'd gone to Sew Easy for the last time had been a bittersweet trip. Saying goodbye to Grace and farewell to her dream had been painful. Yet she'd also been blessed with her first freelance job. On her way back to the *dawdi haus*, she hadn't known whether to feel happy or sad. Then, when she discovered the beautiful cabinet Jake had made her, and when he had swung her around, so thrilled for her, all seemed right with the world again.

Her cheeks warmed at the memory; she wished she could go back to that simpler moment. Now she was happy for Jake and Beth, yet somehow, she couldn't deny a certain sadness, too. She could only hope that when Jake and Beth were living happily ever after, she could still be a part of their lives and the *kinner*'s, too. How she would miss sharing meals with them. Laughing together. Being there for them.

As tears pricked at her eyes, she hugged the piece of fabric to her chest. If only she didn't love them so, she wouldn't be so emotional about missing them already.

But you do love them. Sarah. Clara. Eli. She smiled, envisioning their sweet faces.

And Jake, too.

As a friend. She reaffirmed. *My best friend.*

Determined to keep her wavering heart on track, she paused long enough to take a deep breath. Then she shook out the fabric, straightened it and began measuring. She needed to stay focused on her work.

She needed to create something pretty and fit for a princess.

Beth had given Sarah and the twins way too many biscuits while they were at Kauffman's. Jake had been somewhat embarrassed about the drips of honey and blobs of jelly spread around the table. But the mess hadn't bothered Beth. She only smiled at their joyful faces and the way they enjoyed their treat. Like Hannah, Beth had always been easygoing and kind natured.

And though he'd never wish for anyone to go through what he had as far as a spouse dying, the fact that they'd both faced the same thing seemed to bond them closer. Even though they rarely spoke of their losses, their similar trials deepened the friendship they'd shared as *youngies*.

Older now, they could talk about pretty much anything. The only problem was, as Jake leisurely guided the buggy out to her cousin's farm, the subject Beth most wanted to address was Hannah.

I've always envied Hannah." Beth sighed. "She certainly has a gift, doesn't she?"

"You mean her matchmaking?" He was sure that was what Beth was thinking of. Right before they'd left town, they'd run into Isaiah Glick and Amanda Shetler, a couple whom Hannah had matched up and who had recently announced their engagement.

Beth grinned. "I was thinking more about her sewing talent. But come to think of it, that's two things she's mighty good at. Matchmaking and creating beautiful items to grace people's homes."

Jake crooked his shoulder. "*Jah*, but like Hannah has told me, matchmaking and sewing are much the same. She takes pieces of material and sews them into a whole and brings a man and a woman together to make them a whole couple."

"That's Hannah for you, isn't it?" Beth sounded proud of her friend. "Humble as always."

"But she also thinks she's always right." His voice rose, unfortunately exposing his annoyance. Naturally, Beth instantly picked up on his frustration.

She snickered slightly. "Do you mean she thinks she's right when it comes to knowing what's best for you?"

He nodded. "Mostly."

"Can you blame her?" She eyed him like he was a fool "You've known each other forever."

"But she may not be the matchmaker she thinks is," he bristled. "Her first two matches for me did not go well. Then she said they were only trial matches to get me back out into the courting world."

"Let me ask you this. Did she force you into those situations?" A knowing smile twitched at Beth's lips. "Because that doesn't sound like our Hannah."

"*Nee*, not exactly. I complained, and she made it sound like a solution for me and the children."

"Ain't so?"

"Yes, it is so." He frowned, wishing he'd never spoken his mind.

"That's interesting because I, for one, am not sure if you could ever find the right person, Jake."

"You mean, you don't know if Hannah can find the right person for me."

"*Nee*. You heard me right. I don't know if *you* can," Beth said matter-of-factly.

Slightly taken back, he jerked his head involuntarily. His grip loosened on the reins. "Am I that difficult to get along with?"

He wasn't sure if he wanted to hear her answer. He already knew his past had made him stodgier. But he had every right to be. He wasn't the only one he needed to be concerned with. He glanced over his shoulder to see his children with their full tummies, looking content.

"I just mean it would be hard for you to get involved with someone, Jake, when Hannah is the one your heart wants."

He fell silent for a moment. "I said nothing of the sort."

She shook her head and clucked. "I don't know why you two didn't end up together when we were younger." She laid a hand on the arm of his jacket. "Please, don't take that the wrong way. I loved Lily. You know I did. But when I think of a perfect match, it's always been you and Hannah."

As much as he trusted Beth, there was no reason for him to share everything that had happened with him and Lily or his feelings for Hannah all those years ago.

"It wasn't meant to be," he said simply. "But I'm not sure matchmaking is for me, either."

He could feel her staring at him, and he knew her well enough to know she was sizing him up.

"Oh… I think I know what's happening here. You've asked me to run about with you and the *kinner* lately so

Hannah will think we're a match." Her eyes sparkled with the realization.

"Well, *jah*, but…" He gave her a sideways glance. "Really, Beth, hasn't it been nice keeping busy with us until Caleb moves back to town? And, haven't I been helpful checking out your beau's new store space with you and making remodeling plans?" He paused, happy to change the subject. "You have mailed those ideas to him, haven't you?"

"Of course I did. And yes, I've enjoyed the time with your family. But, Jake…" She looked away for just a moment. "Now you're making me a part of your deception with Hannah."

"Trust me, it's not any more deceptive than she's been." He could feel himself getting flustered again. "You're not as savvy to Hannah's ways as I am."

"Jake, Hannah is a sweetheart and you know it."

"*Jah*, she is. But also, a finagler."

"Hannah?" Beth giggled.

"It's true." His head bobbed decisively. "Remember that first dinner we all had together? I was supposed to be taking a break from matchmaking then, but I realized that Hannah was doing everything she could to push us together." He shook his head, remembering. "Even before you walked in the door that night, she was complimenting the blue shirt she'd ironed for me, telling me it was your favorite color."

"Blue is my favorite color."

"Exactly my point!" he exclaimed.

He glanced at her long enough to see her brows furrowed in thought. "What you need to know, Beth, is that it's not just about me and matchmaking right now. It's about Hannah. With you and me spending time together, we're letting her concentrate on the business she's growing. She's not one to put herself first, you know. Sewing and designing is what she likes to do best, and it's what she deserves to do."

"You have said she's been *verra* busy."

"Unbelievably. Her customers have been growing by leaps and bounds."

He'd been thrilled for Hannah, but also concerned about how worn out she'd been looking lately. So much so that he kept himself at a distance, knowing if he got too close, he'd want to reach out and massage her hunched-over shoulders or let her rest her head on his.

He even wished he could take a turn at the sewing machine so Hannah could put her feet up and rest for a bit. But that would be sure disaster and only cause her more stress. From the sounds of it, even Ruth wasn't much of a seamstress.

He had thought about suggesting that she should take a night off from sewing. After all, wouldn't it be good for her to spend an evening with him the way they used to? Relaxing. Reading. Talking. Sharing their day. But he never brought up the idea. He knew he'd only be asking her for selfish reasons. He missed ending his days that way.

"So you don't think I'm being deceptive, then?" Beth interrupted his thoughts.

"If you have, then you've made me part of your deception, too, Beth. Caleb's father was in Hochstetler's the other day and—"

"You didn't say anything about Caleb moving back, did you?"

"It almost slipped out," he admitted.

"Honestly, I've seen them at worship several times,

and I've almost said something, as well." Her eyes grew wide. "We have to be careful. Caleb is really set on surprising his family."

"They'll be thrilled."

"So then, let's not say we're partners in deception. Let's say we're two friends helping each other and helping those we care about the most."

"That sounds *verra gut*," he agreed. "And true."

"I have to tell you, though…" Beth's voice turned somewhat giddy. "Caleb will be here full-time soon, and I'm thinking I won't have many free days then. I hope." She giggled, and even though she was on the other side of the seat, he could see her cheeks turn rosy. "Did I tell you? He's already asked me to help run the butcher shop with him."

"You two will make a great team."

Jake knew Caleb was planning on asking Beth much more than that, but he'd never say so.

"Once that happens, you may find Hannah trying to make a match for you again."

"When the time comes, I'll figure it out." He gripped the reins tightly knowing that day was coming soon. "Until then, I really do appreciate your help."

She nodded, and with that settled, he concentrated on the road again. Until Beth spoke up.

"I really hope you'll think about everything I've said. I really do want you to be happy. And you and Hannah are a perfect match."

He didn't say a word.

After all, if he and Hannah were so perfect for each other, why wasn't the matchmaker asking him to be *her* match?

Chapter Thirteen

Just as she and Jake had planned the day before, after worship Hannah made sure everything was stowed in the buggy, ready for their visit with the McDaniels. And most everything was—except for her.

The children had grand ideas about what they wanted to take to Katie McDaniel and her brothers—games, cookies and the cards they'd made. Yet as soon as Jake announced it was time to leave, they burst out of the house and climbed into the buggy, leaving all those items behind. Now Hannah stood with her arms full of their gifts, deciding the best approach for boarding the buggy herself.

"Need some help?" Jake was suddenly at her side.

"I'm thinking I do."

She started to hand him a couple of satchels until she realized Jake wasn't reaching for those. Instead, he was reaching for her. His hands hugged her waist, lifting her as if she and her parcels were as light as feathers. Then he settled her just as easily onto the buggy's seat.

"There you go." He smiled before rounding the buggy and getting in.

"*Jah*, there I go…again," she whispered to herself.

Because as soon as he settled onto the seat next to her and took the reins, the lingering feel of his hands made her feel light-headed. She couldn't stop from thinking of another time, a day in late summer when they were teens, walking and talking till nearly dusk. It had been just the two of them. Lily hadn't wanted to come along. They'd almost made it back home when they stopped, and Jake reached around her waist in the same way, hoisting her up so easily onto the stone wall that ran along the Klingers' property. There they sat side by side, watching the sun set, and she thought her heart would melt when he'd reached over, pulled her close and—

"I'm not a baby, Sarah," Clara began shouting. "I know what lions say. Stop asking me. They say *roar*. And I know what dogs say, too. They say *ruff-ruff*."

Hannah turned in time to see Clara grab the lion puppet from Sarah's left hand and the dog puppet from Sarah's right.

"Clara, that's not nice," Hannah reprimanded her. "If you'd like to use the puppets, you need to ask nicely."

"But they're *my* puppets." Clara hugged the cloth animals close, her lips in a pout. "You made them for me."

That was true. Clara had asked Hannah to make puppets, and Hannah had been glad to. She'd deliberately made the cutest lion and dog puppets she could.

Wanting to restore harmony, Hannah decided there was only one answer to give.

"I may have made them for you, Clara, but we're all supposed to share. And I'm not just talking to you, Clara. I'm speaking to you, Sarah and Eli, too. You are family," she reminded them, "and that's a *verra* special thing. Like I've told you before, you need to help each other and share. Just like you are sharing with others who aren't in your family." She held up one of the satchels in her lap.

The children were silent, their expressions serious. The only sound to be heard was the clip-clop of the horses' hooves and a squeak from Jake's seat when he turned to glimpse at his children. "Listen to Hannah. She's right."

"I heard you, Hannah," Clara said. "Here, Sarah." She kindly started to hand the lion puppet to her older sister.

"*Nee*, you keep it." Sarah smiled sweetly.

"I'll take it." Eli grabbed for the puppet.

"Eli!" Clara wailed, shaking her hand. "You hurt me and Leo."

Hannah had to bite back a chuckle. "I tried." She shrugged at Jake, who was staring at her with a strange look on his face. Usually she could easily read his expressions, but this time she couldn't.

"What?" she asked.

"It's just…you are…" He looked like there was something he wanted to say, but then dipped his black hat before quickly settling his eyes back on the road. "Thank you for taking such good care of them, Hannah."

She started to slough off his words and teasingly reply, "It's my job." But she couldn't, because it wasn't that simple. She also couldn't say, "Why wouldn't I? They're family." Technically, that was false, as well.

She plainly answered, "I'm happy to."

Less than ten minutes later, after passing Graber's Horse Farm, they arrived at the McDaniels' two-story home. Jake had warned the children earlier about being

careful and not roughhousing around Katie. He reminded them once again as he pulled the buggy onto
the acre-and-a-half lot, mostly eyeing Eli as he spoke.

As usual when they visited, Jake unhitched the buggy
and let the horse free in the fenced-in yard. After that,
he went to work, retrieving the plastic bags of bedding
from a rear trunk while she and the children walked to
the front porch and rang the doorbell.

Ashley opened the door, with Jeremy, her two-year-
old, hugging her leg, and a shy-looking Michael grip-
ping the hem of her caramel-colored sweater. Then there
was Katie, who stood back, appearing nervous about
getting too close.

This certainly wasn't the outgoing group of kids
Jake's children had played with just a few weeks before the fire. Clara, however, broke the ice right away,
pulling her dog puppet from behind her cloak.

"Hi. My name is Biscuit." She wiggled the puppet,
and Hannah could tell she'd tried to come up with a
puppy's voice. But the sound was still all Clara's, sweet
and peppy, bringing curious smiles to everyone's faces.

"That's a nice name, Biscuit," Ashley said.

"I like biscuits, so I like you, too, Biscuit." Clara's
four-year-old peer let go of his mother's sweater and
stepped forward.

"Do you like jelly on your biscuits?" Clara waved
the puppet, as if it was doing the talking.

"Lots of jelly." Michael nodded.

"Me, too," Clara exclaimed.

With that, all the children seemed to relax more.
When Jake reached the porch, his arms full of bags,
Michael pointed to the largest one. "What's in there?"

Jake leaned toward the boy. "I've been told it's something out of this world," he said quietly, as if sharing a secret. Then he looked at Hannah and grinned. She knew Jake was referring to the boys' bedding, which she'd designed with stars and planets in mind. It warmed her heart when the boys' faces lit up with curiosity.

"Can we see, Mom?" Michael asked.

"We can if we move out of the doorway and let everyone in." Ashley chuckled.

The visitors removed their coats, and the McDaniel kids got a good look at their new bedding. Then all the children happily settled into the family room, playing the game the Burkholder *kinner* had brought.

Hannah noticed Ashley didn't mind a bit that the six of them were getting cookie crumbs on the rug. Instead, as the men sat in a pair of leather recliners, Ashley offered Hannah a cup of tea.

"If I'm being honest, what I'd really like is to see how the bedding fits," Hannah told her.

"I was hoping you'd say that." Ashley grinned. "But I didn't want to put you to work."

Once upstairs, as Ashley pulled each item out of the bags, she oohed over every one of them, complimenting Hannah repeatedly. Working together, they quickly fit pillows into shams and smoothed out comforters over sheets. When they finished, Ashley was beaming with joy.

"Look at what you've done, Hannah!" she exclaimed. "Their rooms are perfect now. My kids can feel at home here. They'll want to be in their rooms again." Ashley's eyes began to grow misty. She reached up to touch the pink, white and lavender lace and chiffon garland Hannah had made to hang between the turrets on Katie's castle bed. "You really can't know how much this means to me. I'm so very thankful to you."

"It wasn't just me, Ashley. The beds the men built were a great inspiration—along with Tom's pet name for Katie." She smiled.

Ashley's chin quivered and her brows arched with sincere appreciation. "I don't know how I'll ever repay you—repay everyone—for the beds, the food and sweets, and the cards and kind thoughts. Plus, the donations from Hochstetler's haven't stopped. It's all so much!"

Hannah gently squeezed her friend's arm. "Everyone just wants the best for your family."

"How blessed Jake is to have you, Hannah. And the children are, too," Ashley said with the utmost sincerity.

"Jake and I, well, we're only friends."

"You mean for now," Ashley insisted. "Tom says Jake talks about you all the time at work."

"He does?"

"And very fondly." Ashley winked. "Why wouldn't he?"

Hannah started to tell Ashley about Beth, but her friend immediately jumped to a new subject—curtains for the children's rooms.

"I'll only allow you to make the curtains if you'll let me pay for them," Ashley told her.

"Fine, but I'll give you my 'friend' discount," Hannah countered.

"Oh, all right," Ashley agreed. "If that's the only way I'm going to get Hannah Miller curtains."

They began writing down window sizes and discussing colors and fabrics. But all the while, Hannah couldn't stop thinking about what Ashley had said.

Had Jake really been talking about her?

* * *

The longer Jake sat talking with Tom, the more uneasy his friend seemed. And the more stilted their conversation became. He wasn't surprised when Tom jumped up from his recliner the minute Ashley and Hannah came downstairs.

"I'd like to show Jake around the property," he informed his wife. "Sound good?" He eyed Jake.

"Sure." Jake nodded.

"No worries." Ashley told him. "We can manage kid duty. Can't we, Hannah?"

"Without a doubt." Hannah shooed them away.

With that, Tom threw on his coat and handed Jake his jacket so quickly that Jake figured the outing wasn't only about exploring Tom's new homestead.

He was right.

"Sorry," Tom apologized as soon as they were outside. "Sometimes I just have to get out of there. It's like I can't breathe. I look at Katie and how timid my boys have become and my heart breaks." He ran a hand through his thick hair.

Jake started to ask how he could help, when Tom abruptly pointed to a level spot in a far corner of the yard past where Jake's horse had settled in.

"This spring, that's where I'm putting a shed for lawn equipment."

"Makes sense." Jake nodded.

"I always wondered why Ashley's dad didn't have a place to store lawn gear. Right now, it's cluttering half the garage."

"Jah," Jake agreed. "When I moved, there were a few things about my parents' property that I thought

could be better. I guess in our line of work, we're always looking for ways to make improvements."

Jake thought he sighed heavily at times until he heard Tom exhale. "Yeah, well. I wish I had thought of making some before the fire. Like rope ladders, for one."

Jake winced, his heart as heavy as it was when he'd first learned about his friend's tragedy. "How is Katie doing?"

"She…she's…the sweetest." Tom's voice cracked. "She tries to act like she's doing fine. But I know she's in pain. I know she still has bad dreams. The boys do, too. But they tell me about them. And Katie? My princess won't say anything because she doesn't want to worry us."

"Our girls are very much alike." Jake clasped his friend's shoulder. "It kills you, doesn't it?"

"So much." Tom dipped his head. "And then Ashley…whew…" His lips tightened. "Sometimes I can barely look at her. What kind of husband and father am I? Because of me, she almost…" He exhaled. "She almost lost her babies."

He turned away. Jake could tell he was swiping at his eyes, trying to get a hold on himself. It took a minute before Tom circled back around. "How could I have been so *stupid*?"

From what Jake had heard, the cause of the fire wasn't a rare case. Tom had drifted off while in his recliner, studying the roster and playbook for Katie's basketball team. Unfortunately, those papers had fallen to the floor near a space heater that he'd forgotten to turn off before heading to bed. It was a simple mistake that had turned devastating.

"I think there are always things we wish we could've done differently." Jake certainly knew that to be true.

"I've scarred everyone I've ever loved the most." Tom threw his arms up in the air. "And I can't stop blaming myself. I don't think I ever will." He gnashed his teeth, staring out into the yard.

"You know, when you'd tell me what you were going through with Lily," he continued, "I remember saying that you shouldn't blame yourself. That sometimes life takes turns that you never expected." He shook his head disgustedly. "I must have sounded callous."

"I didn't really expect you to have all the answers."

"Well, now I have a way better understanding of what you were going through. Unfortunately. The guilt is tearing me up, man. I feel like… I couldn't be a worse father."

A sob erupted from deep within Tom's chest. Jake reached out and clasped him around the shoulders, feeling the clutches of sorrow grab at him, as well.

He cleared his throat. "Tom, you can take some time to be sorry. But then you must get past it. You have a *wunderbaar* wife. *Wunderbaar* kids. Don't let yourself get lost to them. They deserve all of you."

When Jake looked at his own children, it was something he'd had to remind himself again and again. And still did.

Tom buried his head in Jake's shoulder, weeping. Jake patted his friend's back. "Turn to *Gott*. He will forgive you," Jake told him. "He is a *Gott* of second chances. He will heal your heart and give you a new spirit to go forward. That's His promise."

He hoped Tom believed it for himself and the ones he loved. He wished he could believe it, too. As much as he knew *Gott* was a forgiving *Gott*, he still had a hard time completely forgiving himself.

Tom stepped back and wiped at his cheeks.

"I'm grateful to you, buddy," Tom told him. "I mean it. And you know, I have to tell you, you look better to me. And seeing you and Hannah together…" He paused. "It does give me hope."

Jake started to object but then stopped. Was that Tom's voice he was hearing or was *Gott* whispering in his ear?

Chapter Fourteen

The weeks had been passing by quickly. Each day had, too. Hannah had just finished reading time with the children when Jake's buggy pulled into the drive. His timing was perfect as usual. Or maybe she should take a little credit where credit was due, Hannah thought, grinning inwardly. Once again, she'd scheduled the day's activities with the children just right.

"Grab your coats, *kinner*! Your *daed* is home from work. And don't forget the kitty treats we made," she added. "They're in a paper bag by your boots."

"It's my turn to carry the bag," Eli informed his sisters.

Hannah noticed neither sister wasted a minute arguing. Instead, they were all sticking to what had become their new habit.

With winter coming closer to an end and more daylight to be had each day now, they eagerly donned their jackets like clockwork and romped outside to greet their father. Each day, too, she'd gaze out the window with a fond smile.

Jake might've been tired from his day at work, yet no

one would ever guess it. He'd welcome the *kinner* with open arms and take his time lifting each of them into the air, beaming joyfully all the while. Then the children would grab Jake's hands, skipping happily into the barn.

As Hannah watched them disappear into the stable to feed the kittens, more and more each day it seemed like a sign of things to come. Certainly, as time went on and Jake and the children grew even closer to Beth, things were apt to change. Then would she even be needed? The realization tugged at her heart.

Sighing wistfully, she pulled from the refrigerator the ground-beef-and-noodle casserole that she'd prepared earlier in the day. Placing the dish into the heated oven, she was about to start making biscuits, when a knock sounded at the front door.

Quickly, her mind rifled through her list of deadlines. But she came up with what she already knew—it was only Thursday. No orders were due until Monday.

Still, assuming the visitor might be a client, she hurriedly tucked wispy hairs into her *kapp*, wiped her hands on a dish towel and headed toward the door.

Shooting a curious glance out the picture window, she saw a shiny red sports car in the arc of the driveway. It was a car she surely would've remembered if she'd ever seen it on the roads of Sugarcreek. As she opened the door, she realized the *Englisch* woman standing there didn't look familiar, either. Clad in a fancy white wool coat with a fur collar, the lady appeared as if she'd just stepped out of a magazine. She wore pointy-toed black boots and brown leather gloves and hugged a glossy mocha-colored purse to her side.

"Hello." The stranger removed a glove, extending her right hand. "Are you Hannah Miller?" Fortunately, her smile was far more down-to-earth than both her automobile and clothing.

"*Jah*, I am." Hannah rubbed her hands on her apron to make doubly sure they were clean before taking the attractive woman's hand.

"The same Hannah Miller who made the decorative pillows for Julie Caples?—who is my sister-in-law, by the way. And also bedding for the McDaniels, the stool cushions for Kauffman's Kitchen, and the adorable swaddles for Sylvia Wright's new granddaughter?" The woman barely paused before adding, "Yes, I've done some snooping around town and know you have several more satisfied customers. But I suppose I don't need to list everything I've heard about and seen of your work."

"*Jah.*" Hannah blinked. "That would be me."

"Good, I'm in the right place, then." The woman released Hannah's hand. Deftly taking a business card from her purse, she gave it to Hannah. "I'm Madeline Enyart."

Giving the pink-and-gold card a swift glance, Hannah slipped it into her apron pocket. "Nice to meet you. Would you like to come in?"

From the moment Madeline stepped inside, Hannah could see she was scanning the sitting room, eyeing the pillows, cushions and window dressings Hannah had made.

"Everything looks so warm and inviting in here," her new acquaintance commented. "And those are darling."

Madeline pointed to the smaller rocking chairs that Hannah had recently encouraged Jake to purchase for the children. She thought it was time they had their own reading chairs. She had sewn cushions for the chairs and in the middle of the back cushions, she had added a square of fabric with a blessing printed on it.

"*Danke*. And is there anything I can make for you?"

"I certainly hope so." Madeline Enyart's chuckle was a pleasant sound. "Hannah, I'd like to tell you about myself—well, my business actually. I have an interior design studio in Columbus called Decor to Adore, and it's doing quite well. So well, in fact, that I'm opening another studio in Sugarcreek. The thing is—" she paused to remove her other glove, as if getting down to business "—I've been successful using outside companies and seamstresses to create our products. But from what I've seen of your work, there's a warmth, and interestingly, a brightness to your designs that's rare. Just like in this room." She waved her gloves theatrically in the air. "That's why I'd like for you to come work with me."

Hannah squinted, trying to comprehend what Madeline was saying. "You mean do some work for you."

"No, I mean be involved in a partnership with me," Madeline said definitively, raising her brows. "Your work could be in so many homes and delighting so many families, Hannah. And not just in Sugarcreek. Think of all the tourists who come to this town." Her eyes grew wide with excitement. "Decor to Adore, featuring Hannah Miller Designs. It really has a special sound to it, don't you think?"

Stunned beyond belief, Hannah didn't know what to think. Could this really be happening?

"That's a *verra* red car, *Daed*," Eli noted, the minute Jake and his *kinner* exited the barn.

"*Jah*, it is, *sohn*."

Jake wasn't surprised to see an *Englischer*'s car in

his driveway. Automobiles were no longer an unusual sight on his property with Hannah's customers coming and going, picking up their purchases. He'd even been happy to make a few deliveries himself from time to time. As much as Hannah helped him, he wanted to return the favor whenever possible.

"Why aren't buggies a pretty red like that car?" Clara frowned.

"She's right, *Daed*," Sarah chimed in. "If our buggies were red then cars and trucks would see them better."

Though the children had a point, Jake was about to explain how the Amish way was more reserved, when Ruth opened the *dawdi haus* door.

"What have you *kinner* been doing today?" Ruth called out to them, steadying her wheelchair. "I've missed you. Do you have time for a visit?"

"May we, *Daed*?" Sarah asked politely, as always.

"I'll bring them over when dinner's ready," Ruth offered.

"That sounds *gut*, Ruth. *Danke*."

It sounded better than good, actually. While the children scampered into the *dawdi haus*, Jake headed directly home, like a man on a mission. After he washed up for dinner, and Hannah's customer left, he hoped he might have time alone with her.

In the weeks since visiting the McDaniels, he'd been thinking plenty about what Tom had said. If he was being honest, he'd noticed changes in himself, too.

Consequently, he'd been diligently praying, asking for *Gott*'s forgiveness along with seeking guidance where Hannah was concerned. He hadn't exactly heard *Gott*'s voice, but things between him and Hannah seemed more intensified than ever.

The glow of her smile warmed him from across the room. The sound of her laughter lifted his heart, moving him to join in. And when they'd share a look across the supper table, or while playing with the children, or simply saying good-night, he felt as if they were connected more than ever.

Now he wanted to know if she felt it, too.

Slipping in the back door quietly, he didn't want to disturb Hannah and her customer. Typically, he ignored the women's conversations, figuring they were about things he had no knowledge of or little interest in, like thread counts.

But this conversation struck him differently, sounding more serious. He knew he shouldn't eavesdrop, but he leaned against the wall, listening in.

"So, Hannah," the lady was saying, "would you consider moving back to town and working together? I've purchased a house that will become the design studio, and there's a great little house that I bought right next door. You can live there at a very reduced rate so you can be on hand to consult with clients."

"That's the only way I could come work for you?" Hannah asked.

"Not *for* me," the visitor corrected Hannah. "With me."

"But couldn't I just ride into town whenever you need me?"

"How would you know when I need you?"

Jake was curious about Hannah's answer.

"There's a phone shanty across the street," Hannah replied. "That's helped a lot with the business I'm doing now."

He heard the woman sigh. "It's not the arrangement

I'd hoped for. Besides, I hear you're a nanny for Mr. Burkholder's children. When on earth do you have time to sew?"

"I make time," Hannah stated. "At night and on Saturdays."

"I can't imagine you have much time to stop and breathe. And whether you take on a partnership with me or not, I'd be careful about that," the lady advised. "I'm not trying to sound like a know-it-all, but at the rate you're going, it could eventually take a toll on your health and your creativity."

As much as Jake didn't want to take this stranger's side, he also couldn't imagine how Hannah could keep up her pace.

"I haven't been late with a delivery yet." He heard Hannah defend herself.

"And you've truly created some beautiful items," the woman complimented Hannah. "That's why I'm here, and why I'm hoping you'll form a partnership with me. It just requires a simple move to town." Her voice lightened. "Not a trip to the moon or anything." She giggled slightly. "So, please think about it, will you, Hannah?"

Hannah said something softly, but he couldn't hear what.

"I hate to lose you, so I'll be doing some thinking, too," the visitor continued. "The builders are finishing up remodeling work on both houses. So there's still some time, but not much. I'll reach back out to you, and you have my card if you need to contact me."

As the women exchanged goodbyes, Jake knew he should move quickly and act like he had just come inside. He didn't want Hannah to think he was spying on her.

But in his heart of hearts, after what he'd heard—as hard as it was to hear—he felt pressed to address Hannah's opportunity. He stood frozen to his spot.

"Jake!" Hannah jumped when she saw him. "How long have you been in the kitchen?"

"Sorry to surprise you like that," he apologized. "Did I hear what I think I heard?"

She shrugged nonchalantly. "It was someone who needed work done."

"That's not the way I understood it."

She started to walk around him, and he caught her by the hand. "Hannah, what this lady is saying—it sounds like everything you've been working toward since Sew Easy closed."

Unable to contain himself, he took both of her hands into his. As much as he wanted to hold on tight and never let go, he squeezed them gently, encouragingly. "This is your chance to shine. An opportunity to be a partner in a design studio."

"It's nothing, Jake."

He could tell she was trying to muster up an indifferent expression, but her cheeks appeared as heated as the kitchen they were standing in. Clearly, she was flustered.

"Listen, Hannah, I shouldn't have eavesdropped. I realize you have every right to be upset with me."

"Who says I'm upset?" she asked innocently as if it was the furthest thing from her mind.

"Hannah, I know you, remember? Again, I'm sorry."

"I'm not upset with you, Jake."

"What is it, then?" He looked into her eyes, searching for a clue, but she deliberately let her eyes drift from his.

"It's just… I need to finish dinner for everyone." She

slipped her hands out of his grasp. "And afterward, I need to finish sewing pants for Eli. He's growing out of everything these days."

He crossed his arms over his chest. She may have freed herself from his hands, but he was not about to let her brush him off so fast. For her own sake.

"You have to stop this," he said in a sharp tone.

"Stop what?"

"You know what," he insisted impatiently. "You have to stop being everyone's everything. For once, you need to think about yourself and what you want."

Hannah walked past him, headed toward the oven. "Right now, I smell the casserole burning," she quipped, obviously determined to cut the conversation short. "I just need to think about that."

Chapter Fifteen

When Hannah came into the house as he was leaving for work the next morning, it ran across Jake's mind that he'd probably laid eyes on her pretty face thousands of times. That was why, when he saw her hollow eyes and less-than-bright smile, he knew for sure she hadn't slept well the night before.

He could relate. He'd hardly slept himself.

The glimmer of moonlight that had filtered into his bedroom should've been soothing and restful, but instead it seemed to shine a light on everything that had to do with Hannah, leaving him restless. He literally ached, hating the thought of having things change and not having her close…and in his life. About the only time he'd closed his eyes was when he was trying to shut out thoughts of his children. They would be incredibly hurt by her leaving. How they would miss her!

Still, he had to do whatever he could that would be best for Hannah. Yet even after stewing all night, he wasn't sure what that was. And although the sun shone brightly throughout his entire ride to work, he sank into a deep trance. The monotone clip-clopping of the horse's hooves only magnified that feeling.

Thankfully, once he arrived at Hochstetler's, the hustle and bustle of the lumberyard had a way of energizing him. After an hour into his shift, with a plan in mind, he strode into his boss's office.

"Seth, do you have a minute?"

His boss looked up from his paperwork. "Sure, Jake. How can I help you?"

"Is there a way I can get in touch with your mother?"

"This is Friday, isn't it?"

Jake nodded. "Why, *jah*, it is."

"It's easy, then. She'll be here a little later to collect donations from the bins for her weekend deliveries."

"Does she usually stop by to see you when she comes in?" Jake asked.

Seth opened the top drawer of his desk enough for Jake to see baggies filled with cookies and treats. "Where do you think I get all of these?"

Jake chuckled. "Do you mind letting me know when she gets here? I really need to talk to her."

"*Jah*, I can do that," Seth replied. "Anything I can do in the meantime?"

"Only if you want to babysit my *kinner*."

Seth sniggered. "I'll be sure to let you know when *Mamm* arrives."

Two hours later, after a ten-minute talk with Seth's mom, explaining his situation and Hannah's opportunity, Jake had his answer. Mrs. Hochstetler not only assured him that she'd be happy to take care of his children while he was at work, but also offered to help him find a long-term solution. It was everything she had promised months earlier.

Knowing he could offer Hannah a solution, he figured he'd have a sense of relief. Rather, all throughout his shift, everything felt heavy inside him, from his heart down to his feet. He was still feeling that way at day's end when Rosie sauntered up to him at the time clock.

"You're looking at me funny." He swiped his badge to check out. "Am I doing something wrong?"

"I don't know. Are you?" Rosie asked.

"I'm not sure I know what you mean."

"Of course you do, Jacob. Don't play dumb with me."

He shrugged. "No one ever said I was the sharpest tool in the shed. Maybe the handsomest…"

He tried to make her laugh to get her off track, since he figured she'd heard about the setup with Seth's *mamm*. But Rosie crossed her arms over her chest, not one to be easily distracted.

"I hear Mrs. H. is watching your kids so Hannah can move back to town. Is that true?"

"That's the plan. Until I find a long-term nanny." He tucked his badge into his shirt pocket. "Hannah has a great opportunity awaiting her. She needs a chance to do what's best for her."

"But do you think this is really the way to go?"

He cocked his head, eyeing the ever-persistent Rosie, and again tried to make light of her questioning. "My children certainly can't come to work with me. Ain't so?"

"It seems you may want to think of another solution, Jacob. I mean, generally, when you speak of Hannah your eyes light up and a smile creeps across your face. But today, you look like a sad puppy and there sure isn't any light in your eyes."

"Because I didn't get much sleep last night."

"And why is that, do you think?"

Rosie knew him almost as well as his mother ever did.

"I'm doing what's best for Hannah."

"Have you even asked her if that's what *she* wants?"

"You don't understand. You don't know her. She doesn't stop to think of herself. I'm just looking out for her." No matter how much it hurt him and his children—that was what he had to do.

As they exited the building, his surrogate aunt gave one last try.

"Well, you may think this is the best solution," Rosie appealed to him, "but I for one am not sure that having Hannah out of your life is the right one. And vice versa, if you get my drift..." Her lips curved downward before she gave him a weak wave goodbye.

Naturally, he didn't admit to Rosie that for a while he'd been thinking the same way. But after speaking to Mrs. Hochstetler, it was all too easy. Everything was falling into place. Things that were meant to be usually were that simple, weren't they?

As he got into his buggy and turned his horse toward home, he drifted off thinking about Hannah. With her, nearly everything every day just fell into place. And the feelings he'd always had for her were even greater now. It was as if their relationship was supposed to be, wasn't it?

He shook his head, working to be rid of those thoughts. He was being selfish for wanting her to be by his side. This wasn't about him. It was about her. Hannah deserved the life she'd hoped for and the chance to pursue her dream.

Besides, *Gott* knew what He was doing bringing them

closer together than they'd ever been. Jake's deep feelings for Hannah were what made him want to give up what was best for him, so he could do what was best for her.

He only hoped she would see that.

After dinner, when Jake asked if she could stay until he got the children to bed, Hannah was more than happy to oblige. He said he wanted to talk to her, and she wanted to do the same.

She'd obviously acted strangely around him following Madeline Enyart's visit the evening before. She knew Jake assumed she was angry with him for eavesdropping, but that wasn't the case at all. If she was upset with anyone, it was with herself, for feeling so conflicted.

After all, Madeline's offer should've had her thrilled and jumping at the chance to have her dream come true. Yet the idea of leaving the Burkholder household any sooner than she had to filled her with sadness. She loved them all too much to be just one more person who left them. Jake needed to know that she didn't plan to disrupt their lives anytime soon. She wanted to stay until things for him and the children—and his heart's match—were permanent.

Hopefully, Madeline would understand the timing wasn't yet right.

But if not…

Without question, I'll deal with it.

"I'm sorry that took so long." Jake came into the room, settling into the chair across from where she was seated on the sofa. She couldn't help noting how tired he looked. Even more tired than when he'd arrived home from work.

"Let me guess." She smiled. "Eli wanted you to read about horses one more time."

"Jah." She noticed her comment brought a glimmer of amusement to Jake's blue eyes just as she hoped it would. "And then—" he started.

"One more time," they chimed the words in unison.

They chuckled, both completely familiar with Eli's bedtime ploy to delay lights-out. Knowing the children as she did and even being fond of their schemes, Hannah was still smiling and feeling sure about what she wanted to say to Jake.

But the twinkle in Jake's eyes immediately faded.

Before she could speak, he leaned forward in the chair, folding his hands in his lap. "Hannah, there's something I need to say." All lightness had departed from his voice.

"Jake, if it's about last night, I'm sorry and—" She started to tell him what she'd been thinking. What she'd been feeling.

But he stopped her. "I've figured out a way that things will work out for all of us. Starting Monday, Mrs. Hochstetler is going to come watch the children. Her husband will drive her back and forth. She even said she'd start dinners, and she'll be helping me find a good nanny for the long haul. That means..." He paused. "You'll be free to form a partnership with that businesswoman."

Her entire body froze in shock. "What?"

He glanced away for a moment. Because she looked so pitiful and confused?

"Trust me, Hannah. This is what's best for you," he said adamantly. "We can't keep holding your life— you—hostage forever."

Stunned again, she squinted at him. "Have I ever said anything like that? I hope I've never seemed that way. *Jah*, I watch your children, but I also care about them. And in turn, you've given me a place to live. I've saved plenty of money and have grown a business." She shrugged. "I think it's been a *gut* arrangement for both of us."

"And now, you have the opportunity to do even more. To have your dream come true," he said more assertively than assuredly. "You need this. It's not fair to make you stay here, Hannah. And…" He stopped and took in a deep breath, letting it out slowly. "Actually, it's not fair to the *kinner*, either."

"The *kinner*?" She blinked at him, shaken. "Have I done something—"

"Nee." He reached out and took her hand. "Hannah, they've blossomed under your care. I've never seen them so happy."

She almost thought his voice quavered before he continued. "On the other hand, I think maybe they're getting too used to this—to us—to all of our times together. I'm not sure it's *gut* for them to continue that way."

Beth. That was what he was getting at and not saying it. Evidently, they were more serious than she knew and wanting to move forward. Covert or not, her matchmaking had worked again. And ready or not, the time had come. He wanted her gone.

She was trying to be brave. She was working to hold back tears. She didn't exactly know what she'd expected Jake to say, but she hadn't been prepared for this. Or the wave of grief that engulfed her completely.

"You're right. We should…whatever is best for the *kinner*."

"It'll be what's best for you, as well."

"Oh, *jah*." She slipped her hand from his warm grasp and stood up, working to steady herself on her feet. "I…um…should go. I'll…uh…see you…sometime," she mumbled. "The blueberries have been rinsed for tomorrow's breakfast. Don't let Clara eat too many… her stomach sometimes…" She wobbled and he caught her by the arm.

"Let me walk you home," he offered.

"You don't need to." She clenched her teeth, fighting back the tears pooling in her eyes.

"I know I don't need to, Hannah." Jake let go of her arm, then rubbed his hand briskly over his beard. A sure sign he was peeved. "You know, you want to help everyone else. And that's *wunderbaar*. But you never want help from anyone else, and that's not fair. There are people who love you and want to give to you in return. Maybe someday you'll see that."

"*Danke*, Jake," she said simply, picking up her cloak and satchel, anxious to leave.

As soon as the cool night air hit her heated face, sobs came pouring from her. As she crossed the lawn to the *dawdi haus*, Jake's mention of love kept ringing in her ears.

It was a four-letter word that made most people happy, thrilled, complete. Oh, but not her. At least not with Jake. A strangled sound erupted from deep within her. Somehow with him, love was always attached to another four-letter word—hurt. Not that he'd ever meant to hurt her. She knew that for a fact. But somehow, invariably, it always happened that way.

Chapter Sixteen

Hannah was tossing in bed the next day, glumly wondering if the birds' early-morning chirping was ever going to sound delightful to her ears again, when *Aenti* Ruth slowly rolled into the bedroom.

"I heard you stirring and thought I'd bring you some tea."

"Oh!" Hannah instantly sat up and leaned against the headboard, smoothing her disheveled hair. *"Danke, Aenti."* She took the warm mug from her hand.

"You're usually up earlier." *Aenti* Ruth gave her a worried look. "Are you sick? Abram said some people in town are getting an end-of-winter flu. You certainly don't look like yourself."

After the encounter with Jake the prior evening, she didn't quite feel like herself, either. It stood to reason that her aunt would think she was ill. Her eyes had to look red and puffy from crying so much the night before.

She'd taken a detour into the barn once she'd spied Abram's buggy in front of the *dawdi haus*. There, she'd sat pouring out her heart to the kittens and any other animal that would listen. When she finally got a hold of herself, she made her way home, giving her aunt and Abram brief hellos before heading to bed. All through the night, she couldn't stop from whimpering, burying her face in her pillow.

"I'm fine." Hannah took a sip of the tea as if that could prove what she was saying.

"No, you're not," *Aenti* Ruth retorted bluntly.

Not ready to explain, for fear she'd break down again, Hannah changed the subject. "How was your evening with Abram?"

The question caused her aunt's cheeks to immediately turn pink, which brought the slightest smile to Hannah's lips.

"*Aenti*, you're blushing. You two must have enjoyed some special time together."

Her aunt covered her mouth with her hand and giggled. "Abram asked me to marry him."

Hannah coughed, choking on the swallow of tea.

"See, I think you are getting sick." Her aunt's eyes narrowed.

"*Nee*, I'm not." She coughed again before getting her bearings. Then cleared her throat. "What did you tell Abram?"

"What do you think?" *Aenti* Ruth laughed. "I said *jah*!" she exclaimed. "Oh, Hannah, I can't tell you how happy I am!" She clapped her hands together. "I know you don't think much of Abram and me together, but—"

Hannah laid a hand on her aunt's arm. "*Aenti* Ruth, it's not that. I only want you to be happy. And I can see that you're *verra* happy with Abram, which is all that matters. I'm thrilled for you and for Abram, too," she said sincerely, knowing the pair had waited forever to find love. It was the first marriage for them both. "Really, I am."

Out of the corner of her eye, on her aunt's nightstand, she spied the "something" Abram said her aunt had left behind during their move. It was his gift of a forget-me-not plant. She should've realized then that Abram had sweet intentions.

"Honestly, we do know we're different as night and day," her aunt replied. "But Abram says we're like a magnet and a paper clip. Sometimes opposites attract each other and hold close. And we do, too." She beamed. "We have a connection…and it just works beautifully." Her aunt sighed dreamily. "Sort of like you and Jake."

Obviously, her aunt meant no harm. Even so, the words gripped Hannah's heart. She gritted her teeth and looked away, working to hide her emotions. It seemed unimaginable that any more tears could possibly flow from her eyes. Yet they did.

"Hannah, I'm sorry. I didn't mean to upset you," her aunt said softly. She rolled closer, reaching up to stroke Hannah's hair. "What's going on, *kind?*"

"Do you think we can move back to Abram and Susan's house right away?" Hannah asked. "Can you please ask Abram if there's a vacancy?"

Aenti Ruth stared, appearing as shocked as Hannah had probably looked the night before with Jake.

"Hannah, dear, if you and Jake had a squabble, I'm sure you two can work things out. You always have." Her aunt's forehead furrowed. "I don't think we have to move."

"Oh, but I do," Hannah cried. "Jake has asked Mrs. Hochstetler to take care of the children from now on. He thinks it's what's best for me so I can be a partner in Decor to Adore. He didn't even ask what I wanted." She sniffled. "He talked about how I help everyone else, but I don't want help from anyone, and it's not fair to people who love me. And then he kicked me out of his house and life. Does that sound like love to you?"

Setting the mug on the nightstand, she grabbed at the tissue her aunt offered. After taking a minute to blow her nose, she continued.

"And you know what, *Aenti* Ruth? This is exactly the reason why I do go around helping everyone else, whether I'm matchmaking or nannying or—"

"Taking care of an old *aenti*." Her aunt gave her an appreciative smile.

"You mean sharing life with someone important to me," Hannah corrected her. "*Aenti* Ruth, never think that I considered being with you as a job. The years we've had together have been incredibly special for me."

"Me, too, sweet Hannah. Me, too." *Aenti* Ruth patted Hannah's blanket-covered knee. They shared a look that made Hannah sigh.

"Oh, I don't know." Twisting the Kleenex in a knot, she shook her head. "Maybe Jake is right. But this is exactly why I try not to depend on anyone. Because I usually get disappointed." Or hurt. In a huge way. She left that part out.

Aenti Ruth tilted her head. "And I'm guessing you didn't speak up or tell Jake how you were feeling."

"Why would I?" Hannah rolled her eyes. "It was clear he'd already made up his mind. And, well…of course, I want to do whatever is best for him and the children, and him and Beth."

"Beth? You keep saying they're together. But when I've seen them, I don't know how to explain it…" *Aenti* Ruth scanned the ceiling as if she'd find the right words there. Then she focused on Hannah, her eyes wide. "I know. They don't seem magnetic to me. Whereas, when I see you and Jake together, there's such a pull."

"You're starting to sound like there's a science to romance, *Aenti* Ruth." Hannah shook her head doubtfully.

"I don't know anything about science, but I do know what I see go on between you two."

"What do you mean?"

"You've always said you wanted to own your own sewing store. That's been your goal, right?"

Hannah nodded.

"So that didn't work out with Sew Easy. But now you have another answer to your dream. Jake knows all of that and loving you—"

"Uh-uh." Hannah winced.

"Okay, then. *Caring* for you the way he does, no matter what, he wants the best for you. And I've also heard you say again and again that you want the best for him." She smacked her hands together. "I don't know about you, but that sounds like a match to me. It's obvious you both want to do whatever you can to make each other happy. All except for facing your feelings for one another."

"*Jah*, well…" Hannah's shoulders slumped under the weight of disappointment.

Months ago, she'd thought if Jake could find love and make a new life for himself, that she'd also step out of her comfort zone and be willing to put her heart out there again. Now she realized what a challenge that would be, especially since her heart had already found a home with people she loved. A home that she was being vacated from.

Yet, she had to trust that *Gott* had a plan for her life and would see her through.

She had to hold on and believe that He knew what was best.

And in the meantime…

"Do you mind asking Abram about any vacancies, *Aenti* Ruth?" she asked again.

Her aunt squeezed Hannah's hand. "For you, of course I will."

Breakfast was usually the easiest meal with his children, but not so this morning. With a heavy heart, Jake had to explain that Hannah would no longer be with them.

"What do you mean she's going away?"

Clara stopped picking the blueberries off the top of the oatmeal Jake had spooned into each of the children's bowls. Licking her stained fingers, she waited for his answer.

Before he could reply, Sarah spoke up. "Is she taking a trip to see *Oncle* David and *Grossmammi*?"

"Can we go, too?" Eli asked.

While his son's eyes grew wide with excitement, Jake closed his own momentarily, whispering for help from *Gott*. Hannah meant so much to all of them that they'd certainly need His support to get them through the days ahead without her.

The night before, countless times, he'd almost gone out to the *dawdi haus* to Hannah to beg her to not go. But he had to stay the course for everyone. It was only right to do.

Taking a deep breath, he exhaled slowly, and began to explain the situation with Hannah the best way he knew how.

"You all know that Hannah enjoys sewing, *jah*?"

"Jah, Daed." Clara's blue eyes surveyed him like he was silly. "She made us Biscuit and Leo, and—"

"And my new pants and shirts." Eli nodded.

"And besides our clothes, the pretty things she's made for the house," Sarah chimed in.

"True. And because she has this gift from *Gott*, other people outside our family want her to sew things for them, too."

"Like she's doing now," Sarah insisted.

"Jah." He bit his lip, then figured he needn't keep beating around the bush. "But now there is a business-woman who wants to form a company with Hannah. Which means Hannah needs to move back into town. So I've arranged for Mrs. Hochstetler to come watch you. You remember that nice lady, don't you?"

He'd tried to shift them from the subject of Hannah and onto the prospect of fun times with Mrs. Hochstetler. It didn't work. All three were staring at him, the two girls with tears in their eyes.

"Why can't we move to town with Hannah?" Clara wanted to know.

"Life doesn't work like that," he told her.

"Why not?" She sniffled.

"Look, *kinner*, I know this is hard for you. It is for me, as well. But I told Hannah I think she needs to do this. I think it's best for her."

"Did she think so, too?" Sarah croaked. "What did she say?"

Obviously, Hannah hadn't said anything. He hadn't given her the opportunity. "Hannah has been so good to all of us. She's given us her time, her talents and her love. Just because she isn't living in the *dawdi haus* doesn't mean she'll be completely out of our lives. We can visit her. Won't that be fun?"

His children gave him skeptical looks. He didn't blame them. After all, how often had they gone to visit her in the past? Never. She'd always come to them.

"I know this hurts right now, but we need to think of Hannah," he continued. "Her happiness is important. Sewing and creating are special to her. Don't you all have something that's special to you? Something you like?"

"I like horses," Eli jumped in. "I'm going to ride them lots someday."

"I'm going to make puppets like Hannah does," Clara declared.

"Sarah?" He looked at his oldest, who seemed to be thinking hard. "What's special to you?"

"Hannah." Her lips quivered, and he knew she was fighting back more tears.

"I know, Sarah, I know." He got up, crossing the table to hug her.

"Can we do something special for her before she leaves, *Daed*?" his sweet daughter asked between sniffles.

"Of course we can." He gave her an extra squeeze. "After breakfast, let's think about what that could be."

"I think I already know," Sarah said, glancing around the table. "But Clara and Eli and I are gonna need you to help."

"I'm happy to," he agreed, a glimmer of hope filling him as his daughter's expression brightened the tiniest bit.

Maybe, one day, they would all be okay after all.

Chapter Seventeen

A round noontime, sorrowfully packing up her few belongings, Hannah shook her head at herself. When she'd moved from town out to Jake's, she'd been uneasy about giving up her independence. Now she was moving back to town and regaining her independence, but she'd never felt so miserable.

She was wondering what *Gott* must think of her when a knock sounded at the front door.

At once her pulse quickened, and her mind raced. Could it be Jake, asking her to stay?

Working to control her emotions, she hurried toward the entrance, tripping over a box along the way. By the time she opened the door, there was no one to see. Nothing, except for a handmade card that had fallen from the doorframe onto the porch. Surprised, she bent to pick it up.

"What is it?" *Aenti* Ruth wheeled over, just as curious as she was.

"It's a dinner invitation for the two of us."

"To where?" her aunt asked.

"To *Kinner*'s Kitchen. Tonight, at six o'clock. The

card is decorated with crayon drawings." Hannah couldn't help but smile. "I'm thinking Sarah and the twins are doing a takeoff on Kauffman's."

"How sweet!" *Aenti* Ruth grinned. "Does that mean they're doing the cooking?"

"I'm guessing so." Hannah nodded. "Plus, it says an escort will be here to pick us up at five to six."

"Abram is stopping by then to pick up some of our boxes. I'll have to pass, although it sounds like a nice evening." Her aunt chuckled.

A nice *last* evening.

That was why at five o'clock Hannah decided to stop packing. She wanted to take her time getting ready for their last meal together. Or, at least the last one until who knew when. After getting cleaned up, she brushed her hair several times before wrapping it up in a bun. And before donning her *kapp*, tried to choose a dress to wear.

She kept coming back to her violet-colored dress. Mostly because each time she wore it, Jake mentioned how nice it looked on her. Why she was even thinking about pleasing him, she didn't know. But remembering how his compliments made her feel special and especially close to him, after much pondering, that dress won out.

Ready by 5:45 p.m., she sat and waited for her mystery escort's arrival. This time she was at the door the instant she heard a knock.

When she opened the door, she gasped. "Jake!"

Since the evening was set up by the children, she'd assumed one of them would fetch her. But there he was, looking more handsome than ever, wearing her favorite blue shirt, of course, which always intensified his already too-blue eyes.

"Sorry to surprise you," he apologized. "Eli was supposed to be your escort. But he's busy arguing with the girls about which dessert you like best—applesauce, trail mix or ice cream. So you may end up with all three. He sent me in his place. I hope you don't mind."

Jake seemed nervous and her heart went out to him. Like her, he was probably hoping things wouldn't be uncomfortable between them.

"*Nee*, I don't mind having three desserts or you as my escort. I think I can manage both," she quipped.

She'd hoped her humor would put him at ease and it did. His tense jaw broke into a relaxed smile. She was determined for the evening to be a good one. They all deserved that much.

"Well, then…" Being the gentleman that he was, he held out his arm. "Shall we head to *Kinner*'s Kitchen?"

"*Jah*, we shall."

She wrapped her arm around his without a moment's hesitation. But as they began their walk across the lawn, he took her by surprise once more.

"You look beautiful this evening." His words were just as warm as the feel of having him close.

She stopped and stared at him, wishing words like that meant something and were forevermore. But knowing they weren't, once again, she responded airily. "You've seen me in this dress plenty of times. But then, your memory isn't the best." She figured that would get a rise from him.

"*My* memory? I don't know what you're talking about." He scoffed, playfully. "I beat you at the *kinner*'s memory game almost every time. Ain't so?"

Attempting to appear thoughtful, she scratched her chin. "Not that I can recall."

His laughter filled her heart, and in good spirits, they entered *Kinner*'s Kitchen. Their mood carried over to the children, whose faces brightened the minute they saw them.

"Doesn't this look special?" Hannah let go of Jake's arm, clasping her hands together. "The table looks lovely with the candles you all arranged. And look at these place mats." She touched the edge of the one closest to her. "Did you make them yourselves?"

The three nodded. "Eli drew the horses," Sarah explained. "Clara drew dogs, and I drew the flowers and trees."

"I will keep mine forever," Hannah said truthfully, placing her hand over her heart. "The only thing is, I don't see places for you *kinner* at the table."

Clara spoke up. "That's because Sarah said we can't eat with customers."

"Workers eat in there." Eli pointed to the sitting room.

"Hmm." Hannah frowned. "Do you think we can make an exception this time?"

The twins deferred to Sarah, who beamed at the suggestion. "*Jah.* Just give us an extra minute, please," she replied, sounding so grown-up to Hannah's ears.

She and Jake took their seats at the opposite sides of the table while the children put together additional place settings. The three of them grinned proudly as they served hot dogs and baked beans, even though they confessed their *daed* had done the cooking.

"Everything looks delicious, *kinner*," Hannah complimented them. "I'm *verra* thankful for all you've done to make this a special evening."

"And I—we—can't be more thankful for you, either, Hannah." Jake's voice was low and sweet.

The children's expressions seemed to sober as they looked at her, nodding in agreement with their father.

Until Clara spoke up. "Can we hurry and tell *Gott* thank-you? I'm hungry."

Hannah didn't know whether to laugh or cry as a mixture of joy and sorrow welled up inside her. Oh, how she would miss them. Miss all of them. She looked across the table at Jake.

But still, I'm thankful, she told the Lord as they bowed their heads in prayer. *Gott* had given her a new opportunity to use her talents. It was all she'd ever hoped for.

Until these past months…until Jake and his children had become such a part of her.

Now she could barely imagine her life without them. And she wondered why she'd let her fear of being hurt keep her from being true to her heart's longings.

But time had passed, circumstances had changed and she'd missed her chance. Besides, it wasn't right, was it, to be given the answer to her dreams—and then expect *Gott* to grant her even more?

All throughout dinner, with the laughter and chatter at the table, Jake couldn't escape feeling like he'd experienced the same sort of lighthearted, joyful banter before. Even during cleanup and washing dishes—which Hannah insisted on helping with—he sensed a harmonious rhythm, reminding him of something he couldn't quite put his finger on.

It wasn't until they were playing the memory game, which he'd teased Hannah about, and the children were laughing happily, that he realized what had struck him as so familiar. It was togetherness, and the sense of family.

He'd taken those feelings for granted when he'd been growing up, but now he realized that his children might not be able to say the same thing. It was only recently that they'd come out of their shells—and they'd done that through Hannah's encouragement. He would need to remember how important moments like this were when Hannah was no longer living nearby.

He hated for the merriment to come to an end, but glancing at the clock, he knew it had to. "Guess what time it is?"

His *kinner* groaned, familiar with his nightly remark. On this night, he hated the evening coming to an end as much as they did. Especially knowing that, when they all woke up, Hannah would be leaving.

"Will you tuck us in?" He watched Sarah place a hand on Hannah's knee.

"Jah." Hannah gently cupped his daughter's cheek. "I'd love to."

As the children headed upstairs to get ready for bed, he and Hannah gathered up the game pieces.

"Are you sure you don't mind staying to say prayers with them?" he asked after a bit.

Her answer came softly. "Have I ever?"

"No, never." He'd never been so honest.

"We're all ready for bed now," Sarah called from up the stairs.

"Oll recht," Jake called back. "We're headed up. Everyone be sure to be under the covers and settled down."

As he followed Hannah up the staircase, he wondered if there would be a next time that they'd perform this ritual together. His melancholy thoughts were interrupted by Sarah's command to her siblings.

"Quiet! They're coming!" His daughter's excited and rather loud whisper was followed by sounds of rustling sheets and squeaky beds.

As he and Hannah entered the bedroom, he scratched his head. "I don't know, Hannah, it's mighty quiet in here."

"Yes, it's *verra* quiet," Hannah said seriously, playing along. "Maybe your *kinner* are already asleep."

"I think you're right. Guess we don't need to be saying prayers then, ain't so?"

"I guess not. I think I'll head home." Hannah turned, pretending to go, just as giggles erupted across the room.

"We're not asleep," Sarah assured them.

"We were trying to be quiet," Clara said.

"And *gut*," Eli added. "Sarah bossed us into it."

"I'm not bossy," Sarah protested. "That's not nice."

"But it's true, Sarah," Clara noted.

"Daed!" Sarah wailed.

As usual, the quiet had turned to chaos in a matter of seconds.

"Come on now, settle down. And no more comments about your older sister," Jake warned sternly. "Sarah is only trying to keep you two out of trouble."

As the three of them wriggled back under quilts, Sarah looked at Hannah with hopeful eyes. "Will you say that prayer from before?"

"Yeah," Eli added. "The one with the funny name."

"Eeny, meeny, miny, moe or something." Clara got in her two cents.

Hannah chuckled "You mean *'Müde bin ich, geh zur Ruh.'"*

Hearing the name again, his children happily clasped their hands and uniformly bowed their heads. As Hannah recited the prayer, he noticed how her sweet voice created a calm peacefulness throughout the room. But as he sat at the edge of Eli's bed, he didn't hear a word she said. He was far too captivated by the sight of her, observing how the sliver of moonlight coming in the window highlighted the softness of her cheeks and enhanced the golden glow of her eyes.

So it shook him out of his reverie when he heard her ask the *kinner*, "Does anyone want a kiss?"

The children bobbed their heads simultaneously. He watched as Hannah started with Sarah, pushing back a wisp of his daughter's hair before kissing the girl's forehead.

Hannah appeared surprised when Sarah flung her arms around her neck and held tight. "I love you so much," Sarah said, looking into Hannah's eyes.

"Oh, Sarah, I love you, too." He could hear the emotion in Hannah's voice, which gave rise to his own. Finally, Hannah dabbed Sarah's nose with her finger before Sarah would let go.

Next, Clara had her arms outstretched before Hannah even crossed over to her side of the bed.

"We want to move to town with you, but *Daed* won't let us," Clara confided before quickly closing her arms around Hannah's neck and pulling her close, not waiting for Hannah's peck. It was some moments before Clara's grip loosened, and Hannah placed a soft kiss on her forehead.

"I'll be back to visit," Hannah said, bringing a smile to the girl's face.

"Promise?" Clara asked.

"*Jah*, I promise." Hannah's voice quaked and Jake knew her well enough to know she was near tears.

Yet he also knew that no matter what, she was all about putting everyone at ease. She made her way to Eli's bed and said lightly, "Last and certainly never, ever least, good night, Eli."

Bending over the bed, she started to kiss Eli's forehead when his son grabbed her around the neck and yanked her to him. His strength must've surprised her, causing her to nearly stumble off balance.

"*Danke* for being my mommy. Or like a mommy," Eli corrected himself.

"Oh, Eli…"

Jake heard a sniffle escape from Hannah before she put her arms under Eli's small shoulders and hugged him with what appeared to be the same fierceness that he was hugging her.

After a moment, Jake spoke up, his voice slightly hoarse. "It's time for sleep now, Eli. Girls."

Jake could see the tears he'd suspected brimming in Hannah's eyes the moment they got to the bottom of the stairs. His own emotions were also veering out of control.

"Hannah, I'm sorry that was so—" He couldn't think of the right word to say.

"Your *kinner* are sweet, Jake. Too precious."

"And you, Hannah…you make them even better," he said earnestly. "I don't know how to thank you. I don't know what to say."

"Then don't."

She put a finger to his lips, and he gazed hopelessly into her eyes. Before she could move away, he reached for her hand and pressed her palm to his lips. Transfixed by its softness, he turned her hand over and slowly, gently held it against the bare skin of his cheek.

Taking her other hand in his, he pulled her toward him, yearning to hold her close and never let her go.

But seeing the bewildered look in her eyes, for her sake, he knew he needed to do what was right.

He leaned his forehead against hers, still not ready to let her walk out of his life, wishing the moments could turn into an eternity.

It was too soon when she spoke.

"I… I have to go, Jake," she whispered.

"I know." Reluctantly, he let go of his grasp. "I know."

Chapter Eighteen

"It's been two weeks since Hannah moved, Jake." Beth stood in his kitchen with her hands on her hips, shaking her head. "I can't believe you haven't spoken to her even once."

"I'm sure she's been busy getting settled. Besides—" he shrugged "—what is there to say?"

"She and Ruth moved back into the Masts' house, *jah*?"

He nodded.

"Well, then, for openers, you could take that mail to her."

Beth tilted her head toward the countertop and the envelopes he'd set aside with Hannah's name on them. Many of which he assumed contained payments from clients.

Staring at those envelopes that he'd tried hard to ignore, he felt guilt stab him hard. Hannah had likely been needing that money.

Before he could say a word, Beth continued, "While you're there you should also tell Hannah you love her,

Jake. It's time to do that, ain't so?" She arched a brow. "Maybe past time."

"*Jah*, well." It was his turn to shake his head. "*Danke* for stopping by to harass me, friend."

"Harass you?" She shook a finger. "You know I'm only here trying to help, Jake. And, well, also Caleb…" Her tone softened at the mention of her beau's name. "He wanted me to let you know he'll be back in town next week. Permanently." Her face flushed. "He's hoping you can find time to discuss the build-out plans of the store."

"Let him know I'm happy to," Jake replied. "And since you're giving me a piece of advice, let me give you some."

"About what?" Her hands flew back to her sides.

"You better not harass Caleb the way you do me. Not if you want him to stick around," he warned playfully. "Also, Miss Know-It-All, what you don't know is that I *am* planning to take the mail to Hannah."

He knew he shouldn't hold on to Hannah's mail or even the hope of her coming back. But her leaving had taken a toll on him, and he wasn't sure if he was ready to see her. And it wasn't only his own feelings that concerned him.

Glimpsing out the window, he eyed his children lackadaisically kicking a ball around. Since the day Hannah moved out, they had seemed somewhat listless and crankier than usual. Given time and his prayers, he knew they would adjust. But how much time was enough so that seeing Hannah again wouldn't get their hopes up?

"I may even go next Saturday," he told Beth.

She eyed him skeptically. "Hmm, I'll believe it when I see it."

Picking up her shawl, Beth turned to go, then bumped into Eli as he came flying in the back door.

"*Daed*, Hannah's here! Hannah's here!" his son shouted with a grin as wide as his face. "She's coming up the drive!"

Jake had only time to gape before Eli rushed out the door to greet her.

The day before, when Hannah discovered Clara's lion puppet mixed in with her fabric, her aunt had remarked with a smile, "The Lord moves in mysterious ways."

Additionally, *Aenti* Ruth had not been shy about stating that by giving the opportunity to return the puppet to its rightful owner, *Gott* had provided a chance for Hannah to share her feelings with Jake, as well.

But as soon as Hannah pulled in Jake's driveway and saw Beth's buggy, she was reminded of what she'd known all along—her aunt's thinking didn't appear in line with their heavenly Father's. And as much as she'd hoped otherwise, if she didn't want to be totally estranged from the Burkholder household, she would have to be at peace with that.

"Hannah! Hannah!"

The children's delighted squeals immediately drowned out any reservations she'd had about stopping by. At once, her heart warmed, and the world felt like it had set itself right again. At least temporarily.

She couldn't halt her speckled horse, hitch it to a post and grab her tote from the buggy quickly enough so she could run to them.

"How I've missed you!" She pulled the three *kinner* into a tight embrace. "So, so much!"

"We've missed you, too," Sarah murmured, nestling in.

"Are you staying for supper?" Eli was the first to break free from her hug.

"We can make grilled cheese like you used to make us," Clara offered.

Gazing at their earnest faces just about broke her heart. "Some other time that would be *wunderbaar*." Preferably when she'd been invited by their father. "But today I wanted to bring you something."

"Besides you?" Sarah questioned.

"Jah." She caressed the sweet girl's *kapp* before patting the tote hanging at her side.

Eli noticed and, in a flash, stuck his nose into her satchel. "It's a white bag." He looked up at her. "Is it chocolate-covered pretzels?"

"With sprinkles?" Clara stepped closer for a look.

"Yes, with sprinkles." Hannah grinned.

"Can we go inside and eat them? I don't want the kitties to get them."

"Neither does Leo." Hannah pulled the puppet from her tote.

"Leo!" Clara shouted. "He's alive!" She clapped her hands. "I need to show *Daed*."

With Leo in her grasp, Clara took off running into the house. Her sister and brother hurried behind her. Meanwhile, as much as Hannah longed to see Jake again, and hopefully his smiling eyes, all at once her heart pounded. Her legs felt locked in place.

You must get over this. Over him, she scolded herself. *If you want to keep these people in your life, you have to take that step.*

Forcing herself to move, she plodded toward the house. The short distance to Jake's door felt like a thousand miles.

Hopefully, it would get easier. Hopefully, with just one step at a time.

It seemed strange to Jake to be courteously holding the back door open for Hannah. In past months, he'd become happily accustomed to her comings and goings being one of the very best parts of his everyday life.

Their greeting was polite but strained, which bothered him, as well. Forever and a day, they'd enjoyed an easygoing connection with each other.

But while some things changed, Jake thought, some things didn't. Like the way a light, pleasant vanilla scent always trailed behind her, teasing his senses, making her seem so familiar to him. And how her very presence could fill every empty corner of his house. Not to mention the effect she had on his children, bringing out their smiles and lifting their hearts. And his, too.

"*Danke* for bringing Leo back." He chose a safe subject.

"I had to. The little lion was missing his keeper."

She looked from him to Clara, who was busy reintroducing Leo to his habitat. Then he saw her turn to Beth.

"How are you, my friend?" She hugged Beth. "I've been meaning to drop by Kauffman's and visit. I've missed you."

"I miss you, too." Beth smiled. "When can we get together?"

"Well, my schedule is flex—" Hannah started. Before she could finish, his son tugged on her sleeve.

"May we eat the pretzels now?" Eli asked.

"Oh, of course. How silly of me." Hannah chuckled. "I only meant to drop those off and be on my way."

"So soon?" Beth questioned Hannah. "I have to run to work. Why don't you stay and visit?"

"Oh…well…no." Hannah shook her head. "I mean, I think my buggy is probably blocking yours anyway. I was so excited about bringing Leo back home and then rushing to greet the children."

Jake could tell Hannah was uncomfortable and most likely couldn't wait to leave. He wished she'd see in his eyes how much he wanted her to stay.

As she laid out the treats from her satchel, Beth caught his attention, nodding toward his countertop.

"You can't go yet," he said a little too forcefully.

"I can't? Why not?"

"Because…because I have something that belongs to you."

"You do?" She appeared even more curious.

"*Jah. Jah*, I do."

He wished he could say it was his heart that belonged to her, but he couldn't imagine what she would think of that. Instead, stepping toward the kitchen counter, he picked up her mail and handed it to her.

"Thank you, Ja—"

Before Hannah could finish his name, an envelope trickled to the floor. As they both stooped to reach for it, the warmth of her hand touching his caught him off guard.

"Sorry to be so clumsy," he uttered. But that wasn't

true at all. The moment his eyes locked with hers it made him wish he'd dropped every piece of mail.

"You're fine," she said bashfully as they both stood up together. And unless he was fooling himself, he didn't seem to be the only one who felt something. Hannah appeared shaken as her cheeks turned a dusty rose.

"Daed." Sarah touched his arm. "May I go down to the mailbox and see if Hannah got anything else?"

"Uh, *jah*, sure." He nodded. "Just be careful, hear?"

Sarah waved in response and skipped out the door.

In the meantime, while the women resumed their conversation and discussions about Ruth and Abram's upcoming wedding, he settled the twins at the table with their treats.

While everyone appeared to be doing just fine, ten minutes later a sick feeling crept into the pit of his stomach.

What was taking Sarah so long?

Apparently, Hannah was wondering the same thing. Interrupting Beth, she turned to him, her forehead creased with worry.

"Shouldn't Sarah be back by now?" she asked anxiously.

The door slammed behind them as they flew outside, leaving the twins with Beth.

Without a sign of Sarah anywhere, feelings of dread surged through him again and again.

"Sarah! Sarah!" He called down the driveway. He yelled her name in every direction. But no answer came.

"Please, Sarah, say something." Hannah tried a softer approach. "Anything, sweet *maedel*. Anything," she urged, turning left and right and back again.

Still, silence filled the air, except for Hannah choking on a sob. "Oh, Jake," she clutched his arm. "Where is she? Where's our girl?"

Panicked beyond belief, they rushed toward the road, calling Sarah's name. The driveway never seemed so long and endless. It seemed forever before they reached its bottom.

And there she was. His Sarah, stricken down and lying motionless in the gulley. Hurled nearly ten feet from the mailbox, blood trickled down her forehead. Envelopes lay scattered on the grass and over the road.

"Oh, *Gott* in Heaven, help us! Please!" he moaned, breaking into sobs. Bending down, he held his oldest *dochder* close, rocking her limp, unconscious body in his arms.

"No! No! No!" He heard Hannah scream defiantly as if declaring what he was fearing—that Sarah couldn't be close to death.

"No!" she shouted again. Then she rushed across the road to the phone shanty.

Chapter Nineteen

"Mr. and Mrs. Burkholder?"

Like Jake, Hannah had been holding her breath and praying her heart out for the past hour as they sat side by side in the hospital's trauma waiting room. Fearful of what the scans and X-rays would yield regarding Sarah's condition, Hannah found her anxiety intensified by the sound of the doctor's voice as she and Jake stood up to hear the results.

"Hannah is not my wife," Jake clarified. "She is my children's nanny."

"*Was* his children's nanny," Hannah further explained. "Is there any news?"

Looking surprised, the physician who had introduced herself earlier as Dr. Asbury glanced between them before she spoke. "I'm sorry. I had just assumed when I first saw you both..." She shook her head as if to clear it. "Anyway, as I was about to say, considering the circumstances, I'm happy to report that I have good news for you."

"You do?" Jake's voice croaked.

"I'm not saying that Sarah is totally out of the

woods." The *doktah* held up her hand. "She has definitely suffered a mild concussion. But there is no indication of any brain damage or significant trauma to her skull. Also, test results indicate Sarah has a stable tibia fibula fracture of her right leg. It can be painful but will not require surgery. She will need to see an orthopedic doctor so that can be further taken care of."

Hannah let out a sigh of relief as heavy as Jake's, while the doctor continued giving care instructions for the concussion as well as providing orthopedic referrals. Dr. Asbury also suggested Sarah stay at the hospital under their care for a few hours longer until she completely stabilized from the accident.

"Fortunately, Sarah wasn't ejected onto the road," Dr. Asbury continued. "She was thrown onto the grass, and with spring nearly here the ground is softer. Of course, none of us know how fast the hit-and-run driver was going, but considering everything, this could've turned out—well, let's just say much worse."

"Jah." Jake voice quaked as he bowed his head. "I can't even—"

For the first time since they'd arrived at the hospital, Jake's shoulders began to shake uncontrollably. He placed his hand over his mouth and beard as if he could possibly hide his emotions.

"I understand," Dr. Asbury said. "I have young children, too." She paused momentarily. "It will still be a while before they bring Sarah back into her room. You're welcome to wait here or step away for coffee or something."

"We'll wait," Hannah spoke up for them both.

Dr. Asbury smiled slightly. "Again, I totally understand." She started to go, then stopped and turned.

"I'll be going off duty soon, but another doctor will be checking in with you after a bit. My best to all of you."

"Danke," Hannah replied once more since Jake still appeared too overwhelmed to speak. "Thank you very much."

As soon as Dr. Asbury left, Hannah felt the tightness in her chest loosen. Tears began to flow freely down her cheeks as wave after wave of emotion washed over her. Wanting so badly to comfort Jake. Wanting also to celebrate with him. Wishing to be close and feel the reassuring warmth of him.

Taking a bold step forward, she couldn't resist throwing her arms around his neck.

"Oh, Jake. Sarah's going to be all right." She gazed into his eyes, their bright blue color dimmed by his tears—and her own. "Praise *Gott* for answering our prayers!"

Without a moment's hesitation, he placed his arms around her waist and pulled her near to him. Right where her heart desired to be. "I'm very thankful. I am. It's just...for such a little one..." His voice faltered. "She's been through so much, Hannah...so *verra* much."

"I know, Jake, I know." She freed a hand to wipe at his tears and took a moment to dab her own. "But you're a wonderful father," she said sincerely, clasping her hands around his broad shoulders once more. "Your children know you're there for them. They know you always will be."

"I don't know what I'd do if anything happened to her, Hannah." His expression turned even more bewildered. "All these years I've loved Sarah like she's my own—like my very own daughter."

Hannah froze in his arms, his words swirling about her head.

Ever so slowly, she released her hands. As he eased his arms from around her waist, she took a step back.

"Wh-what?" She gasped.

"I've been wanting to tell you, but when you said you didn't want to know anything more about my marriage to Lily, I decided to keep it to myself. And maybe this isn't the right time…" He shook his head, glancing around the room before settling his eyes on her again. "But I don't know if there is a time that's right. I really don't." He held out his hands imploringly. "All I know is that I don't want any more secrets between us. You mean too much to me, Hannah, and to my children. You're closer to us than anyone on this earth."

She started to say she was shocked but couldn't. Not if she was being honest. After all, besides Sarah's blue eyes, she'd always wondered why the child looked so different from Lily and Jake. And for the longest time, ever since Lily and Jake married, hadn't she felt like Lily was hiding something from her? Apparently, it hadn't been just a feeling.

"It was the *Englisch* boy, wasn't it?" she blurted. "The boy from Kentucky who was in Sugarcreek visiting his cousin that summer?"

Until now, Hannah had forgotten how many times that summer she'd come home at curfew only to find the bed next to hers—Lily's—empty. And how many times, before she left to take care of her aunt in Indiana, had she made up excuses for Lily when Noah and Rachel Keim asked about their daughter's whereabouts?

"I know the person Lily was with was an *Englischer* and he was from out of state. But I didn't ask many questions back then," Jake confessed. "Lily was a mess about it all. I think a part of her felt ashamed. But looking back, I think a greater part of her was devastated when that boy left. I think she truly loved him." He paused. "And then, too, the Keim household became such a wreck."

"Noah's health took a turn for the worse around then, didn't it?" Hannah remembered that when she'd returned to Sugarcreek, her friends' upcoming wedding wasn't the only thing to be sad about. That was when she had also learned about Noah's lung cancer.

Jake nodded. "But he was never too ill to remind Lily that you were the perfect daughter and not her."

"Oh, no," Hannah moaned. "I wish Lily had shared this with me," she said. "I wish I could've helped in some way." Instead of praying selfishly for herself and her hurting heart back then, she could've been praying for her friend. "You're a good, caring person, Jake."

"No, I'm a blessed person." He dismissed her compliment. "When I think about Sarah's real father, I feel sorry for him. He's never known about her existence. He'll never know what a sweet, good-hearted child she is," he said quietly. "I'm so thankful she's in my life."

"And as far as Lily…" He sighed. "Her depression and despondency began even before Sarah was born. I thought trying to have another child might make us more of a family. But when the twins came along, things only got worse. Lily kept saying I should have a better life. But I thought I had a good one with children I loved." He sighed heavily. "And then when she started with the painkillers…"

Jake literally shuddered. Hannah placed a hand on his arm. "I'm sorry, Jake."

"I can't tell you how tired I am of letting everyone down." With a sigh, he continued, "First, I wasn't the man Lily needed me to be. Then, I betrayed your trust by not being honest with you." Though he was still visibly shaken, he looked her directly in the eye. "I know this isn't the best moment to speak of the past, but I couldn't wait any longer, Hannah. It was high time I told you."

Right then, a medical assistant wheeled Sarah's bed into the room. As soon as the young man locked the bed into place, she and Jake quietly stepped toward it.

Sarah's eyes were closed, and her body lay still. Hannah noticed that even with all her injuries, the child's face appeared peaceful.

With her eyes welling up again at the sight of this precious child, she slipped her arm through Jake's, leaning her head against his shoulder.

"Jake, what you're saying isn't true," she whispered to him. "Not true at all. You haven't let anyone down. Most of all not your children and not this sweet *maedel*. You could've disowned her. You could've made her feel less than. But instead you chose to love her and hold her close. Like you said, you love her like your daughter."

She smiled up at him and was glad to see some of the worrisome shadows disappearing from his face. Since she couldn't tell him all she wanted to, namely, that he was the best of men and the one her heart adored, she hoped what she had said would somehow bring him peace.

And at that moment, she decided to make her own peace with the past. She needed to stop asking herself and *Gott* why she and Jake never got a chance at love when they were young. Instead, she needed to remind herself that however much Jake loved Lily, he took on Lily's problem and made it his own. Despite all that had happened through the years, he never wavered from thinking of Sarah as a special gift and a blessing.

In truth, Hannah knew exactly what he meant. The time she spent as the children's nanny and now even on the periphery of their lives, was a gift she couldn't deny. And maybe that was what all of this was about after all—being given a blessing she'd be eternally thankful for.

Sarah roused just long enough to give both him and Hannah a weak smile. After that, Jake noticed Hannah appeared more comfortable about leaving.

"I need to go tell Beth and the twins the good news."

"Hannah, I... I can't thank you enough..." He couldn't believe the way his voice quivered, saying those words out loud.

Hannah being Hannah, she pretended not to notice. "I'll see you later, then." She smiled sweetly.

Though he wanted to do much more than merely squeeze her hand gratefully before she departed, unfortunately, that was all he had the nerve for.

Shutting the hospital room door behind her and silencing the hallway noise, he took another long look at his daughter. When at last he knew Sarah was resting soundly, he sank into the bedside chair. He was exhausted and extremely relieved.

Closing his eyes, he couldn't stop his mind from continually praising the Creator who had delivered his little girl from harm. He also thanked *Gott* repeatedly for Hannah's presence through it all and for the chance to bare his secrets with her. Because of the way he cared so much for her, setting things right lightened his heart. He'd been set free.

As he relaxed even more, little by little his thoughts drifted. He began to doze off to sleep when the door to the room opened, startling him. Opening his eyes, he expected to see a nurse or physician. He was shocked to see neither.

"David?" Completely taken aback by his former brother-in-law's appearance, he shook his head in disbelief. "Am I dreaming?"

For as long as Jake could remember, David had been a brash, somewhat arrogant person. Today, however, David all but tiptoed into the room, appearing sheepish.

"No, you're not," David replied. "Though I'm sure you might think so. It's been a while, hasn't it?"

"Nearly two years." Jake nodded.

"Jah." David tugged self-consciously at his straggly beard. "I stopped by your house to let you know I finally closed on my parents' property. You'll be getting new neighbors soon," he reported. "But then Beth told me all about Sarah's accident. I had to come right away and find out how she's doing."

It seemed strange that after all this time, David would be concerned about his niece. He'd hardly reached out to Jake in past years, and he certainly hadn't been good about replying to the few letters Jake had sent. Yet instead of reminding David of that, Jake chose to ignore those things. David had gone out of his way to come, so he gladly shared everything about Sarah's condition.

"She'll be all right, then?" David asked as he stood by her bed, staring.

"Jah, she will."

"She's grown up a lot."

"You have no idea." Jake chuckled fondly.

With that, David turned to face him. "Jake, I—" he started. "Is Hannah still here?"

"No, you just missed her." Jake frowned. "Why?"

"I saw her in town a while ago, and I wanted to say something." David rubbed his hands together nervously. "Actually, I want to tell you both. I can't live with myself any longer if I don't speak up and get this out."

"I know what you're going to say," Jake interrupted. "I know you blame me for Lily's death. I'm sure that's why you've kept your distance." He held out his arms in surrender. "Trust me, David, I have issues with myself. I've been begging for *Gott*'s forgiveness. I also pray you and your *mamm* will forgive me...someday."

"Forgive you?" David scoffed. "You're not the one to blame for Lily's death. I am. It's me." He thumped his fist against his own chest. "It's my lies that took my sister's life. It's my selfishness that kept you and Hannah apart."

Chapter Twenty

Two weeks later

No winter lasts forever. No spring skips its turn.

As Jake hitched his best horse to the family buggy, he could almost hear his mother's voice echoing those words in his ear. When he was a young *buwe*, it was a saying she frequently delighted in sharing.

He was never sure where she'd heard the adage. He'd never cared to ask. In fact, any truths buried in those words were lost to him back then. He was far too busy being a footloose youngster, lighthearted and carefree.

"But I sure understand now, *Mamm*," he said wistfully as he stroked his horse's mane.

Even though twittering birds filled the air with their musical tribute to spring, and the gray color of the landscape was quickly fading, making way for renewing shades of green, he knew more than ever his mother hadn't been lecturing about the change of seasons. Rather, she'd wanted to give him a way to visualize *Gott*'s miraculous display of hope. Something he could hold on to throughout the seasons of his life.

But that sentiment was only helpful, he now realized, if a person was willing to let go of the past. To move forward. And not allow the winter to drag on.

Finally, he was willing—and didn't want to waste any more time.

"*Daed*, I made sure the twins got the bags." Sarah interrupted his thoughts.

It had only been two weeks since she'd left the hospital. Yet even with her cast and crutches, Sarah was the first at his side.

"*Danke* for seeing to that, *dochder*." He squeezed her shoulder lovingly, then looked over her head. Clara was trudging down the walk with her gift bag in tow. Eli had his hands full, too, and was last in line.

"Did you shut the door, Eli?" Jake asked though he could clearly see the answer with his own eyes.

"Uh…" Eli dropped his bag and went running back to the house to close up.

Meanwhile, Jake helped Sarah get settled in the front of the buggy, with her crutches. Then noticed Clara in the back seat, hugging her bag in her lap.

Both girls seemed more serious than usual. He supposed that had much to do with the weighty conversations he'd had with his children throughout the week. But he felt it was only right to let them know what he intended to do. When they agreed it was what they wanted, as well, they all began making plans as to how to go about it.

Still, he made sure to warn them that sometimes things don't turn out as one might wish. However, he hoped and prayed that they remembered the other bit of advice he'd passed on—that whenever they felt *Gott* was leading their hearts in a direction, they shouldn't be afraid to give that direction a try.

After Eli jumped into the buggy with his bag, it was time to go. Jake's hands felt sweaty as he picked up the reins. He wondered if his children were nervous, too.

As he drove past his new mailbox and turned onto the road, he couldn't help but think how Sarah's accident had changed people's perspectives. Even his own. Time, relationships and truth had become more precious. It had been a day of owning up. And though it distressed him to think that Sarah's trauma was the catalyst, he had to believe that was how *Gott* had it planned all along.

That day at the hospital, Hannah had been surprised but understanding when he'd opened up and shared his long-held secret. But even more shocking was David's unprompted visit and confession.

David had revealed that he had come up with his plan to unite Lily and Jake for his own selfish reasons. He didn't want to be stuck in Sugarcreek taking care of an ailing father and a single, pregnant sister. He was smitten with a girl named Mary who was moving to Middlefield, and he wanted to follow her there. That was why David had lied and lied again.

David had given Lily his word that he'd gone to Kentucky and confronted the *Englisch* boy she cared so deeply for about her pregnancy, only to have a door shut in his face. The truth was David never made the trip at all. Regardless of his sister's wants, he'd been afraid that if Lily stepped outside her faith, it would cause a family uproar and his father's ill health would worsen rapidly.

And Jake had taken David at his word back then, too. He believed that David really had heard from a reliable person that Hannah had found her true love in Indiana. And Jake had been so crushed he hadn't even checked out David's so-called source. But then, as David admitted, that was what he'd counted on.

Then, David had sinfully used *Gott*'s name to conclude his deceitful scheme, telling Jake it was His plan that Jake should be free to help Lily. Again, Jake had taken that to heart, and Lily had believed it, too. After all, they were young. They were hurting. They wanted to find something—someone—to hold on to. Yet things never got better for them as a couple or for him as a widower. Not until now, his heart lifted at the thought— now that he had accepted *Gott*'s healing grace.

"Are we almost there, *Daed*?" Eli spoke up.

"We're getting close," Jake replied. Glancing at his twins, he saw their small hands were pressed together, in prayer.

He'd also had plenty to pray about lately. Besides Sarah's healing and his family's future, he'd been praying for David, too. He'd done everything he could to convince David to forgive himself. From experience, he knew David's confession alone would be a place to start. They'd promised to pray for each other and meet again soon. For that, Jake was glad.

Besides, Jake couldn't totally blame David for how he'd lost Hannah all those years ago. Jake had never even tried to go after her. Despite his hurting, he'd truly believed she was happy. Unwilling to risk more injury to his pride, he'd left matters at that.

And then, there he was, doing the same thing only weeks ago. Letting the love of his life go, almost forcing her to leave. He'd taken a blessing that *Gott* had wanted to give him and twisted it into something else, not thinking he was worthy enough to receive it.

Now, he prayed for *Gott* to be gracious and give him

one more chance. A chance to begin a new season in his family's life.

He was ready. His children were, too.

"Keep praying, *kinner*," he said. "We're almost there."

"They're here!"

Aenti Ruth turned from the living room window, appearing mighty happy to give Hannah the news. That was after Hannah had noticed her aunt peeking outside at least a dozen times in the past hour.

"Who is here?" Hannah came close, looking over her aunt's shoulders.

"Jake and his *kinner*."

Her pulse quickened as she watched Jake and the children exit their buggy. She couldn't suppress her smile. Ever since the day she and Jake had spent at the hospital being together through all the bad and, thankfully, all the good, she hadn't been able to stop thinking of him.

"Did you know they were coming?"

Her aunt's hand flew to her chest. "How would I know?"

Hannah tilted her head. "Because even though you say you only have eyes for your fiancé, you seem to know an awful lot about everyone else's comings and goings."

"You say that because you're still wondering why Beth and Caleb's engagement wasn't a surprise to me like it was to you, my matchmaking niece. And I keep telling you it's because—"

"I know. You sensed their magnetic pull a while ago."

"And I was right." Her aunt preened. "Now go greet your visitors."

"They probably want to see you, too, *Aenti* Ruth."

"And they will in a bit." Her aunt began rolling her wheelchair toward the kitchen. "Right now, I promised Abram I'd make a sandwich for him."

"But he just ate breakfast." Her aunt was truly the worst at making up excuses.

"Niece, would you please get out there? Now?" Her aunt shooed her.

Truth be told, Hannah couldn't wait to get her arms around Jake's children. She'd also been missing them in the worst way. Even with plenty of work and clients, life felt empty without them. Day after day, she thought about paying them a visit. But once she knew Sarah was recovering well and Mrs. Hochstetler was having no problems watching them, she'd thought she should back off.

Until now. Her heart raced as she sprinted out the door.

"It's so *gut* to see you," she gushed. "So *verra gut*."

Even on crutches, Sarah made it to the top of the wraparound porch easily via the ramp. Hannah opened her arms wide as Jake's eldest came and laid her head on her shoulder. Never ones to be outdone, the twins ran up the stairs, dropped their bags by the railing, then raced to wrap their arms around her waist. The warmth of the three of them, the joy of seeing them, quickly brought a rush of misty tears to her eyes.

"I've missed you so much." She kissed the tops of their heads. "So much." She squeezed them tight until she heard a sound she knew quite well. It was Jake clearing his throat, playfully.

"Ahem."

Looking up from the children, she saw Jake's blue eyes twinkling as he stood before her. He was also holding his hands behind his back, looking almost like he was hiding something from her. "And what about me?" His golden brows arched. "Have you missed me, too... I hope?"

His voice was both teasing and alluring, nearly seizing the breath from her. She was glad the children's embrace steadied her trembling legs.

"Now that you mention it," she jested, "I suppose I have missed you, as well."

"We've missed you," Sarah spoke up, diverting their conversation. "Have you been busy sewing?" she asked sweetly.

"As a matter of fact, I have."

Jake leaned forward, suddenly looking more serious. "How are things going with the Decor to Admire lady?"

The children gazed up at her, as well. It surprised her that they appeared intent on listening.

"You mean Decor to Adore?" She smiled. "Well, it's a funny thing," she began to explain. "One morning while I was praying, I kept getting the sense that I should stay on my own as Hannah Miller Designs. I mean, I've been blessed to build a *gut* following. And the same question kept running through my mind— did I really want to be partners with someone I didn't know?"

"That doesn't sound funny to me," Jake countered.

"Because that's not the funny part," she mused, recalling *Gott*'s timing. "That very afternoon Madeline stopped by to tell me she was pulling out of Sugarcreek and may even lose her Columbus studio. Evidently, her husband has a gambling addiction. Sadly, because of that, they've recently lost a lot of money."

"That's awful." Jake frowned. "Well, then…" Jake cleared his throat again. This time he seemed more nervous than playful. "We, uh, came by today because we also have a sort of business proposal for you," he said, as a few beads of perspiration began dotting his forehead. "Don't we, *kinner*?"

"A what, *Daed*?" Clara asked, and Eli blinked.

"Just nod your heads yes," Sarah quietly instructed her siblings.

Confused, Hannah shrugged. "I'm not sure what you mean."

"We're hoping you'll change the name of your business," Jake stated.

She lifted her brow questioningly. "You think there's a better name?"

"We do." Jake nodded. "If you would, we'd be mighty happy if you'd choose to call your business Hannah *Burkholder* Designs. And before you decide…" He paused briefly. "If you will change your name and want to continue to live in town, that's fine. We'll pack up and move. Or if you want to live out in the country, that's fine, too. We want to be with you wherever you want to be, Hannah."

Hannah laughed nervously. Was she hearing right? "Jake, are you saying—" She searched his eyes.

"Not just me. We." His smile widened as he took one arm from behind his back, extending it toward the children.

As if on cue, Sarah raised a crutch and gently poked her brother's leg. "Now," she whispered. "It's time."

As Sarah stepped from Hannah's arms, the twins

also moved quickly. Picking up their totes, the two rushed back to Hannah's side.

Eli was the first to open his bag. "We want to give you our hearts," he said in a sweet, sincere voice as he handed Hannah fistfuls of paper hearts.

"All of them," Clara chimed in. Removing more cutout hearts from her bag, she tossed them gently toward Hannah like fairy dust.

"Every one," Sarah said with a hopeful smile as she leaned on her crutches, making a heart shape with her thumbs and index fingers.

As pink, red, white and purple hearts overflowed from Hannah's hands and carpeted the porch, her heart overflowed, too. Tears trickled down her cheeks.

"Oh, children. Oh, Jake." She looked up at him, still not sure what to say.

"Hannah." He answered the question in her eyes. "We don't want to live without you, and we hope you feel the same. And, uh…" At last he brought both hands out from behind his back. In one of them was a sizable bouquet. "I wanted to give you these." He presented the flowers to her.

"They're beautiful, Jake." She sniffed at the roses. "I've never seen anything so pretty."

"I have." His gaze was as soft as a caress, sending a warm sensation tingling up her neck. "It seems kind of silly now, but I got these flowers so I could be a matchmaker myself." He pointed to the bouquet. "The yellow roses remind me of your golden eyes that I love—whether they're lighting up with your smile or eyeing me like I'm out of my mind when I do something silly."

She laughed. "I'm sorry that I do that."

"*Nee*. I generally deserve it." He winked. "The pink roses are reminders of your rosy cheeks."

Hannah blushed at that.

Jake continued. "The red roses are a symbol of all the love that I have in my heart for you. And it's a lot. So much."

"You're going to make me cry again."

"Ah, but wait." He held up a finger. "The white hydrangeas are there because I know you like them."

"Really? You remember that day at Klinger's Farm when we sat on the stone wall and these flowers were everywhere?" She gently touched the fragile petals.

"The day we first kissed?" He smiled sweetly. "How could I forget?" He took her free hand in his. "I have loved you for so many years. There's so much I want to tell you, and I will. But right now, I need to know—will you be my match, Hannah? *Our* match? Will you marry me?"

She glanced at their sweet faces, one after another, and couldn't believe the blessing she'd been given. Every day she would be able to see them. Every day she would be able to love them close up, not from far away.

"*Jah*, oh, yes!" She gazed at them with all the love in her heart. "I love you. All of you. I can't wait to marry you."

As she waved her bouquet like a magic wand, the twins began skipping around the porch, tossing the paper hearts into the air. Sarah stood giggling at the scene.

"What's all the uproar?" *Aenti* Ruth peeked out the door.

"We're getting married," Eli shouted. "We're going to have a *mamm*!"

"That sounds like something to celebrate," *Aenti* Ruth said. "You *kinner* need to come inside right now for a treat." Her aunt winked at her. Right then, Hannah knew her aunt had known about Jake's proposal all along.

The moment the children hurried indoors, Jake took the flowers from her hands, pulling her close.

"This may be the only alone time we have." He gazed at her longingly. "So I need to ask—Hannah, may I kiss you?" He rubbed his thumb gently along her cheek.

"Yes, Jake," she said. "*Jah*, please do."

As his lips met hers, she realized this kiss felt nothing like their first one. There was no hesitation this time, no doubt. The love she felt in her heart was like nothing she could've ever imagined.

Suddenly the door opened again. Clara ran out and tugged on Jake's pant leg and her skirt.

"You need to come in." Her blue eyes were wide. "There's raspberry scones."

As Clara grabbed each of their hands and led the way, Hannah looked over at her husband-to-be. She could feel her heart swell all over again.

"Ready to go inside, Jake?"

"Yes, indeed."

His adoring eyes smiled at her in the most affectionate way, letting her know there was a perfect time for absolutely everything…even for love.

* * * * *

Get 4 FREE REWARDS!

We'll send you 2 FREE Books plus 2 FREE Mystery Gifts.

FREE
Value Over
$20

Both the **Love Inspired®** and **Love Inspired® Suspense** series feature compelling novels filled with inspirational romance, faith, forgiveness and hope.

YES! Please send me 2 FREE novels from the Love Inspired or Love Inspired Suspense series and my 2 FREE gifts (gifts are worth about $10 retail). After receiving them, if I don't wish to receive any more books, I can return the shipping statement marked "cancel." If I don't cancel, I will receive 6 brand-new Love Inspired Larger-Print books or Love Inspired Suspense Larger-Print books every month and be billed just $6.49 each in the U.S. or $6.74 each in Canada. That is a savings of at least 16% off the cover price. It's quite a bargain! Shipping and handling is just 50¢ per book in the U.S. and $1.25 per book in Canada.* I understand that accepting the 2 free books and gifts places me under no obligation to buy anything. I can always return a shipment and cancel at any time by calling the number below. The free books and gifts are mine to keep no matter what I decide.

Choose one: ☐ **Love Inspired**
Larger-Print
(122/322 IDN GRHK)

☐ **Love Inspired Suspense**
Larger-Print
(107/307 IDN GRHK)

Name (please print)

Address   Apt. #

City   State/Province   Zip/Postal Code

Email: Please check this box ☐ if you would like to receive newsletters and promotional emails from Harlequin Enterprises ULC and its affiliates. You can unsubscribe anytime.

Mail to the Harlequin Reader Service:
IN U.S.A.: P.O. Box 1341, Buffalo, NY 14240-8531
IN CANADA: P.O. Box 603, Fort Erie, Ontario L2A 5X3

Want to try 2 free books from another series? Call 1-800-873-8635 or visit www.ReaderService.com.

Get 4 FREE REWARDS!

We'll send you 2 FREE Books plus 2 FREE Mystery Gifts.

FREE
Value Over
$20

Both the **Harlequin® Special Edition** and **Harlequin® Heartwarming™** series feature compelling novels filled with stories of love and strength where the bonds of friendship, family and community unite.

YES! Please send me 2 FREE novels from the Harlequin Special Edition or Harlequin Heartwarming series and my 2 FREE gifts (gifts are worth about $10 retail). After receiving them, if I don't wish to receive any more books, I can return the shipping statement marked "cancel." If I don't cancel, I will receive 6 brand-new Harlequin Special Edition books every month and be billed just $5.49 each in the U.S. or $6.24 each in Canada, a savings of at least 12% off the cover price, or 4 brand-new Harlequin Heartwarming Larger-Print books every month and be billed just $6.24 each in the U.S. or $6.74 each in Canada, a savings of at least 19% off the cover price. It's quite a bargain! Shipping and handling is just 50¢ per book in the U.S. and $1.25 per book in Canada.* I understand that accepting the 2 free books and gifts places me under no obligation to buy anything. I can always return a shipment and cancel at any time by calling the number below. The free books and gifts are mine to keep no matter what I decide.

Choose one: ☐ **Harlequin Special Edition** ☐ **Harlequin Heartwarming**
(235/335 HDN GRJV) **Larger-Print**
(161/361 HDN GRJV)

Name (please print)

Address   Apt. #

City   State/Province   Zip/Postal Code

Email: Please check this box ☐ if you would like to receive newsletters and promotional emails from Harlequin Enterprises ULC and its affiliates. You can unsubscribe anytime.

Mail to the **Harlequin Reader Service:**
IN U.S.A.: P.O. Box 1341, Buffalo, NY 14240-8531
IN CANADA: P.O. Box 603, Fort Erie, Ontario L2A 5X3

Want to try 2 free books from another series? Call 1-800-873-8635 or visit www.ReaderService.com.

*Terms and prices subject to change without notice. Prices do not include sales taxes, which will be charged (if applicable) based on your state or country of residence. Canadian residents will be charged applicable taxes. Offer not valid in Quebec. This offer is limited to one order per household. Books received may not be as shown. Not valid for current subscribers to the Harlequin Special Edition or Harlequin Heartwarming series. All orders subject to approval. Credit or debit balances in a customer's account(s) may be offset by any other outstanding balance owed by or to the customer. Please allow 4 to 6 weeks for delivery. Offer available while quantities last.

Your Privacy—Your information is being collected by Harlequin Enterprises ULC, operating as Harlequin Reader Service. For a complete summary of the information we collect, how we use this information and to whom it is disclosed, please visit our privacy notice located at corporate.harlequin.com/privacy-notice. From time to time we may also exchange your personal information with reputable third parties. If you wish to opt out of this sharing of your personal information, please visit readerservice.com/consumerschoice or call 1-800-873-8635. **Notice to California Residents**—Under California law, you have specific rights to control and access your data. For more information on these rights and how to exercise them, visit corporate.harlequin.com/california-privacy.

HSEHW22R3

HARLEQUIN
PLUS

Try the best multimedia subscription service for romance readers like you!

Read, Watch and Play.

Experience the easiest way to get the romance content you crave.

Start your **FREE TRIAL** at
www.harlequinplus.com/freetrial.